A Hunger

OF

Thorns

A Hunger

OF

Thorns

LILI WILKINSON

DELACORTE PRESS

Text copyright © 2023 by Lili Wilkinson
Jacket art copyright © 2023 by Imogen Oh
Interior art used under license from Shutterstock.com

All rights reserved. Published in the United States by Delacorte Press, an imprint of Random House Children's Books, a division of Penguin Random House LLC, New York.

Delacorte Press is a registered trademark and the colophon is a trademark of Penguin Random House LLC.

Excerpt from *Wild Embers* © Nikita Gill, published by Trapeze, reproduced by kind permission of David Higham Associates.

Visit us on the Web! GetUnderlined.com

Educators and librarians, for a variety of teaching tools, visit us at RHTeachersLibrarians.com

Library of Congress Cataloging-in-Publication Data
Names: Wilkinson, Lili, author.
Title: A hunger of thorns / Lili Wilkinson.
Description: First edition. | New York : Delacorte Press, [2023] | Audience: Ages 14. | Summary: When Maud hit puberty she lost her wild magic and her best friend, Odette, rejected her—but now Odette has disappeared, her magic leading her down dark paths, and Maud knows that to rescue her former friend she will have to tread the same paths into a wild, dangerous world.
Identifiers: LCCN 2021061834 (print) | LCCN 2021061835 (ebook) | ISBN 978-0-593-56266-6 (hardcover) | ISBN 978-0-593-56267-3 (library binding) | ISBN 978-0-593-56268-0 (ebook) | ISBN 978-0-593-65027-1 (int'l. ed.)
Subjects: LCSH: Magic—Juvenile fiction. | Missing persons—Juvenile fiction. | Best friends—Juvenile fiction. | Rescues—Juvenile fiction. | CYAC: Magic—Fiction. | Missing persons—Fiction. | Best friends—Fiction. | Friendship—Fiction. | Rescues—Fiction. | Fantasy. | LCGFT: Novels. | Fantasy fiction.
Classification: LCC PZ7.W652 Hu 2023 (print) | LCC PZ7.W652 (ebook) | DDC 823.92 [Fic]—dc23/eng/20220523

The text of this book is set in 11-point Baskerville.
Interior design by Michelle Crowe

Printed in the United States of America
10 9 8 7 6 5 4 3 2 1
First Edition

For every good girl who has a wild girl inside

They won't tell you fairytales

of how girls can be dangerous and still win.

They will only tell you stories

where girls are sweet and kind

and reject all sin.

I guess to them

it's a terrifying thought,

a red riding hood

who knew exactly

what she was doing

when she invited the wild in.

—NIKITA GILL

1

NAN IS VERY PARTICULAR ABOUT TEA.

She orders a personalized blend from an under-the-counter botanica on the wrong side of town, and it gets shipped to her in bulk, a large wooden crate filled with vacuum-sealed packages. Nan decants them one by one into a floral tin with creaking hinges.

Halmoni bought her an electric kettle years ago, but Nan refuses to use it. She fills an ancient cast-iron kettle with rainwater from the tank outside the back door and lights the gas burner with a match.

Nan doesn't ask if I want tea. The kettle is already on, with curls of steam and faint whistles escaping from the spout. I have made the journey downstairs from my bedroom, now there will be tea. Tea is nonnegotiable.

I push aside five cross-stitched cushions, Nan's knitting basket, and two cats to make a space on the couch, and sit down. Princess Bari stalks away, offended, her tail twitching, but Gwion Bach clambers into my lap and starts kneading my thighs. His claws sink through the thin layers of my dress and the brand-new stockings that Halmoni bought me just for today. I imagine the pinprick holes widening and splitting into ladders, and feel a brief surge of wicked satisfaction. But these stockings are fancy enchanted ones and will not ladder, so I will remain neat and respectable. *Put together* is how Dr. Slater would phrase it. Today, I have to be put together, even though I'm falling apart.

Nan takes a pinch of tea from the floral tin and leans out the back door to sprinkle it on the doorstep, over the deep engraved marks of overlapping circles and daisy wheels that keep our house free of mischief. She opens another tin and fishes out a handful of thrupenny biscuits, which she plunks onto a china plate without ceremony.

"Orright, Miss Maude?" she says to me.

Gwion Bach finally deems my lap sufficiently molded to his requirements and settles himself into a furry brown puddle. I rub behind his ears, and he purrs.

She reaches up to an open shelf cluttered with canisters, vases, and ugly little figurines of big-headed shepherdesses and frogs playing musical instruments, and takes down cups and saucers, painted with pink and yellow roses. A reading, then. When it's just tea, Nan uses Halmoni's Buncheong stoneware cups, but white porcelain provides better contrast for reading tea leaves.

The kettle on the stove begins to whistle in earnest, a plume of steam billowing to the ceiling. Nan briefly holds each cup over the steam—to cleanse them of any deceit—then lifts the kettle and splashes boiling water into the teapot.

Nan's teapot is the stuff of family legend. It's large enough to hold up to ten cups, and it is truly the most hideous thing I've ever seen. It's pastel-pink china, in the shape of a soppy-looking cat's face. Huge baby-blue cat eyes stare unblinking, fringed with curled painted lashes. An open grinning mouth leers beneath feverishly rosy cheeks.

She replaces the kettle, which resumes its shrill whistling, then swirls the water in the teapot to warm it before emptying it over the sink. After that, she takes her tarnished silver caddy spoon, its handle engraved with entwined pennywort and milk thistle, and measures out four spoons of tea leaves—one for her, one for me, one for Halmoni, and one for luck. She fills the pot halfway with boiling water—it's too big to fill all the way, unless we have company. Then she pops on the lid and leaves it to steep.

"Now, then," she says, smoothing the front of her tweed skirt, which flows neat and somber over outrageously pink Lycra leggings. "How you feeling, love?"

Her crinkled, watery eyes see too much, so I look away, over toward her workbench, where bunches of drying rosemary and sea holly hang over row upon row of little jars—crushed eggshell, salt, rusty pins, feathers, bits of bone, rowan ash. There's a half-finished poppet there, button-eyed and bound with red and silver thread. A love charm, probably, for some moonsick client. Or maybe good luck for a student—exams are coming up soon.

Nan's still watching me. "Fine," I tell her. "I'm fine."

She is clearly not satisfied by this answer, but she doesn't say anything. She pulls a bottle of milk from the fridge, and Hangul and Huw appear as if from nowhere, winding themselves silkily around her ankles. Gwion Bach twitches an ear but doesn't move from my lap. Princess Bari slips in from the garden and positions herself next to the milk saucer and makes loud, yowling demands. Nan bends creakily and splashes milk into the saucer, and Gwion

Bach leaps heavily to the floor and pads over to join his siblings, his fat belly swaying below him like a furry pendulum.

Nan carefully pours milk into the teacups. Milk goes in before tea, to protect the drinker from any malicious contaminants that may have found their way into the tea caddy. Always whole milk, never skim or almond or (good people forbid) soy. Sugar, lemon, and honey are strictly forbidden. Also banned from our house is Earl Grey, decaf, herbal teas for anything other than medicinal purposes, and those fancy charmed tea bags where the brew doesn't oversteep and the little paper tab never falls into the cup when you pour the water in.

Nan does allow Halmoni a canister of hyeonmi-nokcha, which I secretly prefer, but Halmoni drinks mostly coffee anyway.

The cats' saucer is emptied, and Gwion Bach leaps back up to my lap and settles down, then decides I've gotten all out of shape again and rises to his feet to knead me back into position. Hangul and Huw tumble out into the garden to chase mice, while Princess Bari cleans her whiskers and watches, aloof.

"Are you ready for today?" Nan asks.

I don't know how to answer that question.

Nan lifts the hideous teapot with two hands and carefully pours tea, first into my cup, and then her own. No tea strainer, of course. A little splashes onto the kitchen counter as she sets it down, and she twitches a smile.

She presents me with my cup and saucer, and offers me the plate of thrupenny biscuits. I take one and dunk it into the tea, pausing to inhale fragrant steam. The biscuit crumbles soggily in my mouth, warm milky tannins blending with sweet apple cider and caraway.

"What even is a vigil anyway?" Nan says conversationally. "Is it like divination? Are they expecting someone to have a vision of her?"

"Dr. Slater is going to lead us in contemplation," I tell her.

Nan makes a face. She's not a fan of Dr. Slater and his well-being regimen. "What right does he have? He isn't her family."

"He's the school principal. A community leader," I offer.

"As if anything that man does is going to bring the poor girl home. And doing it on the eve of an egg moon too. People just don't have any sense."

My mouth is too full of biscuit to reply.

Nan falls silent as she sips her tea, and I glance out the window toward Halmoni's stained-glass studio, wishing she'd come in.

"You don't have to go, you know," she says. "You and Odette haven't been close for years."

Four years. Four years since I got my period, my magic dried up, and my best friend broke my heart.

I've reached the bottom of the cup, the tea turned bitter and lukewarm. A few tea leaves wash into my mouth, and I press them between my teeth.

Nan puts down her own cup. "Right, then," she says, and reaches over to pick up my cup in her left hand. She swirls the dregs three times sunwise, then inverts the cup over my saucer. Muddy liquid seeps out around the rim. She taps three times on the base, then lifts the cup again and examines the remaining tea leaves clinging to the white china.

I shift uncomfortably, and Gwion Bach pauses his rumbling purr and flicks an irritated ear. I look around the little room bursting with overstuffed armchairs, cushions, and luridly colored crochet rugs. The walls are crowded with framed

5

pictures—flowers, more big-headed shepherdesses, and family illustrations. I see Nan and Halmoni's wedding portrait, the oil paint faded with age. There's a watercolor of Halmoni visiting her parents in Pisi-Geiteu. Mam, wearing cap and gown as she graduated from university. Me in pen-and-ink as a fat-cheeked baby.

"Something has been lost," Nan murmurs, squinting into the cup. "You have a wild road ahead, Maude."

I didn't need a reading to tell me that.

"But there are good things too." She turns the cup so I can see it, and points. "See there? That's a rose. Love is waiting for you. And here? This is the sun, which represents power."

She goes small and silent, and I know she's thinking about Mam. Power only leads to trouble. Power is illegal magic, wild and unpredictable. Power makes you end up in a detention camp, your mettle—magical life force—drained to make commercial potions and glamours until there's nothing left and you return as a mindless husk, or a corpse laid out cold on the front door.

Nan lets out a faint, breathy sigh and turns back to the cup. She frowns, and despite myself I lean forward.

"What is it?"

"It's . . ." Nan's eyes dart to mine, as sharp as thistles.

I peer into the cup. "It looks like a bird's wings."

Nan purses her lips but doesn't respond.

I have a sudden, vivid flash of memory, of the chirping song of leaf warblers and the trickle of Cygnet Creek.

I WAS LYING on my back, gazing up at the canopy of Peg Powler, the weeping willow. Odette hung upside down by her knees from

6

a branch, her crackling white-blond hair brushing thick clay and exposed tree roots. We were about eleven, and Odette had just experienced her first-ever kiss, with Omar Courtenay. It had not come close to realizing the romantic fantasies that we'd played out in our games, and Odette was feeling mightily disillusioned.

"The problem with getting rescued by handsome princes," she was saying as she swung back and forth, "is that boys are disgusting."

I nodded in happy agreement. "Vile."

Real boys were nothing like the dashing heroes in the stories I spun for Odette under the willow—all noble, tortured souls with tragic backstories and dark, mysterious eyes. Real boys never spoke in poetry, nor were they utterly devoted to us, and us alone.

"On the other hand," Odette continued. "What if I get whisked away by a dark lord, or kidnapped by a dragon? Who will rescue me?"

"We could rescue each other," I suggested dreamily, watching a leaf warbler flit from one willow branch to another.

Odette kept swinging from the tree branch. "Tell me how you'd rescue me. If I was locked in a tall tower, with no hope of escape."

"Well," I said, sitting up and letting my mind start to weave together the threads of a new story. "First, I'd climb the stairs—"

"There are no stairs, Maude," Odette shrieked. "No stairs, no ladders! The tower is so tall the top is shrouded in cloud. Its walls are so smooth there isn't a single handhold."

I knew the answer even before she had finished speaking. I always knew how a story would go. Halmoni explained to me when I was little that everyone had a gift, and that mine was storytelling. To me, telling a story felt exactly like doing magic—reaching for invisible threads and weaving them together to make something greater than the sum of its parts.

"I'd find a witch to cast a spell on me, to give me wings so I could fly to the top of the tower."

Odette grasped the branch with her hands, then flipped her legs backward until she was standing upright again. Her hair took a second to settle, floating around her shoulders as if it obeyed totally different laws of gravity. Her face was serious. "That sounds like powerful magic," she said with a delicious shiver. "It'd come at a cost."

Odette had no idea what magic was powerful and what wasn't, but I nodded anyway, because in this case she was right. Wings—real, functional wings, not just a glamour—would take an impossible amount of mettle—of life force. Maybe more than there is in the whole world.

"Would you give up your sight?" Odette asked. "Your voice? Your firstborn? A happy memory?"

"To rescue you? Of course."

Odette chewed on a fingernail. "So you fly up to the tower, and I climb onto your back, but before we can jump out the window, the dragon returns. And it's hungry. What happens then? What do you do?"

The gurgle of the creek seemed to dim around us, and the sun went behind a cloud. Peg Powler, always such a gentle embrace of a tree, suddenly loomed over us, long tendrils reaching, searching, clawing. A cold wind moved the branches, bringing the tree alive, a green dragon intent on devouring us, right down to crunching bone. A cloud of glimmer moths bursts from the branches overhead, their abdomens glowing bright blue.

I looked up at Odette. She was beautiful the way princesses in stories are beautiful—big eyes, pixie nose, cascading silvery hair. But there was always something behind her beauty. A raging fire, seething with heat. People were drawn to her, like moths to a candle. But her fire could burn a person right up. Omar Courtenay wouldn't be the last boy who wanted to be with her. Ahead of us, there were parties and kissing and glamours and periods and all the other terrifying obstacles on the hard road to gray adulthood, every step crowded with grown-ups telling us to be nice, nice, nice.

It was far more terrifying than any imaginary horror I could dream up.

"How do you defeat the dragon, Maude?"

In that moment, I wished we didn't have to take that gray road. I wanted to stay a child, playing games with Odette under the willow. We were wild—wild in the way that only little girls can be. No matter how hard people like Odette's mother and Dr. Slater tried to shame us out of it.

I clenched my fists. "I would smash it with my wings."

Odette grinned, tooth-bare and fierce, a growl sounding at the back of her throat.

NAN STANDS UP, still holding my teacup. "Where did you go, just now?" she demands.

"I—I was thinking about Odette," I say. "A game we used to play."

"She took the dark paths," Nan says, her voice oddly flat. "You mustn't follow her."

There's something in her tone that makes me snap to attention.

"Do you know where she went?" I ask, trying to hold back my eagerness.

Nan's hands tremble, and the cup slips to the slate floor, shattering.

"Nan!" I leap to my feet.

The back door opens, and Halmoni appears, tall and graceful, dressed in asymmetrical navy with perfectly applied makeup, carrying an armful of white roses. She pinches Nan on the bum before noticing the broken china and the wild expression on Nan's face.

"Niamh?" she asks. "What happened?"

Nan lets out a breath, and the tension in the room is broken. "Nothing."

I get the dustpan and sweep up the broken china, and Nan turns her face to Halmoni's for a kiss. Despite being a million years old, my grandmothers are still super hot for each other, and it's disgustingly adorable.

The china fragments are tiny, some little more than dust. I tip the contents of the dustpan into the rubbish bin.

Halmoni turns to me, her expression gentle. "Time to go, Maude," she says.

The way she phrases it, it's almost like a question. A sudden chill creeps over my shoulders, but I nod.

Nan takes one of the roses and turns to me. "Pin," she says.

I pull the little bone-pin brooch from my dress and pass it to her. It was my mam's—a thin sliver of bone carved with intricate whorls, scarred with nine pinpricks. Nan gave it to me just after I turned twelve. She said it would protect me from the darkness that took Mam, but that I had to wear it every day or else it wouldn't work.

I let Nan pin the rose to the front of my dress, like she does every morning. It's a ritual I take for granted, but today I wish that I had known how to share my pin with Odette. To protect her too.

"You don't know where she went, do you, Nan?" I ask.

Nan looks me directly in the eye. "Sorry, love," she says, and I know she would never lie to me.

"I just wish I could *do* something," I say.

"I know, love. But promise me you won't follow any dark paths looking for her."

For someone who practices magic for her job, Nan is hugely paranoid about it. Fair enough, I suppose, after what happened to Mam. But I wish she'd trust me. It's not like I'm going to get mixed up in any illegal magic business—I've got no magic, so what on earth can she be worried about?

"Niamh?" Halmoni puts a hand on her shoulder.

"Promise me." Nan's voice is low and firm.

"Nan, you're being ridiculous," I tell her. "I haven't spoken to Odette for months."

But that isn't true. I feel a flush reach my cheeks and wonder if Nan notices. Of course she does. She notices everything. Knowing secrets is her gift.

"Promise."

"Okay, I promise," I tell her.

"Good girl. Now go and fetch a cardigan in case it gets cold."

I still have questions, but the expression on Nan's face says I will get no answers. So I head upstairs to my room.

"We'll be waiting in the car," Halmoni calls after me.

I slip the bone pin from the rose and place it on my dresser while I shrug on a gray cardigan. Then I slide open a drawer and pull out a keepsake box, sandalwood inlaid with mother-of-pearl. It contains bits and pieces from childhood—a broken necklace, a folded paper moth, one of those cheap fortune-telling rings. And a photo.

Me and Odette. We're maybe eight or nine, back when we didn't care about how we looked. We're dressed up like princesses, in long, trailing gowns, our arms flung around each other, gap-toothed, tangle-haired, and grinning.

I hold the photo between my finger and thumb, marveling at how so much life can be captured on such a flimsy piece of paper. Odette had found the camera in her mother's office and brought it over to try out. I'd never been photographed before. I have no idea why Odette's mother would own a camera—there's no way she'd ever let anyone see her without a glamour. We'd gotten Halmoni to take the photo for us, then waited breathlessly for the image to appear on the little plasticky square, squealing as our faces came into focus.

I slide it into the pocket of my cardigan. I replace the keepsake box in the drawer, and reach out to pick up the bone-pin brooch and the rose.

My fingers brush the paper moth. Funny, I don't remember taking it out of the box. It feels fragile under my fingers, like it's very old. The shape of it is so familiar—I know every crease. It's a glimmer moth. Mam used to love watching them flit over the hedgerows at twilight, their little furry bodies glowing bright blue. This paper moth has been here, in my room, for as long as I can remember.

"Maude?" Halmoni calls from downstairs.

I used to be scared of the dark. When I was little—when Mam

used to leave all the time but before she left forever. I would wake up in my bed, surrounded by darkness and silence. My storytelling gift would fill the night with all sorts of horrors—ghosts and goblins and things with teeth and claws.

Halmoni wouldn't let me have a night-light—she said it interrupted circadian rhythms. So I made my own. I would wear my boots to bed, to protect my ankles from under-the-bed monsters, then slip out and clomp over to the window, sticking my head out and drawing on the threads of mettle that I could feel floating in the night air. I called for glimmer moths, but they never came. The candle snails did, though, creeping onto my windowsill, leaving glowing silver trails behind them. It used to drive Nan mad, cleaning the sill the next morning.

"It isn't covenant magic," she'd mutter. "We'll have auditors at the door."

"Leave her be," Halmoni would say. "She's only a babe."

One night, I was watching the snails turn in lazy circles on my sill when a figure appeared in my bedroom doorway.

Mam.

She'd been away for over a month. I didn't know where. Nan and Halmoni wouldn't talk about it in front of me, although I sometimes caught them whispering when they thought I wasn't listening, and one time I saw Halmoni crying, which seemed so awful and impossible to my child-self that I just pretended it had never happened.

Mam pushed the hood of her cloak back, and I saw her high cheekbones, paper-white skin, and dark eyes. As she came closer, I could smell some kind of unfamiliar magic on her—crushed vetiver and disrupted storm air.

I could see it too—threads of mettle that seemed dull and limp—not the bright silver I was used to.

Whatever magic Mam was caught up in was forbidden.

I was expecting a hug, but instead she padded right past me, to my windowsill, and touched a varnished black fingernail to a glowing blue snail shell.

"Did you do this?" she asked, her voice deep and husky.

I didn't know whether I was in trouble or not, but I nodded anyway. "I wanted glimmer moths," I told her. "Because they're your favorite."

Mam gazed out at the night. "Moths won't come here," she said. "But let's see what we can do."

She took a sheet of paper from my desk and swiftly folded it into the shape of a moth, neat as anything. Then she whispered something to it, and its abdomen began to glow cerulean, just like a real glimmer moth. She placed it on my windowsill, then turned back to me, her wine-dark lips stretched past overcrowded teeth in a smile that warmed me to my toes.

She lifted the covers and slid into bed beside me, the rough wool of her cloak scratchy against my skin. Her breath on my face was soft, her fingers cool on my cheeks.

She withdrew a tiny vial from her cloak and showed it to me. It was filled with a bright, silvery liquid.

"This is pure mettle," she murmured. "Pure magic. Can you feel it?"

I nodded. The silvery liquid seemed to be alive, almost throbbing, in the little glass vial. I turned witch-eyed, the way Mam had taught me, and could see the bright threads of mettle swirling inside.

There was a frightening hunger in Mam's eyes as she gazed at it. Her hands trembled as she slid it under my pillow.

"Keep it," she whispered. "Don't give it back to me, even if I ask."

"Why not?"

"You are powerful, Maude," she whispered, kissing my hair. "I'm going to teach you everything—our deep lore—and one day you will be a thousand times more powerful than me or your nan. You will be the greatest witch of our times."

"But witches aren't powerful, Mam," I told her. "Dr. Slater says that's just stories."

Mam hissed at his name. "That man wouldn't know power if it bit him on the arse."

I giggled.

"Maude, people like him have taken our power away. They tied us up in invisible chains and gagged us with iron and steel. There aren't many of us left. But you will lead the resistance, as fierce and relentless as thunder. You'll show those petty warlocks and oath breakers what true power looks like. They will cower before you, grovel for your mercy and your favor. And you will make them pay for what they have done to us."

I was too little to understand what she was talking about. I didn't know about the prohibition years, when the government banned magic completely. I didn't know about the Battle of Goose Spring—a protest that turned ugly when over four hundred magical folk were killed, including my father, before I was even born. There was such roiling hate and hunger in Mam's eyes as she spoke of these things. I remember the chill that ran through me. I wasn't sure I wanted that kind of power.

I didn't want to make anyone grovel. I didn't want to make anyone pay.

"Tell me the story," I said instead. "The one about the swan prince."

I felt Mam relax beside me. "Are you sure you don't want a different story?" she asked. "You've heard that one a thousand times."

I shook my head. "The swan prince."

Mam chuckled and told me about the tyrannical king with a heart of iron and the simple peasant girl who turned him good with a magical knife carved from the breastbone of a swan. The story stained my dreams with rosy wonder, and I woke up the next morning still feeling the glow of it.

Nan found the vial under my pillow—I could never keep a secret from her. She snatched it up and locked it away in a drawer of her workbench. Later, I heard her arguing with Mam.

Irresponsible. She's just a child.

I could hear Mam begging for the vial back, a thick longing in her voice.

You don't understand. If they get their hands on the knife, it will undo us all.

In my head, she was talking about the knife from the story. The magical knife carved from the breastbone of a swan prince.

Nan stayed firm. I thought it was just as well—I would have handed the vial over instantly if Mam had asked.

The threads of Mam's mettle grew more dull, although her face remained as pale and beautiful as it always had. Sometimes I saw her stumble in after being away for months, stinking of hemlock, her eyes bottomless black, and I'd wonder if she was turning into a monster, like the ones from stories. Mam told me that all stories had been true once, that there were real monsters before humans wiped them out. Would it happen to me too, if I gave in to the tidal roar of magic? Better to be a covenant witch like Nan and just do the spells allowed by the government—legal, minor cantrips to boost confidence or find lost keys.

I was almost glad when my magic dried up. Because it meant I was safe, that I wouldn't get sucked under the way that Mam had. Of course, when it happened I didn't realize that losing my magic would also mean losing Odette.

I can still turn witch-eyed and see mettle, but I can't manipulate it anymore. Can't draw the threads together and bind them into magic. So I don't look anymore. What's the point? Better to be like ordinary people, blissfully unaware of the currents of life force flowing through everything.

But I focus my attention on the paper moth in a way I haven't done for years. And I see them, the threads. Dull and dark.

Mam made this moth. It's not the same one she made that night with the candle snails and the mettle vial—Nan threw that one in the bin. This one is folded from what looks like a page ripped from a children's book.

It feels important somehow, but I can't remember why. I close my eyes and get a glimpse of a high stone wall. Dirt under my fingernails. The thick, dark scent of roses.

"Maude!" Halmoni's tread on the staircase. "Are you coming?"

The vision evaporates. "Yes," I call back. "I'm coming."

I slip the paper moth into my pocket, then pin the rose to the front of my cardigan and head downstairs.

2

THE DAY IS WARM, THE AIR HEAVY WITH THE SCENT OF
Nan's roses, but my arms have broken out in gooseflesh
despite the gray cardigan. I can hear birdsong, but it's distant.
Birds never come into our garden. Nan says it's because of the
cats. Jeremiah appears and bolts out the front door into the
garden, nearly bowling me over. He chases Hangul and Huw,
barking furiously, a blur of matted chocolate fur. But when
he comes face to face with Princess Bari, he skids to such a
sudden halt that he tears up part of the front lawn. His tail
descends between his legs, and he slinks back to me, small and
humble.

Princess Bari haughtily watches him go, licks a paw, and
starts to wash herself.

I shoo Jeremiah inside and shut the door, then hurry down
the garden path and climb into the back seat of the car.

Nan looks over her shoulder at me. "Orright, love?"

No.

"Yes."

IT'S NOT A LONG DRIVE into Inglenook, but it feels like it. Halmoni makes a few halfhearted attempts at conversation, but nobody wants to join in. Nan is silent and small in the passenger seat. Away from her kitchen, she seems to shrink, a towering force of nature diminished into a wizened little old lady.

It's a gorgeous day, and people are out in droves, enjoying the sunshine. Couples link arms and bow their heads close to each other. Children race one another on bikes and scooters. The line for an ice cream truck goes halfway around a block. None of them notice me in the car going by. Why would they? I'm nothing special.

We pull up outside the town hall—imposing bluestone and ivy. Halmoni climbs out and goes around to Nan's door to help her.

I open my car door and emerge into the warm afternoon. Rufus Sheldrake is standing nearby, looking gangly and weird, like he always does. He's attempted to tame his mop of orange hair into a ponytail, but it's already escaping into a fuzzy halo. He's wearing a collared shirt and tie, and looks even more ridiculous than usual, all legs and elbows and freckles. He spots me and strides over, giraffe-like.

"Hi, Mrs. Jenkins," Rufus says, grinning a mouthful of braces at Halmoni. He nods at Nan. "You too, Mrs. Jenkins."

"Nice to see you, Rufus," Halmoni replies.

Rufus narrows his eyes at the rose pinned to my cardigan. "Roses still blooming, I see."

Nan winks at him. Everyone in Inglenook knows about Nan's

roses. They bloom all year and never succumb to pests or diseases. Rufus is obsessed with botany, and generally resistant to magic, in the way that all natural redheads are. It's why we started hanging out—we're both social outcasts. Him because glamours don't work on him, me because my mother was a traitor.

"Are you going to take that off?" Halmoni asks, nodding at my cardigan.

"In a minute," I tell her. I'm still cold.

Rufus looks at the ground and scuffs his foot, obviously trying to think of something to say. What is he even doing here? He and Odette weren't friends. I don't think they ever spoke to each other.

"Maude," says a voice behind me, and I turn to see Tilly, Anesu, and Roshni, each clutching a perfectly embroidered lace handkerchief in a white-gloved hand. They look like they've just stepped out of a *Country Idyll* catalog, all pale ginghams and petite pastel flowers.

"Isn't it terrible?" Tilly says, her voice trembling.

Anesu lets out an elegant sniff and dabs the corners of her eyes with her handkerchief. Roshni lays a consoling hand on her arm.

"Her poor mother," Tilly continues. "She must be so worried."

"As are we all," Roshni adds.

Tilly nods. "Oh, indeed. I haven't slept for *days*."

I want to claw their stupid eyes out. They don't care about Odette. They just want to be *seen* here, looking appropriately demure and concerned.

"You and she were friends, right?" Tilly asks.

"When we were little," I reply, awkward. "Not so much recently."

"Of course not," Roshni says. "She got so wild in high school. So . . . lost."

"Such a shame," murmurs Anesu. "So much potential."

As if any of them ever tried to help Odette. As if any of them ever spared a kind word for her—or for me.

The girls glide on by, and I'm grateful for Rufus, who shudders as they pass.

"They're like living dolls," he says. "Horrid."

Nan nods at him with approval.

"What's going on in the lab?" I ask.

His expression brightens with relief, now that we have something ordinary to talk about. "I've been trying to replicate an experiment on plant cognitive ecology," he says, and starts to tell me about how mimosa plants have a sophisticated cellular signaling network that indicates associative learning. He goes all bouncy, the way Rufus does when he's talking botany. His arms fling out as he tells me about dropping the little mimosa plants in order to stimulate their defensive leaf-closing reflex, and his fingers curl and twitch as he explains how after being dropped multiple times, the plants learned that there was no danger and stopped closing their leaves.

"In the original experiment, the plants remembered being dropped for nearly a whole month—that's a longer memory than a bee has!"

Nan snorts. "Don't need an experiment to tell you that," she mutters. "A tree remembers every spring it's lived, and every winter."

My eye is drawn to the steps outside the town hall, to a straight-backed figure with sleek platinum hair. Odette's mother, her features a cold, perfect mask of beauty, a shiny black handbag hanging from the angular crook of her slim arm. I can see the edge of a glamour patch on her bicep, peeking out from under a capped sleeve. She's standing with Dr. Slater, tall and imposing in a black suit and tie.

Odette's mother's gaze shifts, and for a moment we lock eyes. I raise a hand to wave, but her eyes slide over me like I'm invisible. Dr. Slater turns, and his face tightens in disapproval as he sees me in my gray cardigan, unglamoured and plain as oatcakes. It's a familiar expression, one I've been seeing my whole life. *Pull your socks up. Show some respect. Where are your manners? That isn't very ladylike.*

I remember seeing that expression on the first day of grade two. Billy Bass cornered me in the playground, showing me a newspaper with a photo of Mam and the word TERRORIST printed in angry red letters across her face.

The photo was deeply shocking to me—it was barely recognizable as Mam. Her cheeks were gaunt, her eyes small and hollow. My guts churned as I realized the photo had captured her as she truly was—without a glamour patch, the beauty I knew so well nothing but an illusion. She looked weak and haggard.

"My da says they're gonna execute your mam," Billy Bass jeered. "He says good riddance."

I had been speechless, caught between bursting into tears and throwing up my egg-salad sandwich.

Then Odette had appeared, a straggle-haired stranger to me at that point, the frilly ensemble her mother had dressed her in that day already torn and muddied. She wrenched the paper from Billy's hands and stuffed it into the rubbish bin, then launched herself at him.

Dr. Slater strode up, towering above us, severe and radiating authority, his face as cold as stone. "You should be ashamed of yourself," he told Odette. "Nice girls don't fight." My cheeks burned with mortification, but Odette's expression was triumphant as she and Billy were dragged to Dr. Slater's office, Billy sniveling with a bloody nose.

I rescued the newspaper from the bin and headed to the back of the playground, where a hunching crab apple tree provided some privacy. I crouched there, tracing the word *terrorist* over and over with my index finger. I read the article but didn't understand much. *Carys Jenkins arrested on charges of high treason . . . attempting to steal a historical artifact . . . taken from her home by auditors . . .*

By then, Odette had reappeared, wearing an old witch's hat for her punishment, but seemingly unscathed and unabashed.

"Is it true?" she asked. "Is your mother really a resistance witch?"

I shrugged and told her I guessed so.

Odette shook her head in admiration. "That is so cool. I heard it runs in families. Does that mean you're a witch too?"

Nan had told me not to tell anyone, but I wanted to repay this brave, strange girl, this knight in shining armor. I wanted to give her a gift, and what better gift to give than a secret?

I had nodded. "Don't tell anyone."

Odette ran her fingers along her lips like she was zipping them up. "I swear it. I've never met a real witch before. Do you have a magic wand, or a cauldron? Do you fly on a broomstick?"

"No," I had said, laughing. "It doesn't work like that."

"How does it work?" she asked.

It was hard to explain. "There's mettle in living things, and in things that are special," I told her.

"Metal?" Odette asked. "Like iron or steel?"

"*M-E-T-T-L-E,*" I spelled out for her. "It's everywhere. If you are witch-eyed, you can see it."

"Witch-eyed?" Odette asked. "You mean a witch?"

"They're not the same thing," I explained. "People who are witch-eyed can see mettle. Actual witches can manipulate it."

Odette looked around as if expecting magic to leap out of the ground. "Can you see it now?"

"Not all the time," I said. "It'd be too much. Too hard to concentrate on other things. But I . . . sort of focus my eyes differently, and then I can see it."

"Do it," Odette ordered.

I did, and saw the silvery threads spring to life, twining around the crab apple tree, streaming from damselflies that flitted in and out of sunlight patches. Below it, I could sense the vast network of mettle that spread beneath the soil—an intricate lattice of fungi, ancient soil, and stone.

"Do I have it?" Odette asked.

"Of course," I replied. "All living things do."

Odette's mettle was strong—thick and vibrant, swirling around her like a silvery cloud. She looked pleased.

"So how do you get it to do stuff?" she had asked.

This part was harder to explain, but I tried.

"It's like telling a story," I said. "You take all the different threads and weave them together to make something new."

"You touch it with your hands?"

"Sort of. Not my real hands, though. It's like I have . . . another pair of hands that exist only in my mind."

"You imagine them."

I nodded. It wasn't exactly right, but it was close.

"And how do you know what to weave together?" she asked.

I hesitated. I had only just met Odette. Could I trust her?

"You know there's covenant magic," I said slowly.

"The hundred spells."

"Yes. You learn those. There are instructions. Which things to combine, and how to do it."

She could tell I was holding something back. "There's other magic, though, isn't there? Other spells. Do you learn them too? Is there a big secret spell book where they're all written down?"

"Some of them are in grimoires and other old books," I had said carefully. "Others get passed down from witch to witch. And some . . . some I just know. Some things just *feel* right."

Odette's grin was canny and infectious. "Show me."

I had glanced around to make sure nobody could see us. Then I picked up a crab apple that had fallen to the ground and held it in my palm. I reached out with the hands that were not my real hands and gently tugged on the threads of mettle in the soil, carefully explaining to it what I wanted. I felt roots pulse, deep below. The crab apple started to glow, a rosy golden light radiating from it.

"Can I touch it?" she asked.

I passed the crab apple to Odette. The rosy light was reflected in her wide eyes, and I totally forgot my misery from earlier. I felt a swell of pride in my chest, and I knew I was going to devote the rest of my life to making Odette happy.

DR. SLATER MURMURS SOMETHING to Odette's mother, then makes his way through the crowd to us. He nods to Nan.

"Mrs. Jenkins."

Nan nods back, stiffly. Halmoni leans forward. "Nice to see you, Dr. Slater."

"Mrs. Jenkins."

His cold eyes turn to me, and his smugness sours my stomach.

"Poor little Odette," he says. "Always getting herself into trouble. I'm so glad to see you're making wiser choices, Maude."

To him, I am a work in progress. A daughter of witches, made civilized and bland. All the wildness leached out of me and replaced with polite smiles and top grades. I am a good girl. A nice girl. Humbled and forever making amends for my traitorous mother.

Dr. Slater nods over at Tilly, Anesu, and Roshni. "If only Odette could have followed the examples of girls like them."

I wish he'd stop talking about Odette in the past tense.

"I've been meaning to talk to you, Maude," Dr. Slater continues. "I've been watching you closely, and I want the best for you. Which is why I've secured you a sponsor and a place at a settlement institute."

He says it like I've won the lottery.

I hear Nan start to say something, but she gets hushed by Halmoni.

I stare at Dr. Slater blankly as the life he's offering me flashes

26

before my eyes. A year out in the country, learning to be a "good" adult with a bunch of other "nice" young people. Lessons with representatives from all the big magic corporations, where I'd learn which mettle-boosted laundry detergent would get stains out most effectively and which charmed baking soda would ensure that my sponge cakes never fail.

I'd meet some unremarkable young man there who would offer to marry me, and we'd live a safe, unremarkable life.

It's nothing like the possible futures that Odette and I used to spin stories about, full of adventure and glamour, and passionate love affairs.

"This is a simple country," Dr. Slater says. "Simple and green and good. We live simple, happy lives. Nobody gets left behind. Nobody suffers. We are so lucky to live here in Anglyon. Don't you agree, Mrs. Jenkins?"

He directs this last part to Nan, whose lips have gone white with fury. Dr. Slater knows full well that this country wasn't so lucky for our family.

"Think about it," Dr. Slater says to me. "I believe it is the right path for you."

He inclines his head slightly, then heads up the steps and goes inside.

Rufus snorts. "Imagine you at a settlement institute," he says.

Nan looks fit to burst, but Halmoni lays a hand on her arm, and she clamps her lips instead.

Halmoni sighs. "We'd better put on our brave faces," she says. "It's time to go in."

But I can't move. Going in there isn't going to help find Odette.

For the first time today, I really *feel* something.

Anger, white-hot and burning. Anger at Odette's mother. Anger at Dr. Slater and every time he tried to contain us. Anger at everyone here. Because they don't care.

They're acting like she's dead, not missing.

I'm angry at Odette for running away. I'm angry at her for dumping me, four years ago, when I lost my magic and she decided she didn't need me anymore. And I'm angry at her for turning up on my doorstep two weeks ago, out of the blue, begging me to go on an adventure with her.

And most of all I'm angry at *me*, for turning her away. Because *I* was the one who was supposed to save her. I was the one who had to make sure she always got found, who brought her back from the dark paths, who would sprout wings in order to rescue her from her tower.

But I didn't.

I was too busy playing *nice*.

I turn and start walking away—from Nan and Halmoni, from Dr. Slater, from Odette's mother, from them all. Dimly, like I'm moving through water, I hear Rufus calling my name and Halmoni's voice saying, "Let her go."

I don't turn back.

3

CYGNET CREEK LOOKS LIKE SOMETHING FROM A FAIRY tale. The sun glints silver on the water as dragonflies dart and hover. Cabbage moths flit over drifts of violets and milk thistle. The sounds of chaffinches and cicadas and running water drown out the rumble of the nearby highway.

I pause on the footbridge. When we were little, we used to sit right here, dangling our feet, fishing for eels with black thread hanging from a silver spoon, watching hedgewitches gather marsh mallow and lamb's-quarter in string bags. A hedgewitch is a rare sight these days—there aren't many witches left.

I head down from the bridge, avoiding the bike path and pushing through fragrant wild fennel to Peg Powler and the creek.

The willow tree seems smaller than I remember, her limbs bent lower with old age. I've been coming here for as long as I can remember—Mam would bring me when I was just a tiny thing. She'd tell me the story of the swan prince and whisper forbidden magical secrets.

Nan and Halmoni had begged her to stop—Mam's magic was dangerous and forbidden. It was too easy to get caught and get hauled off to a detention center. Why couldn't Mam stick to covenant magic, like Nan did? After the Battle of Goose Spring, an agreement had been reached—a list of one hundred permitted spells that would remain culturally protected and could be practiced by licensed witches. This was Nan's magic—safe and legal.

Mam had just laughed. "Toothless cantrips," she'd said with scorn. "They want you to think that's all magic is. Love spells and good luck charms. Child's play. Or the so-called magic they sell in shopping malls. They're trying to keep you weak, make you dependent on them. Spend all your money on cheap trash and don't ask what's really going on. They want to sever you from the deep lore, the ancient mettle that you can access and they can't."

I could see the hunger in her. The pull of magic. I saw the same hunger in Odette, but Odette didn't understand magic the way Mam did. Odette lived in a sleek, cold house on a street lined with perfectly manicured trees. Her mother worked in a high, glassy office in Scouller. For people like Odette's mother, magic was something you could buy—luxury glamours and poultices made in designer mettleworks, or more delicate pieces of enchantment you could commission from exclusive thaumaturgical engineers.

Odette never understood it either. That's why she needed me.

"You did the right thing."

I spin around to see Rufus standing a few feet away, half obscured by a curtain of willow.

"What are you doing here?"

"I followed you. I—I wanted to make sure you were okay."

I'm startled. Rufus and I don't have that kind of friendship. We hang out at school, and sometimes in the library. We're thrown together because of our status as social pariahs. We're not real friends, though. We don't talk about our hopes and fears and dreams.

I blink. "What did you say just now?"

"I said you did the right thing. Sending Odette away."

I tilt my head to peer at him through the willow curtain.

"I saw her. At your house the other day. I was coming to see you—to talk about something for school. But she was there. I thought I'd just wait in the garden for a moment until she was done. And . . . I heard."

Something inside me unravels, and I sink to the ground, my hand automatically reaching out to grab a twisting frond of willow to steady my descent.

It had been the first time we'd spoken in months, maybe even longer. She hadn't been to my house for years. Not since my magic dried up.

Nan and Halmoni were out, and I was lying on my bed, half reading a novel, when I heard the door knocker. I knew it was her. She had a rhythm, unmistakably hers.

But why was she at my door?

Her golden hair hung limply around her shoulders. She had bags under her eyes, and her lips had a greenish cast. She told me about an Enochian magician in Eastmoor who could graft witch-hands to someone without magic. She just needed to bring him a drop of pure mettle.

She knew about Mam's vial. It was still locked away in Nan's drawer, but I knew where the key was. I'd shown Odette, years ago when we were little. She'd been entranced by it.

"How do you use it?" she'd asked. "Do you drink it? Or rub it on your skin like lotion?"

I'd shaken my head. "It doesn't work like that," I'd said. But I couldn't explain it. I still didn't have the words to describe the feeling of drawing on mettle, tugging the threads of it and weaving them into something new.

"Can I have it?" Odette had asked me two weeks ago, standing there on my doorstep.

I had been dumbfounded. Four years earlier, Odette had given me up. One day, my magic stopped working, and a week later Odette had started sitting with Betty Metanee at lunch. A week after that, and we stopped speaking altogether. I'd been devastated. Odette had been my truest friend—my only friend. I thought we were forever. But it turned out she just wanted me for my magic.

And here she was again. Not here to apologize. Not here to try and patch things up. She just wanted more magic. Even when I had none to give.

"No," I'd told her. "Pure mettle is dangerous. It can make you sick. You've seen the magic junkies in town. Too much can kill you."

Odette had scowled at me. She never liked it when people refused her anything.

* * *

"I SHOULD HAVE ASKED HER IN," I say out loud. "Made her some tea. Maybe she wouldn't have gone."

Rufus parts the curtain of willow, and ducks under it. It feels wrong for him to be here. This isn't his space. It's mine. Odette's, maybe. Mam's, definitely. But it's not a space for boys, and *especially* not for redheads.

"She's not your responsibility," he says. "You don't owe her anything."

But I owed her everything. I'd be nothing without Odette. She was the one who brought me back to life after Mam died.

I sent her away, and now she's been missing for two weeks.

"I should have gone with her," I say. "I could have changed her mind. Brought her home."

Rufus snorts. "Or you could both be dead in Sicklehurst."

I blink. "Where?"

"Sicklehurst. That's where she said she was going."

"The old power plant?" I'd forgotten it existed.

Rufus nods. "First, she asked for a vial of pure mettle, and when you wouldn't give it to her, she said she'd go into Sicklehurst and get some herself."

"Sicklehurst?"

The word feels unfamiliar in my mouth, but as I say it, I realize that Rufus is right. Odette *did* mention Sicklehurst. How could I have forgotten?

You told me there was a lot of mettle in there, she'd said. *Don't you remember, the day you made the dolls?*

"We went there together," I say out loud, slowly, as the memory begins to emerge, like a ship looming out of thick fog. "When we were twelve. She was upset about something, and I wanted to cheer her up. So I showed her the secret way in. . . ."

Something flutters at my side. I look down, expecting to see a cricket or a butterfly. But there's nothing there.

I shake my head. I can't remember what happened next. Just the overwhelming need I had to make Odette feel better, to try and purge the misery that I already knew was taking over.

"It's nice here," says Rufus, looking around at the canopy of green overhead. "Very peaceful. It's a genetic mutation, you know, that causes the tree to exhibit an abnormal gravitropic response."

"You mean that's why it weeps?"

He nods. "Most trees want to grow up, toward the light. This one wants to grow down."

No wonder Odette loved it so much.

Peg Powler had been the nexus of all our games. She was a sumptuous palace, a treasure-filled cave, a mystical temple. We would scramble up into her rough-barked boughs, green cascading all around us like a glowing cathedral, her leaves whispering their secrets to us.

"Make us a story, Maude," Odette would demand, and eagerly I would begin to pull together golden threads to weave beguiling, fantastical worlds for us to inhabit. We became sorceresses, knights in training, orphaned royalty, and destiny-laden heroes. I embroidered the stories with my magic—transforming flowers into glowing talismans and enchanting the willow fronds to look and behave like guardian serpents.

We ran wild, vanquishing dragons and falling in love with handsome princes (or sometimes vanquishing handsome princes and falling in love with dragons). We splashed through the creek as beautiful fishy creatures tried to drown us, and crashed through the undergrowth, fleeing hideous forest monsters. We made witch's brews in puddles and daubed ancient symbols of power on each other's skin with mud. We'd dream and laugh and skim stones over the water, traipsing home at sundown, our hair tangled with sticks and leaves, our clothes caked in filth, our pockets full of cicada husks and magpie feathers.

It's been a long time since I pulled on the story threads. It reminds me too much of weaving mettle—of everything I've lost.

My eyes fill with tears, and it's like my twelve-year-old grief hits me all over again. The shock of losing Odette. The betrayal. The feeling of worthlessness, like she loved me only for my magic and not for *me*. I thought I'd forgotten it. I thought I'd moved on. I was wrong.

Rufus clears his throat uncomfortably, and I realize this is the most personal conversation we've ever had. He didn't sign up for this.

"You should go," I tell him. "I'm fine. Really."

Rufus looks skeptical, but he takes a step backward toward the path. "I just wanted to make sure," he says. "You looked like you were feeling bad about all of it, and I don't want you to feel bad. Because none of this is your fault. Whether or not she went to Sicklehurst."

Sicklehurst. I'd forgotten again.

I feel the fluttering thing beside me once more and move my skirt to the side to see if I've inadvertently trapped an insect. There's nothing there.

I look at Rufus. "Do you think that's where she is?"

It's hard to think about it—my mind keeps sliding away every time I try to focus.

"Maybe," Rufus says. "You could tell Dr. Slater or Odette's mother. They might be able to send someone to check. But it probably won't do any good. People always forget about Sicklehurst."

I look at him. "Except you."

He shrugs.

"It's magic," I say, suddenly understanding. "There must be a spell on Sicklehurst to make people forget about it. A not-noticing spell. But it doesn't work on you, because . . ." I gesture at his red hair, and he ducks his head.

"My dad would know about it, then," he says. "And a few others. Not enough to make a difference, though."

"That's powerful magic." I frown. Magic nowadays is poppets and good luck charms from Nan's workbench. Or it's shopping-mall magic—glamour patches and cleaning potions and period undies that never stain. Not something big enough to make a whole town forget about an abandoned power plant.

The fluttering feeling is stronger now. I look down and realize that whatever it is, it's in my pocket. I reach in gingerly, hoping it isn't a bee. Something dry brushes my fingertips.

The paper moth.

I pull it out of my pocket and stare at it.

It seems . . . alive. Flexing its folded wings. It shudders a little, then takes off, flapping through the willow fronds and out of sight.

I stare at Rufus, who is staring in the direction that the moth went. He saw it too, so it was no illusion.

"Did you make that?" he asks.

I shake my head. "I don't have any magic."

"Are you sure?"

"I think . . . I think my mother made it."

I scramble to my feet and push through the willow branches.

The paper moth has been in my bedroom for years. Why has it come to life now? It's like a dormant spell has been reactivated, here under Peg Powler.

"You're not going to follow it, are you?" Rufus asks.

Is it because of Odette?

I gesture after it. "How can I not?"

Rufus shakes his head. "Come back with me, Maude," he says. "Let's go tell your nan everything. She'll know what to do."

"You tell her," I say. "I'm going to follow the moth."

I plunge into the wild fennel, Rufus's protests fading into the distance.

THE MOTH LEADS ME along a fragrant trail that is familiar to me. Odette and I wandered this trail as lost girls, lost princesses, lost warriors. We were wild and free, unafraid of anything, least of all ourselves. Being lost was the whole point. Being lost was where the fun began. But for me, there was always a moment at the end of the day when I started to long for a hot bath and the coziness of home, the calm comfort of Nan and Halmoni, the busy kitchen and the warm hearth. Not Odette, though. She always wanted to stay lost. The dark paths called to her, sweet and seductive.

The overgrown trail forks, one path climbing to the top of the ridge, where there's a sports field and a colorful children's playground, the other descending until it is swallowed by a dense thicket of tea tree and bracken. The paper moth swoops and swerves into the dark thicket. I follow, trying to shake off the prickling feeling on the back of my neck.

I bend low, picking my way through the tangled, sharp-scented corridors of twisted branches. Mam once told me the wall between worlds is thin in places like this, but Nan only ever comes in on a waxing milk moon to cut branches of pointed leaves for a witch bottle. *Tea tree and brown sugar turns a sharp tongue sweet,* she says.

Odette and I often played in here. I loved the shapes of the trees, bent and gnarled like the limbs of crones, so deliciously spooky and brimming with stories untold. I loved the carpet of crunching gray leaves, and the way the thicket would turn you around and spit you out in a place you weren't expecting. Once, we went in there and found a waxbill skeleton, picked clean by scavenging creatures. I wondered if the bird had got so turned around that it couldn't find its way out, beating its wings against the tea-tree cavern, yearning for the sky, growing weaker and weaker until it died in there, starving and alone. I imagined the same thing happening to me.

"Don't be ridiculous," Odette had said when I confessed this. "I'd always come and find you. We rescue each other, remember?"

The paper moth perches on a wizened gnarl of tea tree before fluttering out of sight again.

I emerge at the foot of the labyrinth, a low circling maze laid out on grass in blocks of bluestone. Mam told me a story once about how it was built by fairies, but Halmoni says it was the Inglenook council. It was a familiar haunt for the games Odette and I played, and we spent many hours treading its twisting paths, hunting invisible minotaurs. Now, the grass has been worn away by traipsing feet, leaving thick clay mud. I see the paper moth perched in the very center of the labyrinth, and step into the first circle, about to tread my usual path, but I stop myself. Mam used to say that walking the labyrinth confuses spirits and keeps the dead in the ground where they belong, but that doesn't feel right for today. This story demands dangerous choices.

I turn around and head in the opposite direction, treading the labyrinth widdershins. The paper moth does a little loop-the-loop, and I get the sense it approves. It feels as if I'm walking with my shoes on the wrong feet, and my neck prickles with unease again. It's like being told off in class. Calling someone by the wrong name. Arriving at an appointment too early or too late. Being too loud, or too passionate, or taking up too much space.

The sun gets chased behind bruise-colored clouds, and the air around me turns cool. More than once, the mud claims one of my good shoes, and I have to slide my stockinged foot back in and tug it out. On the leeward side of the labyrinth, I can see a stand of callery pear trees, their branches crowded with laughing crows telling me to turn back.

But I don't turn back. I'm going to follow Mam's paper moth. To spin this story. To walk the dark paths, even though I promised Nan I wouldn't.

As we grew older, the fire inside Odette began to transform.

It wasn't the wildness of a little girl anymore. It turned darker and more human, infused with resentment and bitterness. I had been fearless as a little girl, but her new rage was terrifying to me. It was a darkness with no bottom. A monster that stared out through Odette's eyes and just wanted to *destroy*. A part of me always knew it would come—rage was Odette's gift. She had always demanded our games go deeper and darker, hunting out every malevolent presence or sinister detail that lurked in the corners of my stories.

After our friendship ended, she started hanging out with older kids who dabbled in curses and gave each other stick-and-poke tattoos with sewing needles and a broken pen. They'd catch the train to Scouller to explore the stormwater drains and to dance at the Witch Queen's balls in caverns deep beneath the city. Odette would disappear for days at a time, turning up at school bleary-eyed and stinking of tobacco and wormwood.

The labyrinth twists and doubles back on itself. Although its path is set only in the earth and I can see the exit a few yards away, I feel a shiver of panic. I could just step over the bluestone walls and stride right out. But I don't.

Every time Odette left, I'd hoped it would be enough, that she'd return to me and the imaginary worlds I spun for us, where lost girls were never confronted by anything more terrifying than treasure-loving dragons and wicked stepmothers.

But she never did.

I double back again and am brought up short. A large magpie is blocking my path. It has a snail in its white-tipped beak, bending over to bash it on a bluestone block.

I think of Mam telling me that every magpie carries a drop of demon blood under its tongue, and duck my head in a bow.

"Hello, Mr. Magpie," I murmur. "How's your beloved?"

The magpie turns a beady eye on me, and for a moment I feel like I'm submitting to some kind of test. Then it ruffles its feathers and launches itself into the air, beating black-and-white wings in my face. I raise my wrists and screw my eyes shut, terrified that it's going to attack me with that wickedly sharp beak, but it has already gone.

I take a shaking breath, inhaling the calming scent of Nan's white rose pinned to my cardigan. I'm at the end of the labyrinth, and the paper moth is waiting, perched on a branch of the wishing tree—a traveler's reward for treading the labyrinth— a wish to be granted by fairies or wood spirits. I step under the low, spreading branches and am surrounded by hanging bits of card and bark, tied on with string and scribbled with wishes.

I wish the bees will not die.

I wish my mam and dad would get back together.

I wish for as many cats as you can have.

I pull out the folded photo of me and Odette, and tie it to the tree, next to a card that says *I wish the wold cood tern into sweets,* scratched in a childish hand.

The path ends here, looping back up to the playground and the sports field. The paper moth swoops down the hill, to where train tracks cross the creek on a gray pipe bridge. The creek narrows to a trickle and disappears among a thick stand of dogwood and prickly gorse. I listen carefully for the rumble of a train, then climb onto the tracks, picking my way across gravel and timber. Before I step onto the pipe bridge, I put my hand over the rail, checking for vibrations, like people do in stories. I don't feel anything.

I glance around, half hoping that someone will come and yell at me, tell me to get off the tracks, drag me home where it's safe.

But there's nobody. I take a deep breath and sprint across the bridge to the other side of the creek, leaping from the track as soon as I'm on the other side and skidding into the bushes.

My heart is pounding, and I can feel sweat on the back of my neck.

The paper moth flits into the dogwoods and vanishes.

The creek has turned muddy, choked with sun-bleached rubbish and drowned tires. A woolly-necked stork stands in the murky water, its crimson eye watching me mournfully. I can smell gasoline and rotting vegetation. Plastic bags hang from the trees like ragged ghosts.

I can see dirty brick through the screen of dogwood— abandoned public housing, a remnant from the days before the auditors came.

Faded graffiti is scrawled across the outside walls, and right before me there is a newer piece—a giant vibrantly red rose, with a little girl's face at the center. It's been glamoured, the scarlet petals shifting slightly on the bricks, color dripping from them and trailing down the wall like drops of blood. The drops run together to form words in a flowing, cursive script.

Rescue the princess.

It feels like a message for me. An admonishment, for what I failed to do. But it can't be. This is the kind of place where you find illegal, underground things. Drug dealers, gutter druids, and catchpenny witches. It's not for nice girls like me.

The little girl in the graffiti rose doesn't look like Odette, but she does look lost. I scramble toward her and peek around the corner of the wall. I can't see the paper moth anywhere.

An abandoned shopping cart leans unsteadily against a red plastic slide, bleached and brittle from the sun. The building is falling down—there's ragged aluminum foil in the windows and a tattered screen door, the lintel black with candle-smoke marks to ward off bad spirits.

I hear a noise coming from inside, and fear floods my veins. This is the hidden part of the world, the part that Dr. Slater pretends doesn't exist, because it doesn't fit into his vision of Anglyon being simple, green, and good.

Something catches my eye, and I turn my head back to see the paper moth disappearing into some scrubby bushes. My knees wobble with relief, and I leave the public housing behind.

The crowded bushes open up onto a stand of white-trunked poplars, underlaid with a thick carpet of glossy green widow's-tears, which crunch under my feet as I walk over them. The names of all the plants come to me unbidden, as they have always done since Mam taught me them so long ago. Mam was always so proud of how good I was with plant magic, but Nan would narrow her eyes and purse her lips like I'd done something wrong.

I'm tired. I'm not exactly sure where I am. My feet ache from walking in my flimsy black flats, and I'm hot and thirsty.

The paper moth flits from tree to tree, waiting for me to catch up before swooping off to the next one. It flies low over Cygnet Creek, skimming the water. The creek is shallow here, but murky—I can't make out the bottom.

On the other side, skeleton weed scrambles over lumpen mounds of pale clay—an old landfill, or possibly even a series of rubble mounds dug up by prospectors long ago. Beyond that is a chain-link fence and, in the distance, a looming red brick wall, like the battlements of a crumbling castle. I have to blink three times before the name comes back to me.

Sicklehurst.

The sight of the wall fetches new memories out of the fog. It was a forbidden place, and Odette wanted to do everything that was forbidden. Her mother went to see a fortune-teller a few times about Odette's behavior—a real Grulle mouse diviner, not one of the crystal-ball franchises that you see in shopping malls. I don't know what they told her, but whatever it was, it wasn't enough.

I slip off my shoes and tuck them under my arm, then wriggle out of my stockings, leaving them hanging from the branch of a tree like some kind of skinny taupe phantom. I feel guilty about leaving them there—the creek is already choked with rubbish—but I promise myself I'll pick them up when I return.

I step barefoot into the creek. The water is cold—colder than I'd expected. Slimy muck oozes between my toes, and my skin crawls. I try not to think about broken glass, used syringes, and the cold fingers of shellycoats lurking below the surface, waiting to scrabble at unsuspecting wanderers.

I tread carefully, feeling first for sharp objects with my toes before putting my weight down, until a string from some aquatic plant wraps itself around my ankle, and I panic and dash across to the other side.

Maybe it's just the effect of having my feet in the water, but this side of Cygnet Creek feels cooler somehow, like I've crossed over into another world. I half remember a story that Mam once told me, about a man who found his way into fairyland by crossing running water three times. Magic is always more powerful in threes.

I slip my shoes back on. Without the stockings, my wet feet make everything feel clammy. I'm probably going to get blisters.

The paper moth flies over a hillock, and I follow. Embedded in the yellowish clay soil are fragments of things lost and forgotten. Bent cutlery and miscellaneous bits of plastic, the arm of a doll, fingers grasping like it's clawing out of a grave. Flecks of blue and white wink up at me, and I bend down to pry a piece of broken china from the soil. It's a willow pattern, a fragment of treetop in one corner, the wing of a flying goose in another.

Odette and I used to collect bits of broken china. We'd find them stuck in the creek bed, and I told Odette they were washed in from a fairy castle upstream.

"Can we go there?" she'd asked.

"If we collect enough pieces," I replied. "We can put them together like a jigsaw, and they'll make a map to fairyland."

"Tell me what it will be like."

I told her stories of how we'd shrink to the size of dandelions. We'd dance in toadstool rings, sip dewdrop wine from acorn cups, ride on the backs of field mice and wood swallows. Odette delighted in the romance and whimsy of it all, a fairyland from a children's book as sweet and innocent as a daffodil. I felt no need to tell her that daffodils are poisonous as well as beautiful, and that a tea brewed from the petals will cause the drinker's teeth to crumble like cottage cheese.

I SLIP THE PIECE of broken china into my pocket and scramble down the hillock into a patch of sticklegrass. It clings to my ankles like Velcro. There's a spot in our backyard where it grows, and Nan is always trying to get rid of it. Sticky jack, she calls it. Cleavers. Goosegrass. Poor man's lice. But Halmoni collects it in great armfuls, straining milk through it, and adding ginger and black sesame to lessen Nan's arthritis pain.

I feel a little tug of longing as I think of them standing there in the kitchen, bickering fondly the way they always do. I close my eyes and see Halmoni, standing over the sink, sticklegrass overflowing onto the floor, where it will inevitably get attached to the dog. *Catchweed,* Nan mutters, as she wrestles it out of Jeremiah's fur with a steel-toothed comb.

I thought you didn't believe in weeds, Halmoni says, her eyes twinkling. She tilts her head and does a passable impression of Nan. *"Weeds are only weeds when we don't want them someplace."*

Nan scowls, but she can't help herself from adding, *Plants aren't good or bad. They just are. We're the ones who make them good or bad.*

It's been less than an hour since I last saw them, but it feels longer. The tug of home is strong—the comfort of the familiar. But if you stay home all the time, stories never happen. Sometimes you have to break something in order for the story to leak out through the cracks.

ODETTE KEPT OUR COLLECTION of broken china in an old jewelry box—one of those ones with a ballerina that pops up and twirls around. One day, shortly after Odette's twelfth birthday, we came home from school and the box was gone. Odette tore apart her room looking for it, hurling books off shelves and emptying her dress-up box onto the floor.

"What's going on?" Odette's mother stood at the door like an ice queen, all pale skin and glacier eyes. She carried a ribbon-handled shopping bag from an expensive boutique in one long-fingered hand.

"My jewelry box." Odette's voice deepened into a growl as the monster inside her showed its teeth. "What did you do with it?"

I never stopped being shocked at how Odette spoke to her mother. If I spoke to my grandmothers that way, I wouldn't be allowed out of the house for a month.

"I threw it away, darling," said Odette's mother, her voice as smooth as glass. "It was babyish, and full of rubbish. Here. It has a charm that will stop necklaces from tangling, and a glamour that hides it from thieves."

She handed over the shopping bag. Odette reached inside and pulled out a new jewelry box, all sharp corners and mirrors. It looked sleek and modern and sophisticated, like a miniature version of her house. Odette turned baleful eyes on her mother.

"I hate you," she said.

Odette's mother's expression didn't slip. I couldn't tell if it was her glamour or if she really didn't care.

"Suit yourself," she said, and shut the door, her light footsteps receding down the hall.

Odette threw the new jewelry box onto the floor and looked wildly around. She grabbed the amethyst crystal I'd given her for her birthday—a large solid chunk of refracting purple and white.

"Odette!" I cautioned as she knelt and raised the crystal above her head.

She brought it down hard on the jewelry box, the mirrors splintering and fracturing her reflection into a hundred wrathful girls. She let out an animal whine and looked up at me. Tears started in her eyes.

"How will we get to fairyland now?" she whispered.

She looked so frightened, as if the prospect of staying here in this cold house with her cold mother was too unbearable to contemplate. And twelve-year-old me realized, for the first time, how hard it was to be Odette, and why it was that she liked coming to the creek and getting lost in my stories. For Odette, being lost was her only escape. The promise of magic, of fairyland: that was the only way out.

And so I knelt next to her on her plush cream rug, among the mirror splinters, and I told her about our lore, the lore that my mother had taught me, that her grandmother had taught her, growing up by the sea in Fishgate. Lore that is forbidden now, tangled and strangled in patents and lawsuits by the auditors and the big magic corporations.

Every culture has its own deep lore. Some of it is shared. Some is secret. Much is forgotten. Magic is a bit different, depending on who you are and where your ancestors come from, but it all accesses the same source of power, the magic deep within the earth, the energy that causes all living things to grow and thrive and wither. In some places, it's called numen, or qi, or mitogenetic emanation. But here in Anglyon, it's known as mettle, and it's found within all living things. It also collects in the places and objects that are significant, the way dust collects on a mantelpiece.

People like Odette have no connection to their heritage, to the secrets of mettlework. Deep lore has been replaced by glamoured nail polish, and charmed self-heating instant dinners, and mindfulness crystals that hum at just the right frequency. Even Nan doesn't speak the deep lore anymore, although I'm sure she knows how. She only does covenant magic. *Measly magic,* I hear Mam say, her voice dripping with scorn. *Tourist magic.*

I distracted Odette that day with stories of the sunken city of Cantre'r Perlog, where strange fishy creatures held court in glittering halls strung with pearls and shark teeth. I told her about Caer Heli and Caer Rhew. I told her about Islaw, the underworld, and saw her eyes gleam. She leaned forward, her tears forgotten.

"Tell me everything."

She wanted to learn the secrets of the moon, about curses, about hemlock and foxglove and oleander. She wanted more and more, the monster inside her always hungry, always *wanting.*

One day, she barged into the kitchen and demanded that Nan teach her how to make a witch bottle.

Nan sent her packing, then rounded on me.

"Are you trying to bring the auditors back?" she asked. "After what they did to your mother?"

I quaked under the heat of her fury.

"I can teach you covenant magic," she said. "If that's what you want. But no more of this make-believe. It's too dangerous. We can't lose you too."

I promised her I'd be careful.

THE PAPER MOTH GLIDES above an old chain-link fence that lines the edge of the landfill. Every few yards or so, there is a sign.

DO NOT ENTER

HAZARDOUS WASTE

On the other side, there is a field of white flowers and, beyond that, the high wall of Sicklehurst. I don't know when it stopped operating—long before I was born. It looks like a fortress, and even though the pull of home is stronger than ever, I just *know* that this is what the story demands. The heroine has to pass three enchanted gates—the creek, the chain-link fence, the brick wall. More threes. Odette must have found a way in, so I have to.

Now that I can see the wall, the compulsion to forget has dimmed a little.

I know there was a time when the forgetting spell didn't work on me, when I was little.

I remember now that *I'm* the one who told Odette about Sicklehurst. An abandoned power plant that had a magical secret. Of course she was intrigued.

"Why have I never heard of it before?" she'd asked.

I told her that everyone forgets it, and her eyes went wide.

"How do you know about it, then?" she asked. "Why don't you forget?"

I wasn't sure.

"Our town has been enchanted," Odette whispered. "There must be a great treasure in there."

"Or a terrible monster," I replied.

We were lying on the back lawn, the sweet scent of Nan's roses hanging in the air. Odette had her hands clasped behind her head, staring at the clouds.

Nan emerged from the potting shed, holding a pair of pruning shears.

"Who told you about Sicklehurst?" she pressed.

Secrets are Nan's gift.

Odette had sat up, her glamoured-black hair falling around her shoulders like a dark lace veil. "Tell us about it, Mrs. Jenkins. *You* must know."

The eagerness in her voice made me flinch.

"Who told you?" Nan said again, her face stony.

"Maude did."

Nan's eyes darted sharply to me. "Never mention that place," she said after a long moment. "Now go inside. It looks like rain."

We left her to the potting shed and went to see Halmoni, who was feeding her sourdough starter in the kitchen.

"Tell us about Sicklehurst," Odette demanded.

Halmoni's eyes widened. "Not in front of the bread!" she hissed, and threw a dish cloth over the jar of starter.

"Nan won't tell us anything," I said.

Halmoni made the sign of the evil eye and spat into the sink. "Some things are best not mentioned."

"Why not?" Odette never let something go once she'd set her mind to it. She was like a dog with a bone.

"No more questions," Halmoni said shortly, narrowing her eyes at Odette. "And your hair looks ridiculous like that. You should stop trying so hard to be something you're not."

A flash of anger passed over Odette's face, but even her rage monster knew better than to take on Halmoni.

"I've got better things to do," Odette declared haughtily, and stalked out of the kitchen.

I scowled at Halmoni. "Why did you have to do that? Odette has a right to express herself however she likes."

"It's time you both stopped playing silly games and grew up. Odette isn't a little girl anymore, and neither are you."

I FOLLOW THE PAPER MOTH along the chain-link fence for what feels like an age. My feet ache, and my head grows dizzy. I'm thirsty and tired, and I think, *Why am I even here? I should go home. Nan and Halmoni will be worrying about me. This reckless behavior isn't like me. I'm a good girl. I should go home, where I belong.*

My nose tickles with the scent of raw magic, and I sneeze. I realize that my exhaustion isn't entirely natural—there is another spell on this place, not just the forgetting spell. I can just feel the edges of it, the mettle somehow strangely familiar.

I look around and see a small clump of feathery pennycress, and I snatch a handful of it, crushing it and inhaling the strong mustard scent. It makes my eyes water, but the spell is weakened enough to make my weariness lift. Up ahead, I can see a small hole in the fence.

It looks as if the chain link has been clawed open by some kind of small but fierce beast. A pair of enormous gymea lilies rise on either side of the opening, twice my height, like bloody spears topped with severed heads. The second gateway.

I should go back.

The hole doesn't look quite big enough for me, but the paper moth flutters through, so I must follow.

I kneel before the hole and try to pull it wider. A broken link scrapes across my left hand, leaving a bright line of blood, but I think now I can fit through. I crawl on all fours, my hair and clothes snagging on the jagged wire. It feels like the chain link is closing around me, holding me fast, and I'm certain it's more than just a fence that's clawing me back. I close my eyes and breathe slowly, moving forward inch by agonizing inch.

And then I'm through. A chill runs over me as I scramble to my feet.

A meadow of purple-and-white onion weed blooms before me, all the way to Sicklehurst's high brick wall, which stretches off in both directions as far as I can see.

ODETTE'S THIRST FOR MAGIC was frightening. Where she had once been enchanted by the whimsy of fairyland, she now craved the dark paths. She'd beg me to show her magic, and for a while she was placated with small tricks and illusions. But she kept pushing me, wheedling and cajoling. She wanted more. Bigger. Darker. She wanted to find the limits of magic, and then push them.

"Give me fairy wings," she demanded one day. "Not a glamour. Real ones."

I shook my head. "I can't."

"Please, Maude? For me?"

I would have given her the moon, if I could. "That kind of magic is illegal. And anyway, mettle doesn't work like that," I explained. "Glamours work by changing perception. Same with curses, and finding spells, and charisma drams. That's easy, and you can use all kinds of mettle—plants or animals or objects. But to change something in the physical world takes an awful lot of mettle. Humans are really complicated, and to physically transform a person, you have to change everything—neurons, and blood vessels, and synapses, all the way down to the molecular level. The big magic companies can do it, but it'd take a huge team of thaumaturgical engineers." I swallow. "And you'd need pure mettle. Feathers and flowers just aren't enough."

I thought of the little vial of silvery liquid, locked away in Nan's drawer.

Something flared in Odette's eyes. "That's what they do in the detention camps, right?" she asks. "Drain people of their mettle? That's what your mother was doing. Trying to save those poor people."

I nodded stiffly. Nan and Halmoni didn't talk about it, but I'd kept that newspaper clipping, in a shoebox underneath my bed, along with everything else I could find out about her. I'd been to the library and read through past newspaper editions, had searched every online database I could find. I knew that Mam had met my father at university, in a mettleworking program. They'd protested the introduction of the magic ban, and my dad had gone to Goose Spring, where he'd died fighting for the rights of magic folk. After I was born, Mam became increasingly involved in activism, eventually joining the resistance witches. She'd protested against detention camps, against the regulation of magic, against the big magic corporations stealing spells from witches with no compensation.

And then she had tried to steal something. I didn't know what it was—some kind of magical artifact. But she got caught and sent to a detention camp. She returned to us in a coffin.

"You could use my mettle," Odette said. "I'll give it freely— I know it works better that way. Could you make me fairy wings then?"

I couldn't believe she'd ask such a thing. Sometimes you see husks, people who have been mettle-drained walking the back lanes—like wraiths, hollow and vague, their eyesight dimmed, fertility dried up, toothless mouths full of ulcers and cold sores.

I had thought of Mam, cold and lifeless, laid out on our front door. At the time, the idea that Odette could end up as cold and as lifeless seemed inconceivable. Nobody had ever been so full of life.

But now there's been no word from Odette for two weeks, and people are starting to whisper that she is probably dead.

WHEN I WOULDN'T TELL HER any more of our deep lore, Odette went looking for it elsewhere. There was no shortage of shady websites with instructions for cursing rituals, or online suppliers of wax figures, baby teeth, and groaning cheese. She raided the library for books about witchcraft and asked Betty Metanee if she wanted to do a seance. Betty's dad ran the local fish-and-chip shop but was also rumored to be a mo phi, who could invoke the spirits of the dead.

One day, Odette came barreling into my bedroom with a black satin bag containing candles, a pendulum, unleavened bread, a handful of bones, and a little bundle of herbs.

"Betty taught me how to draw a summoning circle," she said. "We're going to raise the spirit of your mother."

I felt blanched with terror at the thought of it. Invoking spirits was dangerous magic—utterly forbidden. I didn't know how to do it, and I didn't want to. But I couldn't say no to Odette.

So I faked it. Odette said I needed a piece of Mam's clothing, and I went and grabbed one of Nan's silk scarves. She laid out the bones—leftover from a roast chicken dinner, still greasy—and I didn't correct her when I saw she'd done it wrong. I smudged the circle and didn't tell Odette that what she thought was henbane and clammyweed was actually just sage and cleome. Odette lit the candles and solemnly chanted the words that Betty had written down for her.

I didn't expect anything to happen. Which is why when the candles all blew out I nearly screamed in fear. The skunky smell of the cleome was suddenly overpowered with the scent of roses and blood, and I distinctly heard a screeching, like the wild cry of a demon.

I kicked the bones away, scattering them across the room.

"Why did you do that?" Odette demanded. "It was just getting interesting."

"No more," I stammered. "No more magic."

It was the first time I'd ever stood up to Odette. The monster inside her flared up, and she didn't speak to me for a week. I was plunged into despair without her.

But she came back to me, barging into my room, her hair wild, her eyes full of angry tears.

"I hate her," she spat without so much as a hello.

I knew she was talking about her mother. Odette saved all her most vitriolic spite for her. They'd had a fight. Odette's mother had been through her room again, throwing away what she called "childish rubbish." Odette had retaliated, cutting up her mother's most treasured dress—made of the finest sea silk and embroidered with tiny Langland pearls.

Odette flung herself on my bed, a snarl of tears and rage and clenching fists.

"I just want to go to fairyland," she whimpered. "More than anything."

I was so grateful that she'd come back to me. All my defenses crumbled, and I showed her the deepest magic I knew.

I took her into Sicklehurst.

The forgetting spell hadn't worked on me then. I had known where to go and how to get in.

If only I could remember *how*. Or what happened when we were in there.

All I remember is coming home and finding Nan waiting for me in the kitchen, her face white with fury.

"How could you," she had said. "You *promised.*"

Halmoni was there too, her eyes rimmed red. "Niamh," she said quietly. "Perhaps we should consider . . ." Her voice trailed off, her eyes falling on a drawer in Nan's workbench.

"Consider what?" I'd asked timidly.

Nan shot Halmoni a warning look, but Halmoni had ignored it, opening the drawer and handing me a brochure.

"You've been scouted by one of the thaumaturgical schools," Halmoni said. "They think you have potential."

Nan scowled. "Gossip travels fast in Inglenook," she said. "I warned you to keep your magic a secret."

A thaumaturgical college. I'd move away from Inglenook to board there. I'd seen the brochures—those schools were elite, with every convenience and latest development in mettleworking technology. I'd get a job working for one of the big magic companies in research and development. There'd be an attractive salary and a fancy apartment in the company town, and lots of other perks. I'd be able to take care of Nan and Halmoni. And I could do magic without getting into trouble. It . . . didn't sound terrible.

"Do you think I should go?" I asked.

"Absolutely not." Nan's voice was firm.

"At least she'd be safe," Halmoni said.

Nan's eyes flared with rage. "Those people killed our daughter," she said. "I'm not handing over our granddaughter too."

I blinked in surprise. It was true that the thaumaturgical colleges and the detention centers were all owned by the same three magic corporations—Ilium, Moracle, and Welch. But I'd never really linked them together before.

"Then what?" Halmoni said. "We can't let things go on as they are."

Nan went very still. Then her shoulders squared, and a grim, determined glint appeared in her eye.

"I can keep her safe."

She put her hands to my head, and I felt the whisper of magic as she wove mettle around me. I didn't ask her what she was doing.

I trusted her.

"You won't go in there again, will you, love?" she asked.

I frowned. "Go in where?"

And she had smiled, and I'd smiled back as I forgot all about Sicklehurst.

I wore the bone-pin brooch that she gave me. I wore it every day, because I didn't want her and Halmoni to worry.

It ended up not mattering, because soon afterward, my period came, and the threads of mettle started to slip through my fingers until I couldn't handle them at all anymore.

"It happens," Nan had said. "Magical ability often fluctuates around big hormonal changes. Puberty. Childbirth. Menopause. Gender transition. Sometimes it comes, sometimes it goes. It's probably for the best, love."

I CAN SEE the old cooling tower, grim and gray against the sky, beyond the high brick wall. All I can hear is the huffing of my breath, the fall of my footsteps, and the faint rasping of the paper moth's wings.

Everything about this is foreboding.

I dig my fingernails into the palms of my hands and march

59

across the field of flowers. My footsteps release the pungent aroma of onion, and I'm suddenly aware of the hollow, aching feeling in my stomach. I haven't eaten anything today except the thrupenny biscuit I had with Nan.

Sicklehurst's wall is broken by two enormous iron doors, like a barred fortress. There is no chain, no handle, no lock. The doors practically scream, *Closed, forbidden, leave.* I've turned around and taken a few steps before I catch myself and stop.

I sneeze three times as my nostrils fill with the scent of magic. It's stronger here, and I hesitate for a moment, then turn witch-eyed. I don't do it very often, it reminds me too much of all the magic I can't do any more. It's a triple spell—magic is always more powerful in threes. The first layer is loose and billowy, threads of mettle floating in the air and stretching all the way back to Inglenook. This must be the forgetting spell. The second layer covers the wall like an invisible blanket, woven thick and tight as damask. I place my hands on the brickwork and can feel the strength of it—these doors cannot be opened, nor the walls be broken by any nonmagical means.

The third layer of the spell must be inside, but I can't sense it. I can't sense anything beyond the wall.

This spell is very powerful, but it is old. It smells powdery like dust, with undertones of rich loam and rose petals. The mettle is a little faded, some of the threads starting to fray. Mettle is life force, and life force weakens over time. Whatever this spell is, it's starting to soften at the edges. I can see evidence of patching, though—someone has been maintaining it.

There are designs etched into the bricks around the doors—crescent moons, chalices, besoms, sickles. One of them is familiar to me—four interconnecting loops in a circle, like a knot or a flower. Same as the ones carved on our doorstep at home. It's our family witchmark—Mam's and Nan's. But what is it doing on the bricks of Sicklehurst?

I suddenly remember being here with Odette when we were twelve. I remember sneezing, and Odette taking my hand.

"How do we get in?" she had asked, staring at the doors.

"There's another way," I'd told her. "A secret way."

If only I could remember what it was.

4

THE PAPER MOTH SWOOPS PAST THE GATE AND DIS-appears into a thicket of holly and brambles that hugs close to Sicklehurst's wall.

"You want me to go in *there*?" I call after it.

It looks extremely spiky.

Maybe there's another way. I circle around the thicket, but there's just more wall on the other side.

And there's something about the way the paper moth flitted in there. It triggered something in me, like déjà vu. I've done this before.

I take a breath and push into the thicket. A thorn sinks deep into my skin, and I see a drop of bright-red blood.

The coppery scent of it hits me, and all of a sudden I'm a child again. Mam is crouching in front of me, holding something gently in one hand.

The moth, the paper bright and new, the creases fresh, its abdomen glowing glimmer-moth blue. Mam opens her palm, and it flaps away.

I try to hold on to the memory, but it disintegrates like paper turned to ash. Did I come here once with Mam? Then why can't I remember?

I follow the moth farther into the thicket, trying to avoid the thorns, but they're everywhere. Sticklegrass clings to my ankles, making me stumble. Soon my arms are cross-hatched with scratches, but I keep going until the close press of brambles thins and I find myself in a small clearing, where the endless brick of Sicklehurst's wall is broken by a small wooden door.

Abruptly, the paper moth falls from the air.

I see that the life has gone out of it. My stomach clenches in horror as I look around.

Dead birds litter the ground before me, in varying stages of decay. Woodlarks, starlings, sparrows, and spinifex pigeons stare at me with unseeing eyes and empty skulls. There are dead butterflies too, and bees. The petal-limp corpses of glimmer moths, their glow extinguished forever.

All winged creatures. All dead.

There's a thump as something falls out of the sky and lands at my feet, and I jump away from it, biting back a scream. It's a stitchbird, flapping its gray wings weakly, the yellow band on its chest rising and falling with failing breaths. Heart hammering, I scoop the poor thing up, but it's already dead, its beady black eyes lifeless and dull. The spell killed it. The second layer of the spell, the part that blankets the walls. It's strong enough to kill any flying thing that attempts to enter Sicklehurst. I place it back on the ground and take a few deep breaths, trying to calm my jangling nerves.

This is the part of the story where the hero wants to turn back. But they have to keep going, even though they're scared and they're not quite sure yet where it is they're going or why. They just have a *feeling*, and storytelling rules say those feelings must be heeded.

Odette said she wanted to return to Sicklehurst, and the paper moth has led me here. It *can't* be a coincidence.

She must be here. I have to find her.

I pick my way through the corpses of dead birds until I'm right in front of the wooden door. I try the handle, but I'm not expecting it to open, and it doesn't. A sad-looking wreath is hung on the door, misshapen and withered, with three white feathers sticking out of it, and something dangling from the bottom.

A necklace.

My breath catches in my throat.

Odette's necklace. A silver chain with a half-heart locket.

I have a matching one in my keepsake box at home.

I can't believe she kept it all this time.

The clasp is opened—the locket empty. When we had exchanged them, Odette had insisted on a blood ritual to seal our friendship. We'd each pricked our thumbs and made red smears on a scrap of linen, then torn the cloth in half and each kept a bit in the locket. We wore them every day until Odette turned up at school wearing a black velvet choker and I knew for sure that our friendship was over.

Odette made this wreath. I see thin rose canes, a young whip of apple, and withered devil's snare. This is no decoration. It's magic. Odette isn't magical, but she must remember something that I don't. I guess because Nan didn't make her forget.

I glance back at our family witchmark on the wall.

My mind is like molasses. I pick up the paper moth, turning it over in my hand and unfolding the paper gently. The creases that formed the moth are old and deep. It's a page torn from a book. It's familiar—it looks like it belongs in the book of nursery rhymes that Halmoni used to read to me. There's a rhyme printed on it, and an illustration of a big-headed girl standing by a stream, with a flock of geese flying overhead in a V formation.

Intery, mintery, cuttery, corn
Apple bough and apple thorn
Bramble, briar, limber lock
Three geese fly in a flock
Cranny key is ~~held in hand~~ forged in blood
Open the door to ~~fairyland.~~ the sticklegrass wood

Someone has annotated the rhyme in faded ink, crossing words out and scribbling in new ones.

I know that writing. I'd know it anywhere.

This is Mam's.

As I read the rhyme, a memory surfaces. Not of Mam, but of Odette, and the day I took her to Sicklehurst.

I brought her here, to the secret door. I made a wreath to open it and chanted the nursery rhyme. She had begged me to teach it to her, so I had.

I look down at the crumbling sheet of paper in front of me. There's mettle in nursery rhymes, power that grows stronger each time the charm is repeated, over and over, through the ages. Folk songs too, even pop songs, accumulate mettle if they get played and sung enough.

The memory is already fading, but I've got instructions now. I read through the rhyme a few times until I'm sure of what I need.

I can use the locket and feathers from Odette's wreath, but other than that I'll have to start again.

A yellow rosebush grows by the little door, and I snap off a cane, careful to avoid getting pricked. I can't find any mint, but there's a clump of costmary nearby that will have to do. There's a stunted apple tree in the thicket, its branches gnarled and low. I realize that, along with no bees nor flying things of any kind, there are no flowers here, by the wall of Sicklehurst. I snap off a flexible whip of new growth from the apple tree, then bend to collect a few stalks of devil's snare.

I take my ingredients back to the door and sit cross-legged on the grass.

I have no magic left. But Odette had no magic either, and she did it. After all, the spell to open the little door has already been cast. The wreath is more like . . . a password, or a key. Odette saw me make the wreath, back when we were little. And she remembered. But how had I known? Had I watched someone make it as well?

Mam. It must have been Mam. Had she left the paper moth for me to find? Did she want me to return to Sicklehurst?

Go home, says sensible Maude. *You're being ridiculous.*

But this is where the paper moth led me. I've spun enough stories to know when the hero must heed the call.

I can't go home yet.

I take the costmary, rose cane, apple, and devil's snare, and braid them together, then bend the braid into a circular wreath.

I wrap Odette's necklace around the bottom, and tuck the three feathers in.

Blood. The scrap of linen in the locket has some, but it's old. I slide the bone-pin brooch from my cardigan and prick my thumb, squeezing a single drop to splash on the locket, vivid red against the dull silver.

Then I replace the pin and Nan's rose, stand up, and hang my fresh wreath on the horseshoe nail, over Odette's withered one. I take a deep breath, feeling more than a little foolish.

"Intery, mintery, cuttery, corn
Apple bough and apple thorn
Bramble, briar, limber lock
Three geese fly in a flock
Cranny key is forged in blood
Open the door to the sticklegrass wood."

I repeat the charm three times, then turn around once and spit into a Turkey rhubarb bush growing up against the wall.

Nothing happens, but maybe the air feels a little cooler than before. The shadows are growing long as the sun begins to sink toward the horizon.

I should go home.

I don't belong here.

But I wait.

The shrill song of a cicada explodes from a nearby stand of whiskey grass, so loud that it makes my ears ache.

I am hit with the overpowering scent of rose petals. It doesn't smell soft and sweet, like Nan's roses at home. This scent is rich and bloody, like roses strewn on a battlefield. It's voluptuous, intoxicating, primal, like I'm being suffocated with petals. The sensual, earthy decay of them seeps into my skin, is sucked down my throat into my lungs, and infuses my blood. My whole body pulses with it.

It feels like a warning.

I stand up and reach out a hand to the dark wood of the door. It's ice-cold and seems to throb under my touch, like it recognizes me. Like it's been waiting. My heart judders in response, the blood in my veins running suddenly cold, then hot, then cold again.

I feel a heavy pull in my abdomen, like I'm getting my period.

The pinprick on my thumb pulses, and blood starts to weep from it. I press it to the door.

I can feel the overlapping layers of the triple spell—the loose, floaty forgetting spell over Inglenook, and the heavy blanket over the walls. I can even sense the third layer, deep within Sickle-hurst, as thick and impenetrable as lead.

I should walk away. This isn't me. This isn't what I do. I like my adventures to be imaginary, where I'm able to step out at any moment and return to the comfort of home.

Nan and Halmoni will be worried about me.

But Odette could be in there.

She needs me.

Sicklehurst calls to me, to the wild girl I once was, the fierce creature that roamed Cygnet Creek with a pocketful of pebbles and dreams.

"Open," I whisper.

I take a deep breath and focus my energy on the door, reaching with my witch-hands for the strands of mettle. But as always now, they slip away from me, like I'm a ghost. When it first happened, I thought it was just temporary. That I'd wake up one morning and be able to weave the mettle once more. Every morning, I'd reach out for it. And every morning, the mettle would slip through the fingers of my mind. Eventually, I stopped trying, because it hurt too much to fail.

But Odette got in. I'm sure of it—her necklace is here.

Which means I can get in too.

"Let. Me. In," I command.

The leaves and blossoms on the wreath curl and shrivel in front of me, then crumble into dust that gets whipped away on a gust of wind. What's left of the wreath slips to the ground. Only the feathers are undamaged.

The musky scent of roses hits me again, thick and moist, like rotting vegetation.

Thunder rumbles overhead.

The door shifts under my hand, opening a crack, and my ears pop.

A thorned rose cane spills out of the door, like some sea creature's tentacle. I glimpse velvet-red petals, more than I could have imagined. There is malice in them. They tremble, like they're being ruffled by a breeze I can't feel. I glimpse a shape beyond them, insubstantial as mist, whirling and writhing in wisps of silver and white. I watch as the silvery threads coalesce into a human figure.

Despite his white hair, I don't think he's much older than me. He is stunningly beautiful—a long, graceful neck, sharp cheekbones, and platinum eyes fringed with thick, silvered lashes. He stares at me, his lips parting in shock, and a crease appears between his brows. I have never seen anyone quite like him before, and yet he feels sharply familiar. He opens his mouth to speak, but no words come out, only a strange, inhuman cry. He reaches out a long, fine-boned hand, but the red roses close in, and he dissipates as if he were nothing more than a shadow.

I push the door fully open. There are no roses. No beautiful ghost boy. The abandoned power plant is gloomy, veiled in evening shadow. I see the rising bulk of the cooling tower again, past crumbling buildings, silhouetted against the darkening sky.

There's a faint glow coming from the very top, as if a candle has been lit in a princess's tower. Is that where Odette is?

I look over my shoulder at the holly thicket, drab and colorless under a cold rising slice of egg moon. I imagine walking back along the dark paths—the slimy creek, the garbage-strewn public housing, pushing blindly through grasping branches.

There's no going back now. I step forward into Sicklehurst, through a kind of skin-crawling wrongness as I pass through the second layer of the triple spell, the door falling closed behind me with an ominous *thunk*.

I should have brought a torch. There's barely any light left in the day, and I'm an idiot for coming in here at all. I turn to leave, but the door is gone, replaced by unbroken red brick.

Of course it is. Bloody magic doors.

Everything looks . . . fairly ordinary. Nettles scramble over cracked concrete paths. Garden beds are overgrown with hemlock and wood-parsley. The structures are weathered—windows broken and grimy, paint flaking. It looks exactly how a forty-years'-abandoned power plant should look.

But beneath my feet, I can sense something powerful, huge,

and spreading. It feels like . . . a kind of vast consciousness. It calls to me in whispers that I can't understand, but I get the feeling that it recognizes me, just as I recognize it.

The mettle of it feels somehow oily—dull and gray instead of the usual bright silver.

Something is wrong.

There's a building before me, a squat brick thing lined with broken windows. To one side is a series of storage sheds. To the other is bare earth, raised and chalky, next to a muddy-looking pond. I can see the frames of rusting tanks in the distance and, beyond, a huge barnlike container building. Behind everything is the rising concrete mass of the cooling tower.

It's hard to decide which way to go when you're not really sure what you're looking for. I had expected it to be made clear when I arrived. I'd thought Odette would be here, grimy and grateful to be found. Or I would be greeted by a wise old wizard or a talking animal, or perhaps have the path laid out before me in colored brick.

Maybe the secrets of Sicklehurst aren't available to me. I'm no lost girl, no tragic princess. I'm not the hero of anyone's story. My gift is *telling* stories, not living them.

I feel a rising wave of shame, that familiar feeling of wrongness, like I don't belong. Like I'm inappropriate. I clench my fists and swallow it down.

Not today.

My heart starts to beat faster as I realize there's something moving around the corner of the squat brick building. I can see it, white like a ghost. Is it the boy again? I take a deep breath and head around the corner. I am surprised to discover that it is a clothesline, strung between two wooden poles, pegged out with white sheets. I walk right up to it, not quite believing that it's real. Who is hanging laundry inside an abandoned power plant?

A sudden gust of wind billows the sheets out toward me, and I'm engulfed by waves of bed linen. It smells like sunshine and dittany. I try to step backward but become tangled in the sheets and turned around, so I'm not sure which way is forward and which way is back. The sheets boom and snap in the wind, whipping at my face and shoulders. I push through them, but there seems to be another row, then another, an endless maelstrom of crisp white cotton.

And then I'm out, the sheets behind me. But when I look over my shoulder, there's only a single clothesline, with two sheets hanging from it. I'm standing in front of a ramshackle wooden building, leaning visibly to one side, dittany bushes growing thick up against it. A faded sign over the door reads SECURITY OFFICE. Gauzy curtains float from the window.

Is someone living here?

I touch my fingers to the bone-pin brooch for luck. It feels warm.

A girl steps out of the building, carrying an empty laundry basket on her hip. She's about my age, perhaps a little older, wearing a blue-and-white polka-dot dress that hugs appealingly plump curves, her beetle-black hair swept up into a vintage roll. She looks familiar, but I can't quite figure out why. Her lips are painted red, and freckles are sprayed across the pale bridge of her nose. She turns bright-blue eyes onto me, eyes that widen in surprise.

"This is unexpected," she says, her voice low and warm. "Are you lost?"

5

HER NAME IS GINGER, AND SHE IS A LOT.

She sweeps me along with her to the clothesline, and I find myself helping her to unpeg the sheets as she chatters away.

"I don't get many visitors," she says, attempting to fold a sheet, before giving up and dumping it into the basket as is. "Or . . . any, really. I can't imagine why. Probably the whole magically sealed fortress thing, I suppose. Who knows!" She aims a scowl at the darkening sky. "Why is it so hot? Is it hot where you came from? It's too hot here. Offensively hot, don't you think? Like someone's doing it on purpose, to vex me. I just want to lounge around in a cool bath when it gets like this, but of course I don't have a bath, do I? What I do have is iced tea. Do you like iced tea? I have some inside."

She doesn't pause for an answer to any of her questions, so I don't answer them. I can't tell if she's rude, or nervous, or just totally self-absorbed. She offers no explanation of who she is, or how it is possible that a young woman is living inside an abandoned power plant with a magic forgetting spell around it.

Ginger bends over to pick up the basket. "Come along, then," she says, and heads back to the wooden building, which she tells me over her shoulder is her "apartment." I trail after her, irritated by her patronizing tone, but I feel caught in her wake and unable to escape.

I notice things outside the building. Pebbles grouped in threes. Bits of iron scavenged from the power plant, half buried in the ground. Bits of bone too—I can't tell what kind of creature they came from, or how old they are.

There are six-petaled hexafoils carved into the lintel above the door like spiked daisies, and bunches of rowan and marsh rosemary hanging from the roof. Someone has gone to a lot of trouble to protect this place. We cross the threshold, and Ginger turns to pour a handful of salt on the doorstep from a little pouch at her waist. Then she pulls the door closed and touches six iron nails that are clumsily banged into the shape of a circle. She does this briskly, efficiently, but I can feel an undercurrent of urgency in her.

What is she so afraid of?

"Welcome to my palace," she says with a smile that reveals twin dimples in her cheeks.

The room has a chipped pink enamel sink and a single gas burner, but it's dominated by a double mattress on the floor that is strewn with a shabby embroidered quilt, and more cushions and pillows than any human being should ever need. Suspended above the bed is a gauzy pale pink canopy, studded with silver sequins. An ivy vine has penetrated a crack in the wall and rambles throughout the room, green glossy leaves on spreading tendrils. Dresses of plum, cerulean, and forest green are hung on cheap wire hangers from a sturdy branch suspended from the ceiling with jute string. There's a ratty-looking chaise lounge by the window, upholstered in faded, moth-eaten emerald velvet and piled with yet more cushions and a sizable stack of magazines— mostly *Cottage Weekly* and *Country Idyll,* but I spy some edgier ones in there too, like *Flairy* and *Glistr.* A low wicker bedside table is cluttered with makeup pots and bottles, and a large tin of Talky Toffees, the kind shy people chew at parties and on first dates to loosen up a bit. A breeze lifts the sheer white curtains, bringing with it the lemony scent of dittany from a row of glass jars over-flowing with flowers, lined up on the windowsill. Where did all of this stuff come from?

The whole place is feminine and eccentric and bohemian, like something out of a story. I feel profoundly ordinary in my plain navy dress and cardigan, my utilitarian ponytail, my total lack of ornamentation, save for Nan's rose and the bone-pin brooch.

Ginger dumps the laundry basket on the bed and lights can-dle after candle, filling the room with a cozy, golden glow. Then she opens a little cupboard and pulls out a jug of what looks like iced tea. She pours it out into a jam jar and hands it to me before sinking onto her bed in one graceful movement.

"Toffee?" she asks, indicating the tin.

I shake my head. "No, thank you."

"I'm afraid that's all I can offer you," she says. "Unless you want some salad greens." She sighs wearily, then kicks off her black heels and tucks her legs beneath her. "Now tell me every-thing," she demands.

She doesn't look quite real. She's beautiful, but without the smooth perfection of a commercial glamour. Yet it's not an entirely natural beauty either. She's like a character from a story, larger than life, the room overflowing with the force of her presence.

Where have I seen her before?

I perch on the chaise and sip my drink, my mouth filling with sharp flavors of nettle, orris root, and angelica. I think about how you're not supposed to eat or drink anything in fairyland unless you want to be bewitched, but I am *thirsty*. I'm suddenly overwhelmed by the incongruity of this room, of her.

"Who *are* you?" I blurt out. "What is this place?"

"I'm Ginger, empress of Sicklehurst."

I glance around. It isn't much of an empire. "You live here? Alone?"

Ginger waves a dismissive hand. "Ugh, boring. Let's talk about *you*. You look interesting. Tell me interesting things. Are you sure you don't want a toffee?"

There's a coldness to her voice as she says it, a hint of something haughty and regal. It must be lonely, living in an industrial ruin. I feel an urgent need to please her, to give her what she wants.

"I'm looking for my friend Odette," I tell her. "I think she came in here."

Ginger nods, as if this makes sense. "A lost girl?"

"She went missing two weeks ago."

Ginger looks away. "I haven't seen her."

I hadn't expected any other response, but I'm disappointed nonetheless.

"Nope," Ginger says briskly. "No sadness. Sadness is boring. Let's talk about something else."

She gets up off the bed and comes to sit beside me on the

chaise, taking my iced tea from my hand and putting it by our feet. Then she takes my hand and examines it.

"Can you read palms?" she asks. "I always wanted to try."

I shake my head. Nan doesn't do palms. She says they're not as accurate as tea leaves or throwing barley.

Ginger strokes the lines on my palm with a cool scarlet fingernail.

"I see grand adventures in your future," she declares. "Riches untold. You'll be a hero to all. Rescue princesses, defeat evil toadmen, save the world. That sort of thing."

Rescue princesses.

Ginger looks at me through thick, dark lashes, heavy with mascara. "And romance," she says, her voice a low purr. "I definitely see romance."

I take another sip of the iced tea. It's strong on my tongue. Orris for calm. Angelica for confusion. Nettle for compliance. I realize that Ginger didn't pour herself one.

Her face is inches from mine, red lips parting to reveal a flash of white teeth.

I'm not sure I'm entirely safe here. But I can't look away. I can feel the faintest whisper of her breath on my face. Her eyes flick down to my lips, then back up to my eyes. The curtains stop floating in the breeze. Each ivy leaf stays perfectly still. For a moment, nothing moves.

"You should come and visit me more often," Ginger murmurs. "You could bring me things."

"Things?" I ask.

"Sweets," she says. "Makeup. Magazines."

I feel the sudden sting of memory, bringing two lunch boxes

to school for a whole term, because the housekeeper at Odette's house had quit and Odette's mother was too busy to find a new one.

"You don't have any magazines on you, I suppose?" Ginger says hopefully.

"Magazines?"

Ginger indicates the pile by her bed. I realize then that they look old and ragged, curled up in the corners from water damage.

"It's always mostly the simple-life country ones." She sighs. "But every now and then something more interesting comes in. Of course they're all just catalogs of things I can't buy, but a girl can dream."

"Where do you get them from?" I ask.

Ginger shrugs. "Lost things sometimes find their way here."

Lost things like Odette.

Ginger picks up a magazine and flicks through it. It's *Luminary*—the kind of trashy celebrity mag you get given at the hairdresser, the kind that I snootily refuse to read. But Ginger is enraptured.

"They're so beautiful," she whispers.

The people in the magazine *are* beautiful—really beautiful, not with the fake beauty of glamours. Cameras don't lie, and so celebrities are beautiful because of their imperfections—slightly crooked teeth, too many freckles, a lopsided smile or a high fore-head. It's what makes them so appealing.

I touch my bicep. It's been ages since I wore a glamour patch. Odette and I used to steal the really expensive ones her mother used and visit all the posh shops in town, holding back giggles as shop assistants deferred to our haughty, cold beauty.

When I started high school, I bought cheap synthetic glamours from shopping malls, like all the other kids, smoothing out my pimples and plumping up my lips and boobs. Some of them came with temporary tattoos—glittery butterflies that flapped their wings, or twinkling stars. There was a sameness about them, everyone in my class blending into generic ideas of teen attractiveness. Not Odette, though. She was into black-market glamours. She'd come to class with luminous green cat eyes and pointed teeth, her skin the bluish white of skim milk, hair as black and glossy as ravens' wings. Looking at her like that gave me a queasy feeling, like the floor was heaving beneath me, and I'd feel a guilty surge of relief when she got sent to Dr. Slater's office, then suspended for violating uniform policy.

By the time I was thirteen, I stopped using glamours altogether, much to the satisfaction of Halmoni and Nan, who both despised them.

Fair leaves bear bitter fruit, Halmoni always said.

"Look!" Ginger says, turning a page in the magazine outward so I can see. It's Qilin Lazuli, showing off their tail at some red-carpet event. It's a real tail—not just a glamour—covered in golden fur, with a tuft at the end like a lion's. It moves and everything. That kind of magic takes a massive amount of mettle, and as such can be accessed only by the very, very wealthy. Qilin is wearing a close-fitting bodysuit made of golden scales, showing off the slim angles of their body. Translucent, milky antlers rise from their deep-blue bobbed hair, hung with delicate white lace. Thin, carplike whiskers in the same deep blue trail from just above their gold-painted lips.

Dr. Slater would hate this. It's so far away from his vision of what is green and good and natural. I'm not quite sure how I feel. Qilin is beautiful—*so* beautiful. But I keep thinking about how much time and money it must take to put a look like that together, without glamour. How much mettle.

"So expensive," I murmur.

"I'm sure they can afford it," says Ginger airily.

Something inside me crackles, like it always does when I get too close to thinking about Mam.

"It would have taken literally hundreds of hours of enchantment," I say.

"So?"

"So that magic doesn't come from nowhere. It's the *life force* of the people who made it, in detention camps and mettleworks. Their life force is drained, just to make sparkly accessories for celebrities."

Ginger looks sullenly at the picture of Qilin Lazuli, tracing the line of the tail with her finger. "Way to bring down the mood," she mutters.

I turn my face to the window to hide my embarrassment, but night has fallen, and there's nothing to see. Except for one glimmer of light that pulls my eyes to the tower.

"Is there anyone in the tower?" I ask.

Ginger's eyes flick to the window. "No," she says. "It's just foxfire."

I feel suddenly uneasy. "I should go," I say.

Ginger's sullen expression softens. "No," she says, pouting. "Not yet. I'll be so bored without you."

The enchantments in the iced tea are making it hard for me to say no. And, more than that, I've missed this. Being around someone who takes charge. Someone who will let me quietly orbit around their bright light.

"Please," Ginger says, turning her eyes to me and smiling. "Stay. I promise I won't bite . . . That is, unless you ask me to."

Heat spreads across my face. I really have to go. Nan and Halmoni will be worried. But the nettle makes it hard to refuse, and I can't bear the thought of returning along the creek in the dark, so after a moment of dithering I agree to stay.

Ginger claps her hands. "Sleepover!" she says happily, and pulls out a short lace nightgown, spinning to present her back to me.

"Zipper," she demands.

My fingers brush her pale skin as I undo the zipper. I swallow as she steps out of the dress. She's completely naked underneath, and I look away, blushing furiously. I hear the slide of silk on skin as she puts the nightgown on.

"We can share the bed," she says, her voice a low purr.

Heat flushes through me. I don't know if it's the iced tea, but I can't deny my attraction to Ginger. I'm not here to flirt, though. It doesn't take a genius to work out that she's dangerous.

"I'll be fine here," I say, curling up on the ratty emerald chaise without taking off my shoes.

"Suit yourself," Ginger says.

She positions herself appealingly on her bed, propped up on

her elbows. "Tell me more about this friend of yours. Are you in love?"

I shake my head.

"No," I tell her. "Not *in* love. Things were pretty intense between us, but not like that. Every story had a handsome prince."

We could rescue each other . . .

DESPITE MY DEVOTION to the brooding heroes of my stories, I had managed one crush on a real boy. Mondarius Cole. He was tall and funny and handsome—not as handsome as a storybook prince, but more so than your average teen. In Year Nine, he asked me to tutor him in math, and for one glorious hour each week we'd meet in the library and talk about vectors and parabolas and stem-and-leaf plots. Sometimes his hand would brush against mine, and I'd feel a tingle of excitement. I fantasized about him asking me to the Hollantide Ball, about dancing with him, held in the circle of his arms, about his dark-brown eyes smiling down at me, about him tilting his head to kiss me.

One day in the library as I was explaining irrational numbers, he turned those dark-brown eyes to me, and I saw his usually confident smile flutter in nervous anticipation. My heart skidded.

"Do you know if Odette is going to the dance with anyone?"

I wasn't surprised or disappointed. Of course he wanted Odette. Everyone wanted Odette.

"I don't know," I said. "Odette and I aren't friends."

Saying the words had felt like a betrayal, even though it had been years since we'd played together.

For the Hollantide Ball, Odette abandoned the ripped black

jeans, which had become her wardrobe staple, and the Goth glamours, which made her look so sickly pale. She wore a gauzy dress of pure white, which sat off her shoulders and was wrapped around her waist with silver ribbon. Her sleeves floated long and low from her elbows. Her hair was a white-gold waterfall, woven with snowy heliotrope flowers. She looked like a fairy princess who had stepped out of one of my stories. Mondarius wore an indigo velvet suit that glittered darkly, and when they danced together it was like watching day and night, the sun rising amid the deepest, most glorious midnight sky.

They danced in the center of the gymnasium, and the other students didn't stray into their silver spotlight, as if they were afraid to approach such luminous beauty.

I sat on the bleachers and watched. I was wearing a black dress—it was the first one I tried on at the first shop Halmoni had dragged me to. Nobody was going to notice me, I thought, so why bother making an effort? Rufus Sheldrake appeared, looking like a clown, with his uncontrollable orange hair and an ill-fitting suit with a baby-blue satin cummerbund. Neither of us had a date, or any other friends to hang out with. We talked about school, and Rufus told me about cryptobiosis in mosses.

I had hoped it would be a turning point for Odette, that she would come away from the darkness that fascinated her so. But on Monday, Odette was back in her black jeans and Goth glamours, and I was patting Mondarius on the back as he tearfully confessed that she hadn't replied to any of his messages.

I knew how he felt.

*   *   *

GINGER IS STILL WATCHING ME, waiting for me to go on.

"Boys came and went, with Odette," I say at last. "But me and her, we were supposed to be forever."

"Supposed to be?"

I swallow. "I guess she didn't love me as much as I loved her."

Something flashes over Ginger's face, a glimpse of vulnerability. "Love is a waste of time," she says breezily.

"Who *are* you?" I ask, in case this time she'll actually answer. "Why are you here?"

Ginger smiles sadly. "I'm tired," she says. "Sleeping time."

I'm ready to push her further, to try and get some answers, but she turns away from me and blows out the last candle.

A faint breath of rose scent drifts in through the open window, a heavy rich velvet against the sharp lemon of the dittany. I reach a tentative hand to my chest and brush Nan's rose with my fingertips, for comfort. I hope she knows I'm okay.

Through the window, I can just make out the cooling tower, where a faint light still glows glimmer-moth blue against the velvety night.

Tomorrow, I will explore Sicklehurst. I'll find Odette, and take her home, and fix her. So we can be friends again. I have to believe that it's possible.

I glance over at Ginger. The night is warm, and she has a sheet pulled up to her waist. Her breasts rise and fall with her breath under the thin silk nightgown. There is something about her that is so familiar, but I just can't put my finger on it.

I close my eyes and drift into uneasy sleep.

6

I WAKE TO GRAY MORNING LIGHT. THERE IS NO BIRD-song. Ginger is sitting on the edge of her bed, toying with a hairbrush.

"Oh, good, you're awake. Would you like to brush my hair? I love to have my hair brushed, don't you?"

I sit up. "I should go."

Nan and Halmoni will be beside themselves. I need to find Odette and get home as quickly as I can.

"Fine," Ginger says. "I guess I'll do it myself."

She begins to pull the brush through her thick hair with long, even strokes.

"At least come and sit with me. Maybe I'll tell you a secret."

I hesitate. She's told me nothing so far, and I'm not sure I can trust her. "What kind of secret?"

She gazes at me through her lashes. "Maybe I do know something about your friend."

My mouth goes dry. "Odette? You've seen her?"

She pats the bed next to her, and I come and perch on the edge.

"Shoes off," she says with mock sternness, and wriggles over until she's half hanging from the bed. She slips my shoes off, one by one, and tosses them over her shoulder. Then she gives me an assessing look.

"Now, what else should we take off?"

I grit my teeth. "I want answers."

She gives me a sultry pout. "You're no fun."

"Is it possible for you to just answer my questions without flirting?"

"Well, I suppose it's *possible*. Just somewhat unlikely."

"Stop trying to be cute," I tell her.

"I'm not trying. I can't help it! Cute is my natural state."

My hands clench in frustration. "This isn't a game."

Ginger's eyes narrow, her dimples vanishing. "Of course it's a game. Everything's a game. What else is there?"

"Tell me what you know."

She pauses her hairbrushing, and for a moment I think she's going to say something useful. Then she winks at me. "Has anyone told you that you have lovely posture?"

"That's the third time you've tried to change the subject."

"Fifth."

I stare at her.

"I make it the fifth time," she says. She lays down her hairbrush, and the dimples reappear. "If we're keeping score."

"Enough," I say, standing up. "I'm leaving."

I find one shoe, pull it on, and cast around for the other one.

"You can't leave," Ginger says, rising from her bed and crossing the room.

"Can't I? Why not?"

Calmly, Ginger holds up my missing shoe. She doesn't break eye contact as she drops it into the jug of iced tea.

"Because your shoe is wet."

I let out a frustrated growl. "Why do you have to be so obnoxious? People aren't toys. I'm not your plaything."

Ginger stares at me, then bursts out laughing. "Finally! I was beginning to think there was nothing in there but a little mouse."

"So will you help me?"

"It depends on what kind of help you need."

"Will you answer my questions?"

"Probably not. But I'll tell you what I will do." She fishes my shoe from the jug and lets it drip. Then she grins. "I'll go and put this in the sun to dry."

She sashays out, and I let myself fall back onto her bed with a groan.

I should just leave. But I'm sure now that Ginger knows something about Odette.

I can't cast a spell on her, because I have no magic. But perhaps I can use the spell she's already cast on me—the iced tea that made me so compliant. My eye falls on the toffee tin by the bed.

Ginger reappears, and I smile and pat the coverlet next to me, reaching over to pull two toffees from the tin.

"I'm sorry," I say. "I lost my temper. Peace offering?"

The dimples spring to life, and she flops down next to me, her eyes warm, her wild dittany scent enveloping me. She unwraps the toffee I offer her and pops it in her mouth. I follow suit, and as the sweet caramel spreads across my tongue, I feel the urge to talk rising.

"My grandmothers would be horrified to learn I'm having toffee for breakfast," I say. "They never let me have sweets before lunch. Except jam, I suppose. And a biscuit with morning tea. That was the last thing I ate, you know. A thruppenny biscuit in the kitchen. Nan makes them using her own recipe, and Goody Morgan is always trying to get it, but Nan won't tell for nothing."

I pause to draw breath. Ginger is watching me with a knowing smile.

"Gosh," I say. "That toffee made me thirsty. It's a shame you ruined the iced tea."

Ginger springs to her feet. "I have more."

She produces another jug and pours me a jam jar full of amber liquid. I bring it to my lips, not breaking eye contact with her.

"It's really good," I tell her. "Aren't you having any?"

Ginger shrugs. "I'm out of jars."

"Here."

I lean forward and hold my jar to her lips. She hesitates, and I lean closer, gazing at her with only half-feigned adoration.

She swallows.

I prattle on for a bit, telling Ginger about Halmoni's stained-glass studio and the time that Hangul got stuck in the chimney.

Ginger watches me indulgently, interjecting to ask questions and deliver responses. But I notice that she doesn't reciprocate with any anecdotes about her own life.

"Tell me something," I say, trying to keep my tone casual. "Why is it that you don't want to answer my questions?"

Ginger responds without hesitating. "Because I don't want you to leave."

She claps a hand over her mouth, then turns her head to glare at me accusingly. "You put a spell on me."

"It's your enchanted iced tea," I point out. "And your chatty toffees. Really, you put the spell on yourself."

"That's not *fair!*"

I shrug.

Ginger narrows her eyes. "The little mouse has teeth, as well as a roar. Fine. Four questions. And I've already answered one."

I try not to look smug. "Okay. Have you seen Odette?"

"No. But there's someone else here who might have."

"Someone else? You mean the boy?"

Ginger frowns. "There's no boy in here."

"I saw him," I say, confused. Is he new? Or is Ginger lying to me?

"Impossible. Only one question left."

I have so many more questions, and I know I can't use the toffee and iced tea on Ginger again. I chew on my lip, considering.

"What are you so afraid of?"

Ginger's expression grows bleak. "The Tatterdemalion."

The word is familiar to me, but I can't figure out why.

I start to ask more, but Ginger holds up a hand to silence me. "Enough," she says wearily. "I've already said far more than I wanted to. Just believe me when I tell you that if your friend ever was here, she'll be dead by now."

I feel sick at the thought of it. Am I in danger too? I look at Ginger, empress of her own lonely wasteland.

"Why are you here, then?" I ask. "Why not go to Inglenook or Foxford and have a real life?"

I see the flash of vulnerability as Ginger's mask slips. Then the queenlike haughtiness comes over her again, and she picks up one of her magazines and opens it, gazing at the images of celebrities on red carpets.

I make a few more attempts to engage her in conversation, but she steadfastly ignores me. Eventually, I give up and, resigned to walking with one soggy foot, go in search of my shoe.

Ginger stiffens as we both hear a high-pitched scream, full of terror. A sudden coldness floods through me, and I leap to my feet and rush to the door.

"Don't open it." Ginger is still clutching her magazine.

"It could be Odette."

"Whoever it is, it's too late for them."

I swallow down a wave of terror. "How can you be sure?"

Ginger's voice is quiet. "I just am."

I stare at her. "I'm going."

"Then you'll die."

The scream sounds again, louder this time. I hurry out the door. The morning is chilly and gray.

Something is coming.

I can make out words in the screams now, swearing and cursing.

Then a girl bursts from a nearby building. How many people are living in this abandoned place?

She's no more than a child. She wears what looks like a bridesmaid's dress, all lace flounces and petticoats, but ragged and dirt-smeared. Her eyes are agate-hard, her lips set in a determined thin line.

Her eyes meet mine, and I feel a jolt of recognition.

I know this girl.

But how?

"Run," she says to me in a low, flat voice.

"Winnie!" It's Ginger, leaning out her bedroom window, her face white with shock.

The girl turns her eyes to Ginger and scowls. "Is this where you've been hiding, you filthy coward?"

Something else is coming. I can hear the sound of heavy foot-falls, of undergrowth being crushed and twigs being snapped. A thick fog descends, swirling and sudden.

The girl makes a noise, low in her throat. I can't tell if it's an animal growl or a moan of terror. Whatever it is that's coming, it's not good.

Through the fog, I see what looks like a forest—tall, dark trees that weren't there a second ago, too big and old to have grown so wild since the power plant closed. Then a creature emerges. A creature that shouldn't exist. A creature that makes me freeze in terror. Branching antlers, long twiglike fingers, and curving green tusks. Tree-root feet that sink into the soil with each step.

There's something about this creature.

Something familiar, even though I've never seen it before.

It looks up, and I see gaping holes where eyes should be, wet and slimy. It stares at me for a long, agonizing moment, its head cocked to one side. I get the sickening feeling that it knows me, that it recognizes me, just as I recognize it.

I find that I cannot move.

It approaches slowly, soil showering from its rootlike feet with each step.

I need to run.

I smell hot, wet compost, and rot, and the dusty granite of gravestones.

This is a dream. It has to be. There are no monsters anymore. Not ones like this anyway. Monsters nowadays are merely nuisances. Shellycoats and lubberkins, and pwca who turn milk sour and steal the best apples just before they ripen.

It is close now. Close enough to reach out . . .

It rakes me across my chest, and the pain is real, burning away the dreamlike feeling. I look down to see my cardigan and dress in rags, blood seeping dark into the white petals of Nan's rose.

"Come at me, asshole!" the little girl screams, rushing at the monster with a machete.

I stagger to the side, and the creature snatches the girl in its claws before she can get in a single hit.

I can't look away.

The girl crumples on the forest floor, her dress soaked crimson as the creature tears open her abdomen, digging deep into her body. The scent of roses and rotting vegetation mingles with the hot, sweet tang of blood. Bile rises in my throat, and my whole body begins to shake uncontrollably.

The girl has stopped moving. There's no way she's survived— the creature has torn her apart like a rag doll.

It makes a grunting, screaming noise that is simultaneously high-pitched and deep, both soft and loud. Its twig fingers curl into fists.

There's a crackling sound behind me, and I turn to see the dittany plants surrounding Ginger's apartment burst into flames, like someone had set a match to a gas burner. Dimly, I recall that another name for dittany is burning bush, as it excretes a highly flammable oil, which can catch fire on hot days.

As I watch in horror, the flames spread quickly to the dry gray timber, licking up the building toward Ginger's open window.

"Ginger!" I scream, and run toward the building.

It's already so hot—hotter than I'd thought imaginable. I throw up my hands to shield my face. I see Ginger's gauzy curtains disappear in a flash, eaten by the hungry flames. I hear groaning and cracking as the building is consumed by fire. But I don't hear Ginger.

I can't do this. I can't think, can't breathe. Everything is smoke and heat and heart-hammering fear. I can't feel my fingers.

My lungs are full of smoke as I cry out for Ginger again. I try to gulp for air, my throat burning. I stagger backward as the building shudders and the beams that support it give way. Then the entire thing collapses in on itself in a massive cloud of smoke and flame.

I hear the creature roar from the forest, and my instincts take over. I pelt back to the place where the door into Sicklehurst was and pound my bloody hands against the high red brick wall.

"Let me out!" I yell, my chest burning with smoke and the raking pain of the creature's claws.

And at my command, the door appears, and I stumble through, back into the field of onion weed.

7

NAN IS PACING THE FRONT GARDEN, HER HAIR LIKE a bird's nest, her eyes wild. She's still wearing her pink Lycra leggings from the day before. When she sees me trudging up the lane, her face contorts into a rapid series of expressions—fear, relief, guilt, and finally anger.

"You!" she says, marching down the garden path toward me.

She grabs me by the ear and hauls me into the kitchen, where Halmoni is waiting.

"Niamh, she's hurt," Halmoni says. "She needs a hospital."

"She'll need more than a hospital when I've finished with her," Nan fumes. "Of all the blockheaded, foolish things to do. And on an egg moon, no less!"

"I—I'm sorry, Nan," I stammer, my voice hoarse from smoke.

Nan looks at me incredulously. "Sorry?" she says, her voice rising an octave. "You're *sorry*?"

Halmoni puts a calming hand on her arm. "Niamh," she cautions.

"Don't shush me, Eun-ah," hisses Nan before turning back to me. "Explain yourself."

Haltingly, I tell her about Odette's visit weeks ago. About Rufus reminding me about Sicklehurst. About the paper moth, and the secret door.

As I speak, I realize the forgetting spell has completely gone. I guess crossing the threshold into Sicklehurst broke it, the way it had done for Odette.

Nan shakes her head and goes stomping over to her workbench, pulling jars from shelves.

I tuck my head under Halmoni's chin, like I did when I was little, and listen to the steady rhythm of her heart.

"You should have told us where you were going," she says, her voice resonating in her chest.

"I'm sorry," I say again.

Halmoni draws me over to the couch, and we sit down. "What did you find?" she asks, in her calm, soft voice, and I realize that the forgetting spell doesn't work on her either. Or on Nan. Of course it doesn't.

"I don't know," I tell her honestly.

Nan rounds on me. "Have we not raised you like our own daughter, after your mother died? Have we not given you everything you needed, every one of your heart's desires? Have we not loved you? Do you truly care so little about us that you would just waltz back into that place?"

I shrink away from her. Nan has yelled at me before, heaps of times, when I've forgotten to pick up my dirty clothes in the bathroom, when I got caught skipping out on a history test, when Odette and I raided her workbench drawers for spell ingredients. But never like this. The full force of her anger, turned upon me.

I'm scared of her.

My nan, who wears luridly colored tights and hitches up her skirts to dance around the hearth whenever "Pretty Tonight" by the Baboon Section comes on the radio. Nan, who makes me poultices when I have a headache, and holds my hair back when I have food poisoning. Nan, who makes the best cardamom shortbread in Inglenook.

I don't recognize my nan in the woman standing before me now, glaring and fuming and hurting.

And worst of all, it's my fault. If it weren't for me, she wouldn't be so worried and angry.

I feel my face crumple, and hot tears stain my cheeks.

Halmoni draws me to her once again. Gentle, patient Halmoni, who always knows what to say to make me feel better.

"That's enough, Niamh," she says, her voice firm.

Nan glares at her, then stalks over to the fire and tosses a stick of myrtle into the flames, staring at it grimly until it is glowing red. She withdraws it with iron tongs.

"It's time for this to end," she says. "Your obsession with Odette. I'm not playing around anymore, humoring you. Odette isn't coming back. You won't find her. Grow up."

She drops the blackening stick into her stone mortar and strikes it with the pestle. With a sharp, decisive crack, the stick shatters into ash.

"I will not stand by while my granddaughter runs off on the most foolhardy of quests," she says. "I will not see you go down that dark path, the way your mother did. She abandoned you. She never thought of her family."

Her words hurt my heart. "Why is there a forgetting spell on Sicklehurst?" I ask. "You put it back on me, after I went in there with Odette, so you must know. Is it something to do with Mam?"

Nan turns away from me. She tosses a chunk of wild iris root in with the myrtle ash and pounds it with the pestle, adding a dollop of margarine and mixing to form a thick paste.

"Is it about the thing she tried to steal?" I press.

I've asked before, of course. But Nan won't talk about it, and the crushed look on her face when I did always made me feel wretched. But my heart is beating fast now, and I'm so caught up in my own fear and panic and adrenaline I can't stop.

Nan's mouth grows pinched, and I know I'm not going to get anything from her. And I'm not feeling wretched this time. I'm feeling *angry*.

"You're a hypocrite," I tell her. "You've tried to shelter me from magic my whole life, but at the same time you're doing it right in front of me."

"*Covenant* magic," she hisses. "I have a *license*."

I raise my eyebrows and look pointedly at the salve she's mixing in the mortar. "Is *that* covenant magic?"

I know it isn't. I can see the threads of mettle that Nan is drawing from the ingredients, and an ugly part of me twists with envy to see how easily her witch-hands manipulate it. Whatever she's doing, it's stronger than covenant magic.

"Tell me you still have the bone-pin brooch," she says.

I pull it out of my pocket. "I took it off when my cardigan got ripped," I tell her. "To keep it safe."

"I told you to wear it always."

I feel my cheeks flush. "I—"

"No more excuses."

I'm about to fire off another retort, another accusation, but Halmoni catches my attention and shakes her head.

Nan looks over at me through narrow eyes, then adds a few drops of rose oil to her mixture.

"Undress." It isn't a request.

I slip the torn cardigan and dress over my head and stand there in my bra and undies. Three hot lines are slashed across my front, where a swell of breasts would be if I had anything other than fleshy lumpiness. I feel a deep gut stab of horror and grief as I realize it did really all happen—Ginger, the monster, the fire. A part of me wanted to believe it was just another story I'd made up.

Nan spreads the gritty paste on the lines, and despite the grim expression on her face, her fingers are gentle on my skin.

"Nan," I ask, and I can hear the trembling in my voice. "Why is our family witchmark carved on the wall of Sicklehurst?"

Nan says nothing, but her eyes are as sharp as two pins.

"Was it Mam? Did she have something to do with the triple spell? Or . . . was it you?"

She doesn't reply, just presses a thick square of gauze over the marks and secures it with cloth tape.

"Nan," I say, trying to steady my voice. "You can trust me. I'm not Mam. I'm not going to run off and join the resistance witches. I couldn't even if I wanted to."

It comes out with more bitterness than I'd intended, and Nan's expression softens.

"Sicklehurst is dangerous," she says. "And your mam was always drawn to danger. I tried to keep her away from that place, just like I tried to keep you away too."

She looks so crestfallen, her sorrow at failing to protect Mam etched on her aging face.

"I'm so sorry, love," she says. "I didn't mean to snap. I just . . . I don't know what we'd do without you."

The sadness in her voice undoes me, and I burst into tears. "Please don't be angry with me," I beg.

Nan enfolds me in an embrace. I have to stoop a little to hug her back, breathing in her biscuity rosemary scent. It smells like home. Like everything.

"Oh, love," she says. "Just promise me you'll never go there again."

"I promise," I say. Anything to make her happy.

We eat dinner, and I help Halmoni with the dishes, and we play rummy by the fire afterward and pretend that everything's normal.

In the dead of night, I lie awake, my heart hammering as I relive my encounter with the monster over and over again. I see Ginger's face, and the other girl's—Winnie's. And the ghost boy's. Why do they all feel so familiar? It's like I know them, or I did, long ago. Like we're all connected.

Or at least we were, before they died right in front of me.

FOR THE FIRST TIME in a long time, I think about the marigold.

I don't even remember who gave it to me. It had been a gift— a birthday present from a friend, perhaps. A cheery orange marigold in a terra-cotta pot. I was six and had vowed to look after it. To water it every day and sing to it, because Nan said that the mettle in a song would help it bloom.

But I forgot. Summer was full of distractions, and I forgot about my marigold until I rediscovered it on my windowsill one morning, brown and shriveled. I was devastated. Halmoni had stroked my hair and gently reminded me that plants needed watering. That if I wanted to, she would take me to the nursery and I could spend my pocket money on a new marigold.

But I hadn't wanted a new marigold. I'd wanted *my* marigold. I was overwhelmed with guilt and shame. If it hadn't been for me, the marigold would have survived. It was my responsibility to look after it, and I'd failed. I put my finger to the withered husk and felt its mettle, brittle and crumbling.

In the midst of my torment, Mam came home, trembling with exhaustion, foxglove petals in her hair and chalk under her fingernails. I hadn't seen her for weeks. She gathered me in her arms, and I sobbed and sobbed.

"I can bring it back," she'd said. "But I need the vial."

I showed her where Nan kept the key to the locked drawer and shrank away from the hunger in Mam's eyes when she withdrew the tiny vial of silvery liquid.

She let one drop fall on the soil of the marigold pot. It sat there for a moment, shimmering and bright. Then it sank into the soil. I felt a kind of invisible rush around me as Mam worked the mettle. The shriveled brown unfurled and flushed green once more, the stems plumping with moisture and mettle as the plant came back to life.

"What are you playing at, Carys?"

It was Nan, standing in the doorway.

"Nothing, Ma. Just a small act of kindness."

Nan stepped forward to examine the marigold. Then she

looked at Mam, her eyes cold. "You don't get to saunter in whenever it suits you and put my granddaughter at risk."

Mam stood up, a full head taller than Nan. "Your granddaughter? Last time I checked Maude was *my* daughter."

Nan shook her head. "You've got a funny way of showing it, disappearing for months on end without any word."

Mam put her hands on my shoulders. "Perhaps we can discuss this later," she said coldly to Nan.

Nan glanced back down at the marigold. "Give it here," she said, holding out a hand.

Mam's chin lifted slightly, and I wasn't sure if I was imagining it or not, but her eyes looked darker than they had before. Reluctantly, she handed over the vial.

"You're a fool," said Nan, and stomped out of the room.

Mam was arrested a few weeks later. The marigold stayed green and healthy, but it never put out another flower.

A year later, they brought Mam home in a coffin, and we laid her out on the front door.

"Can you bring her back?" I asked Nan through my tears.

Nan shook her head. "Nobody can," she said. "Magic doesn't work that way."

"But the marigold . . ."

Nan's face crumpled, and she pulled me to her in a squeeze. "A marigold is a simple thing," she explained. "And even that required a drop of pure mettle. A person is . . . so complex. So many organs and veins and fiddly bits. Not to mention the memories. The voice. The love." She kissed the top of my head. "A whole army of witches couldn't do it."

"Can we make an army?"

Nan had sighed. "There aren't enough witches left to make an army, love."

All I can think now is that I need to find Odette, before it's too late.

THE NEXT MORNING, I pull on my school uniform and head downstairs to find Nan in the kitchen, stuffing little jars and bottles into a black leather case. Halmoni is sitting at the kitchen table, drinking tea and ostentatiously reading the newspaper. The air between them is frosty, and I know they've been fighting.

"What's going on?" I ask.

Neither of them reply.

"Nan?"

Nan empties the contents of a drawer into the black case. "We're going away for a bit," she says. "All of us."

"No, we're not," Halmoni says calmly, not looking up from her newspaper.

"It'll do us good to get away," Nan says. "A vacation. We'll go to the cottage at Fishgate."

I stare at her. "I have school," I tell her.

Halmoni takes a sip of her tea. "That's what I said."

"We're going," Nan says. "That's final."

"Maude says she wants to go to school," Halmoni says, her voice still calm.

"Is this about what I did?" I ask Nan. "Is it about Sicklehurst?"

Nan's eyes dart at me. "No," she says, her tone short.

I don't believe her.

Halmoni puts down her newspaper. "Maude will go to school

today," she says. "If you're still determined to go ahead with this nonsense, then we can talk about it tonight."

Nan glances nervously to the door, as if she's expecting a pair of auditors to break it down at any moment. I follow her gaze, remembering the pair that took Mam away. How meek they were. How polite. How implacable. When I look away from the door, Halmoni and Nan are staring at each other. Something unspoken and full of concern passes between them, then Nan's head ducks in a brief nod.

"Off you go, Maude," Halmoni says, not breaking eye contact with Nan. "Have a good day."

I decide not to mention that I have had no breakfast, and that there is no packed lunch waiting for me on the kitchen counter. I'll grab something at the bakery.

"Wait," Nan says before I can grab my bag. She hurries out the door into the garden, reappearing a minute later with a fresh white rose in one hand. She hesitates before she approaches me, and I smile, trying to assure her that our horrid fight is over. She smiles back, a little tight around the eyes, then steps forward to pin the rose to the lapel of my blazer, as usual, with the bone-pin brooch.

"Take this too." Nan presses a smooth blown-glass ball into my hand.

It's one of her witch bottles, the ones that she keeps high up on the shelf in a box, to be used only in case of emergencies. I've never actually held one before, and I look closely at it. It's about the size of a ping-pong ball. The glass is etched with our witchmark—four interconnected circles, like a flower. Inside, I can make out a twig of whitethorn, a dry bit of Halmoni's sourdough, a lock of hair, and something brown and shriveled that looks like it was once living tissue.

This definitely isn't covenant magic.

I frown and look at her. "Are you sure?"

"Only in an emergency," she says. "And don't let anybody see it."

She looks somehow older, more fragile. She reaches up on tiptoes and kisses me on the cheek.

"Hurry straight home after school," she says. "Don't tarry."

I TRUDGE UP THE GRASSY LANE, then turn up Clapcot Road and follow it into Inglenook. The town is as busy as it gets, with traffic stalled on Market Road as everyone rushes to drop their kids off and get to work. I reach the turnoff to school and hesitate. I'm not going to find Odette at school. I need more information. I can't talk to her, but perhaps I can find a clue in her room. I turn up the hill toward the posh part of town.

"Maude!"

It's Rufus, bounding up the road like a gangly puppy, waving an arm in the air to get my attention.

I close my eyes. *Not now, Rufus.*

"Are you okay?" he asks. "Your nan called my house yesterday—she sounded worried. And angry."

"I'm fine," I say, smiling with false brightness. "I'll see you later."

I start walking again.

"Why aren't you going to school?"

He's following me. "I just have something I need to do."

"I'll come with you."

"It's really not necessary."

"Okay."

But he doesn't stop following me. He has this loping, giraffe-like gait that today I find inexplicably irritating. He tells me about the classes that I missed yesterday. About his extra-credit assignment on growing mushroom hyphae in a submerged culture. I don't really listen.

"What happened with the paper bird?" he says at last.

"Nothing," I say, too fast and too defensive.

"This is about Odette, isn't it? Did you go to Sicklehurst?"

I stop walking. Clearly, Rufus isn't going anywhere. "Yeah," I say. "I did. And . . . it was weird. There were people inside. And a monster."

Rufus's eyebrows are knit together in skepticism and concern. "A monster?" he says. "What kind of monster?"

The slashes across my chest burn under my school uniform, and I shudder. "The kind you hear about in stories. Horns and claws and tusks."

"A wild boar?"

I shake my head.

"Maude," Rufus says. "There are no monsters anymore. They've all been wiped out. Even redcaps and lubberkins won't come within ten miles of a town or city. Too much steel and iron. You know that."

"I know what I saw."

He gazes up the road to the top of the hill, to where a sleek, modern building sits surrounded by a rolling lawn. "That's her house, isn't it?"

"I know Odette went to Sicklehurst," I explain. "There's a kind of key that you have to make to get inside, and she'd made it—her necklace was on it. But I don't know if she's still in there. I . . . I need to see if there're any clues she might have left behind, at home."

Rufus glances at his watch, then at me, then back up the hill.

"You should go," I tell him. "You'll be late for school."

He's never been late to anything in his life. But he squares his shoulders and starts marching up the hill toward Odette's house.

"Let's go, then," he says over his shoulder.

ODETTE'S MOTHER ANSWERS THE DOOR, cold and haughty. She doesn't welcome us in, which is no surprise to me. She says nothing, gazing at me with expressionless beauty.

"I came to apologize," I explain. "I ran away yesterday. I should have stayed for the vigil."

Still, the ice queen doesn't speak. I wonder if she takes her glamour off at night. Does she avoid mirrors when she hasn't got it on?

I glance at Rufus and wonder what he sees. Is Odette's mother still intimidating when he looks at her?

I feel totally frozen by the power that she radiates.

Rufus clears his throat. "Is there any news?" he asks.

Odette's mother takes in Rufus, with his orange bird's nest of hair, his too-short school trousers that show his ankles, his shapeless blazer, covered in stains and burn marks from experiments gone wrong. He bounces on the soles of his feet, unable to keep still. Her distaste is obvious.

I swallow. "You must be worried," I say. "I know you love her, in your own way. I love her too. I miss her all the time, every second of every day. I wish I'd been a better friend. I wish I'd listened to her."

A twitch of her top lip. A flicker of emotion in those hollow eyes.

I soldier on. "I wish she were here right now, so I could tell her that I love her."

"What exactly is it that you want?" she asks.

I swallow. "Just a few minutes in her room."

She regards us both for another long moment, and I'm sure she's going to tell us to leave.

Then she takes a step back from the door, opening it wider to let us in.

"Take anything you want," she says. "It's not like any of it meant anything to her."

I want to tell her that I know where Odette went. That I think I can rescue her. But she won't understand. Everything just slides off her, like raindrops on glass.

We head through the foyer, and it is so strange to be here without her. I can't shake the feeling that any second she'll explode through the front door, slinging her schoolbag onto the cold marble floor for the housekeeper to pick up, tramping muddy footprints up the gracefully curving stairs, filling the cavernous, sterile space with breath and warmth and *life*.

Rufus's mouth hangs open as he gazes at the crystal chandelier, the abstract slashes of art hanging on the walls, the hard-edged furniture that we were never allowed to use. I lead him down the corridor and slip into the one space in the house that doesn't feel cold and hard.

It's been four years since I last set foot in Odette's room. But it hasn't changed much. The fluffy rug is still there, as is the gilt-edged four-poster bed with matching bedside and dressing tables. The bed is unmade, the sheets rumpled. Otso, her ancient teddy bear, flops forlorn in the indent where Odette slept.

"Bloody hell," mutters Rufus. "I had no idea Odette lived in a *mansion*. This room is bigger than my whole house."

I glance around. It *is* big, I suppose.

"And her mother . . ." Rufus shakes his head. "No wonder Odette was messed up."

I bite back a defense. Rufus didn't know Odette. Nobody did, not the way I knew her.

Her dressing table is scattered with black nail polish, candle stubs, and glamour patches with names like Lilith's Curse, Black Hecate, and Raven's Fate. Smoky quartz, bloodstone, and obsidian tumble together in a decorative bowl. There are dead flowers in a glass vase—curled brown nightshade leaves, and brittle umbrella-like sprays of hemlock. The water at the bottom has turned to brown sludge, the muddy, rotting scent of it hanging heavily in the air.

I paw through her drawers and find more occult curios—a silver bullet, tarot cards, a little vial of something labeled DOVE'S BLOOD that looks more like raspberry cordial to me. I leaf through her wardrobe. I kneel on the rug and peer under her bed. But there's nothing. No indication as to where she might have gone.

"What are you looking for?" Rufus asks.

"Clues," I say. "A diary. Anything."

Rufus doesn't help me look, just hovers awkwardly in the doorway. "Maude, you have to stop punishing yourself," he says. "Odette wasn't your responsibility."

"I'm her best friend."

"She's barely spoken to you in four years."

I sit down on the bed, pick up Otso, and hold him to my cheek, his worn fur soft as moth wings against my skin. I keep expecting her to walk in the door, her silvery hair full of light, demanding we embark upon another adventure.

"But I might be the only one who can find her."

"You think finding her is magically going to fix her? Do you think she's going to be all sunshine and rainbows again? Is her mother going to suddenly develop a heart?"

"Odette wasn't always like this. She used to be better."

"Did she?"

Rufus's words hang in the air. The room is so full of contradiction. The diamond girl that Odette's mother wanted her to be—beautiful and cold. The girl *I* wanted Odette to be—a princess, trapped forever in the golden haze of imaginary childhood worlds. And among it all, there are hints of who Odette actually is. Not a princess or a diamond. But a girl so full of wildness and passion and rage that maybe she couldn't contain the whole of herself.

Otso's fur grows wet as I hunch over, crying silently, surrounded by reminders of her and our friendship.

Rufus doesn't try to comfort me. He's not that kind of person, and we don't have that kind of relationship.

Eventually, I run out of tears.

I carefully place Otso back on the bed and pull the covers up to his chin.

Then I take a breath and tell Rufus about the marigold. About how Mam brought it back from the dead with a bit of pure mettle.

Rufus frowns as he listens. A few times he opens his mouth as if to say something. There's a sadness to him that I haven't seen before.

"It never bloomed again?" he asks.

I shake my head. "Odette thought you could fix any problem with magic. But you can't. If Odette dies in there, then that's it. Forever. I need to find her before it's too late. Before she never blooms again."

Rufus nods slowly, then looks uncomfortable. "I get it," he says. "And . . . there's something in here that might help. Something hidden."

I sit up straight. "A glamour?" I ask. "Something you can see that I can't?"

"Being a redhead is occasionally useful," he says dryly. "And I'm good at finding things." He goes over to what looks to me like a pile of dirty laundry. It shimmers a little as he reaches into it, pulling out a box.

I snatch it from him eagerly.

It's the jewelry box that Odette's mother gave her, the one that was glamoured to hide it from thieves. Most of the mirrored surface is gone, smashed off by Odette, but there are still a few shards stuck to the outside, reflecting distorted versions of my face back at me.

I open it and see instantly that it contains mementos from her childhood—from *our* childhood—hidden away where her mother wouldn't find them.

I take the items out, one by one. Another glamour patch, sealed in its plastic wrapper, one of the super-expensive ones Odette's mother uses. The hunk of amethyst I gave her for her birthday many years ago. A few silver shards of mirror, and a piece of broken china.

"All she wanted was to escape to fairyland," I say, half to myself.

"Did she?" Rufus responds, a hint of sarcasm in his tone. "Is this how you get to fairyland? With black nail polish and dove's blood?"

I shake my head. "She got lost. I didn't realize how bad it had gotten."

"Yes, you did," Rufus says. "You knew exactly how bad it was. You were scared of her."

I don't know why Rufus Sheldrake thinks he gets to have an opinion about me and Odette. I don't even know why he's here.

There's a notebook in the box. I pull it out, and suddenly my heart feels too big for my chest.

When my magic dried up, I tried to tell Odette that I still had my gift. That even though I couldn't weave mettle for her anymore, I could still tell her stories. I'd waited for her after school and followed her home, begging and pleading.

Odette had cocked her head to the side and considered me, a vague expression of distaste on her face.

"I think we're a little old for stories, don't you?" she'd said, and walked away from me as my heart shattered into a thousand jagged pieces.

But here they were. My stories. Odette had written them down and illustrated them, her childish hand so familiar to me. I saw the two lost girls we always pretended to be.

Their names flood into my memory with a rush, so fast and thick that it makes me dizzy.

"Genevieve and Eilwen," I murmur, tracing my finger over Odette's clumsy drawings.

We never played as Odette and Maude. We were always Genevieve and Eilwen. How had I forgotten them until now? Genevieve, with her sensuous curves and long black hair. And innocent Eilwen in her white lace dress.

"Oh my goodness," I say out loud as the realization hits me.

Genevieve and Eilwen.

Ginger and Winnie.

I remember what happened the day I went to Sicklehurst with Odette.

She had been disappointed by the weathered, abandoned buildings there. I had hoped the gloom of it would appeal to her, but she just sighed and trudged around, the tears still fresh on her cheeks from the fight with her mother.

She couldn't feel what I could feel—the pull of something ancient and powerful under our feet. All she saw was concrete and weeds. Meanwhile, I was nearly drunk on the intensity of it. A vast, profound consciousness spreading beneath us.

But I could sense something wasn't right. The threads of mettle in the soil felt oily, heavy and dull and pulsing with rot.

"Can't you feel it?" I had asked Odette.

She shook her head, frustration clear on her face. "Let's go deeper," she said. "Maybe I'll feel it then."

But I didn't want to go deeper. The deeper we went, the more rotten the mettle in the soil felt. The more malevolent. I was afraid of it, and of the memories it contained. So instead I distracted her, the way I always did. I told her a story.

I knew it had to be better than our usual stories. Odette's misery and rage were stronger than I'd ever seen them before. She was like a kite, whipping around in a high gale, with only one string of attention tethering her to me.

I took twigs and vines and mud and worked them into little dolls.

"This one is you—Genevieve," I told Odette. "And here is Eilwen."

THE TWO GIRLS from the power plant. The girls we had played as for so many years. The girls I had fashioned from twigs and mud for Odette in Sicklehurst.

They were real. Not quite as I'd imagined them. Genevieve was never so sexy and vain as Ginger was, and Eilwen was sweet and childlike, not the growling, snarling creature I'd briefly encountered.

They were alive yesterday. But not anymore. I close my eyes and hear Winnie's screams, smell the hot tang of blood and the choking black smoke.

They were alive, and now they are dead.

"Maude?" It's Rufus, his voice gentle.

"I—I made them up," I say. "Winnie is Eilwen, and Ginger is Genevieve. They're me and Odette. The characters we used to play as. I—I made little dolls for Odette when we went into Sicklehurst. But now they live there . . . They're real people."

To his credit, Rufus doesn't tell me that it's impossible for dolls to turn into people. Instead he asks, "What else did you do?"

"I—I told her a story."

My favorite story. The one that Mam used to tell me about the dying swan prince, the king with a heart of cold iron, and the peasant girl who saved them both. I'd never told it to Odette before. I had wanted to keep it to myself. Something that Mam had given only to me. But I knew I needed something special that day. I took apart the threads of the story and wove them back together in a new pattern: The peasant girl became two sisters, Genevieve and Eilwen. The king with the heart of cold iron became a queen.

Odette's lip had curled as she recognized her mother.

"I hope she gets eaten by a dragon," she growled.

I told Odette about the swan prince, but she looked skeptical. "A swan?" she had asked. "Not a *real* handsome prince, then?"

"He's both!" I'd said hurriedly. "He can transform into a human."

And I had grabbed more mud and twigs and made another little figure—the most noble, tortured handsome prince I had ever created. I poured every scrap of preadolescent longing I could into him, and felt a surge of triumph as I saw Odette's expression begin to clear.

I FLIP A PAGE in Odette's journal and see him. Lyr, our handsome prince. Odette is not a bad artist at all—she's captured his swanlike elegance, his chiseled jaw, his tortured poetic expression, which now seems a little soppy to me.

It's the ghost boy I saw in the doorway to Sicklehurst. No wonder I recognized him.

"Maude?" It's Rufus. "You look like you've seen a ghost."

I let out a sharp bark of laughter. "I think I have."

"How did you do it?" he asks. "Bring them to life, I mean."

I stare at him. "I—I didn't."

Did I?

I HAD MADE MORE CREATURES for Genevieve and Eilwen to encounter on their adventures—a carnivorous tree, and a whole pile of sharp-toothed fishy girls to go in the milky pond.

But I couldn't hold her attention. Odette was shutting down, closing herself off from me, wrapping herself in a cocoon of misery and rage.

"Wait here," I told her, scrambling to my feet.

I followed scented threads of mettle in the air to find wildflowers growing among the weeds to dress the dolls in—larkspur and crocus and cow parsley. A particularly thick braid of threads led me to an enormous rosebush, the blooms blood-red and heavy with scent. Each one was perfect, every petal plump and velvety-soft. Careful to avoid the thorns, I'd snapped off one stem and carried it triumphantly to Odette.

"Look," I said, presenting it to her. "Isn't it beautiful?"

Odette had looked at the rose for a long time without saying anything.

"Sometimes I hate you, Maude Jenkins," she said at last, her voice low and flat.

The words were shocking to me. Where had this come from? I'd given Odette all I had. I'd brought her to Sicklehurst. Told her about our deep lore. What more did she want?

"You don't know how lucky you are," Odette went on. "You have everything."

I could barely take this in. What was Odette talking about? I didn't have everything. My parents were dead. I was a social pariah because my mother was a terrorist. Odette was my only friend. I was the sidekick. She was the princess who lived in a castle. *She* had everything. Not me.

"Your grandmothers. Your power. You'll go to a thaumaturgical college and have this amazing career. And I'll still be stuck here in Inglenook, being a sad, angry screwup."

"No," I said. "That's not true."

She smiled sadly. "Sometimes I think about how lucky you are, and it makes me hate you. And that makes me hate myself, because you are the only person I really, truly love, Maude."

I opened my mouth to tell her that she was the only person I truly loved too. But I couldn't. She was right. I loved my grandmothers. And they loved me in a way that Odette's mother never could.

Odette looked at her fist. She'd crushed the rose into a wet, ragged ball. Her palms were bleeding where they'd been punctured by thorns. Red on red.

"You should probably stay away from me," she said. "I ruin everything I touch."

"Never."

I wanted to fix her. I wanted to make her happy again. I wanted to destroy the monster that was eating her up inside, but the only monsters I knew how to fight were the storybook kind. So gently I took the crushed rose. I could see Odette's mettle infusing it where her blood had soaked into the petals. I took more twigs and mud and strands of cotton grass and bound them around the rose.

And I made a storybook monster, with thorned tusks and branching antlers.

"This is the Tatterdemalion," I told her. "It's hunting Genevieve and Eilwen. It's the fiercest and scariest enemy they've ever had to face. But they'll do it. Together."

Odette had looked at me, and the hope and rage warring on her face nearly broke my heart.

I TURN THE PAGE, and my blood runs cold.

Twig fingers. Bushy back. Branching horns and tusks. And underneath it, in Odette's childish hand:

THE TATTERDEMALION

"Did you meet *that*?" Rufus asks.

I nod, unable to speak. The wound on my chest burns.

Rufus touches my arm. "Maude, you can't have. You must have dreamed it. Or it was an illusion of some kind. A glamour."

I turn to face him and unbutton my school shirt. Rufus's ears turn pink, but then his eyes widen as I pull my shirt open and lift Nan's bandage to reveal the three angry gashes across my chest.

"It was real," I say.

"But *how*?"

I shake my head. "I don't know. I made little dolls in Sicklehurst when I took Odette in there years ago. Somehow, they're still there. But they're not dolls anymore. They're real, living people."

"I know that what they teach us about magic at school is nonsense," Rufus says. "I know it's propaganda, aimed at keeping all the magical power in the hands of the big magic companies. But . . . I didn't know magic could do *this*. This . . . It's storybook magic."

I nod. At school they tell us that real magic never really worked anyway—that it was always too dangerous, too unpredictable. That was why it had to be regulated, why magic could be practiced only by licensed thaumaturgical engineers in safe laboratories. And it wasn't like Nan was doing anything particularly powerful in our kitchen. Maybe hundreds of years ago you could raise monsters and make a village forget a whole power plant. But that was before everything changed—before towns and cities were built from steel and iron, and electric wires crisscrossed the land. Now magic is an industry: commercial glamours, celebrity tails, dust-bunny magnets, or charms to ease a toothache.

I remember the feeling of it, when I went in there with Odette. The throbbing of power under my feet. I remember reaching into the earth with my witch-hands and whispering to the mettle in the soil.

"Oh," I say softly.

THAT DAY IN SICKLEHURST, I had reached deep into the earth and pulled on the mettle threads that flowed through every leaf and stone in the place. And I bound it to the dolls. They had sprung to life, little versions of our fantasy selves, no more than six inches high. The little monster had roared, and tiny Genevieve and Eilwen had seized twigs to do battle with it.

Odette's rage and misery had faded as she watched, entranced. It was working. She was coming back to me. I told her about all the adventures Genevieve and Eilwen had while rescuing Lyr, and then I gave Genevieve a love scene with Lyr that made my face hot and my voice husky. Lyr sacrificed himself trying to save us, and together we bore his body to the kingdom of birds, where we were rewarded with a dagger made of Lyr's breastbone—the Hollow Knife of Uisnigh—which we used to defeat the Tatterdemalion and the iron-hearted queen. We took her lands for our own, ruling happily and bravely for the rest of our days. It was the most epic story I had ever told, and Odette's sigh of satisfaction at the end was all I needed.

We had laced our fingers together, and I had believed that everything would be all right. But only a week later, I lost my magic, and Odette dumped me.

"I THINK I DID MAKE THEM," I tell Rufus. "There's a lot of mettle in there. I used some of it to bring the dolls to life."

They hadn't been *that* alive, though. They'd still been dolls, little animated puppets. Not real people.

Rufus lets out a soft snort. "You're saying the power plant has . . . power?"

"Maybe that's why it closed down," I say. "An accident of some kind."

I return my attention to Odette's notebook. On the page facing the illustration of the Tatterdemalion, I see the now-familiar lines of the nursery rhyme.

Cranny key is forged in blood
Open the door to the sticklegrass wood.

"I think there used to be a forest there," I tell Rufus. "Before the power plant. People called it the sticklegrass wood."

Rufus looks thoughtful. "I wonder if . . ." He shakes his head.

"What is it?"

"Could the *forest* be powerful enough to bring your dolls to life?"

I stare at him. "No," I say. "The forest was cut down more than fifty years ago."

But there's still sticklegrass in there. And that vast, spreading consciousness I felt in the soil. The mettle, dull and oily and wrong.

Rufus leans forward, his eyes bright. "The roots could still be there, dormant. Trees in a forest are linked underground by a network of mycelium—mycorrhizal fungi that allows them to exchange nutrients, and even communicate."

I blink, imagining the wise old talking trees from a story I had once told Odette. "Communicate?"

He nods, and his eyes light up. "Studies have shown that the trees can warn each other of approaching predators, allowing them to respond by closing up flowers or dropping fruit, or releasing certain chemicals that either repel the predators or attract things that are predators of the predators."

"And a fungus does this?"

"Yeah. There are some botanists who now consider a forest to be a single living organism, not just a collection of individual plants."

That deep consciousness I had sensed beneath the ground with Odette. I remember it. I whispered to it, and it whispered back to me. The forest.

"You might not be able to see the trees," Rufus says, "but that doesn't mean that the mycelium network isn't there. The tree roots could still be alive under the soil."

Can a forest do magic? It seems like something from a fairy tale.

The nursery rhyme in Odette's journal is annotated with scrawls and notes from when she had puzzled out the spell.

"But I don't understand how the forgetting spell works," Rufus says. "How come Odette remembered all this?"

"The spell starts to break down when you cross the threshold," I explain. "It broke for Odette when we went through the door."

"But *you* forgot again, and she didn't."

I remember Nan's furious face. Her hands on the sides of my head. "Nan put the forgetting spell back on me," I tell him. "But she didn't get to Odette, because we stopped being friends."

Rufus frowns. "It all seems unnecessarily complicated."

"I have to go back," I whisper. "She's there. I know it."

"Maude," says Rufus. "Didn't you just tell me there is an actual real live monster in there? It's too dangerous. You need to tell your nan."

I shake my head. "I can't," I say. "She refuses to talk to me about any of that stuff."

"Dr. Slater, then. Or the auditors."

I give him a flat look. We both know I'll never do that.

But he's right. The Tatterdemalion killed Winnie right before my eyes, and there's no reason why it won't do the same to me. I'm going to have to be smarter this time. I pick up a black satin pouch and empty the cheap plastic runes inside onto Odette's desk. Then I turn witch-eyed and take a deep breath, letting my mind open to the mettle in the room. I can see it, humming and vibrating in the air, collected on the objects that were dear to Odette.

I take a silver mirror fragment and slip it into the black satin bag. The amethyst crystal. A bottle of glittery black nail polish. A red ribbon. A stalk of dried hemlock. A candle stub. I take nail scissors and snip the fuzz from the tip of Otso's left ear. I pull Nan's witch bottle and the piece of broken china from my blazer pocket and drop them into the bag too. I hesitate over the glamour patch, stolen from Odette's mother's dressing table. It has none of Odette's mettle, but it's powerful nonetheless. Patches this expensive aren't like the tacky ones you can buy in shopping malls—they're produced in workshops using real human mettle. I slide it into the bag, just in case.

"What are you doing?" Rufus asks.

"Taking her mettle," I reply. "I might be able to use it to track her."

"Isn't Odette's mettle . . . inside Odette?"

"Mettle lingers. In fingernails and hair. Bones. Teeth. And it collects in places of significance, the way that rain collects in well-worn ruts in the road. Odette's mettle is here—on Otso, in her clothes, in the things she loves."

In her wardrobe, I find the white dress that Odette wore to the Hollantide Ball. I hesitate, brushing my fingers against the gauzy fabric. Then I kick off my shoes, step out of my tartan skirt, and shrug off my blazer and shirt.

"Maude!" says Rufus, turning his head away from me, his ears flaming pink.

The dress slides smoothly over my skin. It feels cool against the slashes on my chest. I can smell Odette in the fabric—clematis and rockrose and wormwood. Her mettle infuses the fabric, and I feel like I'm clothing myself in armor made of *her*.

I look at myself in the mirror. I don't look like a princess. I don't look beautiful. The dress pulls across my belly, creating lumps where Odette had sleek lines. I'm wearing an ancient sports bra, so the off-the-shoulder part of the dress rides up and turns into a baggy, shapeless neckline. I look like a kid playing dress-up.

I am not the bright, shining star that Odette was.

But perhaps Odette wasn't that bright, shining star either.

I leave my school uniform on the floor in a puddle, like a freshly emerged butterfly shedding its chrysalis. The only thing I take is Nan's rose and the bone brooch, which I pin to the front of the white dress, and my school shoes, because my feet are two sizes larger than Odette's, and saving princesses requires sensible footwear.

"Come on," I say to Rufus, who is now staring at me like I might bite him.

We go downstairs and pass Odette's mother. Her mouth thins to an almost invisible line of disapproval when she sees me clomping by in my brown leather saddle shoes and Odette's floaty dress, the black satin bag looped over my wrist. But she doesn't say a word, and we let ourselves out, Rufus mumbling a hasty thank-you-for-your-hospitality over his shoulder.

WE WALK DOWN the long garden path, past topiary hedges and cold stone walls.

"What does she really look like?" I ask Rufus.

"Odette's mother? Tired. Sort of pinched around the lips. Bags under her eyes. Her hair is thinning. She's still terrifying, though."

I shake my head, unable to picture her as being anything less than her icy luxury glamours. I glance over at Rufus, wondering what it's like to see the world as it truly is.

He shrugs ruefully, anticipating my unspoken question. "I've never known anything different."

"Do you wish you weren't a redhead? Do you wish you could use magic?"

"Not really. When I was little I did, because I felt left out, and nobody seemed to notice. But now I don't really think about it. I wouldn't wear glamours even if I could."

"You don't know that."

"*You* don't use them."

"Nobody's looking at me. Glamour or no glamour."

We walk a little farther, then Rufus clears his throat. "That dress. It's the one Odette wore to the Hollantide Ball, isn't it?"

I don't respond.

He pauses for a moment. "I didn't want to go—my dad forced me, because he thinks I need to be more social. As if going to

124

some awful performative charade of heteronormativity is going to make me suddenly develop social skills. But I'm glad I went, because you were there, and you were so sad, sitting there on the bleachers, watching her dance."

"I wasn't sad," I protest. "I was happy for her. For them."

Rufus snorts. "Keep telling yourself that."

"Fine," I say. "I liked Mondarius. But it never would have worked between us."

"Mondarius?" Rufus sounds surprised. "You like *Mondarius?*"

"I did. Or at least I thought I did."

"Maude . . ." Rufus's voice has gone all careful again. "That night, on the bleachers. You weren't looking at Mondarius."

"Of course not," I say. "I was looking at Odette. I know we weren't friends anymore . . . but she'd been so miserable. I was glad to see her looking happy."

"Happy? You obviously weren't looking very hard. Odette was never happy."

"Of course she was. We were happy when we were kids, and she was happy with Mondarius that night."

Rufus raises his eyebrows. "She didn't go to the dance with Mondarius because she liked him. She didn't wear that dress because it made her feel good."

"Then why?"

"She wanted to be looked at. She wanted people to notice her. To be jealous of her. She wanted to go with Mondarius because he gave her power. He had a social capital that she could leech from him. She wanted to say to everyone in our school, 'Look at me. I can have what you want. I could rule this place if I wanted to, but I don't care. None of you are worth my time.' She wanted

125

everyone there to know that she was the strongest, the most beautiful, the most dangerous. She was flaunting it to everyone. Even to you."

I stop and swing around to face Rufus. "Do you hear yourself?" I say. "Who cares why Odette wore the dress? Who cares why any woman wears anything?"

"That's not what I meant. Odette wanted to hurt you that night, Maude. She wanted to hurt everyone."

"You're wrong."

"She did it all the time. Constantly, since primary school. She was always pushing, testing. She'd run off with the cool kids for a week, leaving you on your own. She'd push you into places where you didn't want to go. She'd push you and push you, even though she knew you were uncomfortable. She'd hurt you, over and over again. Until one day she decided she was bored, and she cast you aside like a broken toy."

I turn away from Rufus's words. He's not wrong, but that doesn't give him the right to act like he knew her. "And how did you come to this conclusion? Why have you been watching her so much? Were you in love with her, like everyone else was? Were you jealous of me?"

Rufus shakes his head and lets out a huff of laughter.

"What would you know about love anyway?" I ask. "You only understand test tubes and microscopes and fly larvae. You don't know about love."

He shrugs, and I know I've hurt his feelings, but I don't stop. "She didn't dump me because she was bored. It was more complicated than that."

Shame rises in my throat as I remember trying to do magic

for her and failing. I remember reaching for the threads of mettle and being unable to grasp them. I remember the look on Odette's face as she watched me try. Disappointment. Pity.

"I know about love," he says. He grabs my arm and pulls me back to him. "Someone who needs you to constantly *prove* your love isn't worth loving. Love should be given freely. It's not an exam, or a bargain, or a threat."

I shake my arm free. "You don't understand Odette," I say. "What she's been through. Who she is."

"Maybe not, but whatever shitty things happened to her don't excuse her being a shitty friend to you. I saw how she treated you. I saw you on the bleachers at the dance. I saw you in the biology lab when she decided that she was done with you. She was a bad friend. You didn't fail her. She failed *you*."

Rufus's voice breaks a little, and tears start in his eyes.

Why does he care so much?

"You don't know her," I say again.

"No, but I know *you*. I couldn't see whatever dreary glamours she was wearing, but I saw *your* face every time she walked into class. You looked so sad. So afraid. So worried about her. She didn't deserve you."

I shake my head.

"Maude, I wish you could see yourself. You still think you're nothing but Odette's sidekick, but you're so much more than that. You're kind and strong and loyal and smart and funny. You know the name of every plant under the sun, and you tell the *best* stories, or at least you used to. Maybe this can be a new beginning for you. Maybe it's time for you to step out of Odette's shadow and stand in the sun."

"You think I should just leave her in there to die?"

"Of course not. But maybe this isn't your problem to solve. Go back in there and tell Odette's mother what you know."

I look at the black satin bag in my hand. He doesn't understand.

I can't give up on her.

"This kind of magic is dangerous," Rufus says. "There's a reason why it's forbidden. What if the monster kills you?"

"It won't," I say. But I don't know that.

"What if the auditors find out what you've been doing? What if they come for you?"

I have a sudden flash of memory: A light knock on the door. A man and a woman, both in impeccable suits, the woman with bright red hair. Their heads bent in politeness. Mild tones, spread hands. There were forms for Nan and Halmoni to fill out.

I didn't understand. I was only seven. They seemed like nice people to me. But Nan and Halmoni were quiet. Stiff. Their movements robotic. I saw Nan reach out and grab Halmoni's hand, her knuckles white.

Then the strangers went upstairs to where Mam was sleeping. I heard the creak of her bedroom door, and the low, mild tones of the auditors. I couldn't make out the words, but I got the impression they were looking for something.

Then Mam spoke, and she didn't sound mild or polite. "Demons take you," she had cried. "You'll never have it."

Then there was silence for a while. Eventually, the auditors came back downstairs, pushing Mam in front of them. Her wrists were bound with iron, a stainless-steel snaffle bit in her mouth to stop her from laying curses. She started struggling when she

128

saw me, twisting against the auditors, her teeth grinding against the bit.

I tried to rush toward Mam, to help her. To keep her with us. But Halmoni held on to me and didn't let me near her.

"Please, Carys." Nan's voice was thin and high. "Please don't make it worse. If you cooperate . . . I'll petition for you."

Mam turned her eyes on me, and I knew she was trying to tell me something, but I had no idea what it was. The auditors pushed her through the front door and into their black van. They were gone, and so was my heart.

Nan did petition for her, but nobody listened. Mam had known what she was doing. She had broken into the headquarters of Ilium—the biggest and most powerful of the magic corporations. She'd done it knowing that this was the risk. That she could get taken away from us.

And yet she still chose to do it.

The next time I saw Mam, she was dead, sent back to us in a cardboard coffin.

I know that what I saw in Sicklehurst was forbidden magic, and by not reporting it to the auditors I, too, am breaking the law. It's exactly the kind of thing I swore I would never do. I swore to myself that I would never put Nan and Halmoni in danger, the way that Mam did.

My resolve wavers.

I also swore I'd rescue Odette.

Tears slip down my cheeks. "I don't know what to do," I say.

Rufus reaches out and touches my arm awkwardly. "Come to school," he says. "Think about it. If Odette really has been in Sicklehurst this whole time, then she'll still be there tomorrow."

I think of the monster—the Tatterdemalion. Odette is in mortal peril. And if Nan gets her way, we'll be on the train to Fishgate tonight. Tomorrow will be too late.

"I'm going now," I say.

Rufus swallows. "Then I'll come with you."

I nearly shout with laughter. "Don't be ridiculous."

"You shouldn't go in there alone."

"I have to."

"Why?"

I shrug. "It's what people always say in storybooks."

Rufus makes a disgusted noise. "That's never been a good reason to do anything."

"Rufus, this isn't your story. Stay out of it."

I start to walk away. He lets me get a few steps ahead of him before he calls after me.

"*I* gave you the marigold."

I stop and turn around. "What?"

"The marigold. The one that died and your mam brought back. I'm the one who gave it to you, because I wanted to be your friend. You were kind to me at another kid's party once, when everyone else forgot about me. You told great stories. I liked you. I still like you. But all you see is Odette. Even now."

"She's in danger," I say. "And I'm the only one who can help."

"I don't want you to get hurt."

"Goodbye, Rufus," I say, and head down the hill toward Cygnet Creek.

8

MY SECOND JOURNEY TO SICKLEHURST IS UNEVENT-
ful. The first layer of the triple spell no longer works
on me, so I find the secret door with no trouble. I remake the
wreath and speak the nursery rhyme. The door feels hot under
my hands, and I see a flickering in the corner of my vision, as if
the etched witchmarks on the bricks are pulsing with white light.
I don't remember that happening last time. I turn to look, but
they're just bricks again. I gaze for a moment at the unfamiliar
witchmarks, and wonder who they belong to, and why our family
mark is there among them.

Inside Sicklehurst, I sense the vast spreading network of mettle under my feet, pulsing with oily wrongness. And somewhere,
deep in the heart of the power plant, I can sense the third layer
of the spell, thick and dense.

Ginger's apartment is a charred ruin, damp ash and jagged
black timber. In among the rubble, I spot the remains of the emerald chaise, a single black shoe, a sooty jar. Her whole quirky
bohemian life, erased in a few minutes. I don't see any sign of a
body, but to be honest I'm not looking very hard.

I don't quite know how to feel about Ginger and Winnie and their gruesome deaths. The horror of it is still fresh in my mind, but were they even real? Ginger certainly seemed real. But she can't have been, because she was Genevieve, Odette's childhood alter ego.

There's a bright-green patch on the path ahead that wasn't there before. When I approach, I realize it's sticklegrass, growing thick and lustrous, where everything around it is gray and brown. It's approximately the same shape and size as a child. A girl. Is this the spot where I saw the Tatterdemalion take Winnie?

I shiver and look around. There's no sign of the monster. Everything is quiet and still.

I'm not sure what my plan is. I guess I need to search for clues—for any sign that Odette was here.

A door marked TO CONTROL ROOM has fallen off its hinges, leaving a gaping dark entryway. The ivy and leaf litter beneath it looks a little trampled. A good start.

I step into a short, narrow corridor, with a pair of heavy solid doors at one end. I push at one, and it groans open. I slip inside and let the door fall shut behind me.

As my eyes adjust to the gloom, I look around at a large room lined with strange-looking machinery and jumbled piles of junk. Old office furniture buckling with age and damp is pushed chaotically against teetering piles of boxes and crates. Beside me, there are banks of knobs, dials, and meters with labels like STATION TRANSFORMER and DIRECT METTLE EXCITER and JETTY CONTROL. Thick ropes of cable and conduit hang from the ceiling, tangled with twisted vines that have broken in through a hole where a part of the roof has collapsed, sunken and leaking wan daylight into the room. It glints from the cracked glass of the innumerable meters. Mint-green paint flakes from the walls, and matching linoleum peels away from a concrete floor.

I sneeze three times. There's something in here. Something magical.

The room smells like burning dust on light bulbs, and red roses.

Whatever it is, it's at the back of the room. I can't quite see it, but there's a presence. Something that's waiting for me.

I swallow a knot of fear and pick my way past stacked boxes overflowing with ancient paperwork. As I get close, I realize the stacks are riddled with silverfish, and I shudder at their tiny feelers and segmented insect bodies.

The roof has caved in near a narrow barred window, and I have to duck to get under it. But once I'm on the other side, I see it.

The rosebush.

It's enormous, taking up almost a whole wall. It has come in through the hole in the ceiling and spread out in all directions, its leaves glossy dark green. Each stem is smothered with fat blooms, tightly packed with petals, red as blood. Long canes snake out from the bush, bristling with thorns, like talons reaching toward me.

There's something unnatural about it. Why would a plant grow *away* from the sunlight? There's nothing in here for it— no food or water.

The scent of it draws me in, and without thinking, I put out a hand to touch one of the blooms, brushing the velvet softness with my fingertips. I let out a startled yelp as one of the canes suddenly moves, winding itself gently around my hand, holding it in place. This rosebush is . . . more alive than it should be. Another cane brushes against my chest, sliding beneath the neckline of Odette's dress and under Nan's bandage. It gently traces the three lines that the Tatterdemalion marked there, and then I feel a sharp sting as it thrusts a thorn deep into the center line.

I let out a cry of pain and leap back away from it.

The bloody thorn retreats to the bush and disappears. The red petals of the rosebush quiver, and I get the sense that the bush is *tasting* me, my blood.

I hear a far-off rumble, and as if in response my hands start to shake.

I touch the white rose pinned to the front of my dress, for comfort. Nan's roses are nothing like this.

The rumbling sound draws closer. I hear snapping branches, heavy stomping, and an unmistakable roar.

My guts turn watery with fear.

The Tatterdemalion is coming.

Rufus was right. I should never have come here.

I can't breathe.

I turn to the doors I came in through, thinking to flee back down the corridor. But I can hear the stomp and roar of the monster outside. The doors are copper, embossed with the stylized image of a man's face surrounded by vegetation, forming his beard, his hair, leaves spewing from his mouth and sprouting from his eyes and nostrils. There is a heavy bolt, which I fumble into place with my shaking hands, hoping it will hold the Tatterdemalion at bay for a little while.

I turn and pace a panicked circle of the room, but there are no other exits. The windows are all barred. There's no way out.

The heavy scent of the roses is making me dizzy, and I wonder if perhaps it would be easier to just lie here on the floor and give into it, let the roses lull me to sleep and let the monster do what it will.

But no hero ever saved a princess by lying down and giving up.

The Tatterdemalion is growing closer. I can hear it prowling around the outside of the building, searching for a way in.

If this were a story, what would the hero do? My storytelling muscles have grown soft from lack of use.

We could rescue each other.

"Odette!" I yell. "Can you hear me?"

But Odette isn't here. Winnie and Ginger are dead. There's no one to hear my call.

No one, except . . .

"Lyr!" I yell. "I need you!"

I feel a breath of air on my cheek, but it stills. The roses seem closer than before. The Tatterdemalion roars again.

I need magic, but I don't have any.

Except I do.

I fumble in the black satin bag until my fingers curl around the smooth blown-glass ball of Nan's emergency witch bottle. I didn't want to use it so soon, but what choice do I have?

I don't really know what it's going to do—whether it will neutralize the danger, or transport me somewhere else, or perhaps summon Nan here to help in a flurry of knitting needles and tea leaves. *In case of emergency, break glass,* Nan used to joke. *Just smash it and tell it what you need.*

I hurl the bottle to the ground, where it shatters into tiny pieces, the braided mettle rushing forth in a whirling silvery gust.

"I need . . ." I am at a loss, and say the first, most obvious thing in my head. "I need a handsome prince to rescue me!"

The thick bloodiness of the rose scent suddenly becomes diluted with stone and frost, and the air around me chills. I spin around. There's something here, something whirling white and silver, made of ice and terror and mettle.

"Show yourself!" I command.

The blizzard spins faster, coalescing into a figure.

It's Lyr, as he was when I glimpsed him through the secret door to Sicklehurst—insubstantial, little more than a ghost. He stares at me, his eyes glittering.

He opens his mouth, and a kind of whistling hiss emerges. He puts an elegant hand to his throat and tries again, his jaw working to produce the right sound.

He stares at me, his face twisted in astonishment. "What witchcraft is this?"

He looks at his own hands, then back at me. He struggles, as if he's trying to turn and run, but he appears to be trapped, held in place by some invisible force. His face twists in misery. The mist that makes him up shudders and eddies as if a breeze were passing through it.

"You called to me," he says.

"Yes," I tell him. "I need your help."

His expression is a strange mix of wonder and grief. A ghostly tear slips from his silvery eye.

"I need help," I say again desperately. "The monster—"

"Shh!" he glances around and holds up a thin finger. "Enemies are close."

I look around. "You mean the Tatterdemalion?"

Lyr jerks his head toward the rosebush. "The roses are spies."

His words make no sense, but I shuffle away from the bush, back toward the door. I can't hear the Tatterdemalion anymore. Could Lyr have driven it away?

"Where are you, really?" I ask. "I know you're not truly here."

Lyr's lips part in a sad half smile, but he says nothing.

I step closer, until I can feel the chill radiating from him.

"Are you a ghost?" I ask.

"I am a prisoner," he says.

He reaches out to touch a rotting cardboard box, but his hand passes right through it, as if he were nothing more than mist.

"How did you bring me here?" he asks. "And why?"

"I didn't," I say. "I just called for help, and you came."

But I can tell he doesn't believe me, which is fair enough. I don't know how, but this Lyr comes from the mud-and-twig doll I made for Odette, just as Winnie and Ginger did, and the Tatterdemalion. But the Lyr that I made wasn't a ghost . . . so why is this one?

He is beautiful. As beautiful as my descriptions of him to Odette. It's almost embarrassing how perfect he is. The embodiment of a preadolescent fantasy—full-lipped and long-lashed. Odette always pushed me to make the romance in my stories more explicit, giggling at my red cheeks as she demanded more kisses, more desperate embraces, more bedchamber hijinks.

"I know you," Lyr says, gazing at me. "We are . . . connected, you and I. But I do not know your name."

"I'm Maude," I tell him. "I'm here to rescue my friend."

"Ah," Lyr nods. "You are a hero."

I feel a sting of shame. "No," I say. "I'm no hero. I've been here for five minutes, and I already need rescuing myself."

"You ventured into danger to save a princess—you must be a hero."

I let myself imagine it. Finding some long-lost crystal or sword that would return Odette to me. All of her weird glamours worn away, leaving the true Odette behind. I imagine the spark of hope in her eyes, the clutch of grateful arms as she embraces me. I imagine her apologizing to me for walking the dark paths. Promising me that it's over, that we can go back to how we used to be.

"There's a monster out there," I say. "I need a way out that isn't that door."

Lyr gazes at me for a long time as he considers this. "You could be a spy," he says at last. "Sent by the witch who imprisoned me here. Perhaps I should let the monster have you."

"What witch?" I ask.

He narrows his eyes at me. "Do not seek to distract me, spy."

"I'm no spy!" I protest. "I swear it. I'm just here to get my friend back."

"How do you swear it?"

"I swear I am no spy, on the egg moon. On the ashes of Ginger's home. On the memory of a happy day with Odette."

"Swear on the sticklegrass."

I spread my hands, in a cross between a confused shrug and a gesture of submission. "I swear it."

"Swear on the blood of witches."

I think of Mam, laid out cold and dead on our front door. And of Nan, bustling around our kitchen, making tea in the big ugly cat teapot.

I hear scuffling, just outside the door. Is it the Tatterdemalion? Or just rats or nesting pigeons?

"I swear it."

Lyr hesitates, then nods. "Very well. I can help you. I know where your friend is."

My pulse quickens. "Odette? You've seen her?"

"She is being held prisoner in the tower."

I *knew* it. I knew it when I saw the light from Ginger's apartment. "The cooling tower?" I ask eagerly.

"The very same."

"How do I get there?" I ask.

"You must be careful," Lyr says. "The Tatterdemalion is not the only danger that lurks within these woods. Eat nothing. Trust no one. Stay on the path. And you should destroy that." He nods at Nan's white rose. "All roses are spies."

I shake my head. "No," I say. "This one is different. It'll protect me."

Lyr snorts but says nothing.

"What other dangers are there?" I ask.

"There is a rotten star at the heart of the sticklegrass wood. A demon core," says Lyr. "It feeds the monsters. It will call to you. You must not answer."

"The sticklegrass wood," I say. "You mean the forest? The one that got cut down to make room for the power plant?"

"It was not destroyed," Lyr says. "Merely suppressed. It grows foul in its slumber."

There's a faint rustling at the other end of the room, and I turn to look at the rosebush. The thorned canes seem closer now, as if they are leaning forward to listen.

"Find your princess," Lyr says, his voice urgent. "Set her free."

At that moment, a deep, animal roar sounds, shaking dust free from the boxes and crates around us. The silver mist that is Lyr trembles. The Tatterdemalion is in the building, crashing down the corridor toward the copper doors.

Lyr spits out an oath. The peeling linoleum under my feet shudders.

"I need to get out," I tell him. "You have to help me."

"Move those." He points.

I kick aside boxes, shuddering as a thousand silverfish burst forth and scuttle away, searching for cracks and folds to hide in.

"Keep going."

I lift a corner of the linoleum and tug it aside. Underneath, there is a circular iron hatch, set into the concrete floor. The iron is corroded, peeling away in great wide strips like sunburned skin.

The Tatterdemalion roars as it crashes against the copper doors.

"Open it," Lyr directs.

I grab the handle and haul it upward.

The hatch squeals and groans, revealing a stone-lined shaft with an iron ladder leading down into darkness.

From inside comes an earthy, sour smell, a bit like the compost bin on our kitchen counter at home.

"Make haste," Lyr urges.

I hesitate. "What happens when I get to the bottom?" I ask.

Lyr starts to speak quickly, his voice low and urgent. "There is little time. Take the tunnel to the lake house. Call the ferry.

From the dock, stay on the path. It will lead you to the tower at the heart of the sticklegrass wood. You will find your princess there, I am sure of it."

I open my mouth to ask what he's talking about. There's no lake or dock in Sicklehurst. But he rushes at me, filling my lungs with ice, forcing me toward the gaping hole in the floor.

The Tatterdemalion begins to pound at the big copper doors. The roses seem to be holding their breath.

I wrap the black satin bag string around my wrist and start to back down the ladder. The rungs are slimy and cold, and none too solid.

"Thank you," I say.

A flash of pain crosses Lyr's face. "You seem brave and true," he says. "You do not deserve this fate."

I start to ask him what he means, but before I can speak, the copper doors burst open, and I catch a glimpse of the Tatterdemalion, all earth and slime and twigs.

Lyr hauls his insubstantial body against the iron hatch, bashing himself against it. Bits of silvery mist burst off him as he breaks apart. The hatch groans, then tips forward and swings closed above me.

I am plunged into total darkness.

9

I CAN'T SEE ANYTHING, AND MY HANDS ARE COLD AND stiff on the iron rungs of the ladder.

There is silence above me, and I don't know if the Tatterdemalion is still there, in the room. I can't risk going back up, though, and I can't cling here forever. The only way is down.

I reach out with one tentative foot, blindly searching for the next rung. The ladder feels unstable in my hands, rusted but with a viscous, slimy coating. I begin to descend. Sometimes, my foot slides on a rung and my heart rate skyrockets as I cling tight with my hands. I don't know how far it is to the bottom. I don't know if the ladder will hold. It's getting more worn the farther I go, chunks of rust coming off, the cold, gritty gunk oozing between my fingers.

Down I climb, down and down.

Occasionally, there is a patch of luminescent fungi sprouting from the wall, ghostly pale and delicate. I linger there, casting about for some sign of salvation. But the light it gives off is faint, and there is nothing but blackness above and below.

I vacillate between longing for the bottom and dreading what I might find. Can I trust Lyr? I can't help but feel drawn to him—he is literally my preadolescent sexual fantasy. But that doesn't mean he's telling me the truth.

I place my heel carefully on the next rung and let it take my weight. With no warning, it gives way beneath me, the iron bar crumbling into nothing. The next rung dissolves too—I scrabble with my hands, but all I grasp is flaking sludge, like wet chalk. I try to brace myself against the wall, but my knees and elbows slide off slimy lichen and wet rock. I rattle down the shaft like a pebble, feeling my flesh grow tender as it bashes and scrapes against the wall.

If there is a stone floor at the bottom, then I will probably die. If I'm lucky, it'll be quick. If I'm unlucky, I'll break both my legs and starve to death.

I take a breath to scream, but my mouth fills with thick sludge as I land in what feels and tastes like a compost heap. The impact of my fall embeds me in it—slimy rotting leaves and carrot tops and soft, warm loam. I struggle to free myself, kicking and pushing against the slippery stone walls of the shaft. I feel things moving around me—worms and millipedes and wood lice. Something wriggles into my ear, and I claw it out with mounting hysteria.

Finally, I break free of the compost, and take great lungfuls of air. Not fresh, but air nonetheless. It's steaming warm in here as microorganisms work hard to break down the organic material.

For a moment, I think I've lost the black satin bag, but it's still wrapped around my wrist.

I can just make out a crack of light ahead, where the shaft widens into a kind of chamber. I wade through mounds of potato peelings and soggy lettuce leaves, slipping and stumbling, the muck sucking at my shoes, worms wriggling between my toes.

Where did all this food refuse come from? Surely, it can't all belong to Ginger and Winnie.

The chamber is long and narrow, with a low ceiling. The crack of light is coming from above, another hatch, this one wooden. I scoop compost into a heap and then scramble to the top of it, balancing on one foot as I stretch up to shove at the hatch. It gives a little, but I sink back into the mulch. I scrape and pile more compost, unearthing more insects, which scurry away from the light to burrow back into darkness.

I climb once more to the top of the heap and heave at the hatch. It shifts and gives way with a shower of ancient splinters, and I shove it to one side as light spills into the pit. Faint sounds pour into the stillness—the sloshing of water, and beneath it, the sound of far-off singing. I grasp the rim of the opening with aching hands, and haul myself into a cold, empty room.

It takes a few moments for my eyes to adjust. The room is small. Ancient wooden floorboards and crumbling gray stone walls. Everything is covered in moss and lichen, patterning over the surfaces like flocked wallpaper. It's chilly and damp, the glass in the single window long gone, the roof collapsed on one side, letting in weak, colorless light. The floor beneath the collapsed roof has rotted away, leaving a jagged hole through which I can see not dark compost, but a giddy drop to cold water below. There's a wooden door opposite the window, the timber soft and swollen. A grimy glass globe sits by the door, probably a buoy or a fisherman's shewstone. Most of the opposite wall is taken up by a stone hearth, with a small wooden counter and an armchair placed before it.

The hearth and the chair are familiar—they are identical to the ones in my own home. This room is like a weird, spartan, mildew-spattered version of our kitchen.

What is going on?

I can still hear the singing—multiple voices raised in a strange, discordant harmony. The sound is distorted, the notes bending and wobbling. I can't make out any words.

Odette's white dress is damp and filthy. My school shoes are full of squelching muck. I pick bits of eggshell from my hair and try to shake the soil free. Nan's rose is still pinned to my chest, though, thank goodness.

Shivering, I make my way over to the window and look out.

The little stone building I'm inside sits high up on a lake, water spreading out maybe twenty feet below me, an opaque, milky gray green, wreathed in low mist that partially obscures the wooded far bank. Petrified trees rise from the water, white skeletal branches draped with beard lichen the color of mildew. The sky is gray and cold.

This must be the lake house that Lyr mentioned.

I cross the room to the door. It's swollen shut, and I have to put my shoulder against it and shove hard before it finally swings open. The rusted hinges give way, and the entire door plunges into the water below. I grab on to the doorframe to stop myself from tumbling after it. The doorstep drops off sharply to water and mist. I peer out and crane my neck, holding on tightly so I don't fall.

The lake is all around me. The building isn't at the edge of the lake. It's in the middle, on tall wooden stilts. Through the mist, I can make out thick woods on one side and rising cliffs on the other, chalky and white.

It seems impossible, but stranger things have happened today. I'm cold and hungry, and I have no idea where I am. Have I slipped into some kind of fairyland? Did Lyr's escape hatch actually take me away from Sicklehurst, to a dark land straight out of one of my stories?

And if it did, how can I get home again?

The strange, warbly song seems louder now, making it hard to concentrate.

I'm beginning to suspect that I'm on a very dark path indeed. The kind of story where roads lead nowhere and nobody can be trusted. I'm pretty sure I'm still in Sicklehurst, which means that someone or something is producing the most powerful glamour I've ever encountered. I didn't think magic *could* do something this big.

Was Rufus right? Could the ancient forest itself still be alive under all the concrete? Could it have a kind of consciousness of its own?

The only person who has given me any kind of answers so far is Lyr, so I guess all I can do is follow his instructions.

Call the ferry, he said.

How? There's no bell or button. There's no ladder down to the water, and no sight of a boat or jetty. I could jump, but then what? I don't know where I'm supposed to swim to, and if the water is as cold as it looks, I doubt I would get very far.

And who knows what might be lurking under the milky surface?

I lean out the doorway and do the only thing I can think to do. I shout, "Ferry? Please?"

The words disappear into the cold lake, drowned out by the singing. It's like a kind of static, covering my thoughts with a blanket of wet nothing. Through the fog of it, I wonder if there was another exit back in the compost chamber. But the hatch I emerged from has gone, replaced by flaking rough floorboards, bleached and ancient.

I guess I just have to wait for the ferry to arrive.

What would Nan say if she could see me now?

You've made a right mess of things, you have. Nothing for it but to put the kettle on. Everything looks better after a cup of tea.

I swallow, sniff, and make my way over to the hearth.

A fire has been laid there, logs below and twigs on top, crowned with a kind of bird's nest of dry moss and bark shavings. Everything is neatly stacked and ready to be lit.

A black cauldron hangs from a bar embedded in the stone hearth. I peek inside and see what looks like stew, cold and gelatinous. I wonder how long it's been there. I can't see any signs of mold or rot, and a quick sniff assures me that it's fresh.

I realize I haven't eaten anything all day. I look at the sky through the hole in the roof, but it gives me no clues as to the time.

Even before Lyr warned me, I was well aware that you should never eat or drink in fairyland. But I'm so *hungry,* and the singing is crowding my head so that no other thought can take hold.

Fuzzily, I look around for something to light the fire with. On the counter, there is a blackened ladle, an earthenware bowl, a short knife with a rough wooden handle, a silver spoon, and a battered tin, the kind that Halmoni keeps horseshoe nails in for making stained glass. I open the tin, hoping for matches, but find a piece of knapped flint sitting dark gray and waxy on a bed of papery punkwood.

Odette and I taught ourselves to light fires with flint. So many of my stories involved girls lost in the woods—Odette said we should learn how to survive, just in case we ever found ourselves on a real quest. We looked it up in a book and scoured the creek for the right kind of stone. We gathered strips of paperbark and dry vetch, and crouched under Peg Powler, striking our stone again and again with one of Odette's mother's very best butter knives.

Odette had knelt and breathed reverently on the tiny flames, as if she were casting a spell. The fire had caught—better than we anticipated. It flashed over the crackling, dry leaves and yellowed tufts of crabgrass and leapt high, singeing the tips of the willow's drooping branches. I rushed to the creek and threw my cardigan in, soaking it, before dashing back to throw the damp wool on the spreading fire. Odette cackled, dancing around the blackened earth on fairy-light toes, her eyes still burning, even after the fire was extinguished.

I take the flint in my left hand and the knife in the other and give the flint an experimental tap with the blade of the knife. Nothing. It takes me a few minutes of trying before I get the angle right and see my first spark. I lean over the blackened punkwood tin and try again. A few strikes, and another spark appears. It lands on the punkwood char but quickly extinguishes.

I try again and again. My forearm aches from gripping the

knife so hard and from the repeated action of striking the flint. Each spark flares for a moment, then vanishes. Why wasn't it this hard when I did it with Odette? I breathe gently onto the punkwood, closing my eyes and seeing her face, alight with wild joy. And I strike again.

The spark lingers, and a spot on the punkwood starts to glow red. I drop the knife and flint and breathe again, and the red spot expands. It keeps growing as I keep breathing until it is large enough to sustain itself.

Gingerly, I reach into the tin, pick up the piece of punkwood, and, sheltering it with my other hand, place it carefully on the bird's nest of moss and bark. I blow some more, and the red spot blazes orange, and the bird's nest alights in a flaring hot white flame.

The twigs catch quickly, and before long a healthy fire is burning cheerily in the hearth, filling the room with an orange glow and the smell of cooking stew.

While I wait for my meal, I drift aimlessly around the room, looking for any signs of inhabitants, or any clues as to how I might escape.

I crouch to inspect the glass globe. It's about the size of a basketball, hollow and encased in a tightly knotted rope net. The glass is translucent green, thick, and filled with tiny bubbles and imperfections. I nudge it with my foot and notice a heavy chain attached to the rope netting. The chain leads outside through a neatly framed hole in the wall, like a miniature porthole. I peer out the doorway and see the chain descending into the water below. I can't for the life of me figure out what it's for.

I crane my neck to see the long stilts that raise the little room so far above the surface of the lake. They are covered in green algae. I wonder how sturdy they are, and if I'm at risk of the whole thing collapsing under me. I lean out the window and see that the exterior sill is encrusted with barnacles. I pry one off with a fingernail and examine the mollusk inside, glistening gray and pulsating. It's still alive, which means it has to be getting water. Could the little room be on some kind of platform that raises and lowers?

Something catches in my mind about this, but I can't quite find it through the dampening blanket of the singing.

Is my dinner ready yet?

There are markings in the lichen on the exterior wall of the building, vertical slashes that look like something has been clawing at the bare stone. Some kind of waterweed is caught in the corner of the windowsill, trailing in like ragged green ribbons.

Do lakes have tides?

A bubbling from the hearth distracts me, and I ladle out some of the stew into the earthenware bowl.

I settle myself in the chair by the fire—a carved wooden armchair that is more comfortable than it looks. The stew is delicious, rich and hearty, and it warms my insides while the fire warms me without. I eat two bowlfuls, then lean back in my chair and watch the fire crackle and pop.

The singing changes tone, becoming slow and somnolent.

My eyelids grow heavy, and I slip into a pleasant doze, where it's easy to pretend I'm at home, Gwion Bach soft and purring on my lap, Hangul and Huw chasing dust motes on the floor at my feet. Princess Bari sitting with Halmoni—the only lap she deigns to grace with her presence—while Halmoni reads one of her detective novels. Nan would be cooking—cockles and speckle bread, or knitting one of an endless series of colorful cardigans, or sitting at her workbench working on a poppet or a witch bottle, humming softly to herself.

My belly is full, and I'm warm, happy, and safe.

Suddenly, an icy wind blasts me in the face, and I hear Lyr's voice.

"Awaken!" he shrieks, his voice the howl of a storm.

I jerk forward, my feet soaking in ice-cold water that's seeping in from between the floorboards.

I don't know if the water has risen or the little house has sunk, but whatever's happening, it hasn't finished yet. The water smells like salt and sulfur and is just as milky white up close.

The singing is still there, but the tone of it has changed again, to something anticipatory.

The fire begins to hiss and spit as the water laps at the hearth, then all of a sudden it's extinguished, with a great gush of steam and smoke, billowing into the room and out the window and the doorway.

I'm going to have to swim. I look around at the water to see if I can find the fallen door—perhaps I could use it as a raft? But it's nowhere to be seen, and there's nothing else in here that will float.

Or is there? The green globe by the door rolls a little as the water comes in under it, and I hear the heavy chain groan as one link slips through the hole.

Another chain link slips through the hole as the green globe rises in the water. Maybe if I can get it loose from the chain, I can use it as a kind of flotation device. I fumble at the webbing that encases the globe, but the rope is old and stiff.

I splash back over to the counter to get the knife, then crouch over the globe, sawing and hacking at the rope. Fraying fibers irritate my grazed fingertips. I loosen one strand, then another, but there are so many, and the water is rising fast.

One more link slips through the hole, and something in the water below makes a thunking noise, like the falling of a heavy lever. Then there's a deep, metallic grinding, and the whole little house shudders.

I look out the doorway and see green globes popping up in the water, one by one, in a straight line leading to the shore. Each is attached to a length of chain that sags in the water between the globes. The grinding intensifies, and another chain rises in the water beside the first one. This new chain is moving, like it's being drawn toward the house.

The water is lapping at my shins now.

The mist swirls and eddies, and I glimpse movement at the edge of the lake. Something is emerging, pulled toward me along the chain.

The ferry. Finally.

It's an old rowboat, its timbers warped and buckled, white paint mostly flaked away. It sits low and unsteady in the water, like at any moment it could fall to pieces. But it's a boat, and perhaps it means I don't have to swim.

Its progress is slow, the prow smoothly parting the milky water as the chain rattles and clanks and groans. I grip the knife in my hand and hear Mam's voice in my head.

An iron blade in a ship's mast will ease a voyage.

This knife is steel, not iron, but chemically speaking it's more or less the same thing, and I need all the good luck I can get right now.

The boat reaches the front door of the house and stops. The grinding noise sounds again, and the chain falls slack.

I wade through the ice-cold milky water—past my knees now—and haul myself into the boat. It wobbles alarmingly, and I brace myself against the sides, trying to find my balance. I crouch in the center, as low as I can. The boat doesn't have a mast, but I thrust the knife into the prow.

Will it go back on its own? Do I have to do something to tell it I'm ready?

"Let's go," I tell it, and feel silly.

But the chain rises in the water and starts to move again—this time in the opposite direction. I feel a surge of relief as the shore draws closer.

The singing voices are louder now and increasing in tempo. They sound . . . hungry.

I hear a splash in the water and peer over the side of the boat, but I don't see anything, just an expanding ring of ripples. A fish, perhaps?

The hairs on the back of my neck stand up.

I realize I should have brought the flint with me. Who knows what I'll find when I reach the shore?

At least I have the knife.

Nan's father was a fisherman, and she told me all about sailors and things that cause bad luck. Whistling, pigs, hares, bananas, women—unless they were naked, in which case they were good luck. Not much I can do about any of that, as I can't stop being a woman, and I don't intend to strip. Still, my journey seems to be progressing. The boat is watertight, and I'm confident I'll make it to shore.

There's another splash, and once more I look into the water, my heart thumping.

A face, just under the surface, watching me with dark fish eyes. A creature, pondweed-green hair fanning out around her, her pale-gray body mostly obscured by the milky water. She watches me, expressionless. I glance around and see other faces, other strange, fishy girls, beautiful but eerie. One reaches a hand out of the water toward the boat. The space between her fingers is joined with a translucent webbing, and her nails are sharp and curved, the color of silt.

These aren't like the shellycoats that claw and snatch from the bottom of creeks and rivers. Shellycoats are just animals—they can give you a fright, but they're mostly harmless unless you get snatched under an ash moon. These creatures look like real girls, but *fishy*. And with a shudder, I remember that I made them too, in the story I wove for Odette. I remember the slip of pondweed between my fingers as I bound the twig-and-mud dolls together.

On the shore, something crashes through the undergrowth. The creatures scatter in the water like startled fish, diving into the milky depths, out of sight.

I peer into the mist and see the silhouettes of trees. Then a ramshackle jetty, squatting in the water on spidery legs.

And a figure.

Dread twists in my gut.

Broad shoulders and branching antlers. It's bigger than I remember, twice as tall as me, and as solid as an ox.

It's waiting for me.

Was it a trap all along? Did Lyr send me here to die?

Or did the Tatterdemalion track me? I touch Nan's rose, pinned to my breast. The lines on my chest throb with heat.

I remember the Tatterdemalion hunching over Winnie's little body, digging deep into her flesh. I remember the hot smell of blood. Hysteria bubbles in my chest. I don't want to die today.

I don't have another one of Nan's emergency witch bottles.

"Lyr, show yourself, you lying bastard!" I shout into the sky, but he doesn't come.

I look at the lake house, wondering if I can swim back, but it's gone. Instead, there stands a line of petrified trees rising out of the water, marking the perimeter of where the house was.

One by one, the fishy creatures reappear. One of them moves closer. Her long hair ripples around her in waves, topped with a wreath of pearls. Her pewter lips part, and she hisses at me, baring sharp, pointed teeth. I draw back into the safety of the boat and look carefully at the other creatures, trying to see past the fishy horror of them. One has a sprig of rue woven into her hair. Another is black-haired with aquiline features. A third is sharp-eyed and homely.

They open their mouths, and I finally realize where the singing has been coming from.

"I made you," I tell them. "Please don't hurt me."

My words are met with a frothing, foaming surge of activity as the girls writhe and thrash in the water. I see cold, pale limbs, sharp claws, and one kicking foot, ragged and bloody on the sole. They surge toward the boat, sharp teeth bared, dark eyes glittering.

My body starts to shake uncontrollably, and I'm finding it hard to take a full breath. "Please," I say.

Webbed fingers reach over the boat, gripping the sides. For a moment, I think they will climb into it and take me, but they don't. Something keeps them in the water. While I'm in the boat, I'm safe.

I ask a third time, for luck. "Please."

The thrashing stops, and the water becomes calm. The singing stops too, and the absence of it is more terrifying. The only sound is the wet grinding of the chain as it pulls me inexorably toward the Tatterdemalion.

I try to tug the knife free from the prow of the boat, but my fingers are stiff and frozen.

The monster stands unmoving on the jetty, a great, hulking shadow of brush and tusk and branch. As I am drawn closer, I see it more clearly. Rags and string and mud. Prickly bushes sprout from its hunched back, and twigs and branches rise from its head like antlers. It stares at me with eyes that are just empty black sockets fringed with milky fluid that drips down what I suppose are its cheeks. I can see slimy sluglike creatures moving around inside its ragged black scream of a mouth. Two long curved tusks protrude from the black hole, glossy green tipped with brown, oddly reminiscent of the thorns on Nan's rosebushes.

The Tatterdemalion shambles forward, the roots of its feet burrowing into the ground with each step.

The fishy girls have disappeared.

Then a pale hand reaches over the side of the boat. It's holding a ladle, identical to the one I used in the lake house for the stew, which it empties with a swift flick of the wrist. Ice-cold water sloshes over my feet. Another hand appears, also bearing a ladle, then another, and another. The boat is rapidly filling with water, up to my ankles now, cold and milky and stinking of sulfur. I keep tugging at the knife, my fingers numb and useless.

The boat begins to sink lower in the water.

The Tatterdemalion roars a sickening roar that is high and low, quiet and loud. It makes my ears pop, and my head aches with a sudden pressure. The jetty trembles. The fishy girls ladle faster. The prow of the boat is nearly below the water now, and long pale arms are reaching over the sides to grasp my ankles. The creatures are swarming around me as the water closes in. Sharp teeth graze and snap at my shins. I try to back away, but my limbs aren't working properly and I can't stop shaking.

Finally, the knife comes free, and I slash at the fishy girls. They draw back and hiss at me, but there are so many, and I can't fend them all off.

The Tatterdemalion roars again, and the boat is almost at the jetty. It's reaching out to me, its long, twiggy fingers black with dried blood. The slashes on my chest are burning hot.

"Stay back!" I shout, brandishing the knife at the Tatterdemalion, my voice thick with fear.

It shows no reaction.

Disemboweled by the monster or eaten alive by fish creatures: either way, it's not much of an end.

What would I do if this were a story? I'd fight the monsters. I'd trick the fishy girls into helping me. I'd cast a spell or call on some giant eagles to rescue me.

I scrabble at the black satin bag hanging from my wrist, but it's too late. And what could I have done anyway, with no magic? All I have is a knife. I grip it in my fist. Perhaps I can wound the Tatterdemalion somehow.

A glimpse of movement across the lake catches my eye.

The mist has cleared to reveal a cloaked figure standing on the far bank, surrounded by buttonwood and white mangrove.

A ripple passes through the lake, and the very top of a fin breaks the surface, causing the water to sluice off into little swirling eddies. The fishy girls stop their relentless advance and look around, glistening eyes darting from side to side.

A golden fish breaks through the water, leaping into the air like a rapturous sunrise. It's enormous—easily twice the size of my rapidly sinking boat. It carves a graceful arc, droplets of water streaming from its long, trailing fins and tail. Its scales are gold, peach, and saffron, and it seems to glow in the chilled, lifeless air above the lake. It plunges back beneath the surface, and even through the milky water I can see it arrowing toward me like a comet. The creatures scatter with shrill screams and hisses, extending claws and webbed fingers as if to try and stop the fish.

I am close enough to the jetty now that I can hear the rattle of the Tatterdemalion's breath, like rustling dry leaves. It is perched right on the edge of the rotting wooden boards. I lean back from its reaching fingers, and the lines on my chest burn brighter.

The fish emerges beside the boat, moving its tail gently to keep it in position. It appears to be waiting . . . for me.

"Jump on, you fool!" yells the cloaked figure.

I have only a few seconds before the boat is swallowed by the water, and before the Tatterdemalion reaches me.

I take a deep breath and fling myself at the fish. It's cold and slippery, and I scrabble for purchase until I wrap one hand around the base of its dorsal fin, my other hand still gripping the knife. With a shudder, the fish surges forward, plunging deep into the milky gray-green water. I have just enough time to gasp for breath before I'm submerged and I feel fingers snatching at me, tearing at my clothes, my hair, my skin. I try to open my eyes, but all I see is murky darkness, so I squeeze them shut again and hold on to the fish as tightly as I can.

Bubbles fizz and pop in my ears, and I can hear the singing again, distorted from the water. It's discordant, but there's a sweetness to it now, something powerful and alluring. I want to hear more, and I turn my head toward the sound of it, my fingers slackening their grip. The song builds, and I can make out a multitude of voices raised in some kind of strange harmony— familiar yet totally alien to me, throbbing with mettle. It calls me, and I let my hand fall from the golden fish's fin.

With a shudder, it lashes its billowing tail up and around me, slapping painfully against my ear, making it thud and ring. It changes course abruptly, and we soar to the surface, breaching into the mist. The music clears from my head, and I grip the fish once more as it dives back underwater.

Now I can hear other sounds as well—snarling and hissing, getting closer and closer.

I feel a cold hand on my ankle, the points of fingernails digging into my skin. I slash at it with my knife. Another hand joins it, and then there are hands everywhere—on my elbows and thighs and hair—pulling and scratching and tugging at me. Cold fingers pry open my own frozen fist, and the knife slips from my grasp. I kick out at the creatures, but the movement dislodges me from the golden fish's back, and I'm grasped by cold, clammy arms that pull me down, deeper than I thought possible.

I open my eyes, and through the murkiness I see silt and gray weeds and bones. Lots of bones. The singing is back, but it's not sweet and enticing anymore. It's urgent and hungry, accompanied by a noise like the booming of a great drum. My lungs are burning with the effort of holding my breath, and I know I can't do it much longer.

I try to struggle against the fishy girl who pulled me down, but she is strong and her grip on me is viselike. Her face is pressed against mine, her gray watery fish eyes staring at me with single-minded hunger.

Then the golden fish is there, barreling into us like a truck. The girl releases me and attacks the fish, clawing at its fins and tail. I kick against the silty floor of the lake and launch myself toward it, grabbing a fin and holding on with everything I have. The golden fish darts toward the surface, the hungry girl left behind in the deep.

Stars dance before my closed eyes, and my lungs spasm. Instinct kicks in, and I try to draw breath, water pouring into my chest and filling me with icy panic. The fish leaps into the air and skims along the surface of the lake. We whiz past the chalky cliffs and slow to a stop in the shallows. I slide off and land on my hands and knees, coughing and retching, my hair plastered wet across my face. I throw up my two bowls of stew and what feels like half the lake, gulping huge breaths of air in between heaves.

"Get out of the water, you ninny."

I look up to see Ginger, pushing the cloak back from her raven hair, utterly and completely alive.

10

I STUMBLE OVER INTRICATELY LOOPING MANGROVE roots, slipping in the slimy mud, as the pale faces of the fishy girls emerge in the shallows.

"But you died . . . ," I say.

I scramble up the bank, and Ginger looks me over as I stand there, shivering. "Wait here," she tells me.

She steps into the lake, and the fishy girls surge forward, grabbing at Ginger's bare legs with long, cold talons. I let out a warning yelp, but she doesn't seem concerned.

The golden fish thrashes its tail in the water, protecting Ginger, and she kicks out at the fishy girls.

"Back off," she snaps.

The creatures lift their heads above the water to bare their pointed teeth and hiss. But they keep their distance.

I look across the lake to see what the Tatterdemalion is doing, but the jetty and the far bank have been swallowed by mist.

Ginger sinks down and embraces the golden fish, her cloak floating on the surface of the water. She lays her pale cheek against the fish's golden one, and it nuzzles her, a shining black eye looking up adoringly. She caresses its long whiskers and leans over to inspect its fins and tail for harm.

"Are you all right, dearest?" she murmurs.

She seems so vulnerable, so un-Ginger.

And so *alive*.

She gives the fish another loving embrace, then stands.

The fish turns in a whirl of vivid gold and tangerine, shudders, and disappears under the water.

The fishy girls hiss from the lake, spitting streams of cold milky water at us.

Ginger gives me a haughty look, then she turns on her heel and stalks away. I'm not sure if I'm supposed to follow, but she lets out an irritated sigh and, over her shoulder, says, "Well, come on, then." So I scurry after her.

"Ginger," I say. "Stop. We need to talk."

But she doesn't stop.

Looping vines twist and hang around us, and at times I'm not quite sure if they are organic vines or electric cabling. Leaves crunch underfoot, but sometimes I get a glimpse of faded linoleum beneath them, as if the glamour of this place is weaker there.

"Are we stopping soon?" I ask breathlessly.

"We stop when we get there," Ginger answers. "Or would you rather be eaten alive?"

"I'm sorry," I say. "I'm just so tired."

She snorts.

The ground grows rocky underfoot. I look up into the green-and-brown canopy and am genuinely not sure if we're inside or outside. It's eerily silent, with no buzzing of insects or chirping of birds. I finally draw even with Ginger, and reach out to grab her by the arm.

"Stop," I say. "Talk to me."

Ginger turns around and narrows her eyes. "I owe you nothing. You burned down my house, and my fish nearly split a fin saving you."

I shake my head. "I didn't burn it down. The dittany . . . and the Tatterdemalion . . ."

"It was hunting *you*."

"How do you know?"

"Because it's never been able to break the wards around my apartment before. You're the new thing in the forest. Things changed when you arrived."

She marches past a long line of filing cabinets embedded in a wall of skunk vine and creeping Jenny. Mildew-spotted paper spills from rusted drawers.

I stare at the back of her head. "I thought you were dead."

She ignores this, and her tone changes to its usual light banter. "Do you like my big fish? I've had him since he was a baby, no bigger than a walnut."

"What happened?" I press. "The fire . . ."

"You're the one whose been having all the adventures," she says. "You tell me."

I hear a nearby rustling, and Ginger freezes, turning to lay a finger over her lips.

I shiver. "Are we safe here?" I whisper.

Ginger's smile is bleak. "Nowhere is safe."

"Where are we?"

"Sicklehurst."

I shake my head. "It's all just glamour, isn't it? I've never seen anything like it. And you . . . Did you escape the fire?"

She must have. Otherwise, she wouldn't be here. But she says nothing.

"Thank you," I tell her.

Ginger quirks an eyebrow. "For what?"

"Saving me."

She ducks her head in the slightest nod of acknowledgment. It's the closest thing to a genuine response that I've managed to get out of her.

"Why did you do it?" I ask. "Rescue me."

Ginger's eyes soften as she meets my gaze. "I'm not a monster," she says.

She leans forward, tilting her head to mine. She smells like wet wool and dittany.

There's so much Odette in her—this character that Odette inhabited for years. But this lost girl is all grown-up. She's sexy and powerful and seems totally in control. I think Odette would be proud of her.

I notice there's a smudge of something brownish green at her temple, and I reach up to wipe it off with my thumb. She closes her eyes as I touch her, and I hear a slight tremble of anticipation in her breath.

I can't do this. She wants me to fall into the same trap I fell into with Odette. Always following, always assenting. Backup. Assistant. Best supporting friend. But I'm not here to audition for a new sidekick role. I already have a best friend, and I'm here for *her*, not for Ginger.

"Tell me how to get to the tower," I demand.

Ginger scowls, and the intimacy of the moment is broken. "What? No. Why would you want to go there?"

"Odette is there. Lyr told me."

"Who?"

I frown. Ginger hadn't known about Lyr when I mentioned him before either. How could she not have seen him? "Lyr. He's . . . a kind of ghost. He helped me escape the Tatterdemalion, earlier today."

And also led me into a trap.

Ginger looks taken aback, as if I had, for the first time, said something she truly wasn't expecting. "There's no one else in Sicklehurst. No boys. If there were boys, I'd know."

"There is," I insist. "He told me Odette was in the tower."

"He can't have, because (a) there's nothing in the tower and (b) he doesn't exist."

I nearly tell her that I created Lyr, that I made him up, just as I made her, but I have a feeling she wouldn't take it very well.

"What happened," I ask her, "back at your apartment, with the monster, and the fire? Where did you go?" I have to know how she survived.

Ginger stands still, her chin tilted away from me in defiance, then says, "Follow me."

She turns and marches down an overgrown path that leads between thick stands of dogwood and birch, interspersed with cracked concrete pillars and crumbling iron joists. I catch up to her at a thicket of sourstone bamboo, and Ginger squeezes between the straight vertical poles, leading me through what feels like a maze. The bamboo forms corridors that twist and bend erratically. Sometimes a wall is broken by a heavy iron door or a twisting mass of rusting pipes and cables. The floor is still a strange mix of linoleum and rotting leaves.

As we move deeper into the thicket, the air grows warm and moist, until it feels almost tropical.

There's something missing, though. Our footsteps sound too loud, crunching and squelching through the leaves. I can't put my finger on what it is.

The maze of bamboo opens out into a wide boulevard, thickly grassed with flea sedge and clumping tangles of sticklegrass. Walls of glossy bamboo poles line either side, grown so close together that they obscure anything beyond. The passage is as straight as an arrow, leading unbroken toward a high concrete wall in the distance.

Above us is a thick canopy of bamboo, golden sunlight just barely filtering through in shifting green-stained patches. The only sound is the faint rustling of leaves overhead, and the *tock tock* of swaying hollow trunks knocking against each other. Suddenly, I realize what's missing.

"Birds," I say out loud.

Ginger turns her head to look at me.

"There are no birds," I tell her.

A wistful look passes over Ginger's face, and she shakes her head. "No," she says. "No birds. I don't think I've ever seen a bird."

Sticklegrass clings to my ankles, and I kick it away, my foot glancing off a smooth, rounded boulder, pale and covered in moss. The path is uneven, the grass obscuring more such boulders, as well as thinnish branches and crunching dry sticks.

"What is this place?" I ask.

"The Bone Road," she answers.

The hair lifts on the back of my neck, and I tentatively nudge one of the boulders over with a toe. Empty eye sockets stare at me. There are no boulders or branches underfoot.

It's all bones. Human bones.

I stumble, pressing a hand to my mouth to stop a scream from escaping. More bones crunch underfoot, and bile burns at the back of my throat.

"W-who were they?"

Ginger hesitates before answering. "Lost girls."

A warm breeze blows the scent of thick earth and compost, and I shudder.

"Come on," Ginger says.

She doesn't bother to avoid the bones, just stomps over them. But I try, picking my way around sightless skulls and grasping white fingers.

"Hurry up," Ginger says over her shoulder.

Eventually, the Bone Road comes to an end, and a crumbling concrete wall looms before us, spilling over with sticklegrass. Ginger leads me through an archway, and we find ourselves in a kind of walled garden.

I can't tell what this space once was—a courtyard, or a building that has since lost its roof. Whatever human-made structures were here before are now completely obscured by a blanket of sticklegrass, forming a thick mat over shapes that could be trees or more power-plant infrastructure. They look ambiguous under the vibrant green froth, organic yet with the promise of mobility, like they might shamble around when you aren't looking. The air here seems purer, and I feel dizzy from the sudden influx of oxygen.

An enormous concrete building lurks on the far side of the clearing, crouching squat and ugly against the sky, its edges blurred with more sticklegrass. A glittering waterfall spills from the top of it and pools into a muddy hollow. There are other pools too, murky and choked with lurid blooms of algae, or floating duckweed. Everything is so violently green it makes my eyes hurt.

"Where are we going?" I ask, but I know that Ginger won't answer.

She leads me over to the edge of one of the pools, and sits down beside it on something oblong, draped with sticklegrass. I sit next to her and realize there's a stone bench underneath all of the vegetation. She looks at me and licks her lips. There is fear in her eyes as she figures out how to begin.

"I don't remember my childhood," she says. "Sometimes I get little glimpses—a convent, a castle, a little cottage by the sea, an orphanage. But they never match, and I don't know whether they are my memories or not. I know things. About the world. About magic. But I don't remember learning them."

I think of all the versions of Genevieve's life I created for Odette. So many origin stories.

"The only thing that's clear is this place. Being hunted by the Tatterdemalion."

A tendril of sticklegrass has wrapped itself around her ankle. She pinches it off and examines it critically before dropping it into the pool. It floats on the surface, then is swallowed by an algae bloom.

"I tried to get out, but there was no way. I couldn't climb the walls, and there were no doors. This place . . . it changes, all the time. Sometimes it's a forest, or a swamp, or a jungle. Sometimes there's a great river. I like that version best because things wash up on the riverbank that can be useful. Once, Winnie and I made a raft so we could float down the river and maybe escape, but we just ended up at the lake with the fishy girls."

"I'm sorry," I say.

She smiles softly. "It's not your fault," she says.

But it is. She just doesn't know it yet.

"I remember other people, but they don't feel like my memories. Other than Winnie, you feel like the first real person I've ever met."

Her words sting like hailstones. She's telling the truth. She hasn't met Odette in here. I see a blazing of hope in her eyes, and guilt rises in me alongside my disappointment. I can't help her. I made her when I still had magic, but I don't have it anymore. She's stuck here, and it's all my fault.

"Are you sure no one else has come in here?" I ask, desperate.

Her gaze slides away from mine. "I haven't seen your friend. Winnie might have. But like I said, if she was ever here, she'll be dead by now. The monster never stops hunting."

I close my eyes and see the hulking shape of the Tatterdemalion, smell its rotting scent, feel its reaching, twiggy claws. I touch my fingers to the three lines on my chest and feel a hotness there.

"It's my first real memory," Ginger says. "The Tatterdemalion. I tried to run, but it cornered me. I remember it so clearly. The tusks. The black mouth. The rotten smell of it."

"How did you get away?" I ask.

Ginger looks at me, exasperated. "I didn't," she says. "Of course I didn't. How could I? You've seen it."

"I don't understand."

"It killed me. It cut me down and drove its hands into my belly and tore out everything that was inside until there was nothing left."

For a moment, the surface of the pool ripples, the duckweed shifting ever so slightly back and forth.

"Then there was nothing, for a while," she says. "Sometimes it happens straight away. Sometimes it takes a day or two—it depends on the season. Then there's mud. The taste of it. The grit of it between my teeth. Then I was here, in this garden. Entrails all on the inside again."

I say nothing.

"Dying hurts," Ginger remarks. "A lot. I don't recommend it."

My mind is racing. If Rufus's theory is right, then it's the forest itself—the sticklegrass wood—that is doing this. Some kind of strange, ancient plant-consciousness, keeping the dolls I made for Odette alive, then unmaking and remaking them, over and over again. But why?

What does it want?

"Tell me more about the Tatterdemalion."

Ginger's face twists bleakly. "What is there to tell? It hunts us. Its sole purpose in life is to destroy."

"Why don't you fight it?"

"It can't be killed."

"How do you know?" I ask.

"I just do."

I press harder. "How do you know if you haven't tried?"

There's a hollowness to her face, a blank terror of something so monstrous that I can't even begin to comprehend it. "We did try."

I wait as Ginger stares at the pool.

"We tried," she continues at last, her voice low and hoarse. "We made weapons out of whatever we could find—branches, bits of broken pipe, old tools. Winnie thinks the source of the Tatterdemalion's power is inside the refinery building, a great gaping black hole leading deep into the earth, like a dungeon. The plan was to try and get down there, to find it and destroy it."

A dungeon. Princesses are sometimes kept in dungeons. What if Lyr is wrong, and Odette is there?

"What did you find?"

Ginger shakes her head. "Nothing. We barely got through the door. The Tatterdemalion was waiting for us. We thought we were ready."

"What happened?"

Ginger's face is as hard and cold as stone. "We died. It tore us to pieces, scooped out our insides. It crushed our bones, our skulls."

"So you didn't enter the dungeon?"

The pool ripples again, more forcefully now, like something is moving underneath. I sneeze, then breathe in a waft of something rich and earthy, and remember being in the compost heap under the lake house. I look at the pool witch-eyed and see that it is a writhing mass of mettle. I've never seen so much before. It's practically *boiling*. I blink, unsettled, and return my attention to Ginger.

"We didn't just try once. We tried again. And again. And again. And every time was the same. Carnage. Pain. Death. There is something buried there, in the dungeon. Something dark and rotten. It makes the Tatterdemalion stronger—too strong. Eventually, I gave up and escaped to my little apartment by the wall. I put up wards to protect myself from everything, even from Winnie. Until you came along and broke it all."

"How did you know how to do it?" I ask. "The wards, I mean."

She shrugs. "Some of it I just knew, in the way that I know things. Some of it I learned from magazines."

There's a sloshing noise as the puddle heaves, and something starts to emerge. Fingers, covered in duckweed and mud. They flex as they rise from the water, reaching, grasping, splayed wide from a flat, filthy palm. Ginger stands up, grips the hand in hers, and hauls. An arm appears, then another. A head. Shoulders. A body.

I scramble to my feet and take a step backward. But Ginger doesn't seem frightened at all. Her face is sad, if anything. She lets go of the muddy hand and wipes her own fingers on her skirt, leaving dark streaks behind.

The mud creature is a girl. She's slick with earth and algae slime, but I can tell she's young—much younger than me or Ginger. Her dark hair is caked with muck, and she is wearing some kind of dress. She doesn't acknowledge us, just coughs violently, spitting out a mouthful of dark soil. She trudges over to the waterfall and stands under it, letting the water wash away the slime and the mud. I watch, horrified, as I see pale skin, a white cotton dress with pearl buttons and lace around the cuffs. I've seen it before. I've seen this girl before. I saw the Tatterdemalion rip out her insides.

I made her.

It's Winnie.

Eilwen.

The plucky, sweet little girl I'd inhabited for years, in every game that Odette and I played, every story I told. Odette always wanted to be older, to be sixteen and nearly a woman. But I never wanted that. I just wanted to be a little girl, for as long as I could.

My heart hammers as I stare at her. She doesn't look anything like me—but that was the whole point. Imaginary play let me and Odette be other people for a little while. Odette could be wild and free and magical, away from the cold diamond life that her mother had laid out for her. And I could be truly innocent, free from suspicion and pity. *That's her. The traitor's daughter. Poor thing.*

"Welcome back," says Ginger.

Winnie doesn't answer. She turns her face to the waterfall and sticks a finger in her ear to clear it of mud. It's like she was buried alive and has just crawled out of the earth.

Except she wasn't buried alive.

She was dead, brutally disemboweled by the Tatterdemalion.

I look over at Ginger. "You died in the fire," I say, just to be sure.

"Of course I did," she snaps. "Haven't you been listening?"

"You died, and you came back . . . here."

There were dozens of skulls on the Bone Road.

Lost girls, Ginger called them. Were they all Ginger and Winnie?

I'm struck by the desperate bravery of them, dying over and over again while trying to escape the horror of this monstrous prison.

I want nothing more than to run home. This is no story. These are real girls, who are really dying.

And it's all my fault.

Maybe if I can save Odette, then together we can figure out a way to free them. Maybe Lyr will know. If I can find a way to communicate with the sticklegrass wood, maybe then we can break this awful spell.

I should tell them the truth about where they come from, and my part in it.

But I don't, because I'm afraid they'll hate me, and I need their help.

"How does it work?" I ask. "What spell is powerful enough to bring someone back from the dead?"

"Death." It's Winnie. Her voice is childish, but her expression is grim. "It needs a death to make a life."

Her words hang in the air. I guess it makes sense. Death discharges a lot of mettle. But enough to resurrect a whole person?

She steps out of the waterfall and wrings out her hair and skirts. She's cleaner now, but not completely. The white of her dress is dull and smudged, and I look at my own white dress, similarly damp and bedraggled. Winnie separates her hair into three sections, yanking and tearing through matted knots. These sections she roughly braids together. She rips off the grimy ribbon sash, using it to secure the end of the plait. She shucks off her black Mary Janes and peels away wet stockings before stepping out of a soaking petticoat, the ruffled cotton streaked with mud. These items she dispatches into a nearby pool with a savage kick, then turns to Ginger.

"Finally decided to come out of your hidey-hole, I see."

Ginger shifts uncomfortably. "Not by choice," she said. "The fire burned down my home."

"I saw. Accident?"

Ginger shakes her head. "Dittany." She jerks her head at me. "Her fault."

Winnie narrows her eyes at me.

"Her name's Maude," Ginger explains. "She has a dead friend."

"Join the club," Winnie says before I can protest that Odette isn't dead. She comes forward to stand before me. The top of her head barely reaches my chin. She peers at my chest and puts a finger to the place where the Tatterdemalion marked me.

"It was after her," she observes.

Ginger nods. "She's wearing a rose, see?"

"Amateur," Winnie snorts, reaching out to snatch the rose from my dress. "This is how they track you, you know?"

I hold on to the bone-pin brooch as she crushes the rose in her fist, then drops it into the mud.

"She ended up in the lake house," Ginger continues.

"How did she get away?"

"My big fish."

"Ah." She wraps her fingers around my throat. "Do you think we should kill her?"

I flinch away, and Winnie chuckles, then turns to the first pool of mud, the one she emerged from. She squats next to it, dips her fingers into the muck, then wipes them across her eyes from temple to temple, so she's wearing a kind of gray-green mask, dark against her pale skin. She turns toward us, tilting her face to the side while she considers us.

"Why are you only coming back now?" I ask. "You died before Ginger did. Shouldn't you have come back first?"

Winnie regards me through eyes that should be wide and innocent, but instead seem flat and uncompromising. "I did come back first."

It takes me a moment to understand what she's saying. "You mean you died *again*?"

She shrugs. "You get used to it."

Ginger coughs. "Speak for yourself."

I stare at Winnie, and she stares back. She bares her teeth at me, and I can't tell if it's a grin or a growl.

"So are we going to kill her?" Winnie asks.

"Not yet," Ginger says. "She might be useful."

"I'm looking for my friend," I say. "Have you seen her?"

Winnie looks at me as she thinks. "Yellow hair? Too much eyeliner? Tragic affect?"

My pulse quickens. "You've seen her."

Winnie nods. "Yeah, I've seen her. She's dead."

"What?"

No. She can't be.

Winnie shrugs. "I saw her running. The monster was hot on her tail. She's definitely dead by now. And she won't come back, the way we do."

"But . . . you didn't *see* her die. So you don't know for sure."

Winnie snorts.

"Where was she?" I ask. "Which way was she headed?"

"I don't remember," Winnie says. "I've died nine times since then. And I owe you nothing, stranger. I don't know you, and I don't trust you. Now if you'll excuse me, I have a beast to hunt."

She walks away without another word, moving with quiet confidence through the tangled sticklegrass and disappearing along the Bone Road.

I turn to Ginger, a mute question on my face.

"So that was Winnie," Ginger says. "She's a bloodthirsty monster."

"But she's just a little girl."

Ginger huffs out a humorless laugh. "Haven't you been listening? She's been here for years, same as me. But she's died nearly every day. Sometimes multiple times. She's determined to kill the Tatterdemalion, no matter how many times it kills her. Now let's go."

"Go where?"

"Somewhere safe. I have to make another apartment. Put up new wards."

I shake my head. "Winnie said that Odette was here. I have to find her. The tower . . . Lyr said . . ."

Ginger rolls her eyes. "Lyr doesn't exist. But the Tatterdemalion does, and if it gets you, you'll die. Permanently."

I shake my head. "No," I tell her. "You're wrong. Lyr *does* exist. I have to get to the tower."

"Or you could not!" Ginger's voice rises. "You could come with me. We could keep each other safe. Even be a bit happy . . ."

And I understand. "You're afraid," I say. "Of being alone."

There's a flash of something raw on Ginger's face, but she quickly replaces it with a sneer. "You have a high opinion of yourself, don't you? I'm not afraid of being alone. I've been alone for years. I'm afraid of *dying*. I want to find another hiding spot and make it safe so the Tatterdemalion won't find me."

"But won't it eventually?"

"It'll buy me some time. Every day that I don't die is a good day in my book. My bar for happiness is low."

"You can't keep running away," I tell her.

"You don't get it. This is a *war*. A war without end. There's nowhere to run. The only choice we have is to fight and die or to hide where it can't reach us. And I choose not dying."

"You're a coward," I snap, then immediately regret it.

Her laughter is humorless and weary. "If that's what you want to call it."

She turns and walks away from the pools, away from me.

11

CONTINUE ALONG THE BONE ROAD ALONE. GINGER and Winnie are long gone, and the grassed avenue of lumpen skulls and bones feels even more sinister without them nearby.

I wonder how many of these skulls belonged to Ginger.

The horror of it strikes me anew, rising thick in my throat.

The call to turn back is strong. I don't want to become one of these skulls.

But I have to find Odette.

I notice now that there's a gap in the bamboo wall that lines the road. It's barely big enough for me to fit through, but on the other side there's a tangled jungle of jade vine, laurel, and Sally Wattle, and beyond that, pale, smooth concrete, rising into the sky. The tower.

Now that I'm closer, I can see that there's something growing up and around it—a dark-leafed vine, perhaps, or a rambling rose.

I angle myself sideways and squeeze through the gap, feeling smooth bamboo press close against my chest. There's no path, just thick, dark greenery. Strangler figs writhe around straight-trunked ribbonwoods and silky oak trees, weaving intricate, choking cat's cradles, which spread to other trees, forming a thick canopy of twisting, gnarled wood, like some kind of ancient organic knotwork. Elkhorn ferns thrust proudly upward from tree trunks, and the ground is choked with white hazelwood and waxflower.

The sticklegrass wood's glamour continues to astonish me with its power. Every detail is there: the humidity in the air, the tropical smell of it. I wonder where I really am, how far I've come. Am I just walking around in circles?

Barely any light filters through the knotted canopy, and I stumble more than once on fat, protruding roots. I'm hungry, but all I can see is toxic ribbonwood fruit and bulbous pink finger cherries, which Mam always said would turn a child blind.

Anyway, I shouldn't eat anything here. I shouldn't have let the fishy girls' song get in my head. I shouldn't have eaten the stew. It's how the Tatterdemalion found me—I'm sure of it. Despite what Winnie and Ginger said, I can't believe that Nan's rose would give me away.

I encounter patches of fungi on dead or dying wood—thick yellow witches' butter, pinkish fingers of bitter coral, luminescent stickycap, glowing eerie green. A magnificent crinoline stinkhorn, as big as my head, sprouts from a rotten tree stump, lacy white indusium spilling from a bell-shaped cap like a bridal veil.

There's a familiar nagging heaviness deep in my abdomen. I glance around, but of course there's nobody watching. I hike up Odette's dress and pull down my undies, squatting on the humus-rich floor to empty my bladder at the base of the tree stump. The ammonia scent of urine makes my eyes water, and I squint in the near darkness to watch it soak away into the earth.

Nan catches urine passed over an iron blade and mixes it with parsley and an earned coin, for a witch bottle to protect against ill wishes. There are other ways to use urine too. Urine and stinging nettle mixed with graveyard soil makes a powerful hex. Mam taught me that.

I pull my underwear back up and walk on.

I walk on and on, hunger and fear gnawing at me. The sight of the cooling tower is long gone, as is the gap in the bamboo leading back to the Bone Road. I'm totally turned around, without even the position of the sun to guide me.

At one point, I encounter the tree stump with the crinoline stinkhorn again, and realize I've been going around in circles. At the base of the stump where I urinated is a thick patch of fresh sticklegrass, vivid green in the half-light. The unsettled feeling grows stronger. I can feel the ancient wood whispering to me, trying to climb into my mind, like ivy seeking cracks in a wall. I ignore it. Silly girls in stories get lost in the woods, but storytelling is my gift. I know the way.

After what feels like hours, the whisper of a sweet-smelling breeze caresses my cheek, and I follow it. There is a glimpse of light ahead, and I quicken my pace. There's a sound too, a human voice. Singing. Not the discordant, wavering singing of the fishy girls.

This is just one voice. A voice I know.

My gait grows unsteady as I feel a tingling in my chest.

It's Odette.

The rain forest opens into a mossy glade, bathed in golden light. In the center of the glade is a spreading tree, branches hanging low and heavy with plump red fruit. I don't recognize the tree, and I don't care, because under it on soft moss is Odette.

I press my hands to my heart to stop it from bursting straight out of my chest. My thoughts scatter, and I want to scream and spin and fling my arms wide in triumph.

She's sprawling comfortably, her lap piled high with fruit. Her lips and fingers are stained red, and she's humming to herself, contented. There's no sign of the bags under her eyes, the black-market glamours, the stringiness to her hair. She looks luminous, like a shining star. She's wearing the white dress she wore to the Hollantide Ball.

But that can't be quite right, because aren't *I* wearing that dress?

Odette raises one of the fruits to her lips and takes a long, languorous bite, savoring it as red juice drips down her chin.

I call out to her, and she looks up. Her lips part in a delighted smile, but she doesn't move.

"Maude!" she says dreamily. "I've been waiting for you."

She pats the moss next to her and takes another bite of the fruit. As I start toward her, I notice that the moss has grown up over her, as if she's been there for weeks. I know that's not right either, but I'm finding it hard to think about anything else.

I found her. She's okay.

She holds out a piece of fruit, and my stomach growls. The fruits glisten, ripe and juicy. I know this tree. I made it, just as I made everything else here in Sicklehurst. Another danger for Genevieve and Eilwen to overcome on their quest.

The tree is dangerous.

But it's *Odette*. My heart can't bear it.

She holds out a hand. "Come on," she says. "I have a secret to tell you."

I take a step forward, but my ankles are wound with stickle-grass, clinging and holding me back, away from Odette and the tree. I tug my foot free of it.

The moss is studded with fruit that has fallen from the groaning branches. Each one is about the size of a pomegranate, fat and round, colored a rich, glistening red. I start to salivate and take another step forward. The sticklegrass winds around my ankles once more, squeezing tight, and it's enough to break the glamour for a moment. The sweet scent drops away, replaced by the smell of rotting flesh. The tree appears gnarled and sinister, thorned canes twisting in its canopy like snakes.

Odette seems to waver too, growing hazy and insubstantial.

"Odette," I say firmly. "Come away from there. It isn't safe."

She laughs, low and lazy. "Don't be ridiculous," she says. "I've never met a fruit tree I didn't like."

"Have you met this one before?"

She shrugs.

"Just come over here," I tell her, reaching out a hand.

"But I need to tell you my secret."

"So come here and tell me."

She looks at the fruit in her lap and considers it, absentmindedly taking another bite from the piece in her hand.

"I think I'll stay here," she says. "I don't really feel like getting up."

"Odette!" I say again. "Come here. Now."

She rolls her eyes. "Fine." She pushes the fruit from her skirt and licks her fingers, then tries to stand. But the moss holds her down, and she wobbles, as if drunk, collapsing back onto the moss with a giggle.

"Oh well." She reaches for another fruit.

I steel myself, rip more sticklegrass from my ankles, and charge forward. The moss underfoot is velvety-soft, perfumed rich and earthy. As I duck under the canopy of the giant tree, the light becomes dappled gold and green, the only sound the gentle rustling of leaves and the creaking of heavily laden branches.

I reach Odette and see that there's a snake wound around her ankles, bright green and no thicker than my finger. Odette's skin is spattered with moss around it. I try to pull the snake free, but it sinks its fangs deep into Odette's flesh. She makes a kittenish noise of protest.

I reach out to knock the fruit from her hand, but she grabs on to my wrist, her movement surprisingly fast. She pulls me down, and we tumble together on the moss. It is as soft as a feather bed. The dappled sunlight is warm, and I haven't felt this comfortable in . . . perhaps in forever.

Odette presses her nose to mine. "Do you want to hear my secret?" I can smell sweetness on her breath, honeysuckle and rose.

"Um," I say. "Okay."

Her voice is whisper-soft, low and tender, and just for me. "I think you're beautiful."

She tilts her head and brushes her red-stained lips against mine, hesitating before pulling away with a twinkling grin.

Without thinking, I touch my tongue to my lips, and I can

taste something so perfect that I know I will go mad unless I get more. I lean in and press my lips to Odette's, and she sighs in contentment.

And in that moment, I let all the walls fall. Every excuse and protest that I was ever happy just being her friend. That I liked watching her dance with Mondarius Cole. That I'd gotten over my heartbreak after she cast me aside without a second thought.

I'm in love with Odette.

I've always loved her. With all my heart. With every single part of me.

This is what I've been longing for. I thought the emptiness inside me was the loss of my magic, but I was wrong. It was Odette. She is my everything.

The kiss breaks off, and I am suddenly ravenous. I scrabble in the grass for the red fruit. My hand closes around a smooth plumpness, which gives a little under my fingers. I raise it to my lips and bite.

The fruit's skin breaks under my teeth, flooding my mouth with thick, sweet juice. It tastes like honeysuckle and rose, and fresh lemon sorbet, and the marble cake that Odette and I used to buy from the bakery, with coins stolen from Odette's mother's purse. I take bite after bite, juice running down my chin, down my wrists, splashing onto my dress and the moss around us. The green snake uncoils itself from Odette's ankle and winds its way around mine.

Odette claps her hands in delight and reaches for another fruit. She holds it to my lips, and I bite. I hold one out to her, and we don't break eye contact. A soft smile blooms on her face, and desire quickens within me.

We keep feeding each other fruit and licking each other's fingers. I know exactly what I want, and for perhaps the first time in my life I'm not afraid to reach out and take it. I kiss her again, drinking the juice from her mouth, pulling her closer, pressing my body against hers.

I forget about the rose canes, Ginger, Winnie, the Tatterdemalion. I forget it all, and it's the best feeling.

Every bite, every kiss, fills me with a contentment I've never known. But as soon as I swallow, the gnawing hunger is back, and I need more. I can't imagine ever being satisfied, ever being able to walk away. I know that we've been ensorcelled by the tree, but I don't care. I don't ever want to be anywhere else. I will stay here, drinking juice from Odette's lips until the day I die.

I follow a trail of sticky red down her chin and neck. She makes little moans of desire, and her fingers tangle in my hair. Juice pools in the hollow of her collarbone, and I lick at it. I rip at her dress to expose more skin, as hungry for her as I am for the fruit. She tugs at my dress, and it tears open at the bodice.

"Maude!"

The voice is familiar. I look up and see someone standing at the edge of the grass a few feet away. It's Ginger. She looks worried, or angry, or scared. I'm not sure. *She should have some fruit,* I think. *It'll make her feel better.*

I close my eyes and kiss Odette again. Her fingers trace the lines on my chest, and I feel the heat there.

When I open my eyes, Odette is gone, and I'm kissing Ginger. Or is it Genevieve? I don't remember. I don't care. Maybe it is still Odette. Maybe they're all the same person.

Does it even matter?

The snake slides across my ankles, but now it's not really a snake anymore. It's a rose cane, winding around my knees, my hips, drawing me down onto the rich moss. I don't feel the thorns. More canes climb over us, our arms, our shoulders, but we can't stop now. Odette/Ginger/Genevieve's teeth graze my shoulder and then sink in more deeply. I respond in kind, closing my own teeth over her wrist, feeling her skin break, and flooding my mouth with blood, as rich and sweet as the juice.

Bright red spills onto the moss, and the rose canes quiver in response, tightening their grip. The thorns sink deep into my skin, spilling more blood, and I know that they are eating us, as we eat each other, and I know that I don't care.

A shadow moves in the corner of my vision, and I hear a noise, like far-off voices. Odette/Ginger/Genevieve murmurs something, then burrows her face into my shoulder again, pulling me tighter against her, tearing at my skin with little gasps of pleasure.

Hands pull us apart, and it's as if someone is ripping off my own limbs. I feel cold steel as a blade slashes the rose canes from me, and every runner that's cut causes me unimaginable pain, as if it's already become a part of me. I scream, as the iron freezes and burns at the same time, and claw at my attacker.

I'm dragged over the moss to the sticklegrass at the edge of the clearing, and my vision swims as the desire to return to the tree overwhelms me. Someone smacks me across the face, and the pain is like a breath of fresh air. A face appears before me. Winnie. She slaps me again, and I shrink from her as I gradually become more aware of the world around me.

Ginger is trying to crawl to the tree now, and Winnie cracks her across the back of the head with the wooden butt of a heavy iron machete, almost as tall as she is, its blade rusted orange. Ginger staggers, and Winnie hits her again. Ginger sinks to the ground with a groan, and I have to go to her, to hold her, to lick and bite and kiss until I don't know where she ends and I begin.

Winnie reaches into the pouch at Ginger's belt, withdrawing a handful of white powder. She crams it into my mouth and forces me to swallow.

Salt.

It neutralizes the sweetness of juice and blood, destroying the enchantment, and I'm brought suddenly, crashingly, back to earth. I can still taste the fruit, and Ginger's blood, but now the taste turns my stomach, and I slump to the side and vomit into the sticklegrass.

Odette was never there. It was all an illusion.

The sound of rustling leaves intensifies, and horror rises in my throat as thorned rose canes descend from the branches of the tree like unraveling ropes. The emerald moss buckles and heaves, like a living thing.

"I'm going in!" Winnie roars, and raises her machete. She charges toward the rose canes, hacking at them and leaving piles of severed greenery behind her. The canes reach for her, but she's too fast. She spins and twirls, the machete a blur of rusty orange. The air grows thick with the scent of crushed vegetation.

I glance over at Ginger, who has raised herself on one elbow and is looking blearily around. Her wrist is slick with blood. Bile rises in my throat once more, and I gag and spit.

"Take. That. You. Evil. Stinky. Plant!" Winnie yells as she slashes at the last cane.

And then it's over.

She flips the machete around in her hand like a gunslinger as she saunters back to us. "And that's how it's done," she says with a cocky grin.

"Errr . . . ," Ginger replies as new canes descend from the canopy, thicker than before and bristling with inch-long thorns.

Winnie doesn't notice until one of the canes reaches around and pins her wrists to her sides, the machete dropping to the ground with a dull *thunk*.

More canes whip at her, tearing at her skin. Bright slashes of blood appear on her cheeks, her arms, the base of her throat. Her dress, already filthy and ragged, becomes flecked with red.

I look over at Ginger. "Do something!" I shriek.

But Ginger is still dazed and sluggish.

I don't know what to do. I'm a storyteller, not a hero.

A monstrous rose cane descends from the center of the tree canopy, as thick as my arm. It winds its way around Winnie's waist, her slim shoulders, her neck, wicked thorns digging deep into her skin. She grunts and struggles, but the more she moves, the tighter the rose cane squeezes, the deeper the thorns sink into her flesh. A bud at the tip of the cane shudders, then bursts open into a full red rose, as big as a dinner plate. The petals press against Winnie's face, smothering her. She jerks, and I hear her muffled cries, but the rose presses harder, filling her mouth and nostrils with velvet petals. Spasms rack Winnie's tiny body.

The scent of the rose is intoxicating. It smells like broken promises, poison-tipped and reeking of death.

I dart forward and scoop a fistful of salt from the pouch at

Ginger's waist, hurling it at the canes, which shrivel and flinch away. I take another fistful and throw it at the red rose pressed against Winnie's face. The flower constricts, closing up into a defensive hard bud, which thrusts deep into Winnie's mouth, making her gag and choke.

This isn't how it's supposed to be. What am I doing here? How did I think I could be the hero of this story? All my stories were for Odette. I can't spin them without her, gift or no gift.

I'm just a pathetic lost girl who needs rescuing yet again.

But there's no one to rescue me this time.

And what if I do it wrong? The old shame rises in me again. The feeling of inappropriateness. Of not belonging in my own skin. Sensible Maude doesn't belong here.

What would wild Maude do?

I crouch to pick up the machete from where it lies at Winnie's feet. Another thorned cane descends from the canopy like a whip, and I slash at it, severing it completely. I then take a swing at the enormous cane that's holding Winnie captive, but it's too thick for me to cut through it. I hack at it, just above Winnie's head, and with every strike I can see it tightening its hold around her, squeezing the life from her. Still, I'm making headway, with a sizable chunk now cut out of the cane.

Ginger appears at my side and starts throwing handfuls of salt at the rose, but it just buries itself deeper into Winnie. She stops struggling and goes limp, and I redouble my efforts, my shoulders aching as I hack at the thick green stalk.

"Hurry!" Ginger pants to me.

I let out a scream and aim an enormous swing at the rose cane. I miscalculate slightly, and the blade of the machete grazes the top of Winnie's head. She doesn't react, and I wonder if I'm too late. My final swing is enough, though. It severs the rose cane, and Winnie falls to the ground, the thorned grip slackening.

I stagger backward and glance over at Ginger. Blood's still flowing from her wrist. I did that. I bit her and kissed her, and I thought she was Odette.

I lost control.

Ginger crouches next to Winnie and gently unwinds the cane, careful not to get jabbed by the sharp thorns. She pulls at the stalk in Winnie's mouth, and Winnie coughs and rolls onto her side, retching until she regurgitates the tightly closed rosebud.

"Motherf—" Winnie rasps, pressing her fists to her salt-crusted eyes.

She touches a hand to the top of her head, where a small patch of hair is missing and a wound the size of a coin is weeping bright-red blood. She glares at me. "Bloody hell, kid."

I start to apologize, but Ginger interrupts. "She saved your life, you ingrate."

Winnie doesn't respond to that. Instead she stands, and crushes the rosebud with her bare heel, grinding it into the soil. Then she turns back to us, scooping up her machete, her eyes sparkling and a look of savage joy on her childish features. "That was *fun*," she says breathlessly.

She has a weird idea of fun.

"You're unhinged," Ginger states.

"We were a team! A squad! We haven't done that for years."

"We were a *terrible* squad," Ginger says. "You nearly killed me with that rusty knife."

Winnie scowls at her. "Well, *you* nearly *blinded* me with salt."

"Exactly. We were a terrible squad."

"We were great!"

Ginger glances over at me, and our eyes meet for an excruciating moment before we both look away. She gets up to inspect the severed rose canes.

"Careful," Winnie warns.

"This was new," Ginger says, nudging the canes with a toe.

Winnie nods. "There's always been a scarlet lissom in the woods, but this is the first time it's teamed up with the roses."

They both turn to look at me, and everything is bleached bright with guilt and shame. I don't know how to tell them. Where to start.

Ginger has torn a strip from her skirt and is winding it around her bleeding wrist. I imagine how I must look—my dress filthy and torn, stained with blood and fruit juice, my lips bruised and swollen.

Dr. Slater's voice is in my head.

You should be ashamed of yourself.

This is what happens when you lose control.

"I still think we should kill her," Winnie mutters.

Ginger sighs. "Maybe you're right. Maybe I should have let the fishy girls have her."

"We could take her back there," Winnie suggests, hefting her machete. "Dump her in the lake."

I don't like the way this conversation is going.

"Help me," I say. "Please."

"Help you how exactly?" asks Winnie.

I explain about Lyr, and how he told me that Odette was in the tower.

Winnie looks puzzled. "There're no boys here," she says. "I would have noticed if there was a weird sexy ice ghost."

"I didn't say he was sexy," I protest, my cheeks growing hot.

"You didn't have to."

"Just trust me," I say. "He's real."

"Prove it."

"What?"

"You said you summoned him. So do it again."

"I can't . . . I had a witch bottle before."

Winnie shrugs. "So just use your magic."

I feel my cheeks redden. "I don't have any magic."

She and Ginger exchange a look. "Yeah, you do," Winnie says. "It's coming off you in waves."

"I have mettle," I tell her. "And I still have my witchsight. But I can't work it anymore."

Ginger frowns. "I don't think that's a thing," she says.

But how would she know? She's not even real.

"Just try," Winnie says, and I am afraid of the stubborn cast to her face, so I widen my stance and raise my hands, feeling foolish.

I refocus my eyes and reach out with my hands that are not my flesh-and-bone hands. There is mettle everywhere here, writhing thick around the scarlet lissom, streaming from Winnie and Ginger, densely packed into the soil of Sicklehurst.

The threads slip through my fingers, as I knew they would, and it hurts now just as much as it did when I'd tried and failed in front of Odette four years ago. My cheeks burn with shame.

"Keep going," Winnie says, her hands on her hips.

"I can't," I say. "It's not working."

She rolls her eyes. "Stop making such a song and dance about it. Ignore the mettle threads. Just *call* him."

I'm not totally convinced she's joking about killing me, so I close my eyes. "Lyr," I say out loud. "I need you."

My heart isn't in it, which is why the breath of cold air takes me by surprise.

I open my eyes again, and he's there, wreathed in mist and looking as perfect as ever.

I hear Ginger whistle. "He *is* sexy," she says.

If Lyr hears her, he doesn't react. His eyes are locked on mine, his lips slightly parted.

Winnie steps forward, thrusting a hand into the center of his chest and wiggling her fingers.

"Yep," she says, shivering from the cold. "Definitely a ghost."

She breathes into her cupped hands to warm them up.

"Have you been here the whole time?" Ginger asks Lyr.

Lyr turns to her and makes a little bow. "I have been here for many years, cursed by a witch and held imprisoned. It wasn't until Maude called to me that I could leave my body and appear as you see me now."

"Huh," says Ginger.

"I don't think we can trust him," says Winnie.

"You don't trust *anyone.*"

"You say that like it's a problem."

Lyr turns to me. "You must journey to the tower at once to save your friend."

"How do you know she hasn't already done it?" Winnie asks, her eyes narrowed. "And how do you know the other girl is in the tower, if you've been locked up this whole time?"

Lyr ignores her. "The tower. You must make haste."

Ginger exchanges a glance with Winnie and nods. "I don't trust him either," she says. "We need more information, Ghost Boy. Tell us more about this so-called witch."

Lyr turns to her. "Her name was Carys."

My hands grow clammy as my pulse speeds up. "My mother?" I say. "She cursed you?"

"She stole something and sought to keep it here, hidden by the spell that binds this place."

"The triple spell," I say, nodding. "Tell me about the third layer—what is it protecting?"

His lip curls. "The third aspect of the spell is found deep inside the heart of this place. It contains the rotten star."

"Did Mam make the spell?" I ask. "Is that why I keep seeing her witchmark?"

Lyr doesn't answer, just gazes coldly at me.

"What did the witch steal?" asks Winnie, her eyes gleaming. "Treasure?"

"Indeed," Lyr says, his face turned mournful. "An artifact of great power."

I had always known that Mam tried to steal something. That's why the auditors took her away. But I didn't know that she had succeeded—and had hidden it here. I wonder, is it still here, this artifact she stole?

But things aren't lining up the way they're supposed to, and I raise a hand, puzzled. "That doesn't make sense, though," I tell him. "I made you, along with Winnie and Ginger. Mam was already dead then."

"That wasn't when you made me," Lyr says. "It's just when you gave me this form." He gestures at his body.

I open my mouth to ask more questions, but Winnie interrupts me.

"Wait," she says, and I flinch. I knew this was coming. "What do you mean, you *made* us?"

I swallow. I don't want to tell her. But it's time.

"I did," I say. "You and Ginger. I made you."

"You *made* us?"

Ginger is very quiet, watching me.

"I came in here, with Odette, when I was twelve years old. I made up stories for her, you see, and we'd act them out. We gave ourselves different names—Genevieve and Eilwen—and I'd create adventures for us. So when we came here, I made these little dolls, and used the . . . I guess it was the sticklegrass wood's magic, to bring them to life. I thought they were just puppets, like shadows on a wall. I'd made similar things before—they only ever lasted for a few hours before crumbling to nothing again. I had no idea when we left that you would . . . stay."

"Are we even real?" Ginger's voice is subdued.

I spread my hands, helpless. "I don't know," I say. "I'm sorry."

"If you made *us*," Winnie says slowly, "you could make more, right? You could make a whole army, and we could take down the Tatterdemalion."

"I can't," I tell her. "I can't do magic anymore. I told you that."

Winnie narrows her eyes, and I can tell she doesn't believe me.

"Did you make the Tatterdemalion too?" Ginger asks in a small voice.

I have been dreading this question. I close my eyes. "I'm so, so sorry."

Winnie nods slowly. "Well, that takes care of that dilemma."

"What do you mean?" I ask.

"I am *definitely* going to kill you now," she says, reaching for her machete.

I take a nervous step back, and Lyr buffets himself at Winnie in a tirade of ice.

"Okay, okay," she says, her hands up. "Calm your farm, Blizzard Boy."

"Swear you will not touch her," Lyr says.

"I swear," Winnie says grudgingly. "But I don't see why you're protecting her."

Lyr looks at me, and I can't help but drown a little in his eyes. He doesn't respond to Winnie.

"Help us," says Ginger to me suddenly. "Help us take down the Tatterdemalion. Help us escape from here."

"I—I can't," I say. "I have nothing to offer. I'm really just here to find my friend."

"You *owe* us," Ginger says. "This is all your fault. You have to put things right. You know how stories go. That's part of it."

Winnie stares at Ginger. "What makes you think she can help us? We've tried to take down the Tatterdemalion a thousand times before, and it's never worked."

"There were only two of us then," Ginger says. "You know magic is more powerful when there's three."

Winnie looks dubious, but she shrugs. "Okay," she says. "Help us, and I'll tell you everything I know about your friend."

I turn to her, eager. "So you have seen her."

She jerks her chin in a nod. "I'll give you a freebie to start with—there's no way she's in that tower." She scowls at Lyr.

"How do you know?" I ask.

Winnie shakes her head. "After the Tatterdemalion is dead. Then I'll tell you everything."

"You must not trust them," Lyr tells me. "They lie. They will lure you to your doom."

"You didn't warn me about the fishy girls," I tell him. "You lied too."

I hesitate as all three of them stare at me. I have to choose. Lyr wants me to take a dangerous path alone to the tower. Winnie and Ginger want me to help them take down a monster. It's not a great choice.

"You can go," I tell Lyr. "I'll call you if I need you."

He opens his mouth, outraged, but he's already fading. Winnie swipes her machete through him, and he evaporates into swirling white mist. Then she turns to me expectantly, as if she's hoping I'll transform into some kind of monster-slaying superhero.

I have no magic to help them with. But I still have my gift.

What would I do if this were a story? I take a deep breath and close my eyes, searching for the glittering story threads in my mind. It's so hard without Odette. Without her to spark the story, I'm adrift. But I have to try.

"We can't destroy the Tatterdemalion with brute force," I say. "But . . . maybe there's another way."

I'm suddenly very aware of my torn dress. My burned and

scratched hands. The weeping, sticky wound on my neck. The deep gouges all over my body from the rose canes. I think about how many times I've needed to be rescued since I came here. The control room. The lake house. The scarlet lissom. There's nothing I can bring to this squad. I have no skills. I can't fight, I can't do magic. I tried to save Winnie and nearly chopped off her head.

What good are stories when the monsters are real?

"She's nothing," Winnie says coldly. "She can't help us."

"I can," I protest. "I just need . . ." I shake my head. "If Odette were here . . ."

Ginger makes a disgusted noise. "*Odette.* Everything with you is *Odette.* I bet if Odette were here, she'd hightail it straight back to the real world."

"No," I say. "She wouldn't. Odette is brave."

And there it is. I don't need to make up a new story for the lost girls. I already know this story.

"We have this teacher at school," I tell them. "Dr. Slater. He's the school principal, but he also teaches history. One day, back when we were little, he decided to tell us about the Battle of Goose Spring."

"The what?" Winnie says.

Of course she doesn't know. How would she?

"How can you not know about Goose Spring?" Ginger says.

I look at her sharply. "How do *you* know about it?" I ask.

"I read magazines," she replies loftily.

"Wait," says Winnie. "There was a *war,* and you didn't tell me?"

"Not a war, exactly," Ginger says. "More of a . . . copyright dispute."

I make a face. "The government banned magic, seventeen years ago."

Winnie blinks. "They can do that?"

"They thought they could. There were lots of protests. Strikes, marches, petitions. But nothing worked. Things got ugly in Goose Spring, where a coven of witches camped outside the governor's office. More people kept joining them—druids, magicians, diviners. It was a peaceful protest until the governor called in the military. Then things got ugly."

I swallow. My father had been one of the protesters. The battle had been over within hours. The protesters had only mettle and spells—no match for artillery and planes dropping explosives.

"So, Dr. Slater was telling us about it, about how dangerous unregulated magic was. How unfair it was for magic people to have all this power and regular people to have nothing. He told us stuff that just wasn't true—about magic folk bewitching non-magic people to be their slaves, or denying them healing. He made it sound like there was a whole secret government running the magical world."

"Was there?"

I shake my head. "There was no great divide. It was all just people. Sure, some were more powerful than others. But there are lots of ways to have power in the world. Nobody was trying to ban being rich."

Winnie nods.

"Dr. Slater told us about how selfish the protesters were, and how noble the governor was for protecting his constituents. There were a few kids in the class who lost family at Goose Spring, and people were getting upset and trying not to show it."

I remember the self-righteous smirk on Dr. Slater's sweaty pink face like it was yesterday. He knew about my father, and Lisbet Jones's aunt, and Yanuar Prasetyo's grandmother. My hands had clenched into fists, and I'd felt tears prickle my eyes.

"Odette didn't have any family at Goose Spring. She didn't really care. But she knew we did. She knew *I* did."

"Did she stab him with a pencil?" Winnie asks eagerly.

"She stood up in the middle of the class and yelled, 'A bee! There's a bee in our classroom! And Maude's allergic!'"

"*Are* you?" Winnie asks.

I shake my head. "Of course not. She leapt at me, knocking me from my desk and onto the floor. She shrieked and wailed, batting at the air and making an unimaginable fuss."

Laughter bubbles up inside me at the thought of it.

"Dr. Slater told her to sit down. He came over to help me to my feet, and Odette shouted, *'I can see it! Dr. Slater, it's landed on you!'* And she slapped him, right on the upper arm. It was a hot day, and he was in short sleeves."

"And did she get the bee?" Ginger asks.

Winnie rolls her eyes. "Have you been listening? There was no bee."

"Right. She used the whole thing as a distraction, and then slapped a glamour patch on his arm."

"A what?" Winnie asks.

Ginger rolls her eyes. "You really should tend to your education, you know. A glamour patch is like a potion. But it lasts longer, and there's no slimy aftertaste. It changes the way you look, but it can't fool a camera."

"It was a chibi patch," I explain. "They were really popular at the time. Dr. Slater looked all short and chubby, with huge eyes, and floppy pink bunny ears."

Winnie cackles with satisfaction. "Genius."

"He hauled Odette out of class and made her wear a witch's hat and scrub the floor of his office until the end of school that day. He hated her and was always looking for an excuse to punish her. He came back so smug and pleased with himself, but he still hadn't noticed the glamour patch."

Winnie snorts.

"Nobody in the class heard a word he said about the evils of magic after that. We were all too busy trying not to laugh. The bell rang, and we went to the auditorium for assembly. It was a big one—the whole school. None of the other teachers said anything. I guess they hated him too. So Dr. Slater delivered his entire speech like that. He ranted and raved about how lucky we were in Anglyon to be protected from danger. About how the best life is a simple life. About the dangers of big cities and technology and magic. The whole time his bunny ears were flopping around all over the place, and his giant baby-blue eyes were shining with conviction."

"But Odette didn't get to see it," Ginger says. "So what was the point?"

"She had me to tell her all about it," I said. "That was enough."

"What happened?" Winnie asks. "He must have found out eventually."

I nod. "He was livid. He called Odette's mother in. Odette was grounded for a month. She wasn't allowed to go to the Pettavel Fair, wasn't allowed to see me."

"Do you think it was worth it?"

"She did."

Her wicked grin. Her self-satisfied cackle. Her lips against mine under the scarlet lissom.

I feel my cheeks flush. It wasn't real. It wasn't her.

"This has all been very entertaining," Ginger says sarcastically. "But I don't see how it's going to help us."

"Well," I say, and hope I can pull everything together. "There are three main threads to that story. One is that sometimes in order to take someone down, you have to give them what they want first."

"You think we should let the Tatterdemalion kill us?" Ginger says. *"Again?"*

I shake my head. "Not you." I touch my fingers to the three slashes across my chest, where the monster marked me.

Winnie is looking at me thoughtfully. "What's the second thread?"

"The second thing is sometimes in order to trick someone, you need a little magic." I manage to catch Ginger's eye. "I'm going to need your help."

Ginger squirms and tears her gaze away from mine. "Why me?"

"You made the wards around your apartment. You know what you're doing."

Ginger kicks the dirt with a sullen foot. "It didn't even work, remember?"

"I can't weave mettle anymore, but I can guide you."

Ginger hesitates just long enough that I know I've convinced her.

"Good," I say.

"And the final thing?" Winnie asks.

I swallow. "I don't know how to fight, but experience has taught me that I make great bait."

Winnie's eyes light up at the idea.

I outline the plan.

Winnie nods slowly. "I like the part where I get to fight it," she says. "Do you think the thing will work? The poppet?"

"Yes," I say, with a confidence I do not feel.

"It could work," Ginger muses.

"It *will* work!" Winnie paces up and down, punching the air in front of her. "We could take it down for good!"

I wish I shared her confidence. But anything is worth trying if it'll lead me to Odette.

"Okay," I say. "Let's get going."

12

WE GATHER IN A WAREHOUSE-SIZED BUILDING WITH a mostly collapsed roof, containing huge ceramic pipes that curve up out of the floor and dive back down again, like the looping coils of a sea monster. It's damp and cold, with chilly moss coating the tumbled concrete blocks on the ground. Around us, iron girders loom, coated in thick orange sludge. Gantries criss-cross overhead, the metal swollen and dissolving in great long dribbles of vivid jellied rust.

"It won't come for us in here," Winnie says. "Too much iron."

"Does everyone understand their jobs?" I ask. "Ginger and I will make the poppet while Winnie locates the Tatterdemalion."

Winnie and Ginger nod.

As soon as Winnie leaves, the thin veneer of my resolve disintegrates. I'm no leader, and faking it is exhausting. I glance at Ginger and feel my throat close over when I see the bloody smudges on her arm around her makeshift bandages.

You should be ashamed of yourself.

I am. I'm sick with it. I can't believe I let myself give in so easily.

I turn to Ginger. "We'd better get started."

"What are you waiting for?" Ginger asks.

I hesitate, putting a finger against one of the iron girders, and push. My finger sinks into the orange sludge, all the way up to my knuckle. I pull it out and rub the sludge between forefinger and thumb. It's gritty, and it stinks of rust.

It's probably not the best place to attempt magic, surrounded by so much iron. But we'll be safer—whatever mettle it is that animates the Tatterdemalion will be weakened in here.

"It'd be better to wait a couple of weeks," I say, half to myself. "Until the fish moon is waxing. A waning egg moon is bad luck."

I sound like Nan. If she were here, she'd dismiss the Tatterdemalion with a wave of her gaudy pink handbag. She'd sort out this whole forest, rescue Odette, and be home in time for tea and biscuits and *Antiques Divination* on the radio.

I swallow. But if Nan were here, she'd know what I did. That I made the girls, and the monster. That I tasted the deep mettle that called its siren song to Mam, all the way to her death.

She'd look at me with the sadness and disappointment and betrayal that she'd looked at Mam.

"I don't like waiting," Ginger says.

I nod and shove my shame and misery somewhere so I don't have to look at it. "I guess we start with the body, then."

I sound more confident than I feel. I haven't made a poppet since I came to Sicklehurst with Odette and made Winnie and Ginger and the others. I've watched Nan make them a thousand times, of course, but Nan's are pocket-sized covenant poppets that just hold a charm. They don't move around or anything.

We head outside and duck into the close green darkness of the forest to gather sticks and twigs. We also gather handfuls of plants that are strong in magic—clover, feverfew, rue, and mugwort—rolling them into fragrant balls between our palms. As we work, I watch Ginger weave the mettle from the plants together and feel the sickening stab of envy. Odette had always insisted that Genevieve be a powerful enchantress—to make up for her own lack of magical ability. She'd longed for the one thing that I'd had, so I guess it's only fair that the situation is now reversed.

We make a few trips back and forth, gathering more armfuls of sticks. Ginger rips up big slabs of grassy sod, the soil clumping underneath, and we carry that to the warehouse too.

Inside, I place the balls of crushed greenery in the center of a mossy plinth, and start weaving the sticks and twigs around it while Ginger weaves the mettle.

We twist and weave and stuff. I still don't really know what I'm doing, but I figure if I just throw everything I know at the poppet, maybe it'll work.

I pull out strands of my own hair and tie them in ossel hitches and dogshanks and oysterlines. Nan taught me to knit, crochet, and embroider, but it was Mam who taught me chanting knotwork. Nearly every culture in the world has some form of knot lore—whether the great power knots of Samalan or Piracles, the Mófâ white thread of death, the cursing knotwork of Læntana, or Rukolon weaving, where incantations are spoken over a loom, the words bound to the knotted thread with a spray of saliva.

Mam taught me to dip red thread in snake fat and knot it twice around a hawthorn tree as a protection from fairy mischief. I tie a clove hitch and hope that it will bind the poppet together and protect it from the Tatterdemalion's grasping twig fingers.

I can feel heat from Ginger's skin near mine and taste the sweetness of the red fruit in the back of my throat. The thought of it makes me want to be sick again.

"I'm embarrassed," Ginger blurts out suddenly. "I let that stupid tree get ahold of me. I should have known better."

"It was my fault," I tell her. "I'm not supposed to behave that way. I'm nice."

She glares at me. "What's *that* supposed to mean?"

I feel my cheeks flush hot. "I—I didn't mean that. . . ."

We knot and weave for a few moments more. Ginger's jaw is tight with tension.

"I'm sorry," I say. "For everything."

She hesitates. "I know."

I have a sudden flashback to being under the tree, and feel heat drench my body. I can't blame it all on the scarlet lissom. I *wanted* Odette, and Ginger too. In my mind, they were inseparable—different yet connected—and my desire for them both felt as twisted and knotted as the poppet growing under my hands.

I glance over at her, and the heat becomes soured with shame and guilt.

Ginger coughs awkwardly and looks at the poppet. "We need mud," she says. "The sticklegrass garden mud is the best."

"I can get it," I say. "Just tell me where to go."

She shakes her head. "You'll get lost. I'll go. You find something for the eyes."

"Okay," I say.

I head back into the forest, trying to shake my anxiety and doubt. Winnie and Ginger are trusting me, and I don't know what I'm doing. What if they get hurt and it's all my fault?

What am I thinking? Of course they'll get hurt. And every time they get hurt, it's my fault.

A stab of longing hits me so hard that my knees almost buckle. I want Odette to be here—more than I've wanted anything in the world. I miss her so much it's like a piece of me has been amputated. I'll do anything to get her back.

Anything.

My eyes are blue, so I need two blue flowers. Not forget-me-nots, obviously. I search through the undergrowth of the forest, keeping to the very edge, where the sunlight can still penetrate. I make sure I can always see the squat bulk of the warehouse—I don't want to get lost in the woods. I stumble across a drift of wildflowers—foxgloves and daisies and tiger lilies all jumbled in together. But none are blue. I notice a trail of scarlet pimpernel leading between two giant wooden reels that once held steel cabling. *Poor man's weatherglass,* Nan calls it, because it blooms red in the shade, and blue in the sun.

A glimmer of light shines in between the trees, and I follow it to a tiny clearing. A shaft of sunlight filters down, and, sure enough, the pimpernel is growing bright blue. I pick two flowers and return through the dark.

Ginger is back already, slapping black mud over the twisted cage of knotted sticks and twigs to bind it together. We make a torso, rough arms and legs. When I get to the head, I bend closer, fashioning crude features from the mud.

I lift a handful of sticklegrass from the concrete plinth and arrange it like hair.

"If only I could get this kind of volume from my shampoo," I comment, and Ginger chuckles.

"The color wouldn't suit you."

The banter is like a cooling balm, and I relax a little, for the first time since the scarlet lissom.

"Have you always known how to weave mettle?" I ask her.

She shrugs. "Pretty much," she says. "I learned the rest from magazines. There's always an article or two for the hipsters. 'Make Your Own Kombucha and Witch Drams!' 'Find a More Authentic Way of Living!' That sort of thing. Then I just experimented." She hesitates. "What about you? Did your mother teach you?"

I nod. "She got taken away when I was seven."

I remember being little and waking up one morning with a sore head, hot and shivery, like I was coming down with something. I'd tottered into the kitchen to see Mam slumped against the kitchen counter, her hands shaking, her pupils dilated. She wasn't wearing a glamour, and for a moment I hadn't recognized her. Her cheeks were gaunt and sunken, her eyes bruised. Her hair fell in thin, matted strings around her face. She looked like a hag from a fairy tale. Nan had come sailing in, took one look at me, and barreled me off, back to bed. But I snuck out again to crouch on the staircase and listen as Nan crashed around the kitchen making some kind of mettle-restoring tea. Mam had slurred an apology, and Nan had snapped at her.

You lost control . . . Should know better . . .

I looked at my hands and noticed that they were stained green and brown, my fingernails crammed with earth.

A few hours later, the auditors came, and took Mam away.

A part of me seethed with resentment at Nan, for yelling at Mam. For not protecting her better when she needed it the most. But I didn't say anything, because the idea of having the blazing eye of Nan's disappointment turned on me was too much to bear.

It's not like Mam was ever around much before that. Nan and Halmoni had raised me from day one. But she was still my mam, and I still grieved when they took her away. I was so angry at the auditors who took her, but even angrier at her. How could she do what she did, knowing that one day it might take her away from me? How could she put the lives of strangers above her own child?

I think about what Lyr said. She stole something and hid it here, inside Sicklehurst. Could it still be here?

"Is it done?" Ginger steps back and admires our work. The poppet is crude, but it's definitely human-shaped.

"Is my nose really that big?" I ask.

Ginger snorts.

I lean forward and place the pimpernel flowers on the poppet's face for eyes, and slash a fingernail across where the mouth will go.

"Needs clothes," Ginger observes. "Unless you want to make it some genitals."

I feel my cheeks color. All I have is Odette's dress, so I rip off a strip from the hem, and tie it around the poppet's neck like a scarf. Hopefully, the glamour we're making will figure out the rest.

"What now?" Ginger asks. "How do we bring it to life?"

This is the part I'm not so sure of. When I made Ginger and

the others, I asked the sticklegrass wood to give them life. But I can't do that anymore.

There's another way, though. Mam brought the marigold back to life with pure mettle.

"Take one of my strings," I tell Ginger.

Her eyes widen. "You're joking."

I don't know how else to make it work. The creature needs to have a beating heart. It needs mettle.

"I'm giving it willingly. It'll be powerful. It'll work."

"But . . . you won't get it back. It's your life force."

"It's just one string. It'll be worth it."

Ginger hesitates. "Tell me what to do."

I'm making it up as I go, but it *feels* right. "We need a vessel," I say. "Something that was alive, that we can bind to the poppet."

"Leave it to me," Ginger says, and slips away to the forest.

Anxiety shudders through me. I know that losing a string is a big deal. It's like a piece of you dies. I've heard it hurts, and that you're never quite the same afterward.

But I can't think of any other solution.

Ginger returns holding the limp body of a dead mouse, one of its legs twisted in an unnatural bend. I hope it was already dead when she found it.

"We need something to bind it to you," Ginger says. "Something from *your* heart, to wrap your mettle around."

She's right. I open the black satin bag and pull out Odette's red ribbon.

"Was that hers?" Ginger asks, eyeing it.

I nod, and Ginger sniffs haughtily. She's jealous. It'd be funny if we weren't maybe about to die. They're practically the same person.

We wrap the mouse in the ribbon, like a burial shroud, and I spit on it.

"I don't suppose you have any menstrual blood available?" Ginger asks.

"No."

"Pity."

Instead, I find a broken shard of glass and drag it across my fingertip and then swipe my finger over the mouse and ribbon bundle. Then I carefully place the whole thing inside the chest cavity of the poppet.

"Okay," I say. "Do it."

Ginger hesitates. "Are you sure?"

I nod and close my eyes.

It takes only a moment. Ginger reaches inside me, her witch-hands brushing my strings. It feels far more intimate than anything we did under the scarlet lissom. I try to keep my breathing steady.

Snap.

A sharp cry of pain escapes my lips as I feel suddenly hollow inside, like a vital piece of me has been removed.

I've felt this before.

Mam, standing over me, her hair falling in matted strings. Her hands trembling.

Just a little. You have so much . . .

I open my eyes to see Ginger staring at me, her face contorted in a mix of horror and concern.

"I'm okay," I tell her. "Let's keep going."

Ginger bends over the poppet and reaches out, the silvery thread of my mettle glimmering in her witch-hand. She wraps the thread around the mouse bundle.

I dip my bloody finger in mud and draw a heart shape on the poppet's chest. The poppet doesn't move, but something about it is different. It's no longer just a scarecrow made of mud and twigs. Faintly, I can hear the pattering of the mouse's heart.

"Now what?" Ginger asks.

I wish I knew. The creature has a beating heart now. What else does it need?

"A mouth," I say. "It needs to breathe."

Ginger reaches into her pocket and pulls out a tube of bright-red lipstick, which she hands to me.

"Try not to use it all up," she warns. "Lipstick doesn't come in often on the river."

I turn to the poppet, but Ginger stops me. "On you first," she says.

"Good idea." But then I offer the lipstick back to her helplessly. "There was a makeup craze a few years ago, when Qilin Lazuli brought out their own smudgeproof line. I bought a lipstick and tried it at home, but . . . well, it might have been smudgeproof, but it didn't stop me from looking like a clown."

Ginger lets out a little huff of laughter and takes it, stepping close to me.

"Let your lips part naturally," she says, then leans in and applies the makeup to my lips. It tastes sweet, like black cherries and buttercream. I can feel her breath on my cheek.

"Done."

I crawl onto the plinth, crouching over the poppet. I bend

down and press my lips to the mud slash of its mouth, suppressing a shudder of horror. A faint breath comes from its mouth, bringing with it the smell of mud and crushed greenery.

"I think it's ready," I say. "Do you have some words?"

Spells often work better if you can speak some words to set them.

Ginger uses her toe to draw a circle around the plinth, then takes a step back and begins to sing.

"Green gravel, green gravel, your grass is so green
The fairest young damsel that ever was seen
Dear maiden, dear maiden, your true love is dead
Your eyes they are blue, your lips they are red.
Green gravel, green gravel, stand up as you should
And whisper your name to the sticklegrass wood."

She repeats the song three times. Beneath the cracked concrete floor, the earth listens. I can feel the sticklegrass wood stirring, stretching, reaching out to me and Ginger and the poppet. Its mettle is raw and green and hungry, surging with power. The oiliness that I sensed is still there too, strange and terrifying.

I can feel it probing at me, but I can't talk to it. I don't know how anymore.

Beside me, the poppet twitches. I swallow a scream as it starts to move, stick-and-twig arms jerking and twitching. Its movements are unnatural, punctuated by the creaking of twigs and the faint scrabbling of the mouse, deep in the creature's chest cavity.

But it doesn't get up. It isn't strong enough.

I shake my head. "It's not working," I say.

Tears form in my eyes.

Did I sacrifice my own mettle for nothing? What would Nan say?

"There has to be something else we can do," Ginger says desperately.

Her brow is bright with sweat. Her cheeks are flushed pink.

"Maybe another string," I suggest, but Ginger shakes her head.

"No way. Too risky."

I spread my hands. "Then I don't know."

I don't know why I thought I could pull off something magical.

Ginger bites her lip. "What about Ghost Boy?" she asks. "Maybe he can do something."

"I thought you didn't trust him."

"I don't. But I'm not sure what else we can do."

I don't want Lyr to witness my failure as well, but Ginger bullies me mercilessly until I relent and call his name.

The space around us grows cold, and frost rimes the edges of the sludgy iron girders. Then Lyr appears, translucent and glowing slightly in the gloom.

"My lady," he says in greeting, his tone as icy as the air around him.

"Get in the poppet," Ginger tells him without ceremony.

He looks startled.

"Can you?" I ask. "Can you animate it?"

Lyr looks uncertain. "I do not know," he says. "Why do you wish such a thing?"

"We need to lure the Tatterdemalion," I say. "We're going to kill it."

"Are you sure this course is wise?" Lyr says. "I would not see you put yourself in the path of danger. Would it not be better to simply journey to the tower and save your friend? She could even aid you in this quest."

"Just do it, Ghost Boy," Ginger snaps. "Enough pretty-talk."

Lyr glances at me, and I reach out to touch his hand, my fingers sinking through his skin. He is ice-cold, and my fingertips turn white and numb.

"Please," I say. "I need you."

He inclines his head. "I cannot refuse you."

It is simply done, in the end. Lyr sort of wades into the poppet, then sinks until he can't be seen anymore. I hear the mouse scurrying even faster, and the poppet's hands grow white with frost. Then it shakily sits up on the plinth.

"Lyr?" I ask. "Can you hear me?"

The twigs inside the poppet rustle, and it raises a hand in response. Then it stands, tall and straight. I scramble off the plinth and stand beside it. We are exactly the same height, the same build.

I turn to it and touch a finger to its lips. "I have made you, and you are Maude Jenkins."

Lyr's presence is the magic that I cannot give it. A shudder passes through the poppet, and suddenly it's like I'm standing next to a mirror. Not a perfect mirror. The poppet still has a certain lumpiness about her, a twiggishness that is definitely not human. But from a distance, one could be fooled into thinking it was me.

Or at least I hope so.

"Wow," says Ginger. "That is . . . a lot."

"You're telling me."

Ginger hesitates. "And you're sure this is what you want to do."

"I'm sure."

"Even though you'll probably die."

"I won't die. The plan will work."

"The plan is ridiculous," Ginger says flatly. "If the Tatterdemalion does come, it'll kill us, like it has every single time before. If you're lucky, you'll die too. If you're unlucky, you'll wake up in the mud."

"Would that be so terrible?" I ask. "Is the idea of me being in here with you so repellent?"

Ginger lets out a frustrated noise. "Of course it isn't!" she growls. "But being in here sucks. It's the worst place in the world. It's cold and damp, and everything wants to kill you, over and over again. I don't want that for you, even though this is all your fault."

"I don't want it for you either. That's why I'm doing this. I'm trying to make it right."

"Bullshit. You're doing it because you think it'll help you find your girlfriend."

"Odette isn't my g—"

"Perhaps you two could save this for another time?" Winnie says acidly from behind us.

Ginger spins around, her cheeks aflame with indignation.

"It's in the tank yard," Winnie says. "Are you ready?"

I nod. Winnie looks the poppet up and down, and then does the same to me.

"Good work," she says. "It looks just like you."

"Except for the nose," I point out.

Winnie shrugs.

"Try not to die," Ginger says, then leans forward to kiss me on the mouth.

It's nothing like the sticky, fevered kiss under the scarlet lissom. It's soft and warm and sad.

"I really am sorry," I tell her.

"Me too," she says. "Also, you're not my type."

I smile. She is *definitely* my type, but I think I need to get a different type.

Ginger takes poppet Maude by the hand and leads it into the forest. She doesn't look back.

"Ready?" Winnie says. I nod, and we head out too.

"Hurry," she says. "Before it moves on."

We run through the maze of conduit and mossy concrete, past towering oak trees and thick stands of bamboo and thorn apple. We cross the Bone Road, and I try not to look at the moss-covered skulls that litter it. We splash through a stream that is so cold I'm surprised it isn't ice. We reach a large open space, littered with rusted tanks of varying sizes. In between them grow flowering jacarandas, the orange-corroded steel vibrant against black branches hanging heavy with purple flowers.

"How much of this is real," I ask Winnie, "and how much just glamour?"

Winnie shrugs. "No idea."

"Aren't you curious?"

"I don't see that it matters if something is real or not. If I can see it and it's trying to kill me, then that's real enough."

The ground underfoot is thick with fallen purple flowers, so everything is purple, above and below. The scent is strong, like sweet honey. But I can smell something else that clamors in my chest like a great vibrating gong.

Rotting vegetation and loam.

The Tatterdemalion.

Winnie bends close, her whisper in my ear barely more than a breath. "You know where to go?"

I nod and try not to let her see how terrified I am.

She melts back into the forest, and I'm alone. I put my fingers to the bone-pin brooch for protection.

I can't see it yet, but I know it's here. There's a chill in the air, my breath coming in clouds. My heart hammers, and I can't believe that I—nice, sensible, dependable Maude—am really doing this.

I straighten up and walk forward. I can smell the rust of the pylons, taste it in my mouth, mingling with the sweet honey scent of the jacarandas.

"Woe is me!" I say loudly. "I'm lost in the woods. Whatever shall I do?"

I hear an animal-like snort, not too far away, and a low rumbling growl.

"Help!" I cry. "Somebody rescue me!"

There's a pause, and I wonder how smart the Tatterdemalion is. Has it guessed that this is all a ruse? That we're leading it into a trap?

And my stomach drops . . . because it is coming for me. I hear the crunching of its branch legs, like the cracking of dry wood.

I run.

A wind picks up, whisking purple blossoms from the branches of the jacarandas, whipping petals into my face until I can barely see where I'm going. But I can't stop. I can run fast, but I know the Tatterdemalion can run faster, and the head start I have won't last forever.

I can hear it behind me, crashing and screaming. My breath tears ragged at my chest, and I pump my legs harder, bursting from the tank yard and scrambling up a steep incline, pushing through bracken and fennel.

The ground grows rocky, and my sprint turns to a scramble. The monster behind me draws closer. The three marks on my chest burn hot and begin to throb.

I hope I'm nearly there.

I swerve right, to vault over a fallen pylon, hoping the iron will slow down the Tatterdemalion a little. Mistletoe scratches at my bare legs. I slip on a patch of rotted leaves, and fall. The time it takes for me to get back to my feet erases whatever time I'd bought from the iron pylon.

I can smell the lake before I come to it—the sulfur and salt of it. I climb higher and higher as the ground turns white and chalky underfoot. I don't have time to consider the impossibility of the landscape that's unfolding beneath me. I know there are no cliffs in Sicklehurst, and yet I appear to be approaching the edge of one. Straight-backed silver birches spring from the white earth until everything around me is as white as it was purple just moments ago.

I burst free from the trees, finding myself on a bare patch of chalky ground, high above the lake. An icy wind whips Odette's now-ragged dress around my legs. From here, I can see the whole power plant for the first time—the charred remains of Ginger's apartment, the building where I first summoned Lyr, the cooling tower, tall and wound with climbing vines like something from a fairy tale. I spot the straight stripe of the Bone Road, and the vivid green tangle of the sticklegrass garden and the mud pools. I can see how methodically the forest is eating the power plant, and how the decay is slower where there are large quantities of iron. The whole site is smaller than I'd expected, encased in the towering red brick wall. And bigger too—the lake is vast, and surrounded by so much forest. My brain struggles to process the entire glamour at once, to comprehend how such great distances can fit into a space so small. It . . . breaks rules.

Ginger is waiting for me, half concealed behind an ancient shipping container, slimy with jellied rust. "Finally," she mutters.

With only seconds to spare, the Tatterdemalion emerges from the silver birch wood. It stops and paws the ground like a bull. I can see the wet blackness of its eyes, the crawling slugs in its mouth. It roars at us, and my heart quakes in response.

"Here we go," says Ginger, and she darts forward, throwing a handful of salt at the Tatterdemalion's face. The wind catches the salt and whisks it around us like twirling smoke, but enough hits the Tatterdemalion.

The slugs shrivel and start to foam. The Tatterdemalion emits a high-pitched shriek and claws at its face.

"Now!" shouts Ginger, dashing into the cover of the silver birches.

I haul the poppet from where it was concealed behind the shipping container. It feels icy to the touch.

"Go," I whisper to Lyr, and the poppet stumbles forward.

I flatten myself against the back of the container, feeling the gritty, oozing rust soak into Odette's dress. My blood pounds so loudly I'm afraid it'll give everything else away.

The Tatterdemalion lowers its twig claws from its face and looks around. It spots the poppet and tilts its head to the side. It sniffs the air once, twice.

Some of Ginger's salt has hit the poppet, and it's starting to sag on one side, twigs and sticks emerging from the skin. There's a wisp of mist, and I worry that Lyr will dissolve and the whole thing will collapse. But after a pause, the poppet continues its unsteady journey toward the edge of the cliff.

The Tatterdemalion peers at it and sniffs again.

I'm sure it's not going to be fooled, yet it springs forward, its twiggy arms reaching for the poppet as it stumbles along.

But the Tatterdemalion is too fast.

It snatches the poppet too early, too far from the cliff edge. A blast of ice hits it in the face. It howls, but it doesn't stop its assault.

I hear Ginger cry out in shock as the twig fingers bury themselves in the poppet's side, tearing it open to reveal the mud and sticks inside.

Hope turns to despair as our plan disintegrates before my eyes.

The Tatterdemalion hurls the poppet to the ground, digging deep into its abdomen with vicious slashes.

I shudder as I hear the wet splatter of mud and the cracking of twigs. That could have been me. It probably will be, in a matter of moments.

I hope Lyr is okay.

The Tatterdemalion scrabbles at the poppet, howling in frustration. Then it looks around, sniffing the air. Its head turns toward me, and I cower behind the shipping container, half-mad with terror.

My body is screaming at me to run, but I'm frozen in place.

I'm going to die.

"Looking for someone?" Winnie asks from the edge of the forest, one hand on her hip, the other lazily swinging her machete.

She's such a badass. I can't believe that I made her up. I feel quite proud.

She doesn't seem worried that the plan has failed, that the poppet didn't manage to lure the Tatterdemalion close enough to the cliff. The Tatterdemalion springs to its feet and rushes toward her. Winnie shifts into a fighting stance and raises the machete. Her eyes gleam with anticipation. She clashes with the monster, carving off a chunk of its shoulder, then rolls out of its way as it clumsily paws at her. She dances on nimble feet as she takes more great swings.

The Tatterdemalion roars and grunts, a deep, animal sound. Mud spatters on the ground as twigs snap and branches bend. It slashes at Winnie's face, and bright lines of blood appear in a diagonal sweep from her right temple to her left ear. She stumbles backward and shakes her head, one hand over her left eye. Blood streams from her face and drips in vivid red streaks on the white chalk beneath her feet.

I'm filled with horror as I realize I'm about to watch her die again.

She's just a child.

In many ways, she's *my* child. And she's me.

Panic hauls me to my feet, and even though all I want to do is run away, I look around desperately for something—anything—that might help.

If this were a story, there'd be . . . something. A sword to pull from a stone. A magical crystal with unknown powers. A bell to ring or a wish to be made.

All I have is a cliff edge.

I wait for the Tatterdemalion to press its advantage and take Winnie down while she's temporarily vulnerable. But it doesn't. It turns away from her, taking a few shambling steps and sniffing again.

My heart hammers.

The Tatterdemalion turns its head and looks directly at me.

My insides turn to liquid.

Steam rises from its back, and hot breath comes snorting from its wet mouth. It spits half-dead slugs onto the ground and takes a step toward me. Then another.

I can't move. It's as if the wound on my chest is holding me immobile, like a moth pinned to a collector's board. The monster comes within arm's reach and bends over me. It flexes its claws and bends lower, brushing one of its thick green tusks under my chin, tilting my head up toward its face. Its rotten breath huffs over me, and one of its mouth slugs drips down to land on my throat.

I can't even scream.

But Winnie can.

She bellows a challenge as she barrels into the Tatterdemalion. It roars at her as they collide, clawing at her blood-slick face. But despite her childlike figure, she's an unstoppable force, and the

Tatterdemalion shambles backward, step after step, as she pushes it closer to the edge of the cliff.

Suddenly, I can move again, and I run out to the poppet. It is barely held together now, mud and twigs spilling from its abdomen. I can see Lyr struggling to control it.

Ginger appears beside me and puts her hands over mine, and together we haul it to its feet.

Winnie and the Tatterdemalion are on the very edge of the cliff, battling, each trying to gain the upper hand.

The poppet goes stumbling toward them both, still shedding organic matter. It nearly crashes into them, and the Tatterdemalion's attention is drawn to it for a moment.

It's enough. Winnie shoves at it, and it teeters on the edge.

But before it can fall, it reaches out to wrap a branched arm around her. With a howl, Winnie kicks off against the cliff, launching herself and the Tatterdemalion over the edge and out of sight.

The poppet crashes to the ground, and a ghostly wisp escapes from it.

Ginger and I run to the edge of the cliff and peer over, just in time to see a flash of orange-gold leap up from the cold, milky water. The giant fish smacks into Winnie and the Tatterdemalion, and with a slash of its tail, it separates them. Winnie's hands wrap around its dorsal fin, and it dives deep with her. The Tatterdemalion crashes into the water with a monumental splash.

I glimpse webbed fingers and long pondweed strands of hair, then the fishy girls have the Tatterdemalion. They tear at it with their sharp nails and razor teeth, dragging it into the depths of the lake in a maelstrom of froth and mud.

Ginger and I dash along the edge of the cliff as it slopes down toward the lake, where Winnie and the golden fish are waiting for us.

"That was *awesome!*" Winnie shouts as we approach. "We did it!"

She's dripping wet, her forehead slick with blood, making her vicious grin all the more terrifying.

Ginger dashes forward and catches Winnie in a crushing hug, spinning her around and laughing. "It's done!" she cries. "The monster is dead!"

They caper around in a little dance, squealing and cackling.

"Is this it?" Winnie asks. "Can we leave now?"

Ginger is crying with happiness. "I don't know," she says. "I think so?"

They turn to me, as if I would know. I don't want to ruin their happiness, so I smile brightly and don't wonder aloud if the forest can bring back the Tatterdemalion, just as it has brought the girls back, over and over again.

Maybe it can't. Maybe the monster is really dead, forever-dead, and the lost girls can leave Sicklehurst with me and Odette.

It's a nice thought.

But I know it's the sticklegrass wood that's keeping them alive. And it's not like they can take it with them when they go.

Ginger disengages herself and wades into the lake to embrace the fish.

"What's the deal there?" I ask Winnie, who shrugs and wrings lake water from her hair.

"Ginger went down to the lake, years ago. We hadn't been here for long. She thought it would be easier just to give in to the fishy girls, let them take her. But they had this golden fish, and they were taunting it. It was just a tiny thing then. She rescued it and started feeding it."

"So they saved each other," I murmur.

Winnie makes a gagging noise.

Ginger lays her head against the fish's golden scales and gently strokes a fin, murmuring to it. It's weird to see her act so tenderly, her haughty, flirty act completely gone.

We sit there for a while on the edge of the chilly milk-green lake, gazing into the thick fringe of forest that surrounds it.

The sky is still gray. The air is still cold. I'd thought things would change, after the Tatterdemalion was dead. I'd thought the sun would come out and the birds would start to sing.

But there are no birds in Sicklehurst.

"So," says Winnie at last. "Your friend. She's kind of a bitch?"

I acknowledge this with a tip of my head. "She's . . . complicated."

"I met her maybe a week ago. She said she'd come in to get something that was strong in mettle, from the darkest part of the power plant. She demanded I take her there."

"And did you?"

Winnie looks at me. "Of course not. I told her to piss off—I'm not a tour guide. But I told her where the darkest place is."

I stare at her. "And where is it?"

She and Ginger exchange a glance. "The dungeon," says Ginger.

"That big black hole in the refinery building," Winnie explains. "It's deep underground. It's the source of all the evil in Sicklehurst."

"And Odette went there?"

Winnie shrugs. "I don't know for sure."

"She didn't mention the tower?"

Winnie shakes her head.

"But why would Lyr tell me that's where she was?"

"Isn't it obvious?" says Ginger. "*Lyr's* in the tower. Your mother imprisoned him there. He wants you to set him free."

She's right, I realize. Of course he's in the tower. Lyr lied to me.

"Why wouldn't he just tell me that?" I ask, baffled.

"Because he can't be trusted," Winnie says, like it's obvious.

I stand up. "I guess I'm going to the dungeon, then."

"There's one more thing," Winnie says, looking at me. "She recognized me. Called me Eilwen."

My heart rises. She remembered. This is a good sign.

"We'll take you there," says Ginger. "But only to the entrance."

"Yeah, there's no way I'm going in there," Winnie agrees. "I'd rather get killed by the Tatterdemalion a thousand times over."

"Okay," I say. "Let's go."

13

WINNIE AND GINGER LEAD ME BACK THROUGH THE birch forest and the jacaranda tank yard. We stop in front of a massive domed building made of thick concrete. It's almost too big to conceive, like a football field that's been encased in a shell. At first it looks like there's no way in, but we circle around it until we come to a small door, emblazoned with a peeling sign:

REFINERY CHAMBER

AUTHORIZED PERSONNEL ONLY

My heart judders.

"This is it," says Winnie.

"You really sure you want to do this?" Ginger asks me.

A part of me is hoping they'll change their minds and come with me. I don't want to go in there alone.

I nod, but I feel like I might be sick. I touch my fingers to the bone-pin brooch. I wish I still had Nan's rose.

"There's a big hole inside . . . ," Winnie says. "Dungeon is in the hole."

"That's it? No more instructions?"

Winnie shrugs. "I've never been down there. I just know that's where it is."

"We'll wait and see if you come out," Ginger says.

"And if you don't," Winnie adds, "I guess we'll see if we can get out of Sicklehurst on our own."

"I hope it works out for you," I tell them.

Then I swallow, open the door, and step inside.

The walls rise around me, furred with black fungus, broken in places where the concrete has crumbled away like a half-collapsed sandcastle, letting eerie greenish light filter in from outside.

Rusted iron girders crisscross above me, although some have buckled and twisted as they degrade into orange mucus, falling to litter the ground like rotting trees.

The floor slopes inward from the sides of the dome. It's a gentle incline at first, but it becomes sharply steeper in the center, where it falls away to nothing, a giant gaping maw, like the entrance to the world's most terrifying waterslide. The rim of the hole is thick with moss, and smells like rich earth and old coins. The sight of it fills me with terror, and I can't believe I'm volunteering to go down there.

But that's what stories are all about, right? Riddles, challenges. Breaking the rules for all the right reasons. I just *know* Odette is there. Where else could she possibly be?

I look at the steep sides of the hole. It looks like a one-way journey, so I hope there's another tunnel or a flight of stairs somewhere.

Mettle tickles the inside of my nose, and I sneeze three times. I can feel the third layer of the triple spell now. It's in there, in the dungeon, thick and strong. I get as close to the maw as I can on foot, but then the incline grows too steep, and I sit down and shuffle forward, inch by inch. The black fungus under my fingers is soft and furry, and it's laced with something else, delicate strings and branches like veins, letting off an eerie silver glow.

I'm hoping I'll have enough courage to jump. To take a leap of faith, sending me hurtling into darkness toward my destiny. But instead the fungus beneath me slides away, and I slide with it, scrabbling for a hold and grazing my elbows as I fall.

I end up plummeting only a few feet before I crash into a steel gantry, spongy from rust. It buckles and groans as I collide with it, bashing my already-bruised knees and wrists. Standing up, I look around. The silvery-veined fungus gently illuminates the space, a round vertical shaft about the size of our kitchen at home. I shudder as I see faint green daylight above and nothing but blackness below. Steel stairs lead down, and I have no choice but to follow them.

My feet sink into the decaying steps, and I don't dare grip the banister too tight, for fear that it will crumble into nothing. I descend one flight, then two, before I come to a tunnel, cut into the concrete, leading away from the shaft and farther into darkness. I take it, grateful to be away from the insubstantial jellied steel. The silver veins lead me down concrete stairs, and the air around me grows warm and moist.

There's something here, in the bowels of Sicklehurst. A malevolence, deep beneath my feet.

There is a rotten star at the heart of the sticklegrass wood. Lyr's voice
echoes in my mind. *A demon core.*

I shiver and run my thumb over the carvings on the bone-pin
brooch.

It will protect me. I know it will.

I have to believe it.

I'm so close now. It's nearly over. I will find Odette in the
dungeon. Then we can go home, and I can go back to being just
plain Maude.

I keep traveling down.

Eventually, I reach a doorway, arching overhead. It appears to
be made of tree roots, erupting from cracks in the concrete above
us. They twist and twine with each other, the glowing threads of
the silver fungus glinting and pulsing among them.

The copper design on the door itself is familiar—a man's
face, vegetation forming his beard and his hair. It's the same as
the face embossed on the door of the control room, but the leaves
and vines are real this time, brown and green and woody. Empty
eye sockets stare at me. I can see something moving inside.

A pinkish-gray worm wriggles out, its mouth probing the air
blindly before dropping to the floor at my feet.

This door is almost pulsing with mettle.

A lichgate, Mam would call it. An entry to the land of the dead.
It's a portal and a warning, the darkest of dark paths.

There's no turning back now.

The arch looks like it's moving, a trick of the silver witchlight.

But as I draw closer, I realize that the doorframe really *is* moving. It's covered in hundreds of thousands of crawling creatures—wood lice and millipedes and silverfish and firebrats. They cover every inch of it, squirming and streaming in patterns that I can't discern.

This is earth magic, deep and powerful. There's a reason why Mundi hags perform their rituals in caves and the Witch Queen holds her ball in the sewer. Mettle is strong here, away from iron and steel and electricity.

I reach out and lay my hands against the copper face. Tiny white shoots sprout from the eyes, nose, and mouth, twining and searching, reaching for me. At first I think it's mettle, but I'm not witch-eyed, so it can't be. It seems to be some kind of fungus. *Mycelium,* Rufus's voice echoes in my head.

I try to step back, but brown vines wrap around my hands, holding me in place, even as I struggle against them. The white tendrils reach for my own face, tiny threads, searching and branching out like the most delicate network of roots. I screw my eyes shut and try not to scream.

I feel them enter me. Almost invisible filaments, slipping up my nostrils and down my throat. Something electric and tingling passes through my body, but I'm not sure if it's the tendrils or my fear. It's not forceful or painful. At most, it tickles—a gentle exploration. And with it, I sense the most incredible power. The power of the sticklegrass wood, huge and ancient, but tainted with slick, greasy corruption. It's probing at my mettle—asking me to join it, to open myself up to it.

"I can't," I tell it. "I don't have any magic."

The filaments retreat, out of my body and back into the face.

My breath is coming fast, adrenaline spiking in every part of me.

The heavy door groans open.

I close my eyes, hold my breath, and take one, two, three steps forward. Earwigs drop from the lichgate like fat raindrops, falling into my hair and on my shoulders. I bite back a scream as they scuttle and scrape on my skin. One burrows its way under the thin fabric of Odette's white dress and slips into my sports bra. I convulse and shake it free.

The door falls closed behind me with a boom of finality.

I sneeze again. The wet-wool-and-eucalyptus scent of mettle is overpowering, stronger even than the metallic taste that lingers at the back of my throat, and I know I'm getting closer to the third layer of the spell. I lift my hand and bend my fingers slightly, watching white sparks fly from the tips. Mettle coats my tongue in fuzz and forms a thin film over my eyeballs. It wants to change me from the inside out, and I am terrified.

I have no magic to protect myself from it.

It's hot on this side of the door, as hot as a sauna. I thought the air was supposed to get colder the farther you go underground. Sweat pours from my brow, stinging my eyes. Odette's dress is soaked and clinging. Each breath feels like I'm just filling my lungs with moisture, and I long for the chill and bite of outside air.

I reach another door, a simple one this time, just iron set into concrete. I push it open, and am met with a gust of warm, wet air so full of malevolence that it nearly drives me to my knees. I step through at last into the refinery chamber.

The ceiling is so high that I can barely see it. The walls are thickly furred with the black fungus that coated the entrance to the hole. Running through it like veins is the bioluminescent fungus, but it is brighter here, and pulsing as if blood runs through it, pumped by the beating of some great heart. The silvery veins all converge on two great thorned rose canes that run down opposite walls and across the floor.

This isn't what I'd expected.

Complicated machinery lines the walls, but in the very center of the room is a circle made of thousands of square plates. It puts me in mind of the casting circles that Odette used to attempt, drawing witchmarks and pentacles on the floor of her garage in chalk. Sometimes the candles would gutter and go out as Odette chanted, but other than that nothing ever happened. She'd kick them over in frustration, then beg me to do it for her.

And even though the magic frightened me, I'd do it, because I couldn't bear to lose Odette to the rage that always threatened to consume her. I'd light the candles and recite familiar ditties. I'd make the candlelight change color, or raise little Genevieves and Eilwens made from smoke, and let them do battle with dragon shadows on the walls of the garage. Odette would clap her hands, her eyes shining, and I'd feel so relieved to have subdued the monster inside her.

In the center of this circle, there is a pool, maybe thirty feet in diameter. I recognize the liquid inside—it's pure mettle, more than I knew existed in the world. But it's like no mettle I've ever seen before. Instead of the bright silver in Mam's tiny vial, this stuff is a dull gray, shot through with a kind of oil-slick sheen of acid yellow, lime, and violet. Brownish scum collects at the corners.

The two massive rose canes wrap around and over the pool before meeting in the middle.

This is the rotten star that Lyr spoke of, the poisoned heart of Sicklehurst.

It was never an electric power plant.

It's a mettle refinery. Whoever built this place was trying to extract the raw mettle from the ancient forest.

But something happened. The mettle is poisoned. Corrupted.

The triple spell has been protecting this. The forgetting spell. The impenetrable wall around Sicklehurst. And this, the third layer.

It's a kind of membrane—a thick web of silver spun over and around the pool to contain the mettle. So how is the mettle getting out? I've seen this corrupted mettle elsewhere in Sicklehurst—it's infected everything. How is it getting through the seal?

I can't shake the feeling that I've been here before. Or . . . not here exactly. I close my eyes, and over the thick scent of corruption, I can smell roses and thruppenny biscuits. I know this place. Understand it well enough to know that something is wrong.

I peer at it witch-eyed. The membrane is so thick it's clear that whoever made it had incredible skill and power. I take a step forward, and then I notice it.

A hole, made by one of the great black thorns, long and sharp like a spear.

The corrupted mettle is being drawn into the great black rose canes and carried out into the rest of Sicklehurst. That's what's poisoning the sticklegrass wood, turning its mettle oily and strange.

I take a step toward the roiling venom of the pool, then another. My footsteps ring hollow on the floor as I approach.

"Odette?" I say out loud, my voice bouncing and echoing off the walls, returning over and over again to mock me.

There is no Odette down here.

There is nothing.

The realization seeps through me, as sour as nightshade.

Perhaps she was never here. Perhaps Winnie lied.

Perhaps all of this was a ruse, designed to send me to my doom.

The power of the leaking corrupted mettle takes my hope and twists it into something else. Something bitter, like wormwood and betrayal. My breath chokes with despair. I want to plunge into the pool—let it take me, dissolve my bones into sludge.

I sink to my knees.

Once again, I have found myself in a situation that I cannot escape from.

I close my eyes.

Tell me a story, Odette's voice whispers.

I'M ELEVEN ONCE MORE, sprawled under the crab apple tree at lunchtime, eating peanut butter sandwiches with Odette. We weave garlands of celandine and forget-me-not, giggling and exchanging secrets. We can say anything to each other. We have no boundaries. We're basically the same person. After school, Odette will come to my house until Nan or Halmoni coughs and suggests it's time for her to head home. As soon as she gets there, she'll message me. She's the first person I greet in the morning, the last person I say good night to. We are each other's everything.

We're deep in a story about two apprentice sorceresses, Genevieve and Eilwen (of course), who have to dress as boys in order to study magic. There's an evil chancellor, a prophetic crone, and several talking animals. We've just gotten to the bit where a mysterious knight arrives at court.

"Mysterious . . . and *handsome?*" Odette suggests.

"That's the thing," I tell her. "We don't know, because he's on a quest that means he can't show his face. He appears at court in full armor and won't raise his visor."

"But he *is* handsome, right?" she whispers.

I wink at her, and she squeals.

"He's on a quest to find the lost Shard of Tranquility, rumored to be somewhere far beyond the Howling Reaches."

I spin the threads of the story as the sun filters golden through the snowy white-and-pink blossoms of the crab apple. Odette listens, enraptured, clapping her hands over her mouth when Genevieve and Eilwen assist the knight with his quest and his helmet is finally removed to reveal an appropriately handsome face.

There is a kiss, and I get caught up in the description of sensual lips, beating hearts, and trembling hands. We don't hear the bell ring. Don't hear approaching footsteps across the playground.

But we do hear the disapproving clearing of a throat as the sun is blocked. It's Dr. Slater, scowling down at us.

"I *will not* have that kind of filth spoken in my school." Spittle flies from his lips, his breath sour with coffee and halitosis.

A shudder of rage passes through Odette, and I speak up before she can. "It was just a fairy tale, sir."

"Girls in fairy tales don't behave like that," Dr. Slater states. "Girls in fairy tales are sweet and good. That . . . that was *smut.* You should both be ashamed."

I feel it then. The hot rise of shame. The idea that Dr. Slater can see something perverse and monstrous in me. I'm drowning in guilt and mortification, and all I want is to be good. To be approved of.

But Odette looks at me with sparkling eyes, and that look cuts through everything else. An unspoken understanding passes between us. We will be good, for now. On the outside. We will lengthen our skirts and pull up our socks and be seen and not heard. But on the inside, we are still wild as wild can be.

"Sorry, Dr. Slater," I say, meek and contrite.

"You shall both wear witch's hats for the remainder of the day. Perhaps that will remind you how a sweet, good girl should behave."

I try to keep up that feeling of secret, wild defiance. But the black pointy hats are itchy and they stink of stale sweat, and they draw the eyes of other students. I catch snatches of rumors from Tilly, Roshni, and Anesu, who giggle and whisper behind my back.

She had porn in her locker.

They were trying forbidden spells.

They were caught smoking mugwort behind the bike shed.

They were caught fingering each other behind the bike shed.

I can't bear it. The hateful gossip. The judging eyes. Witches never even wore pointy hats, but I know what everyone is thinking.

Just like her mother, the traitor.

I flee my history class and cry in the bathroom until the bell rings for the end of the day.

We return the ridiculous hats to Dr. Slater's office, and, thankfully, he is on the phone, so we don't get another lecture.

"Ugh," says Odette once we are free of the school grounds. "Slater is such a *toad*."

I giggle as the shame evaporates in the sweet glow of the

afternoon. That sets Odette off, and our giggles turn into cackles as we traipse home.

THOSE GIGGLES AND CACKLES FEEL very far away in this foul, lonely place, but I can think again.

"Lyr," I whisper. "I need you."

A faint breath of ice on my cheek, and I can move. I rise to my knees. Water drips from the tip of my nose and slides down my body, onto the floor, where it joins little rivulets running from every part of the refinery chamber.

Lyr's face is cold and cruel, his eyes full of scorn. "I told you not to come here."

I stand up and reach out to touch him, but my hand passes through his body as if he were nothing more than one of my candle-smoke warriors. Little eddies of icy mist cling to my fingertips, and I shake them free.

"You did not heed my instructions," Lyr says. "You are no hero."

"I never said I was," I tell him.

Lyr's eyes glint with madness, and his breath grows shallow. "Now you are a prisoner like me, trapped by the rotten star."

"I just want to find my friend. Then afterward I can free you. I promise."

Lyr laughs bitterly. "It is too late."

"Why?" I ask. "What's going to happen to you?"

A thin chuckle escapes from his lips. "Not to *me*. There's nothing that could happen that would be worse than it already is. I mean that it is too late for *you*."

The hair lifts from my arms. "What do you mean?"

Lyr's gaze is steady. "You know what this is?" He gestures to the pool. "The rotten star?"

"It's mettle," I say. "I think Sicklehurst was a mettle refinery. That's why they built it over the sticklegrass wood—they knew how powerful the forest was. They stripped the magic from the soil, from the roots of the trees, and refined it into pure mettle. They stored it here, in this pool. But . . . it's gone bad. It's corrupted. It must have been like this since they closed the plant, forty years ago."

"Forty years is nothing for a star," he says. "The blink of an eye. This star will burn for thousands of years before it fades."

"Why do you call it a star?"

"It has the power of a star. The energy of one."

"Can't it be purified?" I ask. "Surely, modern technology—"

Laughter spills from Lyr's mouth, sparkling, cold, and hard, like glittering jewels.

"You are naive," he says. "Have you learned nothing on your little adventure in the woods?"

"What do you mean?"

"The sticklegrass wood was here long before the refinery. It has been here forever, much longer than humans. This is a place of deep magic. Old magic. Slow magic. But then humans came and cut it down. They wanted to harness the power of the forest, to trap the pure mettle in barrels like oil and sell it. But magic like that cannot be contained. The pool of refined mettle grew foul and corrupted, burning and roiling with the power of a star. Everything around it grew twisted and poisoned. The witches sealed it up with their triple spell and hoped it would stay that way. Then you came here."

"Me?" I say.

His eyes bore into mine, and in them there is a memory.

MAM, GAUNT AND STINKING OF MAGIC, shaking me awake in the middle of the night. She was unglamoured, and I shrank away from her ghoulish face, sunken and pinched and gray, her hair hanging thin and lanky from her sweating brow.

Mam, bundling me into my coat and shushing my questions as we tiptoed past Nan and Halmoni's room.

Mam, dragging me down the lane and across moon-drenched fields until we reached the high brick wall of Sicklehurst.

The paper moth in her palm, she led me through the holly thicket to the little wooden door. She'd gathered brambles and devil's snare and a young whip of apple bough. She bound them into a wreath, with three white feathers, and clicked a padlock around them, then dragged a knife across her palm and dripped dark blood onto the feathers.

She hung the wreath on the wooden door, on a horseshoe nail, and muttered the nursery rhyme.

"Intery, mintery, cuttery, corn
Apple bough and apple thorn
Bramble, briar, limber lock
Three geese fly in a flock
Cranny key is forged in blood
Open the door to the sticklegrass wood."

The door had swung open under her fingers.

As I passed through the doorway, I felt . . . something. I'd always been aware of the mettle in the earth—the roots of plants and the branching networks of fungi in the soil. But this was different. Something was whispering to me. Something deep and ancient, in a voice like the trembling of leaves in a thin mountaintop breeze.

"Mam, what is this place?"

She didn't answer, just led me past crumbling buildings into the heart of Sicklehurst.

"Listen carefully, my darling," she murmured. "I don't have much time. I need to hide a treasure so no one will find it."

I asked her what it was, this treasure. I imagined a jeweled crown, a gnarled magic wand, a diamond-hilted sword.

The thrill of being outside at night overwhelmed any fear I had. After all, I was with Mam. She would protect me.

"It's something very powerful," she told me. "It once belonged to a prince."

"A handsome prince?"

"The prince of swans."

"Like in our story?"

The story of the swan prince and the peasant girl. The king with the heart of iron. My favorite story, the one I begged for every time I saw Mam.

She nodded. "The very same."

"But it's just a story."

"Nothing is just a story."

"Are you saying it's true?"

Mam didn't reply. I gazed around at the deserted refinery and saw the cooling tower, smooth and pale under a bread moon. I imagined the swan prince at the very top, guarding his treasure.

"What's his name?"

Mam was distracted, laying out sprigs of hawthorn and barberry in a circle. "Whose name?"

"The swan prince."

Mam shook her head like it didn't matter. "I don't know, Maude. Make one up, if you like."

This seemed like an awesome responsibility. "Lyr," I decided. "His name is Lyr."

Mam was muttering to herself, but her words faded from my consciousness. All I could hear was the whispering from under the soil. I felt the threads of mettle down there, more than I could have ever imagined. I brushed my hands—my witch-hands—against them, and felt them stir at my touch. Slowly, as if waking from a long slumber, they started to reach for me, just as I reached for them. Tiny shining filaments, tickling at my consciousness. As more of them came to life, I let my own mettle entwine with them until I couldn't tell where it began and I ended.

It felt like coming home.

I STARE AT LYR. "I came to Sicklehurst with Mam. Before I came in with Odette. That's why I could remember how to get in when I took her. That's how I learned the nursery rhyme."

Lyr's lip curls. "Your human memory is so frail. Even now, you don't remember what you did."

"What *I* did?"

Lyr's gaze slides over the two great rose thorns. "It doesn't matter now anyway," he says. "The forest is poisoned."

"Because of the corrupted mettle," I say, and Lyr inclines his head.

The whole of Sicklehurst smells like roses. They're everywhere, in everything, carrying poison in their roots.

I think of the stew I ate in the lake house. Of the scarlet lissom. All of it, poisoned.

But I would know by now. If I had mettle poisoning, I'd know. I'd have a headache, nausea, a fever.

And I feel fine.

"I have protection."

I look at Lyr and touch my fingers to the bone-pin brooch. His eyes follow my hand, and the room grows cold, my sweaty skin prickling into goose bumps.

"Where did you get that?" he hisses.

I swallow. "From Nan. She said it belonged to my mother."

Lyr can't seem to take his eyes off the brooch.

"What is it?" I ask. "Have you seen it before?"

It looks like he wants to answer, but nothing comes out. His face twists in pain, and a tear slips down his cheek. He closes his eyes and puts the heel of his hand to his brow.

"Are you okay?"

He doesn't answer me. I see his chest rise and fall, and hear the shaky tremor of his breath.

"Lyr?"

"Do you know the story of the swan prince of Uisnigh?" he asks abruptly.

"Of course," I tell him. "It was my favorite growing up."

"Tell it to me now," Lyr demands.

Finally, a task that I am up to. I take a breath and gather the story threads in my mind.

"There was once a king named Badb, who ruled over lands that were green and good. But a curse turned his heart to bitter iron, and he became cruel. The land grew barren, and ruin befell all. One day, a peasant girl named Aoife came across a swan that had become stuck in a befouled swamp that had once been a clear lake. She freed the swan, but he was too weak from the fetid water. He told her he was a prince of swans and begged her to return him to his home. Aoife did so, carrying his fragile body to the peak of Mount Pitys, where she climbed a white-bark pine to reach Uisnigh, the kingdom of birds. There, the bird queen greeted her and held the swan prince to her breast until he gasped his last breath."

I remember Mam sitting beside me in my little bed, her dark hair falling over her beautiful face as she spoke.

Lyr gazes at me, his eyes bright. "Keep going."

"The bird queen thanked Aoife for returning her son. Aoife told her about King Badb, and the curse on his heart. The bird queen took the limp body of the swan prince and fashioned his breastbone into a knife that she gifted to Aoife, telling her that it could cut out the coldest of hearts."

In my memory, a shadow loomed in the doorway, and Mam had glanced up.

"What now, Ma?" Mam asked wearily. "What did I do this time?"

Nan stared at her, stony-faced. I looked anxiously from her to Mam, trying to understand the current of anger that was sparking between them.

Halmoni appeared and read the situation in a heartbeat. As quick as a rabbit, she sent Nan to the kitchen to make tea and told Mam to take the rubbish out. Then she smoothed the hair on my forehead and kissed me good night.

"Why do Mam and Nan always fight?" I wanted to know.

"They're too alike," Halmoni said. "Having them both here is like having two stags over for tea. They can't help but lock horns."

"Nan doesn't like the story about the swan prince, does she?"

Halmoni had hesitated before answering. "There is truth in some stories," she'd said at last. "Your nan would rather they stayed stories."

LYR IS STILL WATCHING ME, his pale fingers trembling. "Finish it."

"Aoife returned to the human world and made her way to King Badb's palace. She lied and cajoled her way past his guards, and when she came face to face with the king, she whipped out the knife and cut the coldness from his heart with a single stroke. King Badb became good once more and was so overcome with shame and remorse that he gifted his kingdom to Aoife and wandered off into the mountains to live as a hermit for the rest of his days."

Lyr smiles a sad, lonely smile.

It's something very powerful, Mam told me. *It once belonged to the prince of swans.*

"The knife . . . ," I say. "But . . . it's just a story. It isn't real."

Nothing is just a story.

"Is that what Mam hid in Sicklehurst?" I ask Lyr. "The Hollow Knife of Uisnigh?"

Lyr sighs but doesn't answer.

"What about Odette?" I press.

"She had no protection," Lyr says. "If she came down here, then she surely perished."

I can't believe that. I can't.

"I don't know who I am without her," I whisper.

"You must learn."

I shake my head.

"Say it," Lyr demands. "Speak the truth, and it will set you free."

I want to clap my hands over my mouth. To squeeze the air from my own lungs so I won't have the breath to speak. I can't say it.

But my lips part, and the words slip out, as evil and powerful as the rotten star beneath my feet.

"Odette is dead."

Saying the words out loud is the worst thing I've ever done. I feel like I've killed her myself. And maybe I have.

I could have saved her. I could have given her the vial of pure mettle when she asked for it. Or I could have gone into Sicklehurst with her, and maybe we could have escaped together. Maybe I could have convinced her to turn around, to come back with me, to play under the frothy green hair of Peg Powler, like we used to.

Maybe.

Maybe.

"Leave your grief here," Lyr says. "Cast it into the rotten star and watch it sink into oblivion."

Misery wells in my throat, choking me. I fall to my knees and brace myself against the floor as water drips from my hair into the very heart of the refinery.

I look to my fingers again, see the square plates around them glowing faintly. The great black rose canes seem to throb with mettle.

"What do I do now?" I whisper.

"Haven't you done enough? You created those girls, condemned them to a life of eternal suffering. Sent a beast to torment them. You drove your friend away, to her death. What else can you possibly do?"

He leans forward to make sure I can hear every syllable of what he says next.

"*You* are the true monster, Maude."

And then he is gone.

This is what happens when I try to make a story on my own. I ruin everything.

I thought I could defeat the Tatterdemalion and save Winnie and Ginger, but I didn't. They're still trapped here, and they will be forever.

I thought I could rescue Odette, but that was nothing but a story.

Without my magic, all I have is my gift. I'm just a storyteller, dabbling in fantasies. Odette was the one who always wanted to *do*. I only ever wanted to *tell*.

That wild girl I buried is gone. I have no magic. I don't belong in this world.

I wish I'd stayed under the scarlet lissom. At least that way I would have died, drunk and happy, with Odette in my arms.

But she's gone. My mother's cold in a coffin. My father was dead before I was even born. Magic has taken everything from me.

Maybe it's time to take something back.

I stagger to my feet and over to the pool. The giant rose canes are wickedly thorned, each one buried in the mettle membrane. There's only one hole, but perhaps it could be bigger. Big enough for me to reach through.

I don't try to manipulate any mettle—I know I can't. But I also know that the roses are listening to me. Waiting for the word.

"Do it," I whisper to them.

The rose canes pulse and contract, the long thorn digging deeper into the membrane, wiggling back and forth, working at the tiny hole until it is perhaps three feet wide.

I hear my mother's voice hissing in the darkness.

Greenwitch.

Mettle pulses in the black moss on the walls, throbs in the floor beneath my feet. The air is thick with it.

I dig around in the black satin bag.

I take the mirror fragment and the chunk of amethyst and drop them through the hole into the oily liquid. They slip under the surface without so much as a ripple.

"I made Winnie and Ginger," I tell the pool. "I made Lyr and the Tatterdemalion and the fishy girls. And now I will make again. Odette. I will make Odette."

I don't need to manipulate mettle with my witch-hands here. I can use my real hands.

I get down on my knees and plunge my hands through the hole in the membrane and into the pool, up to my elbows. The corrupted mettle feels slippery and heavy, but not actually *wet*. It sucks the warmth from my skin, and my mouth fills with metallic-tasting saliva.

There's no whimsy this time. It's not like making the dolls, or even making the poppet with Ginger. The mettle flows darkly in my veins, streaming from my brow and nostrils. I feel it tugging at my own strings, the pressure enough to make them all snap.

Let them. If I can't leave here with Odette, then I'd rather not leave at all.

I am choking on the mettle. It's leaking out my eyes and ears now. The three lines where the Tatterdemalion marked me split open and start to weep black blood.

The oily pool stirs, and the rose canes begin to thrash like tentacles.

"Odette," I gasp.

I fix her in my mind, hanging upside down from the willow bough, the tips of her white-gold hair brushing the ground. Odette as she was, fierce and free and utterly devoted to me. Laughing at Dr. Slater. Skimming stones in the creek. Pulling me closer to her as she growled with desire under the scarlet lissom.

The liquid mettle heaves, slippery waves of it escaping through the hole to splash onto my knees, then run off in skittering drops.

And then my heart catches in my throat as fingers emerge from the scum-lined pool.

I reach out and grab her hand, and it is *real* and solid. I rock back on my heels and haul, and she rises through the hole in the membrane, oily mettle running from her skin in thick, viscous rivulets.

But just as the hope springs up in me, it crashes back down, dissolving into horror and despair.

This is not Odette.

The creature before me is the color of sour milk and yellow-green bruises. Its fingers are webbed, cold, and clammy, and I snatch my hand back as it rises to its feet.

It is not Odette, but also it *is*. It has her pale hair, but it falls in sparse, slimy strings. It has her features, but they are bloated, its skin waterlogged into ridges and furrows. Milk-pale fungi sprout along the swollen hump of its spine like half-moons.

It opens its mouth, and a wet groan emerges. It reaches for me, and I skitter back. My stomach heaves at the sight of it as it shambles forward. It doesn't move like a human. It stumbles, thrown off-balance by its distended belly and sagging breasts. It stares at me, unblinking through clouded eyes. It groans again, and lurches toward me.

"Get away from me," I stammer. "You're not Odette. You're a monster."

You are the true monster, Maude.

The not-Odette creature is relentless, reaching for me with its limp, spongy fingers. As it stares at me, a millipede falls from one of its gaping nostrils. The creature doesn't seem to notice.

I slip on one of the rivulets of oily mettle, and Not-Odette looms over me. It lets out a wet, wheezing bellow. A string of greenish slime dangles from its mouth and lands on my cheek. It reaches for me, its fingers clammy on my skin.

The sheer horror of it overcomes me, and I kick out at the creature, which staggers backward. It lets out another cry, and I see misery in its face. Longing.

Finally, I have created a version of Odette that wants me, and I am disgusted by it, disgusted by myself.

I reach out and push it toward the pool, and the creature looks confused. Betrayed.

"I'm sorry," I tell it, and give it one final shove.

Its pitiful wet moans are swallowed up by the corrupted mettle, and it sinks below the surface. The rose canes writhe, the pool heaves, and then all is still.

I sink to my knees, so full of revulsion and self-loathing that I am tempted to hurl myself in after the creature. I close my eyes and weep bitter tears.

And then I hear a voice, bouncing around the chamber like a breath of fresh air.

"What the actual *fuck* is going on."

It's Odette.

14

SHE LOOKS GRIMY AND EXHAUSTED, WITH BAGS UNDER her eyes and thin, pinched lips. She wears the same black jeans and tank top as she did when she came to my house two weeks ago, except now they are filthy and torn. Her hair is tangled with twigs and leaves.

She stares at me with cold, hard eyes that contain no warmth, no affection.

"*You* did this," she states. "You made this place. These horrors."

"Odette," I say, my voice weak with relief and shame. "You're alive."

"No thanks to *you*. I've been trapped in here for days. I don't even know how many. In this sick shrine that you built."

"I didn't . . . ," I say. "I just wanted to rescue you."

She makes an impatient, furious noise. "Of course you did. That was all you ever wanted. No matter how many times I told you I didn't want to be rescued."

I stare at her, dumbfounded. She's alive. Odette is alive. She's not a glamoured illusion, or a lumpen horror. Odette. The real, true Odette.

And I think she hates me.

"I met Eilwen," she says with a sneer. "She's a real piece of work. And I saw Genevieve, but you've clearly made some changes since we were kids. Bigger boobs, sexy outfits. Are you sleeping with her? Is that what all this is about? Have you been sneaking in here for the last four years, into your weird theme park, to fuck your fantasy version of me?"

"N-No," I stammer. "It's not like that at all. . . ."

But I think about what happened under the scarlet lissom, and the words dry up in my mouth.

"You're *obsessed* with me," she says. "You always were. I grew up, Maude. You never did. You just wanted to keep being kids and playing make-believe. And even after we stopped being friends, you never went away. You were everywhere, staring at me with those big sad puppy-dog eyes. Guilting me. Judging me. Then the *one* time I actually needed your help, you went all high-and-mighty and sent me away. And now this?" She gestures to the mettle pool. "I saw that thing you made. It was supposed to be me, wasn't it? Was Genevieve not enough for you?"

I try to explain, but my words come out as babbling nonsense. I start to cry, sobs coming in great hiccups and snorts.

She looks me up and down, shaking her head in disgust. "Are you wearing my *dress*?"

"I'm sorry," I say, sniveling and pathetic. "Tell me how I can make it up to you."

Her expression is ice-cold. Despite the grime and exhaustion, she's never looked more like her mother.

"Just get me out of here," she says. "That's all I want."

I LEAD HER UP the crumbling stairs, the silence between us excruciating. A corridor leads past the huge funnel-shaped hole that I fell down, ending in a gritty iron ladder just like the one under the control room. The humidity from the refinery chamber drops away suddenly, and by the time we get to the top, I'm shivering and damp from the cold.

We emerge into a silvery early evening. Winnie and Ginger are there, startled as we stumble out of the door. They look between us, and Winnie blows air through her cheeks.

"Looks like the reunion went well," she says dryly.

"Shut up," says Odette sharply. She glares at me. "Can't you make them go away?" She waves a hand as if to suggest some kind of banishing spell.

I shake my head. "It doesn't work like that."

Ginger says nothing, but she and Odette size each other up, dislike clear on their faces. This place is not big enough for the both of them.

"You didn't get your mettle," Winnie says to Odette. "Wasn't that the whole reason you came in here?"

Odette shakes her head. "I want nothing from this place. I just want to go home."

I lead the way.

Sicklehurst looks different. The glamour has dissolved, and it's just an abandoned industrial site again. There is no Bone Road. No sticklegrass garden. No bamboo forest. No scarlet lissom trees. No brilliant purple jacarandas blooming amid the rusting tanks, only skeleton weed and spiny broom.

My mouth tastes acidy, like tarnished spoons.

We pass a large pool of stagnant water, maybe thirty feet across. The water is milky white and smells strongly of sulfur. In the center, there is an old shipping crate. The water holds no underwater girl monsters or giant golden fish.

I show Odette and the girls to the secret wooden door, which has, thankfully, reappeared in the high brick wall. Sticklegrass clings to my ankles, like a weak last plea, but I push through it and swing the door open.

Odette elbows past me and marches right through without a word. She doesn't look back.

I watch her go, then turn to Winnie and Ginger, who are staring at the door with hope and fear carved into their features.

"I guess this is it," Winnie says. "The real world."

Ginger glances at me. "Will it work?" she asks. "Can we leave?"

I answer truthfully. "I don't know."

I stand back to let them try. Winnie reaches out to Ginger, and they clasp hands. Then they step through, shoulder to shoulder.

I hear Winnie whoop in exultation. Ginger's eyes are shining as she looks over her shoulder, back at me.

But the excitement doesn't last.

They take one step, then two, then they both collapse in on themselves, their skin splitting open and compost spilling out, until they are each nothing more than a pile of rotten leaves.

15

NAN AND HALMONI ARE SITTING ON THE COUCH, holding hands, when I enter. A silver shawl is wrapped around Halmoni's shoulders like a spiderweb. The creases on Nan's face seem particularly deep.

They look up as I walk in, their faces twin masks of fear and hope.

There's someone else there too. Standing with his back to the fire.

"Maude," says Dr. Slater. "Thank goodness you're safe."

I blink slowly at him. "What are you doing here?"

Nan springs to her feet like a jack-in-the-box. Halmoni rises more slowly, gracefully.

"Dr. Slater saw you leave the vigil," she says. "And then you didn't turn up at school. . . . He was concerned."

"You're cold," Nan says to me briskly.

She whisks a lurid crocheted afghan from the back of the couch and wraps me in it, pausing for a moment with her arms around me.

"It's fine," I tell her. "I'm fine."

Nan's eyes are as beady as a robin's. She nods, but we both know I'm lying. Knowing secrets is Nan's gift.

They don't deserve this. They've lost so much already. I shouldn't have frightened them.

There are so many things I shouldn't have done.

"You took your rose off," Nan says, touching the bone brooch, still pinned to the front of Odette's dress.

"I thought . . ." I shake my head. I don't know what I thought.

I remember Winnie crushing the rose and dropping it into the mud, and I feel another stab of guilt and grief for her and Ginger.

I'd expected to arrive home to a torrent of anger and recrimination, but Nan and Halmoni are both silent and watchful. I'm confused but grateful. I have no energy for apologies or reassurances.

"Your grandmothers have been very worried, Maude," says Dr. Slater. "You owe them an explanation."

His presence feels wrong in our cozy little home. He looms large, taking up too much space.

I turn to Nan and Halmoni. "I—I found Odette."

Halmoni claps a hand to her mouth. "You did? Is she okay?"

"She's okay."

Dr. Slater bares his teeth in what I suppose is meant to be a smile. "Have you thought about my offer, Maude?" he says. "The settlement institute? After all this drama, perhaps a simple life is exactly what you need. After all, we don't want you ending up like your poor mother, do we?"

My chest tightens. All of a sudden, a fresh start doesn't sound so unappealing. Away from Odette. Away from the walls of Sicklehurst and the guilty secrets contained inside. Away from the sad, worried eyes of my grandmothers. I don't want them to worry about me. Maybe this is what I need to do. Put aside adventures and hero business and become the predictable, unremarkable adult that everyone seems to want me to be. A good citizen. A productive consumer. The only magic I'll interact with will be safely packaged in plastic. Stable magic. Predictable and mundane. A simple life.

I look at Dr. Slater. "Yes," I tell him. "I'll go."

Nan looks sharply at me, her expression unreadable.

He smiles again, revealing coffee-stained teeth and too much spittle. "Good girl," he says.

He takes his leave, and I avoid Nan and Halmoni's questioning gazes and drag myself up to the bathroom to shower, letting the hot water strip me of Sicklehurst and its shadows.

The Tatterdemalion's mark is swollen and purple against the skin of my chest, three diagonal slashes. I press a finger to it. It's still hot, like a burn.

I pull on my pajamas with what feels like a herculean effort. A light knock sounds on my door, then footsteps retreat down the hallway. I open the door to find a tray with a cup of tea and a toasted sandwich. Cheddar and kimchi—my favorite. I take a bite, ravenous, but it tastes like ashes and coins. Nausea rises in my throat, and I put the sandwich down.

I can't think about Odette. The disgust on her face. She definitely hates me now. And I deserve it.

I'm just so tired.

I can't get comfortable. I keep falling asleep and then jolting awake again. My pajamas twist tight around me as I toss and turn. My tongue is sore. Did I burn it on the toasted sandwich?

When I do slip into sleep, I dream of birds. Black wings beating at my window.

Odette, trapped in a tower, guarded by a dragon.

I would smash it with my wings.

I dream of thorntails and bellbirds and silvereyes and starlings. I dream of a goldfinch, furiously beating its wings against the bars of a gilded cage. A black-crested partridge, carefully building a grassy nest in a hedge. A white swan gliding silently on glassy water.

I dream they are all engulfed in a fire that turns their bones to ash, a fire so hot it can melt the heart of a star.

I SIT UPRIGHT in my bed, my head pounding. My mouth is dry. My skin feels like thin paper, drawn too tight over my bones.

I can't shake the dream free, so I go over to the window and pull back the curtains. The daylight stabs at my eyes, and I flinch away from it.

A blob of black sits on a branch of the rowan tree in the front garden. As my eyes adjust to the light, I see that it's a raven, watching me with one black shining eye.

Birds never come into our garden.

My mouth tastes disgusting. I need to brush my teeth.

The tattered remains of Odette's dress have been taken away, along with my bra and undies, no doubt whisked into the washing machine, then Halmoni's mending basket.

There's a clenching in my bowels, and I sit down on the toilet. A sharp pain stabs at my gut, and I discharge something watery and foul-smelling.

I shower again, and the water on my back feels like needles. My hands and forearms ache where I plunged them into the mettle pool.

I'm fine, I tell myself. *I'll be fine.*

I dress in loose, soft clothes, and head downstairs.

NAN IS IN THE KITCHEN, trying to act like it's just an ordinary morning. Hangul and Huw wind around her ankles, hoping for treats. They flee out the back door when my foot reaches the last step. I must have startled them. Princess Bari is nowhere to be seen. Gwion Bach is asleep on the hearthrug, but his ears twitch as I approach. He leaps to his feet, his fur and tail sticking out sharply and his back arching. His ears flatten against his head.

"It's just me," I tell him, reaching out a hand.

He hisses at me, a low growl in his throat. His tail swishes angrily from side to side. Then he's gone, a black blur streaking past my legs and out the back door. I've never seen him move so fast.

I look up, and Nan is watching me. She smiles, too bright.

"Tea?"

My stomach recoils at the thought of it. I shake my head.

"You don't look well, love," Nan says, and it sounds like her voice is miles away.

"I know," I say. "I think I'm going to go back to bed."

The staircase swims before me as I climb, and I pause at the top of the stairs, where the telephone sits on a little table.

Her number is as familiar to me as my own heartbeat. I dial

it, the phone rings, and anxiety claws into my throat. What if she isn't okay? What if she's sick, like me?

It rings for a long time. Then finally, there's a click, and I hear her voice, flat and cold.

"What do you want?"

"I just wanted to check on you. To see if you're okay."

There's a long pause. "No," she says. "I'm not okay. I'm grounded, my mother is sending me to boarding school, and I'm going to need about a million years of therapy to get over all the shit you put me through."

Self-loathing twists in my gut, but I persevere. "You're not sick, though?"

"I'm sick of *you*. Don't call me again."

The line goes dead. I don't feel any better.

I crawl under the covers and stay there all day. Halmoni brings me food—ginseng porridge and bowls of kongnamulguk—but I don't eat. Everything is a blur of sickness and misery and guilt. The raven on the branch outside watches me with its beady eye, and I turn my head away so I don't see it.

RUFUS COMES TO SEE ME, his face drawn with worry. Halmoni sends him to my room, with firm instructions to be nice.

He sits in the armchair by the window, his brow creased.

"You did it," he says, picking at his cuticles. "You found her."

I nod.

"Are you okay?" he asks.

"Why do you care?" I ask bluntly.

"Because we're friends."

"Are we?" My voice is as bitter as the taste on my tongue.

I have no friends. How could anyone love someone as pathetic as me?

Out of nowhere, a memory emerges. Rufus, coming over to my house when I was little, just after Mam left for the last time. He brought a bug catcher and a magnifying glass, and we spent the afternoon in the hedgerows, looking at crawling creatures. He identified each moth and beetle, and I spun tiny stories, sending ladybugs on quests to defeat evil hoverflies.

I think about the way Rufus sat next to me at the Hollantide Ball. About his freckled, braces-filled grins in the biology lab. The way he was always so polite to Nan and Halmoni.

He came to Odette's house with me.

He offered to come to Sicklehurst.

Rufus was there the whole time, and I was too busy being obsessed with Odette to notice it.

"I'm sorry," I tell him. "Of course we're friends."

"What happened?" Rufus asks.

The mark on my chest feels so hot. Like it's burning through my skin, all the way to the bone. My forearms are itchy, and I rake at them with my fingernails. Flakes of papery skin come off like snow.

I glance out the window. The raven is still there, watching me. I've never seen one so large.

"I wouldn't know where to start."

"Take your time. I'm here."

But I can't. I can't tell him about what happened in the

refinery chamber. About Not-Odette, and the disgust on real Odette's face when she saw what I'd done. I can't tell him about the wild hope on Winnie's and Ginger's faces as they crumbled to compost, reabsorbed into the forest, ready to be mudborn again.

I feel a pang of guilt that I've neglected Rufus for so long, that I overlooked his friendship and loyalty in favor of Odette. But I still can't tell him.

The pang deepens into the now-familiar spasm in my bowels, and I excuse myself, racing to the toilet before more foul liquid streams forth.

I wash my hands thoroughly, even though the pressure of the water hurts. My skin is still cracked and dry.

Rufus watches me as I return and clamber back into bed.

"You need to go to the hospital," he says.

"I'm fine. Just tired."

I can tell he doesn't believe me. "If you won't talk to me," he says. "Then talk to your nan. She'll know what to do."

I smile at him. He's such a good egg. "There's nothing to be done," I say. "It's over. I'm leaving in a few weeks anyway."

"Leaving?" Rufus's voice is steady. "Where are you going?"

I tell him about the settlement institute, and his mouth twists in distaste.

"No," he says. "Not you. You don't belong in a place like that."

"Maybe I do."

"But, Maude, you're *interesting*. You're smart and funny. You don't want to become one of those homesteading automatons, all blueberry pies and hand-stitched napkins and Ilium catalogs."

"I like blueberry pie."

"But you also like *physics*. And stories. Don't you want to go to university?"

I shrug. "I don't really know what I want."

"The settlement institutes aren't much better than the detention camps. They're owned by the same people. All they do is brainwash you into buying their magic junk."

"I need a fresh start."

He narrows his eyes at me. "You're running away."

Anger flares up in me. "And why shouldn't I?" I ask. "You don't understand what it was like."

"Because you won't *tell* me."

I can't handle him anymore. His worried eyes. His faith in me.

"I need to rest," I say. "I'll walk you to the door."

Rufus hesitates, and I see his natural politeness warring with his concern. But he gets up and follows me down the stairs.

Watching him disappear down the garden path, I think about calling him back, but I don't. Instead I linger on the doorstep, breathing in the warm scent of the afternoon. I glance up to see the raven, still there, ruffling its feathers and staring at me with that beady black eye.

The flowers on Nan's rosebushes are fat, many-petaled whorls of pink and white. Which isn't surprising, since they bloom even when there's frost riming the hedges.

I think of the monstrous rosebud choking Winnie.

I remember the puncture marks on Lyr's throat and wrists.

The roses are spies, he said.

Is that why Nan always makes me wear a rose? Has she been spying on me?

I reach out and cup one with my hand. Breathe in its per-fume. They are nothing like the red roses at Sicklehurst. These roses are sweet and pure, but nonetheless I am reminded of that other scent, heavy with malice.

I can still taste old coins.

I slip back inside and shut the front door.

Nan is watching from her workbench. "You're not well," she observes.

"I'm fine."

"I heard you arguing with Rufus. He's right, of course. You can't go to that ridiculous place. It's run by the people who killed your mother, and you know it."

"Mam made her own choices. I'm making mine."

She comes over and sniffs me, close enough that I can smell her biscuity rosemary scent. She runs practiced fingers over my brow, pausing on my temples. She peers into my eyes, one by one, and takes my left hand and traces the lines on my palm before letting my hand drop and stepping back to take me all in.

"Your mettle is poisoned," she says, and a tremble in her voice betrays how serious it must be. "Are you ready to tell me what happened?"

I shake my head, unable to meet her gaze. I feel exposed, vivid with shame and self-loathing.

Nan sighs. "Strip," she says.

I obey without thinking, pulling off my loose T-shirt and track-suit pants to stand before her in just my underwear. She leans in and peers at the three slashes on my chest. Then she turns to her workbench and pulls out linseed, dandelion, horseradish, and comfrey, crushing them with her mortar and pestle, moistening the mixture with milk as needed to make a thick paste. Then she coats her hands in the paste and faces me.

"May I?" she says.

I nod.

She presses her hands firmly against the Tatterdemalion's mark, and I let out an involuntary gasp as the lines burn even hotter than they have before. Nan grunts, and as her witch-hands touch my strings, I am seven years old again, in Sickle-hurst under a bread moon with Mam.

She is frail and frightening, her skin gray and her hands trembling. She opens her mouth to speak, and there is blood on her gums, on her teeth. She's trying to get to her feet, but it's like she has forgotten how to walk properly.

"Mam?" I whisper, crouching beside her. "Mam, are you okay?"

She grips my hand, her teeth clenched. And I feel her tug at the threads in me. She takes my mettle—a single thread snapping like a bowstring. I gasp and cry out—it *hurts*. A piece of me breaking, gone forever.

"I'm sorry," she murmurs as she gets to her feet. "I just needed a little bit."

I can't stop shaking.

"SHE TOOK MY METTLE," I tell Nan. "She didn't even ask, so it was barely worth anything."

Nan takes her hands from my chest, her face crumpling. "I'm so sorry, love," she says. "She never should have."

Nan knows. She's always known. That was why she was so furious with Mam when we got back.

"I would have given it to her freely," I say, and my voice comes out small and childlike. "If she'd asked."

Is that why my magic dried up? I wonder. *Did Mam take it all?*

But I know that she can't have. I had magic for years after Mam died.

Nan sighs. "Your mam . . . she thought she was doing the right thing. But she lost her way."

I have no words. She took my mettle. Her own daughter's.

Nan holds up her hands. "I'm going to help you," she says. "You can trust me."

I swallow and nod, and Nan presses her hands to my chest once more, her witch-hands on my strings. Her touch is gentle. Cool. Healing. My strings stay intact, but Nan strips the oily corruption from them. The pain subsides, but as Nan presses on my chest, my hands and forearms start to burn. My ears are ringing, and I try to pull away. But Nan holds me firm, fixing me with her beady eyes.

My fingernails feel like they are melting.

Eventually, she releases me. I see sweat on her brow, her own chest rising and falling with rapid breaths. Her pupils dilate, and she wobbles, like she's about to faint.

"Nan?" I ask.

She waves me aside and takes a slice of bread, spreading it thickly with honey before pressing it against my chest. Then she binds me up with brown paper and sticky tape before stepping back to inspect her handiwork.

"Are you okay?" I ask.

She nods once. "You should be safe now."

"Nan, there's more. I should tell you—"

She holds up a hand to stop me. "Not now, love," she says. "I have a headache. We'll talk about it later. We'll fix everything—I promise."

I think about our family witchmark on the bricks outside Sicklehurst.

The roses are spies.

I call Odette again. I have to know she's okay. But she doesn't answer.

FROM THE GARDEN, Halmoni's studio looks fairly ordinary—old clapboard and tin. I open the door and slip inside into a glittering fairyland.

Rows of shelving hold panes of glass, organized by color and texture. Other shelves are stacked with jars and boxes and containers holding grinders, groziers, cutters, and heavy spools of silvery lead. One entire wall is made of stained glass, brightly colored and fitted together as neat as a jigsaw. It's a reproduction of our garden, the afternoon sun streaming in and lighting it up like a cathedral. I see in colored glass the rowan tree, the cherry, and the spiky juniper with its purple-black berries. The blueberry bushes and raspberry canes. The veggie patch. Hollyhock and sage and hellebore and peppermint. Nan's roses are there, of course, pink and white. No birds, though. Never any birds in our garden.

Except now there is a raven in the rowan tree.

I stand in the doorway, breathing in the volcanic scent of molten lead and black putty. Halmoni is working on a finely detailed piece for a client, a trailing vine of clematis set into clear glass—a sidelight, by the shape of it.

She takes a small pane of milky jade green and scores it with her cutting wheel, a straight line down the middle. Then she takes the pane in both her hands and snaps it neatly in half. One half goes back onto the shelf. The other she lays on her light table. She slides her design—black lines on tracing paper—underneath the glass, and then carefully follows the lines with her cutting wheel.

She lifts the pane up and gives it a sharp rap on the underside. The scored piece breaks off, perfectly formed, a milky-jade leaf.

"Are you feeling better?" she asks without looking up.

"Yes," I reply, and I'm surprised to find that I'm not lying. I feel lighter. The pain in my hands and wrists is still there, but it has faded to a dull tingle.

"Good," says Halmoni. "We were worried about you."

"I know," I say. "I'm really sorry."

She smiles at me. "I'm just glad you're okay. You walked a dangerous path."

"You know about Sicklehurst," I say. "You and Nan didn't forget."

She inclines her head in a slight nod. "You shouldn't have gone back there," she says. "There's a reason why it was sealed up."

"Tell me."

The jade glass slips between Halmoni's fingers and shatters on the concrete floor. She bends to sweep it into a dustpan, and I notice her hands are shaking.

"It's not my story to tell," she says, at last.

"Please," I say. "I have to know. I have to know what happened there."

Halmoni puts the dustpan on her bench and gestures to me with her elegant fingers. I cross the room, and we sit together on the battered couch, the brown paper dressing crackling under my shirt.

"I don't know the whole story," she says. "When your nan and I first moved here after we were married, Sicklehurst was under construction. Environmental groups protested—the site was an old-growth forest. Very old. Very powerful. But corporations don't care about folk stories. They ripped up every tree, covered the forest with steel and concrete. A new age, they said. A bright future. They said it was an electrical power plant, but your nan knew the truth. All the witches did. They knew it was a mettle refinery, stripping raw mettle from the earth and transforming it into something commercial."

"What happened?"

She gazes out through the stained-glass window, out over the fields and hedges that stretch from our back gate to Cygnet Creek and the rising dunes of Black Larpent Bay. "Sicklehurst operated for ten years, and then accidents happened in other mettle plants—Glidź and Carrowdown. The decision was made to seal the site. But the timing was too close to the other accidents—everyone suspected it was a mettle plant. In the end, they had to call in the witches. Not officially, of course. Officially, women like Niamh are just quaint old biddies, kitchen witches dealing in superstition and placebos. But men can't do magic that strong, no matter how shiny their boots are."

She pauses, like I should understand where the story is going.

It takes me a moment to catch up. "I didn't know," I say. "I thought Nan was just a kitchen witch."

Halmoni raises her eyebrows. "Your nan was one of the most powerful witches of her generation."

Nan? My nan, with her lurid tights and her crocheted cardigans? I blink, my gaze unfocused as I try to put the pieces together.

"She made the triple spell," I say. "The forgetting spell, the wall, and the membrane over the mettle pool."

Halmoni hesitates, then nods. "There were thirteen witches. Your nan is the only one still alive."

"What did they do?"

"It was a strong spell," Halmoni says. "A difficult spell. I don't know what they had to do, and at the time I didn't want to know. Carys was a baby, and all I wanted was for us to be safe. When the accidents happened at Glidź and Carrowdown, I wanted to move away. To go back to my family in Gojoseon, or maybe to Oenotria or Spitzbergen or Snæland. Anywhere but here. But your nan said she had to stay, to help shut up the power plant and make sure it stayed safe. When she got home, after the spell, she went straight to bed and slept for a week."

An uneasiness creeps through me. The mineralized, brutal taste of the refinery rises in my throat, and I remember the waves of oily malice emanating from the pool.

"Will you go back?" Halmoni asks.

I shake my head. "Never."

"Good."

I mean it too. I'm done with magic, with lost girls and adventures. I saved the princess. My part in this is over.

I just wish I knew that she was okay.

16

THE NEXT MORNING, THE RAVEN IS GONE. THE SUN IS out, and I feel like a person again. I shower, and the water doesn't feel like knives. I get dressed, and my clothes are just clothes.

I call Odette again, but she doesn't answer.

Whatever Nan did to me clearly worked.

Halmoni makes breakfast—kongnamulguk with steamed rice and fried eggs. Nan is still avoiding me, claiming she's not feeling well. I know she's lying—Nan is never sick.

I'm starving, and I shovel my breakfast into my mouth, marveling at the fluffiness of the rice, the pillowy eggs, the salty umami of the bean-sprout soup. After several days of tasting ash and old coins, real food is a revelation. I had no idea it could taste so good.

"You're feeling better," Halmoni observes, her eyebrows raised.

I nod, my mouth too full to answer.

The cats still won't come near me, but Jeremiah does, slinking toward me on his belly, his tail wagging nervously. I scratch behind his ears, and he grunts in appreciation.

Maybe it's over. Maybe now I can get on with my life.

Back in my room, a single black feather lies on the window-sill, in the place where the candle snails used to dance for me.

NAN LOOKS TINY in the big four-poster bed she shares with Halmoni—like a child—her chest rising and falling with each breath. Her lips are chafed and dark like bruises.

I think about her dilated pupils as she pressed her hands to my chest. She's not used to doing strong magic—it must have exhausted her. I feel a pang of guilt to have put so much strain on her. But she must have known what she was doing. After all, Halmoni says she was one of the most powerful witches of her generation. I tell myself she just needs to rest, because I can't bear to think about the alternative.

Jeremiah is curled up on the end of Nan's bed, asleep.

I sink into the overstuffed armchair by the bedroom window and wait for Nan to wake up.

Does she know what I did in Sicklehurst? Are the roses really her spies?

Finally, she opens her eyes and looks over at me.

"Orright, love?" she says, her voice hoarse.

"Nan." All I want is to gather her in my arms and tell her I love her. But I don't. "I'm sorry," I say instead.

A sad smile appears on Nan's face. "You shouldn't be sorry," she says. "I'm the one who should be sorry. I . . ."

Her jaw works, trying to make words, but nothing comes out. She sighs in frustration. "Your mam . . . ," she says, and her voice trails off. She looks at me helplessly and points to her throat.

"You . . . you can't tell me?" I ask.

She shakes her head.

"Did Mam put a geas on you?"

Her face crumples slightly, and she nods. What did Mam *do*? What possibly could have been so important she'd bind the tongue of her own mother?

It doesn't matter. She's gone now. Time to move on.

A rumbling from outside makes me glance out the window. A sleek, shiny car is pulling up, brandishing a silver badge shaped like a sharp-tipped fountain pen, and I feel a twisting in my gut.

"Auditors," I say out loud, and Nan lets out a low moan.

They must know I went to Sicklehurst.

Or maybe not. Maybe it's just a standard audit. They visit all the licensed witches from time to time, to make sure they aren't using illegal ingredients or doing spells that aren't from the covenant list.

Maybe they're here to tell us they've fixed everything. Found whatever wretched thing my mother stole and put it back where it belongs.

But my heart knows that nothing good happens when auditors knock on your door.

Nan makes a choking sound and tries to rise to a sitting position.

"Don't, Nan," I tell her. "You have to stay in bed."

"They mustn't come in," Nan says, still struggling with the bedspread.

I try to keep my voice calm. "Maybe they're just here for an audit."

But Nan is no more fooled by this line of reasoning than I am. "No," she rasps. "They'll take you. Like they took Carys."

I put out a hand to comfort her, and she shrinks away.

"Let me take care of it," I tell her, with a bravado I do not feel.

"You can't," Nan rasps. "You're just a child."

I've already put too much strain on Nan. "I can deal with them."

"They are *not to be trusted*," Nan says. She's writhing beneath the covers, her breath coming in terrifying hitches.

"Okay," I say calmly. "Okay. I'll send them away."

"Promise me," she begs.

My palms are sweating. "I promise. Just stay quiet. I won't let them in."

I turn to leave, but Nan reaches out to me. In a smooth movement, she slides the bone-pin brooch from my T-shirt, clenching it in her fist.

"Nan?" I ask.

She hesitates. "They mustn't see it," she says, but she doesn't meet my eyes.

Through the window, I see the auditors get out of the car. A pair of them, as always. Clad in exquisitely tailored black suits. Briefcases in hand. A chill runs down my spine at the memory of their mild tones and quiet politeness.

I slip down the hallway into my room, and empty Odette's black satin bag onto my bed, hunting around until I find the glamour patch I took from her room, the one stolen from her mother.

ESTEEM, it says on the label. A SUBTLE YET POWERFUL BLEND OF ELEGANCE, INFLUENCE, AND PRESTIGE, CRAFTED BY THE WORLD'S FINEST CHARISMA ARTISANS.

I know it won't work. Auditors always travel in pairs. One mettleworker. One redhead. The redhead will see through the glamour in an instant.

But I tear open the plastic wrapper anyway and slap the patch on my upper arm. It smells of bitter almond and ambergris. I glance at my reflection in the mirror over my dresser and watch as I transform from a grubby teenager, with sunken eyes and sallow cheeks, into a vision of elegance and authority.

My skin smooths and blurs into flawlessness, erasing pimples and scratches and freckles and replacing them with a luminous glow, as soft as moth wings. My lashes lengthen, and previously invisible cheekbones provide my face with a new dimensionality, the light highlighting sleek contours. I'm still me, but now I'm beautiful. Older, wiser. Powerful. I'm still wearing jeans and a T-shirt, but now the jeans seem perfectly tailored to my suddenly long legs, the T-shirt draping silkily from elegantly postured shoulders, flowing over my perfectly proportioned breasts. No bra strap slipping over my shoulder. No soft belly. No unsightly lumps, bumps, or marks. I seem taller, although I'm not. Thinner, although I'm not.

This young woman in the mirror is everything I am not. She is confident and poised. Assertive but demure. She would be able to wind men like Dr. Slater around her little finger, bending them to her will while they were distracted by her refined beauty.

This is nothing like the cheap glamour patches I'd tried years ago, and I can see now why people are so attached to the better-quality ones. The selfish relief of looking into a mirror and seeing something flawless, something that cannot be nitpicked. Something that brings with it no shame, no regret, no disappointment.

I get it, why some people refuse to leave the house unglamoured. Why they avoid redheads and security cameras, and never, ever let anyone take their photo, lest it produce a permanent record of what they truly look like.

A polite knocking sounds at the front door, and I tear my gaze away from the beautiful girl in the mirror, suddenly afraid. This glamour is a good one—the best. But it won't fool the redheaded auditor. All it can really do is help *me* feel more confident.

I head down the stairs, careful not to hurry. The girl whose face I'm wearing is not given to hurrying. As I pass Nan's workbench, I reach up to the high shelf and take one of her emergency witch bottles. I have no idea what it'll do, so I hope I don't have to use it. I'm hopeful I can talk my way out of this. Actually attacking an auditor—with magic, no less—would land me in a detention camp for sure.

I lift my chin and open the front door, but not too wide.

Do not let them in.

They are nondescript in a bland, authoritative kind of way. Immaculately dressed. Neither tall nor short, thin nor fat. Handsome nor ugly. Young nor old. They are forgettable but impossible to ignore. After they are gone, it will be impossible to describe them, except to say that one of them has a dark ponytail and the other is a redhead.

"Good morning," says the ponytail woman. "Please excuse the disturbance, but we're here to see your grandmother."

My instinct is to apologize. To match their politeness. To be small and humble. But I fight it. It doesn't matter that the redheaded man can't see the glamour. *I* can see it, and I'm going to act the part.

No apologies.

"My grandmothers aren't here," I tell them, and offer no further excuses or explanations.

The redheaded auditor shifts his head slightly, trying to see around me into the kitchen. "Do you know when they'll be back?" he asks.

"No," I tell him.

"Do you know where they are?"

"I couldn't say."

Being confident is exhausting. How does Odette's mother do it all day? A glamour can only change the way you look. How does she keep up that coldness? That refusal to bow to societal pressure. Never giving an inch or letting a moment of vulnerability slip past that mask.

"Perhaps we could come in and wait for her," the redhead suggests.

My resolve wavers. The auditor smiles at me, an expressionless smile of gentility. There is no warmth in him. There is no emotion at all. I wonder how the auditors do it.

Maybe they're scared too. Or maybe they want to go home. Do auditors have homes? Families? I can't quite imagine them sitting down to tea in the evening, chubby kids climbing on them and leaving smears of mashed pumpkin and spittle on those perfect suits.

The thought of it makes me want to giggle, but I bend it into a polite, emotionless smile to match the ones on the auditors' faces.

"No," I say.

They blink, taken aback. Did I go too far, defying them openly? My fist tightens around the witch bottle, held concealed behind the door. I don't know what to say next. What would Odette's mother do? What cold but polite way can I refuse to let them enter my house?

The dark-haired auditor's shoulders round a little. She's trying to make herself look smaller, more humble, less threatening.

Perhaps I should do that too.

"My grandmothers forbid me to let strangers into the house," I say. "It wouldn't be . . . appropriate."

"Of course," ponytail auditor says. "We understand perfectly."

There's an awkward silence, which every mote of me itches to fill with apologies, concessions, compromises. But I hold firm. The auditors are holding on too, waiting for my counteroffer. It's agonizing.

"If there's nothing else . . . ," I say, with haughty civility.

The auditors exchange a glance, suddenly unsure. I imagine they aren't used to having their deferential authority blocked, over and over again. If they want to come into my house, they'll have to force their way in, and that's not the way that auditors operate. Auditors will not instigate a scene. If someone tries to make one, they will neutralize it, but they only ever react.

"What can you tell us about your mother?" the dark-haired one asks, breaking the standoff.

I blink. The question is unusually direct, coming from an auditor.

"Very little," I say. "She died when I was young."

Because you took her away.

"She stole something," the redhead says. "Something of great value. Do you know where it is?"

Have they been watching us somehow? Why are they here

now? The auditor's eyes bore into me, seeking out all my most secret and hidden places. But maybe I can use him, just as he's using me.

"Oh," I say casually. "You mean the knife?"

His eyes gleam. "Yes," he says. "The Hollow Knife of Uisnigh. You know where it is?"

So that *is* what Mam stole. The Hollow Knife from the story. Carved from the breastbone of a swan prince. It was true all along. No wonder Nan didn't like her telling it to me. But what does it *do*? In the story, the knife cut the coldness out of the king's heart. Why did Mam steal it? What did she want it for?

The auditor is still watching me, waiting for a response.

I shrug. "Sorry," I tell him with a regretful smile. "Never heard of it. Why is it so important?"

They don't answer my question. I didn't really think they would, but it was worth a try.

"Where did you say your grandmother is?"

"I didn't," I reply.

There is another agonizing pause. Then the auditors exchange a glance.

"Please let your grandmother know that we called for her," the one with the dark ponytail says, bowing her head.

Before I can respond, they turn and retreat down the garden path.

I close the door and lean my back against it, trying to still my galloping heart.

* * *

NAN IS WIDE-EYED in her bed, the quilt pulled up to her chin. "Are they gone?" she says, her voice childlike. Her hands are blackened, and I finally admit to myself that Nan isn't just tired. When she took the corrupted mettle from me, she absorbed it.

And it's killing her, as it would have killed me.

"Tell me what you need," I say. "To break the geas. I can't do it, but I can help."

Nan coughs and raises a shaking finger to point at the linen chest at the end of the bed. I fly to it and yank out sheets and patchwork blankets and pillowcases. At the bottom, there is a book. A grimoire.

I know that it's forbidden. I can *feel* it. Can smell the faint whiff of brimstone and jonquil on the pages. There's no covenant magic in here. This is the magic that was outlawed.

Nan has her eyes closed. I don't know if she's asleep or unconscious. I have to work fast.

I open the book and leaf through the ancient pages. I see spells for cursing, for binding, for ashwork and poisoncraft. And for setting a geas—tonguebinding, the grimoire calls it.

There are no instructions for breaking the geas, but I think I can reverse engineer one. I need blood. It's supposed to be Nan's blood, but I don't want to hurt her, so I'll use my own. I need to draw out the blood "with insight and betrayal."

I hurry downstairs and open the kitchen drawer. None of our knives seem to fit the bill—and they're all steel, so that obviously won't do. I pick up the silver scissors from Nan's crafting table, but they're not right either. There's no insight or betrayal in them.

I put my hand to my chest, looking for the bone-pin brooch—perhaps I could use that. But it isn't there. Nan took it off.

They mustn't see it.

I should put it back on again. But it makes me think of something. Nan pinning a rose to my chest every day.

The roses are spies.

Was Nan really using her roses to spy on me? Were her roses here in our garden somehow connected to the roses in Sicklehurst? Did she use them to monitor what was going on in there?

I shudder as I remember once more the monstrous rose cane that tried to choke Winnie to death.

I open the front door and pluck one of the white roses that grow by the doorstep, dragging the stem across the palm of my left hand so that the thorns scrape and drag at my skin. Blood starts to ooze from the wound, dark and sticky, and I drop the rose, heading upstairs to collect the raven feather from my windowsill. It's night-black and shining. Ravens are the keepers of broken oaths and secrets, so the feather should also help Nan to break the geas.

I clutch it in my left fist, then return to Nan.

"Here," I say, and hand her the bloodied feather.

"Take that thing off," Nan mumbles, squinting at me. "You look ridiculous."

I had forgotten about the glamour patch.

"Later," I say. "Tell me what Mam did," I command. "Tell me about the knife."

Nan's lips clamp shut. Her fist tightens around the feather.

"Tell me," I say again.

The geas is strong. I turn witch-eyed and see Nan struggling to weave the mettle together—she's so weak. But the raven's feather is strong and was given freely by the raven.

"Tell me," I say a third time, and channel all the authority of the glamour into my words.

Nan gasps as the spell breaks, and I can smell burning wool and eucalyptus in the air.

"Thirteen witches," she says. A look of relief passes over her face as the story starts to spill out. "One hundred and thirty-seven witch bottles, buried around Inglenook. We filled them with pearl-headed pins, flying rowan ash, hartshorn, knuckle-bones, stillborn caul."

"The first layer of the spell," I say. "To make people forget. Then what?"

"Unbroken salt and wolfberry vinegar baked into the bricks. Oak-fired and inscribed with our witchmarks under a hunter's moon, laid with mortar mixed by youngest sons only, no red-heads."

"The wall," I say.

Nan nods. "We caught three hundred birds and buried them alive in the soil of Sicklehurst. Then we built the wall around it, so deep and so high that nothing could escape. No burrowing or flying creatures—" She breaks off into a spasm of coughing. Red-flecked spittle flies from her mouth, spattering the patch-work quilt. "We had to make sure that no flying creature could leave Sicklehurst and take the corruption with it."

There are no birds in Sicklehurst. No birds in our garden either.

"And the third layer?"

Nan's face turns pale and hollow. "The membrane, to seal the poison in. An adder stone. Bladderwort. Nails stolen from a good man's coffin. Wax from a candle burned at both ends. And . . ."

I gaze at her and recognize that hollowness. "You used one of your strings, didn't you?"

"Each of us gave one," Nan says. "Thirteen witch strings, given freely."

No wonder it was so powerful. Until . . . until it wasn't. Until the rose canes ripped it to pieces on my command. And now it's gone.

I swallow. "What about Mam? What did she do?"

Nan looks at me, her eyes full of sadness. "She stole a knife."

"The Hollow Knife of Uisnigh. Why? What does it do?"

"It can cut the mettle out of any living thing. Your mam joined the resistance witches when she was not much older than you are now. She learned that the knife was more than just a story, that Ilium was looking for it."

Ilium. The biggest magic corporation. It runs the detention camp that Mam was sent to.

"Ilium wanted it so they could use it on *people*?" I say. "Cut the mettle from them?"

Nan inclines her head. "The knife would allow them to take it out whole—full-strength mettle, cut from a person against their will."

I remember the sundering feeling, when Ginger had taken some of my mettle. And Mam . . . It makes my heart ache to think about it.

"Your Mam believed it was too much power. That the auditors would carve the magic out of this world, would stifle any dissent with the knife. And so . . . she stole it."

"And she hid it in Sicklehurst," I add.

"She tried to destroy it first," Nan says. She starts to cry softly.

"Nan?" I say. "What did she do?"

"She was pregnant again. A baby sister for you. She . . . she made a blood sacrifice, to destroy the knife. I found her in her bedroom, half-dead, thighs bloodied, with a tiny purple thing lying still, where it had slipped from within her."

We are both crying now. I grip the counterpane in my fists. "Keep going," I tell her. "The knife. What happened?"

"The sacrifice was for naught. She broke only the smallest sliver off the knife. So instead she decided to hide it, somewhere where nobody would find it. And where better than Sicklehurst, the place that everyone forgets?"

"How did Mam remember it?"

Nan swallows. "Her gift . . . she inherited it from me. It was easy for her to learn my secret."

"And why did she take me with her?"

There's something else Nan isn't telling me. Her eyes slide away from mine. "That last spell broke her," she says. "Even if the auditors hadn't taken her away, I'm not sure she would have made it."

I think of the roses and ask the question I've been dreading. "The roses are spies, right? Your spies."

Nan hesitates, then nods.

I can see the answer to my next question in her face before I've even asked it. But I have to know for sure.

"Did you know that Odette went to Sicklehurst?"

Nan goes suddenly still and closes her eyes briefly. Then, slowly, her head sinks to her chest in a single, sorrowful nod. I flinch away from her, the betrayal making my throat close over with stinging bitterness.

"You told me you didn't know," I say. "You lied to me."

She shakes her head. "I just wanted you to be safe."

"You could have gone after her yourself."

Nan hesitates, and I know this is true.

"And you let *me* go in there," I say. "I nearly died. The Tatterdemalion . . . the lake house . . . all of it. Were you just sitting here watching me the whole time?"

She shakes her head. "It doesn't work that way, love. The roses just report if the second layer of the spell has been disturbed. I can't see anything beyond the wall. So I knew you'd gone in there. I believed that this would keep you safe."

She unfolds a tightly clenched fist, and I see the bone-pin brooch.

"But it didn't," I say. "It didn't keep me safe."

Tears slip from Nan's eyes. "I—I was wrong. I don't understand what happened in there. The third layer of the spell should have held. Should have kept the poisoned mettle contained. Everything you described in there, the monsters, all of it. It's wrong. Something went wrong."

Mam, crouching beside me in the dark.

"Nan, why did Mam take me into Sicklehurst?"

"She needed your power. She wasn't strong enough to do it on her own."

Mam, reaching inside me and snapping one of my strings. The sundering of it. The pain.

But there's something else. Something else happened in there. I remember the scent of loam and a rustling, leafy whisper.

"Put the brooch on," Nan says. "And take the glamour off. Then I'll tell you the rest."

I peel the patch from my arm and slide the pin onto my T-shirt.

"There," Nan murmurs. "You'll be safe now. Never take it off."

Then her eyes roll back in her head, and she starts to convulse.

There's movement behind me, and then Halmoni is there by my side, gathering Nan in her arms, laying her lips to Nan's forehead. "Shh," she murmurs. "It'll be all right. Everything's going to be fine."

I hear the catch in her voice, see the worry etching lines into her skin.

Nan collapses onto her pillow and goes quiet and still, her breathing shallow.

Halmoni glances over at me, tears slipping down her cheeks, and I know she knows what is coming.

We each take one of Nan's hands, and we wait.

The sun grows low in the sky. The rise and fall of Nan's chest slows, and eventually stops.

And then we sit there for a while longer, because this is the last time the three of us will ever be together like this.

17

WE OPEN ALL THE DOORS AND WINDOWS AND cover the mirrors with linen. We put iron nails in the butter and milk to stop them from curdling. We send the cats outside.

I help Halmoni remove Nan's clothes, and we gently wash her. I am shocked at how light she is, how small and fragile.

I rub her skin with rose hip oil and cardamom, and braid her hair with columbine. We dress her in her wedding gown— a simple linen shift embroidered with hyssop and daisies, turned inside out to confuse the fairies. Then we add hot-pink Lycra leggings, because it's what Nan would have wanted.

She looks peaceful. Beautiful.

Except for her hands, which are purple-black and flaking, where they pressed against my chest.

Every time I look at them, I am overwhelmed with guilt.

Halmoni takes the front door off its hinges, and we prop it flat on four dining chairs, then gently lift Nan to lie on it, just as we did with Mam.

Halmoni does this all calmly, although I know inside she is as much of a mess as I am. We don't talk much—there'll be time for talking later.

We bake soul cakes with oats, currants, and a pinch of saffron, then put out bottles of wine spiced with cloves and star anise. I take great care in lining up the plates and glasses on the sideboard—they must be perfectly spaced.

Finally, all the preparations are done, and the only thing left to do is to sit and watch.

I take Nan's right side. Halmoni takes her left, closest to her wedding band.

And we watch her as the sun cartwheels over our little house.

PEOPLE COME TO PAY their respects.

Rufus and his dad come first, both of them ginger-haired and awkward as they stoop under the low lintel. Rufus pats my shoulder.

"Your nan really was something," he says. "A true force of nature. And she was always kind to me."

I smile at him.

Rufus's dad nods to us. "I know the work Niamh did for our town, and the strength it took. I remember, and I am grateful."

Halmoni nods elegantly. "Thank you, Alan," she says.

Other visitors come. Alejandro from the botanica. Nikita Chamovitz from the Inglenook council. Jim-the-bus. Goody Morgan. The Osgood twins, peering at Nan over their spectacles and bowing their white-capped heads.

They each bring something for the table—cakes and fresh bread and flowers and ale. Everyone helps themselves, and before long, the walls of our house ring with laughter and stories and kind wishes. I am proud that Nan was so respected in our village. So loved.

Tilly, Anesu, and Roshni come too, arm in arm, their lace handkerchiefs at the ready. Their parents mill around and chat, but the three girls make a beeline for me. Tilly wears a brand-new dress of pale muslin, and I just know it's one of those Ilium-enchanted fabrics that resists staining and wrinkles.

"Such a tragedy," she murmurs, even though she never spoke a word to Nan in her life.

"Indeed," agrees Anesu, who once made the sign of the evil eye when Nan crossed her path.

"You poor thing," says Roshni, laying a gloved hand on my arm, as if she hadn't refused to sit next to me in grade three because my mam was a traitor.

"Thank you for coming," I say, because even though I'd love nothing more than to kick them out of my house, this is Nan's wake, not mine, and I must be polite.

"We heard you were coming to the settlement institute," Tilly says. "You're so lucky to get a place. I didn't even know you'd applied."

"It's going to be *such* fun," Anesu adds.

I will learn to be like them at the settlement institute. Demure and proper. Unwrinkled and unstained. Free from wildness and adventures.

Tilly and Roshni exchange a look, then lean forward conspiratorially.

"Odette is back," Roshni says, her voice low. "And they're saying you're the one who found her."

I open my mouth in the hope that some polite words will come out, but none do.

"Of course you're here for gossip," says a dry voice from behind them.

It's Odette.

Odette is here in my house.

Tilly, Anesu, and Roshni draw back, as if Odette is some kind of wicked wraith who might suck the goodness from them.

"Get out of here, you carrion crows," Odette tells them, and they scatter.

She is alone, of course. Her mother would never come to our house, let alone to Nan's wake. She's wearing a simple black dress, her hair pulled back into a ponytail. She's thin, and I can see scratches on her forearms from her time in Sicklehurst.

I search her face for any signs of sickness. There are dark circles under her eyes, and her skin is sallow. But that's to be expected . . . isn't it?

We stare at each other.

I thought I'd want to hurl myself into her arms. To weep with joy.

I'm glad she's home. Glad she's safe.

But this girl standing before me isn't the Odette I'd held in my head. The fantasy Odette that I'd nurtured and obsessed over.

This girl . . . I don't really know her. I'd thought she was a shadow of who she used to be, but I was wrong. She's grown into a whole new person.

I have, too.

The grief of realizing that I have truly lost the Odette I held in my heart isn't the same as the grief of losing Nan. It's smaller and sharper, a vicious sting instead of an overwhelming blanket of sadness.

I just feel so tired.

"I hate those girls," Odette says.

I nod. "Me too."

There's an awkward pause. From the other side of the room, I can see Rufus pretending not to watch us.

"Sorry about your nan," Odette says.

I nod. "Thank you."

"I'm not staying," she says. "I just wanted to pay my respects."

She shifts on her feet, not meeting my gaze. Then she nods and is gone.

Rufus is looking openly at me now, a question in his eyes. I smile weakly to tell him I'm all right.

Goody Morgan lets out a cackle of laughter at something that Dan from the fish shop said. Halmoni is smiling, a genuine smile, not the polite one she wears so often. She's on her second glass of spiced wine and is starting to relax.

I can barely keep my eyes open.

Dr. Slater appears in the late afternoon, his expression disapproving as he takes in the wine and food and general merriment.

"Mrs. Jenkins," he says to Halmoni. "I'm sorry for your loss."

There's a pause in the chatter of the room, a sudden tension. Nan would have sent him packing. But Halmoni is as polite as always and thanks him for coming.

Dr. Slater makes his way over to me.

"Maude," he says. "I expect you'll want to stay here for a week or two to help your grandmother with the necessary arrangements. Your place at the settlement institute is assured, though. I'll drive you up myself."

Stain-free. A good girl.

Dr. Slater leaves, and after a moment the volume in the room returns as people start to talk again. Ginny Johnson appears with her fiddle, and before long, voices are raised in song and feet pound the floorboards as our friends and neighbors dance around Nan.

My head spins. Rufus brings me a soul cake and some bread and butter, but I manage only a single bite, which sticks in my throat.

It is well after midnight when everyone leaves. The house shows no sign of the festivities—Goody Morgan and Alejandro made sure that every dish was washed and put away, the floor was swept, the empty bottles were removed.

Halmoni and I light three fat candles and place one at each of Nan's shoulders, and one at her feet, over the witchmarks on the door that Nan herself had carved when Mam died. I take a small bowl and ladle in three teaspoons of salt, then place it on Nan's chest. Halmoni places more bowls—empty ones—beside each of the candles.

Then we settle into our chairs and watch as the world grows very silent and still, the night erasing everything around us until all that exists is the three of us, illuminated by a circle of candlelight.

I remember sitting on Nan's lap when we did this for Mam. Falling asleep in the safety of her arms, knowing that she'd always be there for me, even in the darkest times.

I remember Nan dancing around our kitchen, singing at the top of her lungs.

I remember her exchanging dirty jokes with the Toadmen that came around on Whitsuntide Eve, her cheeks shining apple red.

I remember the care she took each morning, pinning a white rose to the front of my shirt.

Exhausted, I slip into a strange dream, where Nan is lying in a garden bed, surrounded by marigolds. I have a watering can full of pure mettle, and I'm pouring it over her, trying to bring her back to life. But as the bright silvery mettle hits her, it turns oily and dull, rainbow-slick and scummy. The soil dissolves into the corrupted mettle, swallowing the marigolds. Nan slips under the surface, and I drop to my knees and plunge my hands into the oily pool, scrabbling to grab hold of her.

My burning hands jerk me back to the present. The candles are low and guttering, and the faintest tinge of predawn light is coming in through the open windows to the east.

As the light grows stronger, Halmoni meets my eyes and nods. We stand up, stiff from sitting all night. Then as the candles sputter and hiss, we circle Nan three times and chant.

"Thrice the candle, thrice the salt
Thrice the dishes empty for praise
Thrice the door we walk around
Be at rest within the ground."

The candles go out, three plumes of smoke rising from three puddles of wax. We wrap Nan in soft white linen, and Halmoni lets out a little sob as we wind it and see Nan's face for the last time.

As dawn breaks, Alan, Alejandro, and Goody Morgan appear to help us move Nan into Alejandro's van. We follow on foot as it rumbles down the lane through a thin drizzle. A hole has been prepared in the graveyard, and she is lowered in. Halmoni and I take turns with the shovel to fill the hole, then linger by the grave while the others leave.

Later, there will be a headstone. We'll plant flowers, and this place will be beautiful. But today it is muddy bare earth under weeping gray skies.

"Come along, Maude," Halmoni says at last. "Let's go home and get some rest."

She tucks her arm in mine, and we return home, painfully aware that now we are two.

"She was so proud of you," Halmoni says as we turn into our lane.

A raven cries from its perch overhead, and all I can think about is that Nan would be alive right now if it weren't for my foolishness.

18

I **CAN'T SLEEP, EVEN THOUGH I WAS UP ALL NIGHT.**
Whenever I close my eyes, all I see is Sicklehurst. The oily roil of the corrupted mettle. The grasping fingers of the fishy girls. The ragged scream of the Tatterdemalion. The shambling fungal bloat of Not-Odette.

It's just past midday, and the drizzle has cleared to let sun stream in through my bedroom window.

Am I really going to leave this place? Abandon Halmoni and go off to start anew as a good girl, a goodwife? A productive consumer?

I peek my head into Nan and Halmoni's room. Halmoni is asleep. The bed seems too big for just her.

I remember being little, crawling in between them in the deep of the night and sinking into sleep, warm and utterly safe.

I remember the way they would look at each other with such unspoken love.

It's too much to bear.

* * *

I LEAVE HALMONI A NOTE in case she wakes up, and then head down the lane toward the edge of the village. The cobblestones feel solid under my feet. Birds are singing in the hedge, and bumble-bees hang lazily in the air over corn cockles and billy buttons.

It's a beautiful day in Inglenook. One of my last.

When I return here, I'll be an adult. All this will be behind me.

Unthinking, my steps lead me to Peg Powler.

The old willow looks smaller, more ordinary. She's not a cas-tle anymore, or a dragon's lair. She's just a tree like any other. I guess this is what growing up feels like.

A white swan glides serenely along the creek, leaving a gentle wake behind it. Moorhens call from the rushes.

It really is a beautiful day.

I lie on the soft earth beneath the tangled branches of the wil-low and stare up into the green canopy.

I remember Odette, hanging upside down by her knees.

Tell me how you'd rescue me. If I was locked in a tall tower, with no hope of escape.

The worlds I made beneath the willow weren't enough to contain Odette. No place was. She was everything that people like Dr. Slater despised—wild, untamable, unladylike. She filled a room with her presence, instead of demurely fading into the background. She was loud and unrepentant and boundless, her head thrown back, grinning wide into the open sky.

I couldn't contain her either, no matter how much I tried.

The monster inside her had always been there. I'd thought I could tame it. That I could coax her from the dark paths. I wanted to bend her to my will, just like her mother did.

I hope Odette knows how sorry I am.

I look at my hands and see that they are red and shiny, like they've been scalded. I feel a wave of dizziness, and I *know*.

The corruption has returned. Nan leached it from me, but she didn't get it all.

She died for nothing.

And now I will die too.

At least I won't have to go to the settlement institute.

I'm startled from my reverie by a snowy-white blur hurtling toward me from the creek.

Its wings are spread wide, wider than I can spread my own arms.

The swan is not as elegant on land as it is on water, but it is fierce. It charges forward, beating those enormous wings at me, its orange beak snapping, a savage honking sounding over and over, like a siren.

I scramble to my feet, but not before one of the beating wings cracks into my shoulder blade, a powerful blow that makes me see stars. The size and force of the creature is shocking, its great feathered chest thrust forward, its long neck stabbing at me, its dark eyes glittering.

The wings batter me, landing blow after thudding blow, always on my back, my shoulders, like it doesn't want to face me directly.

I cower under Peg Powler, and through the hissing and thumping of the swan, I hear my own child voice echoing from the past, making my best friend a promise.

I would smash it with my wings.

Then there are footsteps, and I hear someone yelling, *"Gie, go on, git!"*

The swan flees to the creek, where it crouches in the shallows, still hissing and growling, its neck curved in an aggressive question mark, wings half-raised.

I turn to see my savior—Rufus—brandishing a eucalyptus branch in one hand like a cudgel. Behind him, improbably, is Odette, unglamoured, in black jeans and a black T-shirt, her hair pulled into a ponytail.

Rufus helps me to my feet. I feel bruised and tender. The swan retreats farther, then glides away down the creek and out of sight.

"What are you doing here?" I ask them both.

"I needed to see you," Odette says. "You weren't at home, so I asked Rufus. I think finding you is his gift."

She says it lightly, but the tips of Rufus's ears turn pink. "Finding anything," he mutters. "I'm good at finding things."

Odette steps under the canopy of Peg Powler. The green sunlight filtering through the leaves makes her look elfin and delicate.

"Why did you want to see me?" I ask.

Odette reaches out and grabs a strand of hanging willow. She doesn't meet my eyes. "I think I made a mistake."

I wait for her to continue.

"Dr. Slater came to see me," she says. "He had a lot of questions. And . . . and some auditors came, a few days ago."

I taste sourness on my tongue, and I feel myself turning away from her, as if to shield myself from what she's about to say.

"I told them about Sicklehurst. I told them how to get in. About what was in there. About the pool and the corrupted mettle. I told them everything, Maude."

I hear Rufus suck in air through his teeth. He knows what this means for me. But he doesn't know what it means for Sicklehurst. For the forest. And the knife.

"I'm sorry," Odette says, tears standing in her eyes. "I was just still so angry at you. And they . . . Well, you know how they are. It's hard not to give them what they want."

I have no words. I can't be angry at her—she doesn't deserve that. But . . . the auditors know. That's why they came to my house. They know about Ginger and Winnie and the pool of mettle and the knife.

They know where the knife is.

The knife that can cut the mettle from a person.

My mother gave her life to ensure that that knife would never fall into their hands.

And now Nan is gone, unable to help.

But why didn't they take me then? What are they waiting for?

"Anyway," Odette is saying. "My mother is sending me away. To some boarding school that she says specializes in 'children like me.'" She says this with a sardonic quirk of an eyebrow, but there's real fear behind it. "You probably won't see me again. I just thought I'd tell you. So you don't rush off on another adventure in search of me."

It's a joke, but nobody laughs. I won't be rushing off anywhere. Now that the auditors know about me . . . about what I did, they'll take me. Like they took Mam.

They'll use the knife on *me.*

I guess it doesn't matter, since I'm dying anyway.

Rufus puts a hand on my arm. "I think you'd better go," he says to Odette.

Odette nods and turns to leave, but she hesitates. "How did

you do it?" she asks. "Genevieve and Eilwen. How did you make them so real?"

I remember being there with her that first time. The sticklegrass wood whispering to me beneath the soil.

"I—I'm not sure," I say.

Odette sees the expression on my face. "Can you try to explain?" she asks. But she isn't eager this time. Her fingers don't flex at the mention of magic.

Rufus nods. "Tell us. All of it."

Maybe it is time.

WE SIT UNDER THE WILLOW, the three of us, and I weave them a story.

"Sicklehurst was built fifty years ago," I say. "The locals were told it was an electric power plant, but that wasn't true. It was a mettle refinery."

"A what?" Odette asks.

"It was supposed to extract pure mettle from deep in the earth."

Rufus leans forward. "There were only a handful of them built. It was supposed to revolutionize the mettleworking industry."

"But it didn't?" Odette asks.

I don't know much about this part of the story, so I nod at Rufus for him to explain.

"The plants were erected over sites that were strong in natural mettle," he says. "They were supposed to extract it from the earth. But because the mettle wasn't given freely, it . . ." He spreads his hands. "It went wrong. There were big accidents at

Glidź and Carrowdown. Hundreds of people died, poisoned by the corrupted mettle. The other sites were all closed immediately, as a precautionary measure."

I nod. "The extraction process poisoned the mettle," I say, thinking of the horror-filled oily scum in the pool. "Witches were called in to seal the plant, so that none of the corrupted mettle could escape."

"Your nan was one of the witches?" Rufus guesses.

I nod. "They used a triple spell—you know magic is more powerful in threes. The first layer was a forgetting spell. The second made the wall around Sicklehurst, so no living thing could go in or out—no humans, no animals, no birds or insects. The third layer kept the corrupted mettle contained."

"What does it do?" Odette asks. "The corrupted mettle."

My forearms burn and throb. I can't look her in the eye. "It— it makes spells go wrong," I say. "It poisons everything."

I feel her gaze upon me. "You used it, didn't you?" she says. "The corrupted mettle. That's . . . what I saw down there. You used it to make that . . . thing."

I want to burrow into the earth to avoid Odette's cool gaze and Rufus's curious one.

"What thing?" Rufus asks.

"There's a pool underground at Sicklehurst," I tell him. "Full of mettle. More than I ever knew existed in the world. But it's poisoned. The third layer of Nan's spell was around the pool— it created a kind of magical membrane that would contain it, stop it from leaking out into the ground and the water."

"Did your nan teach you the way in?" Odette asks. "To Sicklehurst, I mean?"

I shake my head. "My mam," I explain. "She . . . was a resistance witch. You both know that. After the mettle refineries didn't work out, the government tried to ban magic altogether. After Goose Spring, they opened detention camps to imprison dissidents, and they started extracting mettle from *them*. But it wasn't enough. Mettleworking was becoming industrialized, and demand for mass-produced glamours and charms was high. They needed more. Then they found out about the knife—that it was real."

"The knife?" Rufus asks.

"The Hollow Knife of Uisnigh," Odette says, and I look at her, startled. "The auditors asked me about it," she says guiltily. "I knew the story. You told it to me."

"The knife has the power to cut the mettle from someone," I explain to Rufus. "It doesn't need to be given willingly. It's incredibly powerful."

"Dangerous," says Rufus thoughtfully. "Especially in the hands of the auditors."

I nod. "That's what my mam thought. She stole it from them."

Odette chuckles. "I knew your mother was cool," she says.

"She tried to destroy it at first," I say. "It nearly killed her, and she only managed to break off a sliver. So she decided to hide it. She took it into Sicklehurst, and she took me with her."

"Why?" Rufus asks. "You must have been just a kid."

"She . . ." I hesitate. "She needed some of my mettle. She was too weak to do it alone."

Rufus frowns. "Did you give it willingly?"

I shake my head, and Odette gasps softly.

"The auditors knew that Mam had taken the knife. But they

didn't know where it was, and she wouldn't tell them. They took her away to a detention camp, and she came back in a coffin. She was already very weak."

I close my eyes and see Mam laid out on the door. Then Nan. Our family has lost so much.

"What happened next?" Odette asks.

"I took you in there," I say. "When we were twelve. I made those little twig-and-leaf dolls of Genevieve and Eilwen and Lyr."

She nods. "I remember," she says.

"They were just little poppets," I say. "I assumed that they'd crumble to dust at sunset, like they usually did. But . . . they didn't. They turned into real living beings somehow. The magic of the forest kept them alive."

"And we all know what happened next," Rufus says tartly to Odette. "You dumped Maude when her magic ran out, because you were a bad friend and a terrible person."

"Rufus," I chide.

Odette looks away, uncomfortable, and I remember the words she said to me in the refinery chamber.

You're obsessed *with me. You always were.*

I swallow and taste old coins.

"Then you went back in there," I say to Odette.

She bites her bottom lip and takes up her own part of the story. "I met a kid in the drains who said there was a magician in Eastmoor who could give me witch-hands if I could bring him a drop of pure mettle. And I knew, from you, that there was pure mettle in Sicklehurst. I remembered the things you did to get in, but I wasn't sure it would work because I have no magic."

"The spell was already cast," I explain. "The wreath and the nursery rhyme are just the key. That's how I can still get in too."

"I saw Genevieve—Ginger—from a distance," Odette says. "I recognized her straightaway. But the monster came before I could talk to her."

"The Tatterdemalion?" Rufus asks.

"How do you know its name?" Odette asks him.

"I saw it in your notebook," he explains. "In your room."

"You were in my *room*?" Odette's face twists with distaste. "Ugh. Never mind. I ran away from the monster and got lost. I don't know how long I was in there, but I couldn't find the door again to let me out. I was so *hungry* and tired. After a few days I ran into Eilwen—Winnie. She told me that the pure mettle was deep in the refinery building, but she warned me it was super-dangerous. She wouldn't tell me how to find it, so I wandered around some more. I found some fruit and berries to eat, but it was a pretty rough time."

"You were missing for two weeks," I tell her, and she nods.

"Ginger and Winnie found me eventually," she says. "They told me you were nearby, that you'd gone into the refinery build-ing. They showed me the way." Her eyes meet mine.

Rufus looks from Odette to me, curious.

I swallow. "The corrupted mettle . . . ," I say. "It—it messes with your brain. Makes you think terrible things. I got all swept up in it, in losing Mam and my magic. I thought Odette was dead, and I kept thinking about the marigold. I thought I could bring her back if only I had the magic. And here was this pool of mettle—more than I thought could exist in the whole world."

Rufus's eyes are wide. "You tried to use the corrupted mettle?"

"I didn't need my witch-hands to do it. It was so strong I could just . . ."

Reluctantly, I show him my hands. The skin is angry and blistering.

"But I thought the pool was sealed. Isn't that what your nan did? The membrane? The third layer of her spell?"

"There are two rose canes wrapped around the pool," I explain. "One of the thorns punctured the membrane and is absorbing the corrupted mettle. That's what has turned Sicklehurst all strange."

"And you made the hole bigger," Odette adds.

"You *what*?" Rufus turns back to me.

"I didn't," I say. "I just . . ."

"You told the roses to do it," Odette says. "And they did."

"I didn't think they would. I have no magic."

I remember the shambling horror of Not-Odette, and I am flooded with shame once more.

"What does it mean?" Rufus asks. "If the hole in the membrane is bigger."

I swallow. "It means more of the corrupted mettle can get out. A lot more. Eventually, it'll find its way past the walls. If the auditors don't get to it first when they go looking for the knife."

Rufus is still staring at my hands. "Is this what killed your nan?" he asks.

Something unlatches inside me, and I start to cry. "She tried to drain it from me," I explain. "It was too much for her. She died for nothing."

The enormity of what I've done stretches before me.

310

Nan is dead. Mam is dead, and everything she sacrificed will be for naught. The auditors will find a way into Sicklehurst and take back the knife. The corrupted mettle will leak into the creek, poisoning Inglenook and its residents. And who knows what will happen to Winnie, Ginger, and Lyr once the auditors get their hands on them.

Everyone will suffer.

I stand up. "I have to go," I say numbly.

"Go where?" Odette asks.

I don't answer. I just turn and walk away from them both, toward home.

But they follow me, like lost sheep—Rufus right on my tail, Odette a few steps behind. She seems quiet. Subdued.

"Maude," Rufus says after a few minutes of walking in silence. "What are we going to do?"

"You should go home," I tell him.

"Are you serious? You're not going to do anything? About the spell? The knife? The corrupted mettle?"

"What could I possibly do?" I ask. "I have no magic. I'm no match for the auditors. They will take the knife, and it will be done."

"But your mam—"

"My mam was a terrorist who thought she could save the world. She was wrong."

"What about the mettle? The pool? What will happen to Inglenook if it leaches into the ground? Into the creek?"

Nothing good—I know that. I imagine the village growing as twisted and dark as the sticklegrass wood, full of monsters and dangers and carnivorous magical trees. I think of how the oily surface of the mettle pool whispered to me, pulled on my ugliest parts and soured my thoughts.

"And what happens if Ilium get their hands on it?" Rufus persists. "Or any of the big magic corporations. You said it was more mettle than you knew existed in the world. What might they do with such a supply of corrupted power? They're not going to use it to make more magical cleaning products, that's for certain."

"Shut up," I say to him. "Leave me alone. You don't have any magic. You don't understand any of this."

He recoils, stung. "I understand plenty," he says. "You're a coward. Willing to put lives in danger because you're embarrassed about what happened in there."

His words bite deep.

"You're right," I say. "I *am* a coward. Let Sicklehurst be someone else's problem."

"Whose, though?" he says. "Who can fix it?"

"I don't know. The auditors. Thaumaturgical engineers. They must teach them something in those schools."

Rufus snorts. "How to make self-shining shoes and dish towels that don't stain. You know as well as I do that they don't let the engineers near any real magic."

"Well, there must be someone."

Rufus stops walking, his face set. "If you won't do something about what happened, then I will."

I laugh coldly as I pass him. "What are you going to do?"

"I'll call the papers. I'll tell everyone."

"They won't remember," I say over my shoulder. "The forgetting spell is still in place."

Rufus lets out an infuriated growl as he runs to catch up with me. "How can you be so calm?"

"You're angry," I observe.

"Of course I'm angry!"

"Why?"

Rufus puts his hands to his head and curls his fists into his ginger hair, as if to tear it out. "I'm angry because you have mettle poisoning. You're going to *die*," he says, his voice high with anxiety. "You went in there and you shouldn't have, and now you're out here and you're *dying*, but you won't *do* anything about it."

"I'm sorry," I tell him.

"Don't be *sorry*," he says. "Sorry gets us nowhere."

"What do you want me to say?"

"I can't believe this. I thought you were different."

"Sorry to disappoint you," I tell him.

The sun has retreated behind a gray, overcast sky, and the birds have stopped singing in the hedges. The gentle dreaminess of the day is gone. My body aches, and my lungs rasp and scrape with each breath. When I trudge up the garden path to the front door, I pause and lean against it, breathing in Nan's roses.

Pink and white.

And red.

There is one red rose, in the center of the bush. As big as a dinner plate. I reach out a finger and touch it, and the rose seems to shudder a little. As if it recognizes me.

I look at my hands and notice that my fingernails are turning black, like I've slammed them in a door.

"Maude."

It's Odette. I hadn't realized she was still with us. She didn't speak the whole walk home, while Rufus and I were fighting. I turn to look at her, and my heart thuds dully.

A dark trickle of blood is seeping from her nose.

I refocus my eyes and look at Odette with my witchsight. It's faint, but her mettle has an oily tinge.

I take a shaking breath and square my shoulders grimly. "I'll put the kettle on."

19

THE KITCHEN IS EMPTY, MY NOTE ON THE TABLE UN-touched. Halmoni must still be sleeping.

The fire is out, the hearth cold. No kettle sings on the stove. There is no scent of biscuits or bread baking in the oven. The animals are nowhere to be seen. More than anything that has happened, the emptiness of the house fills me with dread. It's like a portent of what could come.

I light the stove and fill Nan's kettle. It feels wrong to do it without her. I take down the big ugly teapot with the cat face, and empty three spoons of tea leaves into the pot, then add a fourth, for luck. We're going to need it.

We sit at the kitchen table—Rufus, Odette, and I.

My hands are mottled with purplish bruises, which also spatter my wrists and forearms.

"We need a plan." Rufus has produced a notepad and pen from somewhere and appears to be writing a to-do list.

If I had the energy, I'd laugh at him.

He holds up the list. His handwriting is as tangled and

impenetrable as any enchanted forest, but I know it well enough
to decipher.

-Fix Maude.
-(And Odette, I guess.)
-Repair hole in magical membrane.
-Figure out how to deal with the auditors???

He and Odette both look at me. Thankfully, the kettle starts
to sing, and so I busy myself with filling the teapot and finding
cups and saucers for everyone.

When the tea is finally made and poured, they're still waiting
for me to say something.

"I have no idea what to do," I confess. "I'm not a witch anymore. This is . . . It's too much."

Odette narrows her eyes. "That doesn't sound like the Maude
I know," she says.

"Maybe you don't know me very well."

There's an uncomfortable pause.

"What about the knife?" Rufus says suddenly. "If the knife can
cut the mettle from someone, could it cut the corruption out too?"

I stare at him and think about the story that Mam told me,
over and over again.

I meet Odette's gaze over the table, and she nods. Aoife, cutting the coldness from King Badb's heart.

"We need to find Lyr," Odette says. "He's guarding the knife."

"Or he *is* the knife," Rufus says. "This magic business is
confusing."

I shrug. "I guess we'll find out when we get there."

Odette takes a sip of her tea and then makes a face.

"It doesn't taste right," she says.

The corruption in her is spreading.

"Okay," says Rufus, looking at his list. " *'Go back to Sicklehurst. Find Lyr and use the knife to cut out the corrupted mettle.'* Then what?"

"Then I fix the membrane over the mettle pool," I say. "Keep it sealed."

"How?" Odette says. "You can't do magic."

Odette is just stating the truth, but from her it stings.

"I don't know," I say. "Maybe Lyr can help me. Or Ginger. She helped me do magic before."

I notice a pinching in Odette's lips when I mention Ginger. It makes her look like her mother.

"How do we find Lyr?" Rufus asks.

"There's no *we*," I tell him. "I'm going alone. It's too dangerous for you."

Rufus waves a hand dismissively. "Ridiculous," he says. "We're all going. You said yourself that magic works better in threes."

Odette looks hesitant, but then she nods.

I feel an overwhelming sense of relief. I don't have to go back there alone.

"I thought I needed to rescue a princess in a dungeon," I say with a rueful smile. "But maybe all along it was a prince in a tower."

"They're the same thing," Rufus says with a sigh, because he can't help himself. "Towers and dungeons. The word 'donjon' means 'keep.' The main tower of a fortress."

I smile fondly at him, and the skin on my lips splits with a sharp sting.

"So when are we going?" he asks. "I need to pick up some supplies first."

"Better to get it over and done with," Odette says.

I nod. "Let's meet back here in an hour."

I PULL ON a loose cotton sundress with deep pockets, soft against my newly sensitive skin.

I place a four-leaf clover in my left shoe. I turn my socks inside out, and put the right sock and shoe on first. I take the black satin bag and add things to it, grabbing items from Nan's workbench at random—oakmoss, knucklebones, snakeskin, dried skullcap mushrooms, silver coins, horseshoe nails, and buttons, and little vials of graveyard dust, urine, red wine, and petitgrain oil. I take a spool of red thread from Halmoni's mending basket. I unlock Nan's secret drawer and hesitate for a moment, then slip the vial of pure mettle into the bag.

"You promised you wouldn't go back," Halmoni says, and I turn to see her on the stairs, blinking sleep from her eyes, pulling her robe tight around her shoulders.

"I have to," I say, shrugging. The movement causes the world to spin around me. I put a hand out to steady myself, and notice that my fingernails are now completely black, my skin shrinking away from them.

"You're not well," Halmoni says. "Wait a day or two to recover. You know it's bad luck to start a journey on a Friday."

She presses her fingers to her temples, and I want to curl myself into her arms and tuck my head under her chin.

I glance at Jeremiah, who is lying on the hearthrug, whale-eyed and panting. The fur behind his ears has fallen out, right where I scratched him two days ago.

I didn't think the corrupted mettle could be passed on so easily. But maybe I'm wrong.

Halmoni wrings her hands. "You could die."

Her words hang in the air. I don't need to reply. She knows the truth. I'll die if I don't go. I'll probably die either way. And she knows that I don't need her permission to go.

She kisses me on both cheeks, even though I tell her not to touch me. Then she goes out to her stained-glass studio, because we both know it's bad luck for her to see me leave.

I arrange bread and salt on the dining table. One plate, and three spoons, one each for me, Odette, and Rufus. So we'll all come back.

Rufus appears on the front doorstep, and I burst out laughing when I see him.

He's wearing jeans and a fisherman's vest over a plaid shirt. The pockets of the vest are bulging—with what I don't know. He's also wearing a large backpack, sensible-looking boots, and a peaked cap.

"What?" he asks, defensive.

"You look like you're going on a hike."

He scowls at me. "I'm a redhead," he says. "I don't know what you're supposed to wear on an adventure."

"What's in there?" I ask, eyeing the backpack.

He winks. "Supplies."

I look out the window to see if Odette is approaching.

"I bet she won't come," Rufus says.

Despite everything, I still believe in Odette. "She'll come."

I armor us while we wait, shaking a palmful of salt from the silver cellar in the pantry and putting it in our pockets. Then I duck behind the cherry tree to where the juniper skulks, clumping and spiky. I twist off two sprigs and shove one into my pocket and one into Rufus's, along with the salt. I slide the bone-pin brooch onto my dress, because Nan isn't there to do it for me. No rose, though. It doesn't feel right.

"It's been more than an hour," Rufus says. "We should go."

He's right. Odette isn't coming. I wish I wasn't disappointed.

We head down the garden path to the lane. There's a figure coming toward us, and my heart sings.

"Did you think I wasn't coming?" Odette says. "That's probably fair."

She's wearing the same jeans and T-shirt she was in before, and she's not carrying anything.

"I didn't go home," she explains. "I went to see the auditors. I told them I'd seen you."

Rufus stiffens beside me, and I know he thinks she betrayed us. But I can see a familiar glint in her eye.

"I told them that you found the knife," she goes on. "And that you had taken it to bury it in Deeping Fen, beyond Scouller. It should buy us some time."

She's proud of herself, and I'm proud of her too. A glimmer of the old Odette.

"Let's go," she says over her shoulder as she strides off down the lane.

20

THERE'S NO POINT IN WALKING THE DARK PATHS TO GET
to Sicklehurst, so instead we take the train two stops down the
line, then walk past the abandoned public housing and follow a
dusty, overgrown road littered with empty beer cans and bleak
dead saplings, silhouetted gray and gaunt against the sky.

Walking is painful. My feet are swelling up, pushing at the
restraints of my shoes. My hands throb, as if the blood in them
has grown thick and sluggish.

Odette tsks as we pass great drifts of rubbish. I see multiple
Ilium products, faded and filthy, the mettle in them all used up.
Those disposable dust bunnies that collect all the dust from your
house like a magnet. Odor- and leak-proof nappies for babies.
Discarded packaging for glamour patches, hair-curling papers,
and the chewing gum that helps you focus. Empty bottles of
clurichaun wine and woodruff mead.

"People can be so selfish," Odette says, looking around at it all.

"You'd know," mutters Rufus.

Odette turns to him. "Is there something you want to say?"

Rufus hesitates, but he shakes his head.

We walk on, then Odette stops and puts her hands on her hips. "I don't use any of this commercial rubbish," she says heatedly. "Disposable synthetic magic. It's disgusting. It's turned an ancient and sacred art into consumer trash."

Rufus nods slowly. "Right. And your indie-Goth glamours really honor that ancient and sacred art, right? I hear the benandanti witches were really into sparkly purple nail polish, back in the day."

We cross the creek, and in the distance, I hear splashing and the screaming of wild geese. My shoulders feel bruised and tender where the swan battered me.

The light has turned yellow and watery as gray clouds swoop in to swallow the morning sun. Thunder rumbles in the distance, which feels appropriately ominous.

Odette and Rufus are still bickering, but I'm finding it hard to focus on their words.

"You think that wearing black and hanging out in the drains makes you some kind of countercultural hero," Rufus is saying. "But you're just a spoiled brat, messing with stuff you don't understand. Dangerous stuff."

"At least I'm not part of the capitalist machine," Odette retorts, her voice dripping with scorn.

Rufus lets out a bark of laughter. "Yes, you are! You—"

"Stop," I say as the earth tilts beneath me. I reach out for Rufus, but he isn't where I think he is, and I stagger and fall to the ground, which continues to lurch, the sky wheeling overhead.

"You don't look so good," Rufus says, crouching beside me. "Maybe—"

I interrupt him with a stream of vomit. Odette stares at the stinking, steaming splatter on the ground, her face blank and gray.

I wipe my mouth with the back of my sleeve.

"Come on," I say, struggling to climb to my feet. "We'll gain nothing lounging around here."

Rufus grabs my hand and pulls me upright, and I pretend I don't see him flinch when his hand touches mine. I swallow down a surge of guilt along with more vomit, and we continue.

The road leads us to a gate, crisscrossed with heavy iron chains and padlocked thirteen times.

"How do we get in?" Rufus asks.

"It's this way," Odette says, and I can see how smug she feels to know something that Rufus doesn't.

Odette leads us along the fence until we reach the gymea lilies and the torn hole in the chain-link. We scramble through, and this third time it's easy, the barrier totally dissolved.

Rufus pulls my arm over his shoulders, helping me past the lumpen mounds crawling with sticklegrass. I can feel the warmth of his body against mine. He feels alive in a way I do not.

"Do you think Dr. Slater's right?" I ask him.

"Rarely," he replies. "About what in particular?"

"That magic is too dangerous to be allowed. That it needs to be regulated."

Rufus considers this. "Regulation is good," he says. "But what they did to the witches—it's not really regulation. It's prohibition dressed up as regulation. And prohibition never works. You can't ban who people *are*. We don't restrict people from being clever or strong or creative."

"But you do think magic is dangerous."

He lets out a bark of bleak laughter. "Evidently."

"What's the answer, then?" I ask.

"Science is dangerous too," he says. "There's tremendous potential to do harm. But we don't ban science. We have codes of ethics. Regulations that don't inhibit new discoveries. Dr. Slater is always banging on about how the industrialization of magic was its democratization—that now magic is for everyone. But that's not true. Magic belongs to Ilium and the other big magic companies. Slater says that no one should ever have as much power as the witches had, but Ilium has far, far more power than any single magic user. That kind of power is the real danger."

I shake my head. "How are you so sensible, Rufus?"

He shrugs. "I don't know any other way to be."

Odette makes a gagging noise.

We cross the onion-weed meadow and push through the holly thicket. Rufus recoils at the ground littered with the corpses of winged creatures.

"What happened to them?" Rufus asks. "Is this part of the triple spell?"

I see the flash of a vision, of thirteen witches in parkas and rain boots, working here in this field, laying bricks under the light of the hunter's moon.

"Yes," I say. "The witches had to stop any flying creatures from getting in and carrying the corrupted mettle out."

Odette's pace slows a little as we approach the wall of Sickle-hurst, and her fists clench.

"Are you okay?" I ask her.

She doesn't look at me, just stares fixedly at the wall. "I'm fine," she says, her jaw tight.

I don't bother with the wreath this time. Instead I press my palm to the wooden door.

"It's me," I tell it simply. "Let me in."

The door opens under my touch, as if it is expecting me.

Rufus narrows his eyes. "Are you sure you don't have any magic?" he asks.

"I didn't make the spell," I tell him. "But it knows me now."

Inside Sicklehurst, everything is different.

There are no buildings, no lake. No bamboo corridors or jacaranda groves. Just a dark, dense tangle of thorns, so thick that I cannot see a way through it.

Odette swears under her breath. "What happened?"

In fairy tales, the forest of thorns parts at the prince's touch. But in this story, the prince is locked in the tower. The forest gives me nothing but brambles and barbs and numberless shadows.

Rufus is staring straight ahead, his jaw slack.

"Is this a glamour?" I ask him. "All I see is thorns."

Rufus shakes his head. "Me too," he says. "It's no glamour."

Impossible. I was here only three days ago. Could the stickle-grass wood really have thrown up a forest of thorns so quickly?

I think about the pool of corrupted mettle, and the giant rose canes that now have free access to it.

"How do we find our way through?" Odette asks. "We could get lost in there. Go around in circles for days."

There's a hollowness to her voice. She's been lost in Sicklehurst before. For the first time I realize how brave Odette is being, coming back here. I'm proud of her.

"I can find the tower," says Rufus firmly, and I remember that his gift is finding things.

"Lead the way," I tell him.

WE PUSH IN, finding gaps to crawl under and step over, weaving ourselves into the thicket like a tapestry. It's exhausting work for my already exhausted body. I keep an eye out for a glint of Winnie's machete or a flash of Ginger's skirts. But there's nothing. No sign that there were ever girls trapped here.

The silence of it is oppressive. No scratching of insects. No birds. No breeze moving the spikes and spines. Just the crunch of dry twigs underfoot, the soft rise and fall of Rufus's and Odette's breath, and the rattle of my own.

"Wait," Odette says. "I need a minute."

She's starting to deteriorate. The corrupted mettle inside her is worsening in this horrible place. Her skin is gray. Her pupils are dilated. Her hands tremble. She sits with her head between her knees, and I wonder what I can possibly say that will make her feel better. Probably seeing me at all makes her feel worse—I am what she will become.

"I'm so sorry," I tell her. "This is all my fault."

Rufus makes an explosive noise and stares pointedly at Odette, waiting for her to lift her head and assure me that she bears at least some of the blame for our current predicament. But Odette doesn't move. I'm not even sure she heard me.

Rufus huffs and shuffles away from us, bending to examine

a fallen iron girder, almost totally obscured by the dark thorns. The iron is crumbling into gritty orange jelly.

"And I'm sorry for being obsessed with you," I say. "I didn't know . . . I guess I needed something to focus on, after Mam . . ."

"Stop apologizing, already," Rufus says from over by the girder. "She doesn't deserve it. Come and look at this instead."

With some considerable effort, I haul myself to my feet and join him.

"*Talaromyces flavus*," he says, pointing to the orange jelly. "It's a fungus that eats iron. I've never heard of it actually corroding it, though."

He's genuinely excited by it, and in that moment I am just incredibly grateful that he exists in the world.

"You're delightful," I tell him, and the tips of his ears turn pink.

Odette is still curled in on herself. She looks like a child.

"Do you remember going to Kit Kulkarni's birthday party when we were six?" Rufus asks me abruptly.

I shake my head, trying to dislodge a pounding, thudding noise coming from somewhere inside me.

"It was a typical kids' party," he says. "Pass the parcel. Musical statues. Robin runabout. After we sang the song and cut the cake, Kit's father handed out the party bags. They had those kiddie glamours in them. Do you remember?"

"The bubblehead ones that made you look like a cartoon character?"

Rufus shrugs. "I wouldn't know."

I remember Kit's party now, everyone giggling and bouncing around with our huge eyes and brightly colored hair. I remember the taste of fairy bread and elderflower cordial. I remember the bright ache of color as I looked at balloons bobbing in the sky.

And I remember Rufus, sitting inside and watching us out the window, his expression wistful.

"They all forgot about me," he says. "Except you. You pulled your patch off and came inside to sit with me. You told me you were sick of glamours. You asked me if I wanted to hear a story. I told you I did, and right there you spun the most incredible tale, about goblins and fairy rings and a mouse who set out to save his homeland, riding on the back of a loyal chicken. I couldn't believe you'd just created it from nothing, just out of your head. We sat there all afternoon as you spun the tale, and we ate honey joys and popcorn while everyone else danced outside."

"I wouldn't have taken you for a lover of fairy tales," I say. "You're so science-y."

There's a flash of silver braces as Rufus smiles. "That's why I love your stories so much. They show me a world that I can't imagine on my own."

From the corner of my eye, I notice that Odette's head is up and she's watching us quietly. But she doesn't say anything, just climbs to her feet.

My feet have swollen beyond recognition, my shoes cutting deep into the engorged flesh. I pull the shoes off and leave them in the thicket. Every step is like walking on knives, and I'm annoyed that I don't even get a handsome prince to help me—only Rufus, who looks like he might throw up when he sees my purple-gray toes, the nails peeling off, the skin stinking of rot.

But I'm beginning to think that perhaps a true friend is worth more than a thousand handsome princes.

My vision blurs, and the thudding in my ears grows louder, like someone is beating a drum inside my skull.

"You get this look when you tell a story," Rufus says. "Like the real world just falls away, and you're really *there*. The rest of the time you're just regular old Maude, but when you get that look, it's like you're lit from within, all radiant."

My lungs feel like a wet paper bag. I struggle to draw breath as blackness rises before me, and everything is the *thud thud thud* of the drum.

Dimly, I hear Odette groan and say, *Ugh, just kiss her already*.

Then there is nothing, and the nothing is so quiet and calm that I sink gratefully into it. I forget I have a body that is falling to pieces. I forget about my home and Halmoni, and Odette and Lyr, and Rufus, who is shaking me, holding me by the shoulders, saying my name again and again, forcing me back into my body, back into the thudding, disintegrating horror of it all.

"Maude!"

I open my eyes to see Rufus leaning over me, his face blanched white.

"What happened?" I ask.

He shakes his head.

"You had a seizure," Odette says from behind him. She's sitting down again, her knees drawn up to her chest. "It was . . . bad."

The hollow look in her eyes is back again, and I know that this place is waking up the monster inside her.

I haul myself upright into a sitting position. I feel a wetness on my face and put fingers up to it. White foam, presumably from my mouth. My eyes are leaking a kind of gray gunk.

"Are we doing the right thing, Maude?" Rufus says. "You

should be in a hospital. There must be treatments. Rehydration. Things that might help."

"We're here now," I say. "We're so close."

He looks torn. "I don't know if I can watch you literally fall to pieces in my arms."

"If we don't . . ." I glance at Odette.

The darkness reaches for me again, but a voice cuts through it from the other side of the clearing.

"Gosh, the whole gang's here."

It's Ginger.

I prop myself onto my elbows, and we take each other in.

She looks gaunt and haggard, dark circles under her eyes, her skin raked with scratches. But it's better than the last time I saw her, crumbling to compost as she crossed Sicklehurst's threshold.

I wonder how many times she's died since then.

"You look terrible," she says, frowning at me.

"It's good to see you too," I say. And it is. "Is Winnie here?"

Ginger nods, a sharp, tight movement. "It's been hard. Really hard. I can't . . ." She shakes her head. "It's not like it was before. The sticklegrass wood has turned. I mean, you can see . . ." She gestures around at the tangled thorns, her hand falling when it gets to Odette. "You again."

Odette scowls at her. "I'm not exactly thrilled to be seeing you either."

They both turn and look at me, with identical expressions of disdain on their faces. I wince. Then Ginger jerks her head at Rufus.

"Who is he?"

"A friend."

"Why is he here?" she asks.

"I'm here to help," Rufus says, and there's a hint of defiance in his tone.

She ignores him and turns to me. "Nice of you to lead us to our deaths the other day."

"I'm sorry," I say. "I didn't know for sure."

Ginger's eyes flick away from mine. "It was nothing, really," she says, with blustering detachment. "I popped back up in the mud a few hours later, like always."

She looks fragile, like a gust of wind would be enough to break her.

"I went home," I tell her. "I thought it was the right thing to do."

"It was," she says. "You shouldn't have come back. I wouldn't have."

"Did the Tatterdemalion come back?" I ask.

"Of course it did."

We stare at each other.

"We have to find Lyr," Rufus says. "Maude and Odette are sick. We think Lyr has something that can fix them. Maybe he can help you too."

"Uh-huh," says Ginger dubiously.

She and I both know that Lyr is no wizard, bestowing fantasy wishes at will.

She knows that I'm not here to save her.

She knows that she'll never get to walk out of the forest.

"I'm sorry," I tell her again. "I really am."

"Come on," she says. "I'll take you to Winnie."

She leads us through the tangled brambles, ducking and weaving and clambering. Rufus has to help me, waiting patiently for me to move my stubborn, aching limbs, guiding and supporting as Ginger charges ahead and then waits, making irritated little sighs of impatience. Odette follows behind, quiet and blank-faced.

I can't believe Ginger knows where she's going. Everything looks the same in here, close and sharp and gloomy, the dark branches twisted in over us, obscuring vision in all directions. But eventually we emerge in a sort of hollow in the brambles, like a bird's nest in a hedge.

Winnie is sprawling on the bare earth, her skin hatched with scratches, her expression leaden-eyed and bleak.

"Maude is back," Ginger says. "And her girlfriend. And . . . some other person who I don't think is important. It's a real party."

"Bloody hell," Winnie says, looking at me. "What happened to you?"

"Magic poisoning," I tell her. "It's no fun."

Rufus peers at Ginger and Winnie. "There's no sign of the corruption in them. I wonder if the forest can leach it away when they become reanimated. Fascinating." He turns to me. "Did you say that Ginger had compost inside her when she dissolved outside Sicklehurst, but under the carnivorous tree, she had human blood?"

"*Excuse me,*" says Ginger, haughty and queenlike. "How *dare* you discuss my insides."

Rufus's ears turn pink. "Sorry," he mumbles.

"Why did you come back?" Winnie asks.

"I have to find Lyr," I explain. "Odette is sick too. We think that Lyr has a knife that can help us."

Winnie narrows her eyes at Rufus. "What about you?"

"Apparently, he's here to help," Ginger says, sarcasm heavy in her voice.

Rufus glances over at me. "This is the one Odette used to pretend to be, right?" he says. "I can see the resemblance."

"Shut up, Rufus," Odette mutters.

I run a shaking hand through my hair, and a clump comes out, limp and colorless in my fingers.

"I need to get to the tower," I say.

Winnie lets out a short, sharp laugh. "No way."

Odette stands up. "Let's go," she says, her voice tight. "We don't need their help. Rufus can find the tower."

Rufus makes a face. "I think I can," he says. "But any extra information we can get from Winnie and Ginger would surely be—"

"Rufus, nobody *cares* what you think," Odette snaps. "Let's go already."

I can see it now—the rage monster that burns inside Odette. Her terrible gift. I was more afraid of it as a child than anything else. Even more than auditors. Afraid that one day she would turn her rage on me, and I would be obliterated.

"Odette," I say, trying to keep my voice light. "Rufus is right. If we can find out—"

"No," she says, and I can hear the thickness in her throat as the monster starts to claw its way out. "We go *now*."

"Bloody hell," Winnie says. "Calm down already."

Heat flushes Odette's pale face, and the tendons stand out on her neck. "Do *not* tell me to calm down," she growls.

A roar sounds in the distance, huge and bellowing and horrifyingly familiar. I glance at Ginger, but she's staring at Odette, a frown creasing her forehead.

"It's the Tatterdemalion," Winnie says. "It's in the tower. And . . . well, come and see."

Odette takes a shaking breath as Rufus slings my arm over his shoulders again, bracing himself against my weight. We stagger out of the hollow with Odette following close behind, and Winnie leads us through the tangle of thorns, along a barely discernible path, the wicked barbs tearing at us, shredding me even further.

Eventually, the gloom eases, and Odette hastens forward to break free of the choking closeness of the thicket.

Winnie puts out an arm to stop her. "Don't let them see you," she says.

"Who?" Odette asks.

Winnie nods her head to a gap in the wall of thorns, and we lean forward to see.

The thicket ends abruptly, the ground sloping away to a large open space below us, grassed and gray. The cooling tower is in the center of this space, wound tightly with two thick black rose canes, identical to the ones in the refinery chamber. The tower is only a few hundred yards away. If I could run, I would be there in seconds.

Except the tower is encircled by a field of roses.

Thousands of bushes, each about the height of a human and studded with red blooms. The scent of them is overwhelming, bloody and sickly-sweet, as a breeze ruffles leaves and petals gently.

"They can't be stopped," Winnie says, her voice low and bleak. "When you chop them down, they grow again behind you, penning you in. They squeeze and choke and slice and smother. Ask me how I know."

She picks up a rock, hefting it in one hand before lobbing it out into the open. It collides with one of the rosebushes, releasing a flurry of petals and a rich green scent. The bush *shudders,* and the movement ripples out to the other rosebushes until they are all quivering.

"They're guarding the tower," Winnie explains as she throws a second rock. Each bush springs to life, focusing attention on the rock, flowing fast and lithe, slashing with outstretched canes and thorns in a blur of violent destruction.

Odette lets out a low moan. "You'll never make it through that," she says.

"*We'll* never make it," Rufus corrects sternly.

Ginger snickers. "I think maybe I like this one."

Odette's lips narrow and whiten, and the Tatterdemalion roars again. I can tell now that its cries are coming from the base of the tower, which is wrapped tightly with rose canes, each as thick as my arm and wickedly spiked.

"I need to get in there," I say. "I need to find Lyr."

Ginger is watching Odette through narrowed eyes. "It must be hard for you," she says. "Looking at me and seeing everything you always wanted to be."

Odette's lip curls, but she doesn't look at Ginger, just stares fixedly at the ground.

"I guess I'm like the upgraded model," Ginger continues. "And you're just a rough draft."

"Ginger," I say. "Now isn't really the time—"

"Obviously, Maude felt that way," says Ginger, leaning forward conspiratorially. "When we made out under the scarlet lissom. It was . . . intense."

I clap my hands over my ears as the Tatterdemalion roars again, so loud this time that the ground shakes under my feet. The roses rustle and pulse in response.

"It's her," Ginger says to the rest of us, pointing at Odette. "She's making it angry."

Odette flashes a look of hatred at Ginger. "What are you *talking* about?" she snaps, and the creature bellows again.

Ginger is right. "Rage is your gift," I tell her. "Remember when we first came in here and I gave you a rose? You were so angry that day. At your mother. At everything. You crushed the rose, even though the thorns cut into your hand. And I—"

"And you made the crushed rose the heart of the Tatterdemalion," Odette finishes bleakly.

The Tatterdemalion is made of Odette's rage, and it's responding to the monster inside her.

"She might be able to control it," Winnie muses. "If you can get her in there."

"I don't want to put her in any more danger than I already have," I say, touching my fingers to the marks on my chest.

"Who cares?" Ginger says. "She's gonna die anyway, right? Better it be doing something useful for once."

"Use her," Rufus says, nodding. "Like she used you."

The thought of it makes me feel sick. I glance at Odette. Her eyes are black with rage.

The creature bellows again, and this time it doesn't stop. Its cries shake the forest of thorns around us and make my eyes water.

"Make it stop!" Winnie yells, her hands over her ears.

Odette turns to me, and I see the monster gazing balefully at me through her eyes.

"I can't stop it," she says, her voice strained. "I—I think I have to go to it. Face it."

I swallow and look out at the rose army. Just a single one of those bushes could tear a person's throat out. But it's the only way to Lyr.

Ginger squares her shoulders and looks briskly at Winnie. "Well, you know what they say about dying: it's like riding a bike. And we've had plenty of practice."

"I don't know how to ride a bike."

"But you *do* know how to die."

Winnie frowns, puzzled, then her eyes light up. "Does this mean we get to fight the roses?"

I want to hug them both. "Thank you."

Winnie hefts her machete. "Let's go, then."

"Don't be ridiculous," Ginger says. "We need at least some semblance of a plan."

Everyone looks at me.

They don't know that I'm making it up as I go along. They don't know that blackness swims before my vision, that it is taking so much effort just to stay upright.

"We defeated the scarlet lissom," says Winnie. "Let's just do that again."

"We can't." Ginger turns the pouch at her waist inside out. "The lake has gone. It's where I collected the salt."

"Ah!" Rufus exclaims, shrugging his backpack from his shoulders. He undoes the zipper and rummages inside, withdrawing a plastic bag of fine pink flakes.

"It's the fancy stuff my dad uses on his avocado toast," he says. "It costs a fortune, and he is definitely going to kill me when he notices it's missing."

He tosses the bag to Ginger, who dips a finger inside and touches it to her tongue. "It's good," she nods, and pours the salt into her pouch.

Winnie gazes speculatively at Rufus.

"What else have you got in that magic bag?" she asks.

"Oh, there's no magic in here," Rufus says with a grin. It's good to see him smile.

He pulls out a pair of thick pink rubber gloves and two unmarked spray bottles.

"Glyphosate," he says, raising one, then the other. "And pelargonic acid. Both powerful herbicides."

He hands one glove and one bottle each to Ginger and Winnie.

"What about you?" she asks him. "You don't have a weapon."

"I have this." He points to his wild ginger curls.

Winnie snorts. "I guess redheads are good for something after all."

"What about me?" Odette asks, her voice small. "Do *I* get anything to protect myself with?"

"Sure," Rufus says tartly. "What did you bring?"

The howling of the Tatterdemalion intensifies, and Odette's cheeks flush.

"Chill out, princess," Ginger says. "You can have my spray. I have . . . something else that might be useful."

She passes the bottle and glove to Odette but doesn't let go of them straight away.

"Thanks," Odette says, tugging at the bottle.

"Don't think that this means I like you," Ginger warns. Then she lets go.

I open my mouth to try and mollify Odette but am silenced by a preemptive scowl from Rufus.

Ginger disappears into the thicket for a moment, then re-emerges, hand in hand with a staggering figure that once looked a little bit like me but now looks like sagging mud and twigs. It still has the scrap from Odette's dress wrapped around its neck.

"What *is* that?" Rufus asks.

"It's your girlfriend," Ginger replies, and then glances at Odette. "Or is it *her* girlfriend? There's a lot going on here."

The blue pimpernel flowers have shriveled, making the poppet look like it's squinting. The red lipstick slash of its mouth is lopsided and sneering. The whole effect is deeply unsettling.

"How did you animate it?" I ask. "Without Lyr."

"I soaked it overnight in the pool where we get mudborn," Ginger says. "And filled its chest cavity with sticklegrass. It can't really move independently without falling over, but it will follow if you hold its hand."

"What exactly are you planning to do with it?" Winnie asks, looking at the poppet with distaste.

Ginger shrugs. "A diversion."

* * *

WE STAND ON THE EDGE of the thicket. Winnie looks ridiculous in her tattered frilly dress, spray bottle clutched in one pink-gloved hand, machete gripped in the other.

Ginger glances over at me. "You won't make it," she says, bluntly. "You can barely stand, let alone run."

"I'll carry her," Rufus says simply, like it's an obvious solution to our problem. "Odette will cover us."

When did Rufus turn into such a badass?

He crouches down, and I clamber awkwardly onto his back, feeling like an oversized kid.

"You okay?" he asks.

I don't respond, because there is no good answer to that question.

Rufus looks at Odette. "And you?"

She nods, white-lipped and pale.

"It's a bit exciting, isn't it?" Winnie says. "I mean, even though we're all going to die. The squad is back together!"

Ginger and Odette both roll their eyes, then scowl at each other.

"Okay," says Winnie. "Let's do this."

Ginger walks the poppet around the edge of the rose field until she's a reasonable distance from us. Then she gives it a shove, stepping back.

The poppet staggers drunkenly forward, right into the thick of the roses, waving its arms in the air and shedding clumps of mud as it goes.

The rose army turns as one and converges on it in wild fury.

Chunks of it go flying in all directions, and I glimpse one staring pimpernel eye before it is crushed by a green whip.

Winnie charges forward into the gap created by the poppet. Some of the rosebushes notice her and wheel around. Winnie slashes and sprays at them, and they shrink back from her.

"Go!" Ginger yells, dashing in alongside Winnie and hurling fistfuls of salt. "We'll hold them off."

Rufus begins to gallop toward the tower, with me clinging helplessly to his back. Odette rushes after us, pumping away at her spray bottle.

The cooling tower rises before us, impossibly tall and choked with monstrous rose canes. The top is obscured by low-hanging black clouds. I remember it from Ginger's apartment window, far off and glinting with witchlight. I should have known then that it's where I'd find all the answers.

I glance over my shoulder and see Winnie slashing fiercely at the roses with her machete. Ginger reaches into her salt pouch, but it's empty. With a howl, she attacks a rose creature with her bare hands. Thorned canes wrap around her legs, winding their way up her torso. They reach hungry tendrils into her mouth, her ears, her nostrils. She struggles against it, her body convulsing, but they hold her fast. Her eyes lock onto mine, urgent and firm.

Behind me, Odette stumbles, her chest heaving with rapid, panicked gasps.

"Get up!" I call to her.

Rufus keeps going. We're shielded by his red hair—so far, the roses haven't noticed us.

"Stop!" I yell to Rufus. "We need to go back for her."

"Are you sure?" he says, between gritted teeth.

"I'm sure."

He wheels around and runs to where Odette is cowering, her hands over her head. I slide off Rufus's back and pull Odette to her feet. She cries out as she tries to put her weight on her left ankle.

"I c-can't," she stammers.

"You have to," I tell her firmly.

There's nothing but fear in her eyes. But as I speak, something about her face hardens, and I see the rage monster flicker to life. Her lips thin to a narrow line, and she looks just like her mother. She gives a short, sharp nod, and the three of us hobble, clutching each other, toward the tower.

It isn't far now.

But we've alerted the rose army to our presence, and the writhing wave rises and descends toward us, rushing and whipping and reaching with hungry tentacles.

"Maude!" Rufus yells as a rose cane nearly takes off his ear.

The vegetative sound of battle fills the air—whips and cracks and crunches. Rose petals and leaves rain down around us, turning the world red and green.

"I can't do it, Maude," Odette gasps, her voice strained. "I don't want this. Any of it. I want to go home."

"I know," I tell her. "Me too. But we're nearly there."

It's only a few steps to the tower. Odette slumps to the ground again, and I reach into the black satin bag and pull out horseshoe nails and silver coins, scattering them in a semicircle in front of us.

The roses slow, unwilling to cross the barrier of silver and iron.

"That should hold them for a moment," I yell to Rufus over

342

the bellowing roar of the Tatterdemalion, which is so close now that I'm afraid my ears are bleeding.

I turn to face the tower. I can barely make out the smooth concrete behind the thick tangle of rose canes. At least these ones don't seem to be mobile. Still, we have to get through.

I touch the bone-pin brooch on my dress. The musky scent of the roses is rich and ruthless, stinking of blood and powdery grave dust. But it also carries with it the aroma of Nan's garden, the memories of a thousand roses pinned by Nan's gnarled fingers. *For safety, for luck.*

Nan made these roses, as part of her triple spell. And I can feel Mam here as well, crouching beside me in the dirt, whispering in my ear.

Three layers sealing Sicklehurst.

Three witches, linked by blood.

"Maude?" Rufus's voice is wobbly. "Hurry. Please."

I reach out to one of the rose canes, and wrap my hand around it, squeezing tight. The thorns bite into my palm, but I squeeze harder, until blood drips from my hand and runs down my wrist, down the canes, into the soil.

"This is Niamh's blood," I tell the roses. "It is Carys's blood. It is my blood. You know me, and you must stand aside."

And meekly, miraculously, the roses do. The canes shrink away on either side of me, shriveling back and climbing up to form a thickly leafed tunnel leading to a small, unpretentious door, caked orange with slimy rust.

I press forward, with Rufus and Odette at my back, leaning heavily on each other.

Behind us, the rose army grows still again. I don't want to think about what that means for Ginger and Winnie.

At the end of the path, I discover that the door is locked.

Rufus reaches out to rattle at the rusted iron door handle, and it disintegrates to orange sludge in his hands.

"What now?" he asks.

I think about spongy iron girders dissolving into jelly. "We have to break it down."

Rufus nods and aims a kick at the door. It doesn't budge. He tries again and again, but with no success. He backs up and starts hurling his body at the door, grunting with effort every time he does it.

It isn't enough.

I take a few steps backward and grab his hand. Together, we run at the door.

As I make contact with it, the papery skin on my shoulder splits open like a bag of wet cement, and red and purple and black splatter against the rust of the door in a rainbow of pain. I can feel air on my muscles, on my bones, and I let out an involuntary grunt of agony.

Odette lets out a noise that sounds a bit like retching.

I don't want her to look at me when I'm like this. "I'm sorry," I tell her.

"No, you're not," Rufus growls.

I need a spell of some kind. Opening magic. I try and remember what Mam taught me. Charcoal. Raspberry leaf. Breath on a cold mirror, straight from the fridge.

None of it will work anyway, because I don't have any magic.

"Maude." Odette is staring back out at the rose army. A thin cane snakes past my iron and silver barrier, followed by another, and another. The roses move on shaggy, earth-crusted roots, terrifyingly nimble.

"We have to get in there *now*," Rufus says, his voice panting, urgent.

I put my hands to the door.

"Open," I command it.

Nothing happens.

My own dark blood is now on the door along with the slimy rust. I rake my fingernails through it, swirling the rust and blood together into a dark, viscous muck.

I use my nails to gouge out my family's witchmark on the door, four loops to form a flower.

"Open," I command again, placing my palm against the door.

A single rose cane winds around my ankle.

"Maude!" Odette cries.

She pulls thorns from her shoulders. A spiked cane is winding around Rufus's neck. Even his red hair can't protect him forever.

A lashing rage rises within me. Magic has taken everything I love.

"You will not take them," I scream at the roses.

I feel silvery filaments inside me, weak and dull. I sense the throbbing of magic beneath my feet, the power of the sticklegrass wood, the ancient magic buried deep in the earth. Near the surface, the mettle is awake and foul with corruption, swelling and growing and becoming murky, engorged, drunk, and vicious. But the forest goes deep. Very deep. I feel the threads of it like spider silk, but I cannot grasp them.

I close my eyes and see Odette and me trudging home after a

long summer day of playing, bedecked in mud whorls and feathers and daisy crowns. Odette's dress is torn, mine soaked through from an impromptu adventure in the creek.

Dr. Slater is there, his face drawn and pinched in disapproval. "You girls should be ashamed of yourselves," he says. "Carrying on like a pair of wild things."

I felt the sting of it. The shame. Yet Odette just laughed at him.

Be a wild thing once more, the ancient forest whispers to me now.

But I can't be that wild girl again. Not without my magic.

The real Odette stares at me, her face a mask of misery and fear. She's not a wild girl either. Not anymore.

But I'm not giving up yet.

I push my hand into the door, driving it in until it is buried to my wrist in gritty, jellied rust. Rufus and Odette stand on either side of me, their hands on the door too, pushing.

"By the horn moon," I tell the door. "By the tides. By raven's feather and juniper berry. By the blood in my veins and the candle snails on my windowsill. By Nan's teapot and Halmoni's sourdough. *You. Will. Open.*"

The door swings so suddenly that we fall inside—just as the tide of rose warriors surges toward us. Rufus slams the door shut, pressing his back against the rusted thing. There are still rose canes clinging to him, though severed and wriggling feebly, and he rips them from his face, his body, then claps his hands to his ears to muffle the noise of the Tatterdemalion.

It stands in the center of the tower, filling the space with its hulking shape, its breath steaming in the frosty air. Its wooden antlers quiver in anticipation, the bushes on its back trembling.

It doesn't try to attack us. It doesn't move. It just bellows, so loud that I can't think of anything else, can't move, can barely breathe.

The inside of the tower looks less like a concrete cylinder and more like the kind of fairy-tale tower that has a princess at the top of it. It's made of bluestone blocks, worn smooth with time and coated with black fungus. Carved stone steps spiral up and up until they disappear in darkness.

I glance at Odette, and she is staring at the Tatterdemalion, horror on her face, her fists clenched by her sides, her whole body shaking uncontrollably.

"You have to calm down," I tell her. "You're the only one who can make it stop."

She shakes her head.

"You can do it, Odette," Rufus yells, and he almost means it.

"I can't," she says, and I can barely hear her above the howling of the Tatterdemalion. "Because everything about me is shit," she finishes.

"It doesn't have to be," Rufus yells. "Change, if you want to."

"How can I?" she asks. "I hate everything. I hate myself. I don't care about anything or anyone. Even my gift is shit. It isn't fair that Maude gets stories, and you get finding things, and even my mother gets being an intimidating bitch. But I get rage? That's not a gift. It's a curse."

The Tatterdemalion's cries shake the tower around us, and rubble rains from above.

It's going to bring the whole tower down if Odette doesn't do something soon.

Veins stand out on Odette's neck, and her hair is wild around her face. "I can't stop it," she cries. "It's who I am."

"Then *use* it," I say. "Rage doesn't have to destroy. It can create things too. Great things. Rage can be a fire that inspires. That motivates."

Odette turns pleading eyes on me. "Tell me a story," she whispers.

So I do. I wrap my arms around her and press my flaking lips to her ear. I whisper a story—Genevieve and Eilwen reunited at last. Battling the Tatterdemalion together. Genevieve carries a powerful magic inside her, a magic so strong it could tear the world apart if she doesn't learn to control it. But with the help of her best friend, she does learn. She wields the magic and saves everyone. She's a hero.

Odette takes a deep, shuddering breath, and the Tatterdemalion stops bellowing.

My ears are ringing, and my body is still vibrating from the creature's awful cries. Its twig-and-root muscles clench, and the holly bushes that sprout from its back quiver, red berries trembling.

Odette takes a step forward, out of my embrace, toward the monster. I can smell it, hot and moist, the dirty-dark truffly richness of a compost heap. Little slimy creatures burrow and squirm in its mouth. Odette reaches out a shaking hand and touches a green tusk.

The Tatterdemalion's body is bound together by strips of bark and knotted grasses. Odette takes a corner of the bark and starts to pull. It comes away easily in her hand, a long, filthy strip. The Tatterdemalion shivers, and newly exposed grubs wriggle away from the light and air, retreating into the warm safety of mud.

Odette lets the bark drop to the floor and tugs at a whip of grass from the creature's body, the knots unraveling at her touch. She grabs another, then another, speeding up as she goes, until she is wrenching at it, taking great handfuls of stinking bark and muck and hurling them at the ground.

Her breath comes in great, gasping sobs as she works. Her hair falls into her eyes, and she brushes it aside impatiently, leaving a brown-green smear across her skin.

Still, the creature doesn't move, save for the occasional trembling shudder and the rise and fall of its breath.

Odette yanks at the holly bushes, which come out by their roots, showering dirt everywhere.

The Tatterdemalion is smaller now. Odette's sobs deepen as she scrabbles at it, pulling and peeling until she's howling at it. I glimpse something smooth and pale underneath. Something impossible.

By twig and leaf and branch, Odette dismantles the Tatterdemalion until all that is left is a pile of broken sticks and mud, and a naked human figure, shivering before her in the cold.

Odette scrapes mud from the figure's yellowish skin, from its stringy white hair. She uses the hem of her T-shirt to wipe its face, revealing green lips and clouded eyes.

Odette stares at it, and it's like she is staring into a mirror.

Not-Odette has made some improvements. The line of fungi still sprouts along her spine, and her fingers are still webbed. But she's not a grotesque, shambling monster anymore. She looks exactly like Odette, just slightly more . . . vegetative.

"What's going *on*?" Odette whispers to it.

Not-Odette doesn't answer her. Instead, she shuffles toward me, opening her mouth and letting out a noise like the creaking of swaying branches.

I swallow. I don't want this now. Not here. The shame I felt in the refinery chamber rises in me once more. I was selfish. I was stupid. If I hadn't made Not-Odette, then Nan would still be alive.

"Maude?" Not-Odette's voice is the whisper of weeping willow catkins brushing against cotton grass. "Is it really you?"

She reaches for me with shaking hands.

I touch a hand to her cheek, my bloated, blackened fingers smearing filth onto her mud-streaked skin.

"I knew you'd come for me," she says. "I knew it in my bones."

I feel nothing but pity for this creature I made. I wish I'd never done it. I wish she had died down there in the refinery chamber.

Not-Odette lets out a little cry. "I'm so sorry, for everything. Everything I put you through."

She enfolds me in an embrace, her skin clammy and fish-cold. She smells like roses and pond scum. I'm painfully aware of Rufus and Odette watching me. Watching my fantasy come to life.

"Do you ever miss being a kid, Maude?" Not-Odette asks.

"Um," I say, unsure of how to respond. "Sure."

"Me too. I miss how easy everything was. You and I would spend all summer roaming wild. The creek, the willow. We'd play and play, fierce and free. I was so happy then. Without a care in the world."

The smile on her face is serene. I think about Odette's mother and their sterile, elegant house, and I hear Rufus's voice in my head.

Odette was never happy.

I can't bear to look at the real Odette. At Rufus. I feel completely frozen with humiliation. How do I stop Not-Odette's talking? How do I make her go away?

"We could have that again," she says. "We could stay here. Just us. Summer forever. Just playing and being free."

"That sounds nice," I say gently, not wanting to hurt her feelings. "But I'm afraid I have things I need to do. I need to save my friends."

Not-Odette laughs, a tinkling crystal chime. "Oh, Maude. Never mind them. It can be just like it was when we were little. We can fly on the backs of sparrows through the forest, defeating evil wizards by the dozen. Every story gets a happy ending. As many handsome princes and dragons as we could wish for. Just you and me, Maude. Fierce and free."

"I just can't," I tell her. "I'm . . . I'm sick. I need to get to the top of the tower or else I'll die."

Not-Odette takes my blackened hands and raises them to her lips. "I can save you," she whispers. "You know I'm made of magic, right? We can make you a new body in the mud pool, just like the other girls."

I swallow. "But then I'd have to stay in here forever."

"Would that be so bad?"

I pull my hands away and take a step backward.

Not-Odette's eyes narrow, and she bares her teeth at me. I glimpse oil-slick mettle in her mouth.

"I'm really sorry," I tell her. "But I have to help my friends."

Not-Odette lets out a growl of frustration, deep in her throat. "Make a Rufus in here, make a Halmoni. Make *Nan*. Why can't you give yourself this? Be *selfish* for once. Take what you want, and stop being so *good* all the time."

"I can't," I tell her.

Not-Odette's expression falters. Then she rushes forward and crushes her lips to mine, pressing her naked body up against me.

"This is what you want, isn't it?" she murmurs into my mouth. "You can have all of me. Every inch. I'll make you see stars."

I close my eyes, almost hoping that I drop dead this very moment. How can I ever look Rufus or Odette in the eye again? Perhaps I should just give in to Not-Odette after all. The grassy, rose-scented closeness of her makes me giddy, and I think that maybe this is what I *do* want. Maybe this is what I always wanted. The idea of Odette—beautiful, perfect Odette, dancing luminous in the spotlight—wanting *me*. Devoting herself to *my* pleasure. I could *own* her. Command her. She would worship me.

Not-Odette doesn't care about how broken I am, about my purple, swollen skin, my slimy black insides. She kisses a trail down my neck.

I disentangle myself, my heart pounding.

She stamps her foot. "What *do* you want, then?" she asks. "Name it, and it will be yours!"

I remember the longing and despair I felt when I made her. I just wanted her to love me. To be as devoted to me as I was to her. Not-Odette will give me anything, but there's nothing I want from her anymore.

"No," I tell her, and my voice sounds firmer than I feel.

A red fleck appears at the corner of her mouth.

She reaches for me again, her movement as lithe as a sapling bending in the breeze. "Please," she whispers, and rose petals slip from her lips. "Stay with me."

I put my hand to her cheek. "No," I tell her a second time.

"Love me," she begs, her voice the cracking of dry twigs. More petals flutter from her mouth.

"No," I say, for the third and final time.

Rose petals explode from within her, pouring out of her mouth, her eyes, her nostrils. They stream from her like a torrent, splitting her skin open like a burlap sack. Her cheek collapses under my hand, and the air is thick with lusty rose, intermingled with the scent of ancient trees and moss-crusted stone.

And then she's gone—nothing left but rose petals fluttering to the flagstones underfoot.

I'm not sure I can face Odette and Rufus. The shame bleaches me bright and exposes all my vulnerabilities. Not-Odette was my fantasy. All my pining, my suppressed desire, my *longing* to own Odette, to make her want me.

And now they know.

I hear Odette's breath hitch in pain, and that's enough for me to turn my head. She's slumped on the bottom step of the spiraling stone staircase, her hands wrapped around her injured ankle.

She says nothing. I feel as naked under her gaze as Not-Odette had been.

"I'm sorry," I whisper.

She doesn't reply, just shifts her attention to the floor. The rage monster in her is exhausted, and all I see is the coldness of her mother.

"Look at this," Rufus says, his voice falsely bright.

He's bent over and peering at the black fungus that coats the walls of the cooling tower.

"I've never seen anything like it before. It looks like *Exophiala dermatitidis,* but look at these sporangia."

Thank goodness for Rufus and his ability to always find something to talk about, even in the most awkward of moments. I join him and examine the fungus. It's black and velvety, almost like a kind of moss. Erupting from it are tiny little sprouts, silvery and glistening, each with a black cap.

I touch one of the sprouts gently with a finger. "They look more like *Pilobolus crystallinus,*" I observe.

Rufus looks at me thoughtfully. "Can a person have two gifts?" he asks.

"I don't think so," I say. "Why?"

"You're just very good with plant names. Too good, maybe."

His assessing gaze makes me feel vulnerable again, and I turn back to the fungus. "Actually," I say. "It could be *Cladosporium sphaerospermum.*"

"Fascinating," mutters Odette, her voice heavy with sarcasm.

"You're right!" Rufus says, ignoring Odette. He starts to pace around the room, excitedly, with his great giraffe lope. "*Cladosporium sphaerospermum.* Of course!"

"What am I missing?" I ask.

Rufus rocks on his heels. "An investigatory team of scientists found *Cladosporium sphaerospermum* on the inside of the refinery at Glidź. There's a theory that the fungus is feeding on the contaminated mettle and converting it into melanin."

"Wait, what?" Odette says, looking up.

Rufus still doesn't respond to her. "I read a study about how the genomic DNA of flatland pines became considerably hypermethylated after the disaster at Glidź," he tells me, like we're eating lunch together outside the biology lab at school. "Plants are just much better at adapting to their circumstances than animals are, because plants can't just get up and move if conditions become unfavorable." He hesitates and glances at the door. "Not usually anyway. The thing about plants is, almost every cell in a plant has the capacity to make new cells of any other type—which is why you can grow new roots from a stem or a leaf cutting. Animal cells can't do that. You can't grow a new brain from a bit of liver or bone."

"Right," I murmur. I tilt my head to look up the hollow core of the tower. I can't see the top.

"So after Glidź, these pine trees changed their DNA. They learned to isolate the corrupted mettle, trapping it in their roots—literally eating the poison. And they actually started growing *faster*."

"The black fuzz can eat the corrupted magic?" Odette says.

Rufus nods.

"Why aren't we more excited about this?" Odette asks. "Isn't this how we save the day? Purify the corrupted mettle in the pool?"

Hope sparks in my chest, but Rufus shakes his head.

"I'm afraid not," he says. "There's just too much mettle there. The whole sticklegrass wood couldn't do it. You would need a thousand such forests."

Odette scowls at him. "Thanks for getting our hopes up."

Rufus's eyes are bright—he's bursting with knowledge and theory and excitement, lit up like a candle. He looks so hungry. He wants to know everything, to unlock every secret, to learn all there is to learn. He leans forward until he's only inches away from the fungus. One of the tiny silver sprouts shudders and explodes, launching into the air and spraying an almost invisible silver dust.

"Amazing," breathes Rufus. "I'm taking a sample."

He digs into one of his fisherman's vest pockets and pulls out a little plastic vial.

Odette snorts. "You're a walking science lab."

"Always good to be prepared," he answers.

We all fall silent. Odette looks again at the endless spiral of stairs.

"What now?" she asks.

"Now I climb the stairs," I say.

"And then?"

It's a fair question, and one I've been avoiding. "I don't know," I admit. "I have no idea what's up there. I know that somehow with my storytelling I mixed up Lyr and the knife. I'm not sure how I can separate them again."

"You have to kill him," Odette says.

Rufus and I look at her.

"That's how it would work in a story," she says simply.

She's right. I have to sacrifice the handsome prince in order to save the princess. It's elegant. Symmetrical. The way stories should be.

"This isn't a story," Rufus insists.

But it is, because I created this nightmare land, and my brain runs on stories.

"Besides, then what?" Rufus asks. "What happens to the knife?"

I feel uneasy. There are too many loose ends. The story threads aren't coming together the way they should.

Rufus is watching me carefully. "Is this story going to have a happy ending?"

I swallow, and even though I don't say anything, Rufus reads the truth on my face. I don't think I'll be leaving Sicklehurst alive. I'm too far gone, even for a magical swan knife to fix.

"Isn't there another way?" he asks. "You're a storyteller. How do we get a happy ending?"

"Rufus, you're a scientist," I say. "You know that there's no such thing as happy endings."

He looks puzzled. "Why do you think the two are mutually exclusive?"

"Happy endings come from a world of fairy tales and make-believe," I tell him. "You believe in rules."

"Stories have rules too," he replies. "One of the rules is that if the hero completes their quest, they get a happy ending."

I sigh. "Some stories have tragic endings."

"I just can't help thinking that there must be another way. If this were a story, there would be."

I take a breath. It's a long way up.

"You have to stay here," I tell Rufus and Odette.

Rufus snorts. "No."

"Odette can't walk on that ankle. You need to protect her."

"You can *barely* walk," he says. "How will you climb all those stairs?"

I shrug. "One foot in front of the other," I say. "That's how it goes, isn't it?"

"I'm coming with you."

"Rufus, please. Stay with Odette. Look after her for me."

"I don't need looking after," Odette protests.

"I'm not here for you," Rufus tells her. "I'm here for Maude. And I'm going with her."

As he says it, I notice the hollows under his eyes that weren't there before, his fingernails turning black. So I don't argue.

I turn to Odette. She looks small and scared, one hand wrapped around her ankle, her face pale.

"Good luck," she says.

"I'll come straight back with the knife," I tell her. "It'll be the first thing I do."

She nods, and I can see a trembling in her chin as she tries not to cry.

"Nothing you want to add, Odette?" Rufus says pointedly. "You don't want to maybe thank Maude for sacrificing her life for you?"

"Shut up, Rufus," I tell him, remembering the humiliation of Not-Odette. "Let's go."

But I hesitate, just in case she says something. I don't know what I want. An apology? An acknowledgment of her part in all this? An explanation of why she dumped me and never looked back?

She turns her head away from us and picks at the stones embedded in the mossy ground.

21

WE CLIMB SLOWLY. MY BODY RESISTS THE MOVE-
ment. My muscles scream. The stone staircase winds around the inside of the cooling tower, the treads smooth gray against the walls, which are thickly furred with the black fungus that Rufus is still fascinated by.

It takes only a dozen steps before looking down makes my stomach lurch.

Why did it have to be a tower?

I pause, my hand against the wall as I wait for my head to stop spinning. The fungus feels like velvet beneath my fingers.

"Are you okay?" Rufus asks.

"Great," I reply. "I'm having a wonderful time."

"Good to hear."

I keep climbing. The wind whistles, carrying with it snatches of something. A voice.

Find me.

I redouble my efforts, marching up the steps as thunder rolls outside and rain begins to trickle down the walls of the tower. My thighs burn as I climb step after step after step.

"Still okay?" Rufus asks.

"Yep," I say, and I can hear the strain in my voice.

"Don't want to take a break?"

"Nope."

The storm begins in earnest, the thunder clapping overhead. Rain pours in through the hole at the top of the cooling tower, making every step slippery and treacherous. I press my hand against the wall so hard that the tips of my purple fingers start to weep black blood and yellowish pus.

Rufus starts to sing, his voice hearty with false cheer.

"Down in the Lye where the kittiwakes fly
Where sparrows will sing you a song for a penny
There lives pretty Sally, the pride of the valley
Her cockles and mussels are better than any."

We keep climbing. Mist and rain fill the tower with a gray haze. I can't see the bottom anymore.

The stones have become so slick that suddenly my feet go out from under me. I windmill my arms, reaching blindly for some kind of purchase so I don't go toppling over the side of the staircase and tumble to my death.

Rufus grabs me and holds me until I'm steady again. Then he returns to singing.

"Better, butter, oh!
Better, butter, oh!
Singing cockles and mussels
Better, butter, oh!"

I vomit, stringy bile and chunks of something dark and purplish. I lean my back against the wall and sink into the spongy
black fungus, then slide slowly to the floor. Around me, the tiny
silvery sprouts clench and burst, releasing their glittering spores
into the air.

And it isn't Rufus singing anymore. It's my mother, stroking
my forehead as I sweat through a fever dream.

Mam, reading me the story of the swan prince at night, her
voice low and melodious.

Mam, frowning, hunched over the radio, listening to the latest news bulletin, her dark eyes glinting.

Mam, arguing with Nan and Halmoni. *They will wipe us out,*
she says. *Cut out our strings until the only magic left in this world is under
their control.*

Think of Maude, Nan hisses. *What will happen to her if you get
caught?*

Mam sighs. *She'll always have you two.*

"She's bonny, she's fair, with robin-red hair
She wrestles with fishes and eels."

Mam, sneaking me down to the creek to spin stories and teach
me deep lore secrets, away from the ears of those who might turn
us in to the auditors. She was the one who showed me the secrets
of Peg Powler, about how if I concentrated I could hear the tit-
ters of fairies in her rustling branches. She showed me how to
weave catkins to make thunder charms, and how to soak the willow's pliable green branches in running water for more powerful
wickerwork. She taught me the names of plants and was always

delighted when I could remember every single one. She told me about hexes and curses and blood magic. She told me about my father, who had died in the Battle of Goose Spring, desperately fighting to preserve the rights of mettleworkers and witches, when I was still a tiny thing swimming in her belly.

I did everything she asked, because there was nothing in the world greater than Mam's smile of approval. The warmth of her embrace when I demonstrated my skills.

Mam. Her hair stringy and her teeth blackened under a bread moon. Staring at me, her expression awed and hungry. Her lips moving to form an unfamiliar word.

Greenwitch.

Mam, reaching inside me and breaking one of my strings.

"She can beat a man down from his feet to his crown
Before kicking him right where he feels."

I shake the memory from my mind, crawling on hands and knees away from the wall until I can haul myself upright.

The ground spins beneath me, and I hear a sound descend from above, through the roar of pounding rain. It could be the mournful cry of a swan.

That's when I notice that Rufus isn't singing anymore.

"Rufus?" I say, looking around.

I can't see him.

I hear nothing but the dripping of rain, and a muffled, leafy rustling from far below.

Did he fall?

Steadfast Rufus, who gave his friendship and asked nothing

in return. I think of him lying broken at the bottom of the tower, the door bursting open, the roses crashing in and devouring him and Odette

"Rufus?" I yell, my voice high and thin with fear. "Can you hear me?"

"I'm right here, Maude," he says calmly. "You don't need to shout."

He is still by my side. He was there all along.

We climb.

Blood pounds through me, pumping corruption into every corner of my body. Hallucinations dart at the edges of my vision as the fungus continues to release its spores. Shadows weave around me, dim wraiths and taunting memories.

We pass a doorway in the thick stone wall, opening into an impossible corridor. I can hear Odette, as she was when we were little, laughing and calling to me. I hesitate on the threshold. Torches flicker along the wall, leading off to unknown places.

Rufus gently takes my elbow. "Not down there," he says. "We're here to find Lyr, remember?"

We keep going.

More doorways appear. A figure in a bright polka-dot dress disappears around a corner. Ginger. Or not. Another door opens into a room. Odette's bedroom, just as I left it. Another door reveals the biology lab at school, Rufus's backpack slung over a chair.

Rufus sighs longingly, but we keep going.

One doorway opens into the kitchen at home. A fire burns cheerily in the hearth. Gwion Bach sleeps, fat and happy on the battered sofa. The kettle is boiling, whistling a merry tune. Nan's hideous teapot is on the counter, and I just know that if I go in there Nan will come bustling in to fuss over me. She'll be whole and healthy and *alive*, not cold in the ground.

I take a trembling step forward. My legs are like jelly. I want it so much. I want to quit. I want this to all be over.

I want my nan back.

"Maude," Rufus says. "Let's keep going."

Gwion Bach turns yellow eyes onto me and hisses, his fur standing on end, and I notice that the room isn't right. The colors are too bright. The fire is burning green instead of gold. And there's no smell. No biscuity, rosemary scent of Nan. No lead-putty and camellia trace of Halmoni. No sun-warmed brown fur of Gwion Bach.

The whistle of the kettle becomes a discordant scream.

Something breaks inside me, but I can't tell anymore what are my true emotions and what is a result of the corrupted mettle, turning me into nothing but a husk, a decomposing sack of skin and meat.

We keep climbing. Step after step after step. I go into a kind of daze, where I'm not sure if I'm asleep or awake, alive or dead. I just keep taking step after step after step.

"Maude!"

Rufus's sharp tone cuts through my stupor, and my vision blurs and shifts. Something is wrong. The tilt of the world is off.

I'm climbing down, not up.

I stop and close my eyes, counting to eleven, trying to make my breaths slow and even. Then I open them again and grit my teeth, turning around and heading back up the stairs to where Rufus is waiting.

"You won't get me that easily," I mutter to the tower.

The rain is still falling, thick and heavy, obscuring everything above and below. I can only make out the few steps ahead of me. The air glitters with rain and silver spores. I feel like we've slipped out of time, climbing endlessly, with no idea how to gauge our progress. I pause to cough up more slimy purple chunks. Rufus awkwardly holds my hair out of the way.

How many days have we been climbing? How many lifetimes?

I raise one foot after the other. The aching, burning feeling in my muscles has gone, replaced with an almost total numbness. Up and up and up. Until all at once, instead of meeting the next step, my foot lands on nothing, and I lurch backward to rebalance, falling down a half dozen steps before Rufus catches me.

"Is it over?" I ask. "Are we at the top?"

"I'm afraid not," he says.

The stairs still spiral away, out of sight above us. Long, vibrant ropes of goosefoot vine descend from where they are wedged in cracks in the stone walls, the glossy green leaves almost glowing in the gloomy damp of the tower. The eight steps before me are gone, crumbled away to nothing, destroyed by the rampant goosefoot. It's too wide a gap for me to step across. Too wide even to jump.

Rufus reaches out to tug on one of the vines. "It's not woody," he says. "So it could snap. But I think maybe we could swing over, up, and onto the next section of stairs."

I look around, but no other solution presents itself.

"I'll go first," Rufus says. "Make sure it's safe."

He grips the vine, takes a few steps back, and then does a running leap, out over the edge of the broken section of stairs and up onto the ledge formed by the next uneroded step. I hear him let out a little *tssss* of victory.

"Okay, your turn."

As the vine takes my weight, it comes free from the gap in the stone wall, unraveling like Nan's knitting when Hangul and Huw get hold of it. Rufus is on his knees, holding out a hand for me.

He grips my wrist, and I scream at the pain of the pressure on my rotting fingers. I can feel the flesh start to slide away from the bone, tendons screaming and snapping.

It would be so easy to let go.

"Maude."

The voice doesn't belong to Rufus. I feel a feather-soft breath on my cheek, as cold as ice.

"Lyr?"

"You're close," he says, his voice the hiss of the wind down a chimney. *"Set me free."*

"No," I whimper. "I have to kill you. I'm sorry."

"Maude," Rufus says. "Grab my other hand."

The gentle whistle of wind becomes a howl.

"Do we have to talk about it right now?" I say to Lyr through gritted teeth as every spare ounce of my energy directs itself to not plummeting to my death.

"Swear to me you'll set me free."

I don't understand, but I don't have the mental or physical capacity to think about it. "I can't."

I try to swing myself up to grab Rufus's other hand. The howl becomes a scream, and I'm suddenly buffeted by ice, a furious, raging gale, laced with needles.

"Stop it!" I yell. "I have to stop the auditors from getting the knife! It's not like *they'll* set you free!"

The gale doesn't let up. My fingers go numb, and my hand slips through Rufus's fingers.

I fall, and even though I know I'll almost certainly die, all I can think about is the waste. How it took me so long to climb these steps, only to plummet past them in mere seconds.

Will I fall right down to the bottom? Will my body splatter and break on the ground beside a horrified Odette? The thought of that, of her having to experience that, fills me with enough regret that I reach out an arm to grasp at a hanging vine. My destroyed fingertips scrape the green leaves, and I cry out in pain. My wrist tangles in it. And while I don't manage to get any purchase, the vine does somehow swing me over to the side of the tower, depositing my crumpled body on the stone steps like a sack of wet flour.

I lie there, winded, wondering how many bones I have broken. Wondering if I will be able to get up or whether I'll just slowly die, clinging to a slippery stone step. Perhaps I could go through one of the doorways now. Perhaps then I could die in peace.

"Maude?" Rufus's voice comes drifting from above, high with panic. "Are you okay?"

I decide that perhaps I won't die after all. Or at least not at this precise moment.

"Never better," I croak.

I try to move, starting with my fingers, then arms and legs and neck. Miraculously, I don't seem to have any broken bones. My wrist burns where the vine tangled around it, and my fingertips are still ruined, weeping black and yellow slime. But I'm alive, for now. I haul myself onto my hands and knees, and crawl over to the edge of the staircase, trying to figure out how far I fell. It's still a long way down. I can't see to the bottom, only mist and rain disappearing into blackness.

Not quite blackness.

There's something moving down there.

"Odette?" I call. "Can you hear me?"

I lean out as far as I dare, straining my eyes, trying to make it out. It's something writhing. Moving. Growing.

The roses. They've made it through the door.

"Odette!" I call again.

I have to go to her. She needs me.

My hands are ragged, bone protruding from the tips. Black slime is leaking from my eyes, my ears, my nostrils. I can feel my organs shutting down one by one.

I'm dying.

"Maude, what's going on?" Rufus calls.

"It's Odette," I say. "The roses are in the tower. I have to go back down."

The fungus around me quivers, and I can sense the roses trembling in anticipation.

"You can't," Rufus says. "We've come too far."

"She needs me," I tell him.

There's a pause while Rufus considers this. "Let me help you across the gap," he says. "Then I'll go down to Odette."

It doesn't feel right. I need to be the one to save her.

"You need to get the knife," Rufus says. "Otherwise, we'll all die."

He's right. I haul myself to my feet and start to climb again. One foot in front of the other.

Step by agonizing step, I climb.

I don't look through the doorways.

I don't look at the roses. Don't think about what might be happening to Odette.

I just climb, and climb, and climb, and climb, until my vision grows small and focused. Just the one step in front of me, and the one after that.

Everything else stops existing.

There's just that one step, on and on and on. Up and up and up.

Eventually, I reach the place where the stairs crumble into nothing.

Rufus's worried face peers out from the ledge. "I don't want to keep asking you if you're okay," he says, "because you're clearly not."

"I appreciate that."

"I made you this," he says. "Catch."

He swings out a sturdy rope made of several vines twisted together.

"There's a loop at the bottom that you can put your foot into," he explains. "All you have to do is hold on, and I can pull you up."

I want to weep with gratitude. "You're the best," I say.

"Just try not to die, okay?"

I slip my foot into the loop and grip the vine with my ruined hands, then step off the edge of the staircase. Rufus swings me out and then uses my momentum to pull me upward. He reaches out and catches me, his arms going around me and staying there. I close my eyes and lean into him.

"Now go," I tell him. "Help her."

Rufus sighs, and I can tell he doesn't want to leave me. But he nods curtly and holds me for a moment longer. Then he scrambles back down the vine and disappears into the mist, his mop of red hair like a receding lamp.

My legs wobble with relief, and I slump onto a cold stone step. I'm not sure I can get up again.

Who do I think I am anyway? It took thirteen of Anglyon's best witches to make the wall around Sicklehurst. They toiled and sweated over it for eleven days and nights. And I had somehow genuinely managed to convince myself that I—a magicless teenager—could just waltz in and save the day with a purse full of nail polish and teddy-bear fur?

A terrible realization looms in the back of my mind. I had convinced myself. I'd convinced myself that I could do it. That I could save everyone. And even now, even after I'd lost Nan and sentenced myself to death, I still want to play the hero and rescue Odette. Still, after all this time, I'm tangled up in the false fancies of childhood.

Dr. Slater's voice echoes in my mind. *You should be ashamed of yourself.*

I hunch there, cold and wretched, on the staircase, a bloodied bag of slime and bone.

What would Nan say, if she were still alive? If she could see me now?

Life gets tough sometimes, love. But you have to just fix yourself a strong cup of tea, put on your big girl panties, and go out to face it head-on.

I can't argue with Nan. I never could. I wish I had a strong cup of tea.

I pull the vial out of the black satin bag. The mettle in it glints bright silver. I have no idea what it will do to me, or even what to do with it. I'm pretty sure I shouldn't drink it. Instead, I pour it into my cupped hand. There is maybe five drops' worth, and it sits quivering in my palm. I pass my other hand over it and rub gently, like it's hand soap. The mettle covers my hands in a thin silvery sheen, and I feel a breath of fresh air. The fog in my brain clears, and I stand up.

Everything still hurts, but I can go on for now. I don't know how long it will take this new mettle to become corrupted, like the rest of it, so I'd better hurry.

I keep climbing.

And climbing.

And climbing.

Finally, there are no steps left to climb, and I'm at the top.

I collapse onto the landing and surrender myself to the blackness inside.

I DON'T KNOW how much time has passed, but eventually I raise my head and look around. The open top of the tower is gone. Instead, there is a domed roof over my head, built from close-fitted bluestone. The landing that I collapsed on is only a few feet across, ending at the stone wall and a door.

Yet another bloody door.

I shudder in recognition. It's exactly like our front door.

Well, not exactly. Our door is made of ash, whereas this one is clearly oak. Ours is painted a cheery yellow, with a brass knocker shaped like a fox, and this one is bare, weathered wood. But it has the same witchmarks scratched on it in the corners.

We'd laid Mam on ours first, long before Nan, when her body was sent back to us from the detention camp. We lit candles to show her the way through the darkness and put bits of iron in the butter to stop it from curdling. We dressed her in white linen turned inside out to expose the seams and guard against fairies. We put out salt and wine and soul cakes. We covered the mirrors, stopped the clocks, and put the cats outside.

Then we waited, sitting with her, not leaving her side until the moon had passed over our house and been replaced with the sun.

Nobody came to see us, to watch alongside us. There was no fiddle playing, no celebration of a life.

I was seven years old.

I spit bloody saliva into my cupped hand now and paint over the witchmarks in the corners, tracing the familiar patterns with my finger.

I lean forward and breathe on them. I don't bother with words. The door knows who I am and what I want.

It swings open, and I step inside.

22

THIS ROOM IS DARK AND FEATURELESS, THE WALLS HEWN from massive slabs of bluestone. It contains nothing but black rose canes erupting from the walls.

And a swan.

I let out a gasp as I take it in, huge and white and suffering.

It's almost as tall as me, from the webbing of its feet to its orange beak. Its wings are spread wide, a span of at least ten feet, pinned in place by black rose canes, thorns biting deep into wounds that weep crusty dry blood, dark trickling streaks against snowy feathers. The canes stretch from wall to wall, holding the swan upright and immobile.

I remember Mam whispering to me in the darkness of Sickle-hurst, telling me about the treasure in the tower that had once belonged to a prince of swans.

Its beak is bound tight with red thread. Its eyes roll in terror. It's been here all this time.

Buried in the swan's chest is a knife. Yellowed bone, carved in intricate lines and whorls, a brownish toadstone set at the hilt.

The Hollow Knife of Uisnigh.

The swan's chest rises and falls, and I hear the sharp, panicked rasp of its breath and the thudding of its strange heart, beating faintly in its feathered breast.

"Lyr," I whisper.

And I finally remember what I did, the first time I came to Sicklehurst, with Mam.

I'D BEEN SO ENCHANTED with the story of the swan prince— with Lyr—and his treasure that Mam was trying to hide. And I was desperate to see it, to learn more.

Mam had brought forth a rough bundle of linen, hidden in her coat. She'd laid it on the ground reverently, and gently peeled back the cloth to reveal the bone knife.

"Is that it?" I had asked, disappointed.

It wasn't the kind of treasure I'd imagined. No glittering jewels. No gold. Just an old bone knife with a carved handle and a single brown stone.

Mam had sat cross-legged in her circle of hawthorn and barberry, the knife on the ground in front of her. She went into a kind of trance, leaving me alone. I wasn't frightened. I could feel the forest beneath me, whispering to me, telling me secrets. I whispered back. I told the forest about Lyr and his great treasure. And the forest had shown me what to do.

I took sprigs of young rowan, tasselweed, and sticklegrass and bound them together. The forest brought him to life, a little swan, no more than five inches high. I played with him happily until Mam opened her eyes again.

She looked pale, her skin clammy and her lips chapped. Her pupils were huge, and I could see from her expression that she hadn't been able to do whatever it was she was trying to do.

"Who taught you to do that?" she asked, frowning at the little toy swan, which flapped its wings under her gaze.

"The sticklegrass wood," I told her.

Her frown had deepened. "The forest? You can talk to it?"

"Can't you?"

Mam didn't answer. She just stared at me, her expression intense and calculating. "Maude," she said at last. "Your nan made a spell in this place, a long time ago. I want to use the magic of that spell to keep the treasure hidden. Do you think you can help me do it?"

I nodded, eager to please. "I'll ask the forest to help."

Something strange passed over Mam's face. But she smiled and nodded, taking both my hands in hers and guiding me to lay my palms on the ground. "Close your eyes. I'll guide you."

I closed my eyes and let my consciousness sink into the deep forest that lay beneath Sicklehurst. Mam was talking, but I stopped listening to her. I could *feel* Nan's spell, now that I was looking for it. It almost *smelled* like her, familiar and safe, sweet like thrupenny biscuits and the roses that grew in our front garden. I felt the three layers of it—the gauzy layer outside the wall that floated all the way to Inglenook. The layer embedded in the walls. And the third layer, underground, in the very heart of the place.

The magic there was so thick it was almost solid, a membrane of mettle surrounding the . . . whatever it was. Something deep in the ground. Something oily and foul.

With my witchsight, I could see the knife for what it really was now. It was beautiful. Powerful. And strangely swanlike. Mam was still whispering instructions to me. She told me to bury the knife, but I ignored her.

Buried treasure was for pirates, and Lyr wasn't a pirate. He was a prince. His treasure needed to be kept at the top of the tallest tower. And he would guard it with his life, because that was the kind of loyal and true prince he was. I told the forest everything. I opened myself up to its power, and for a wild, glorious moment I merged with it. I became the forest, and the forest became me, tangled and thorny and vast.

I took the knife in one hand, and my little swan doll in the other, and braided their mettle tightly together. Then I had taken the braid, and reached down to the thick membrane of mettle, the third and strongest layer of Nan's spell. I bound the braid carefully to the membrane.

"Make sure the connection is strong," I could dimly hear Mam saying. "As strong as you can."

The biscuity, rosemary scent of Nan was all around me now. But the spell needed structure. Something for the braided strands of mettle to live inside, to keep it alive. I imagined a rambling rose with cheery yellow flowers, winding itself tightly around Nan's spell and then climbing all the way to the top of the tower, where Lyr guarded his treasure. The rose could sustain the spell, drawing on the power of the sticklegrass wood through its roots, keeping it fresh and strong.

But was it enough? A rose might not survive a particularly cold winter or dry summer. What then?

"It cannot fail." Mam's voice drifted into my awareness.

I didn't want to let Mam down. She needed me.

What I really needed was a powerful source of mettle to keep the rose alive. Like a deep pool of roiling mettle.

I knew the membrane was sealing the pool for a reason. But surely a little tiny hole wouldn't matter. I let the rose grow over the top of it, and whispered sharp, pointed suggestions. One of the thorns of the rose cane grew long, like a rapier. The membrane resisted it like rubber. But I whispered to the sticklegrass wood, and together we put our strength into that one thorn, and with the tiniest *pop* it sank through the membrane, the tip of it touching the mettle underneath.

I felt the mettle flow through the rose, turning it dark. The yellow flowers shriveled and died, but the canes and thorns became as thick and strong as iron. I knew it would keep the spell strong. Keep the knife hidden. The power of Nan's spell, the sticklegrass wood, and the oily mettle—magic is always stronger in threes.

When I opened my eyes, the knife was gone, as was the little toy swan. Thorned rose canes wound their way up the tower, each one as thick as my arm and bristling with thorns.

Mam was staring at me, and I realized my arms were buried in the earth up to my elbows.

"How did you do it?" she asked, her expression full of hunger.

I couldn't explain. "I just asked the sticklegrass wood for help," I said.

Mam's breath drew in sharply. *"Greenwitch,"* she had whispered.

I didn't tell her about the little hole I'd made in Nan's membrane. I didn't want her to be disappointed in me. Surely, one little hole wouldn't matter.

IT WAS ME.

I'm the one who made the hole in Nan's spell. I'm the one who let the corrupted mettle leach out, poisoning the sticklegrass wood.

I made Lyr. This swan, who suffers here in the tower. I'm the one who bound him to the knife. I tied them to Nan's spell to keep them hidden, and fueled the whole thing with the power of the corrupted mettle. He's been here for nearly ten years, a living, breathing, suffering creature.

He cannot fly. He cannot move. Cursed to just hang here, thorns biting at him, imprisoned by a spell cast by three generations of witches—me, Mam, and Nan.

The swan draws another rattling breath.

He watches me, and I realize he wants to die. Of course he does. No creature would choose a life like this, frozen and tortured, for year upon year upon year.

"I'm so sorry," I whisper to him, and to myself.

Because now I know what I have to do.

I have to make it right. I have to atone for what I did. I made the hole. This nightmare is all because of me.

I need to take his place. Center the power of the knife on myself. Become the locus of the spell. Only then can I wield the power of the knife and save my friends. And I can contain the corrupted mettle. I can reanimate the Tatterdemalion—make a whole army of Tatterdemalions—to keep the auditors at bay.

I'll just be trapped here forever in this tower.

Beneath Lyr there is a mark. Our family witchmark. It has talismans placed at certain conjunctions of lines—rue, obsidian, oleander, and something shriveled and black that I think must be the heart of some long-dead creature. Lyr's blood falls at significant conjunctions too, where it has crystalized into dark-red shards, like cinnabar.

The mark is faded, the rue and oleander almost crumbled to dust.

I wish I'd had more time with Mam. I wish I'd read some of the old grimoires in the chest at the end of Nan's bed. I wish I was anywhere but here.

The witchmark makes a kind of grid for the spell—like a template for mettle to be woven around. I can't weave the mettle, but perhaps the grid will be enough.

A low rumbling sounds, far beneath my feet, like thunder from below.

No point in lollygagging, Nan says in my head. *Get to work, love.*

I kneel and tip the black satin bag upside down, scattering its treasures on the hard stone floor. I turn witch-eyed and watch the silvery threads of mettle coalesce around each object.

I breathe deeply.

Magic is felt, Mam says. *It's in your blood. You feel it beneath your fingernails.*

The weak thudding of the swan's heart is in my head, pulsing and pounding. My own heart slows to match it. I reach out and touch a hand to a wing feather.

Lyr's watering eyes roll in his head.

"Not long to go now," I murmur.

Over the top of the witchmark, I lay out a five-pointed star, with a new talisman at every point—the broken china, the candle stub, the tuft of Otso's fur, the snakeskin, and the hemlock stalk. Beside each talisman, I place a guardian. Knucklebones for the broken china. A drop of petitgrain oil for the candle stub. A three-holed button for Otso's fur. Oakmoss for the snakeskin. A pinch of graveyard dust for the hemlock.

Then, using the glittery black nail polish, I paint over the looping rose knot of our family witchmark to reignite it.

The rumbling sounds again, and I feel it this time, the tower shuddering with the pressure of it.

My ears pop.

I stand up, wrapping the red thread from Halmoni's mending basket around Lyr's beak—once, twice, three times over the crumbling string—before tying it off in a figure-o'-nine. Lyr flinches at my touch, and my heart aches for him, for his fear and pain and suffering. I hate that I am to be the architect of it, that I can't save him. That the best thing I can give him is death.

The sticklegrass wood trembles beneath me. I feel the sheer strength of it under my feet. Throbbing with barely restrained power. I feel the oily pulse of the corrupted mettle, seeping into the forest, spreading through its network of underground roots and fungal matrices.

I think of Odette, her lanky hair and wormwood-stained fingernails.

I think of my mother, laid out cold on our front door.

I think of Rufus, steadfast and earnest.

I can't help thinking there must be another way.

I think of Halmoni, up to her elbows in sticklegrass and as happy as a squirrel.

I think of Nan.

Plants aren't good or bad. They just are. We're the ones who make them good or bad.

I have to reseal the pool of corrupted mettle. Repair the damage I did.

I grip the handle of the knife in both hands and pull.

But it won't budge.

Lyr's breath grows shallow, the thudding of his heart quickening in his breast.

I pull harder, putting my weight against it.

Nothing.

I look at the five-pointed star with my witchsight and see the mettle drifting uselessly around each talisman. They aren't woven together, nor have they attached themselves to the grid of the witchmark.

Of course they haven't. I have no magic.

It took all the strength of the thirteen witches to complete the triple spell that sealed Sicklehurst. Halmoni said that Nan didn't get out of bed for a week. And Mam nearly died trying to hide the knife. And here am I, almost dead from mettle poisoning and totally devoid of magical ability.

What's left of my heart sinks. I'm useless. Powerless.

I'm ready to bind myself to the spell, to take Lyr's place, but I can't do it.

"I'm sorry," I tell Lyr. "I'm sorry for all of it. I wish I'd never come here."

Maybe Rufus and Odette got out. Maybe they can tell people, before it's too late. Maybe they can send some thaumaturgical engineers to fix the spell.

Why didn't I do that? I ask myself. *Why did I think I could solve this problem on my own?*

But I know why, deep in the most jealous, ugliest part of myself.

"I wanted to be the hero," I whisper to Lyr. "I followed Mam, then Odette, for most of my life. Then they were gone, and a part of me was a bit glad, because it meant *I'd* get to be the hero, instead of the storyteller. I'd get to rescue Odette, the way that she once rescued me. I thought I could rescue her, rescue *you*. Princes and princesses in towers. But I've failed."

This doesn't happen in fairy tales.

I thought I'd stopped telling stories. But I haven't.

I dash the useless pieces of my spell away with a furious swipe. They clatter and spill across the little room.

Junk. It's all junk. Silly games made up by silly little girls who wanted to find a way to fairyland.

My stomach heaves, and pieces of dark purple slip from my mouth. I've used up whatever extra time the pure mettle in Mam's vial gave me. I find that I can no longer take a full breath, and I don't really care.

I curl up on the flagstones of the chamber beside Lyr, and I close my eyes, knowing that I will probably never open them again.

There's another rumble beneath me. I am sure it is the refinery chamber, unable to contain the dark mettle any longer.

I breathe with Lyr, shallow and rattling. Our twin hearts beat unsteadily.

I feel Lyr's pain, his despair, his fear, and he can feel mine.

There's a kind of brutal intimacy in it. I feel the long stretch of time that he's been here, imprisoned in this stone cage, pinned cold and hard by black thorns. I see, through his watering eyes, the dim, unchanging despair of stone walls.

I see myself through those eyes, a bloody demon made of boils and sludge, with peeling skin the color of Halmoni's lead putty.

I feel the ache in his wings, the pain of immobility.

I feel the longing in him—dulled by his endless imprisonment, but still there. A deep, unbroken yearning for blue skies, for the buffeting of wind beneath outstretched wings. For sunlight. For air. For freedom and flight.

The yearning awakens something in me—something tiny and weak, like a newly sprouted tendril. It comes from somewhere deep and secret, a place that even the rotten star cannot touch.

I remember the story of the king with a heart of iron. Of the swan, trapped in a stinking mire. The peasant girl who rescued him. She couldn't save his life, but she took him home to Uisnigh so he could die at peace.

I reach out with my useless witch-hands, down to the earth where the rotten mettle pulses viciously. The forest is still there. It remembers me, even without my magic.

"I need you," I croak.

I couldn't save Nan. I can't save Odette, or Rufus.

I can't save Lyr either.

But perhaps I can help him see the sky, one last time.

I open my eyes as the floor creaks beneath my feet.

I manage to get onto my hands and knees. It is the hardest thing I've ever had to do. But I'm pretty sure this is the last thing I'll ever do. And then I can rest, knowing that I did one good thing.

With a rumble that almost knocks me over, the patch of stone where the witchmark is painted cracks, tendrils of green emerging through from beneath, pushing, tearing, wrenching the stone open.

It's sticklegrass.

The floor tilts, and my scattered talismans and guardians slide and slip through the cracks, disappearing into the empty darkness below. The black satin bag drops away as well, leaving me with nothing. No protections, no wards.

They were useless anyway.

Huge sticklegrass runners—as thick as my arms—fly up from the cracks, plunging into the walls as if the stone were as soft as butter. They spiral around the rose canes and squeeze, forcing the thorns out of the wall like splinters popping from skin.

The rose canes unravel, and Lyr collapses to the floor with a thud. He struggles weakly, using muscles that have been immobilized for years, trying to flap wings that are broken in multiple places. His beak is still bound, and his neck curves and flops. A desperate, muffled honking sounds from his throat as he flails, like a fish exposed to air.

The black rose canes lash up like whips as the sticklegrass continues to rise, burrowing into the mortar of each stone and pushing. The rose canes reach for me and Lyr. I hear his panicked honk once again, and the sheer animal terror of it spurs me to action. I wrap my arm around him and rise to my feet. I kick away the rose canes.

The sticklegrass has torn a hole in the ceiling, and a shaft of brilliant sunlight falls down on us. I heft Lyr in my arms, his feathery bulk awkward but not heavy, and I clamber onto the rising sticklegrass tide. It surges forward and up underneath us, carrying us unsteadily toward the very top of the tower.

As we explode into daylight, I stagger free of the tangled mass, tumbling onto powdery white stone, Lyr still clasped awkwardly in my arms. The hilt of the knife digs into my side where it protrudes from Lyr's breast, and I hope I'm not hurting him. I stumble to my feet, squinting and blinking in the blinding light.

We are at the summit of the tower, and it seems to be made from huge shards of glittering crystal, white and purple, like the chunk of amethyst I gifted to Odette all those years ago.

The air up here is ice-cold, as cold as Lyr's breath on my cheek. The storm has passed. The sun is piercingly bright. Crystals rise around us from the tower, their dazzling light reflecting and refracting, shattering into a thousand rainbows. Lyr shudders in my arms, as waves of sticklegrass keep erupting from the darkness below. Then vicious whips of rose cane shoot out.

I run, because there's nothing else to do.

I can hear the crashing of the sticklegrass and the roses behind me, smell the foaming leafy rise of it—oakmoss and pine pitch, untamed grassy plains, and wet rain-forest boughs. The white stone buckles under my feet as the tower is torn apart by the hungry grass.

Lyr pants and struggles in my grasp, trying to free himself with his broken limbs and atrophied muscles. I half drop him and have to pause to adjust my grip.

Green tendrils shoot up around me, bursting from the floor, wrapping around the crystal shards, squeezing and shattering them into glittering fragments. A thorned black whip catches me around the ankle, and I am aware that my skin is splitting open, although I feel no pain. Lyr moans—a low, desperate sound in his throat—but I just grip him tighter and keep running.

The tower is shaking beneath my feet, the sticklegrass crushing everything it can reach as the roses fight back, trying to halt the destruction and prevent our escape.

I keep running.

The glittering floor slides under me, and the whole tower starts to tilt.

Lyr's heart thuds weakly against mine.

I run, even though I can't see where I'm going. Everything is shattering crystal and brilliant blue sky and white feathers and slashing sticklegrass. I close my eyes against the glaring brightness of it all, and just run.

One foot in front of the other. That's how it works, isn't it?

I run and I run and I run, and I don't notice the edge approaching, don't notice as the crystal floor below me falls away and I run straight off the edge of the tower and into the empty sky.

23

MY LEGS PUMP AWAY AT NOTHING, AND AIR ROARS in my ears. My stomach lurches as I realize what I've done. I am in the sky, surrounded by blue, plummeting downward, my arms still clutching the feathered weight of Lyr.

The world stretches out all around me, far, far below, the dark thorns of Sicklehurst, surrounded by a patchwork quilt of forests and fields and glinting water. I can see the sticklegrass crashing against the walls of the tower like a tidal wave. I spot the refinery building, crouched in among thorns that spread from it like poisoned veins, glinting oil-slick violet and lime as they pulse with corrupted mettle.

I feel Lyr's muscles bunch as he tries to flap his broken wings. But he cannot fly, and neither can I.

We are both going to die. There's no way we can survive this fall.

But we were going to die anyway, so better to do it out here in the air and sunlight. At least this way it should be quick.

The tower cracks and crumbles, huge blocks of stone tilting

and sliding to crash to the ground, where they throw up great clouds of earth and dust.

"I'm so sorry," I shout to Lyr, but the wind snatches my words away, knowing how utterly inadequate they are.

Sicklehurst is a choking tangle of thorns devouring bleak industrial buildings. But something shifts, and I get a glimpse of the forest as it once was, ancient and powerful, moving through time with slow grace. Every tree, every blade of grass, is strung together with every other tree and flower under the soil in a network of glittering mycelium, the delicate white fibers exchanging water and nutrients and information.

The forest now is nothing like it was. It has grown twisted and bulging from its confinement, from the corruption of the rotten star. The poisoned mettle has infected its roots, speeding up the growth cycle of the forest until it moves in human time.

It's been calling to us.

To *me.*

It's been calling for help.

Rufus was right all along. He said that plants can feed on the corrupted mettle, can lock it away in their roots and turn into other things. But everything has a limit. Each plant can only hold so much. And the corruption has been accumulating as the rotten star continued to burn, its foulness leaking out through the hole I made.

You would need a thousand such forests.

"Is there anything to be done?" I ask Lyr as we fall. "I wish you would turn into a human again so you could tell me."

If only I had my magic, I could transform Lyr. Maybe he'd have an answer, a last-ditch plan that could save us all.

But we have no time. The ground below is drawing closer.

The sticklegrass continues to rage and crash against the walls of Sicklehurst, but Nan's spell is holding. It cannot tear down the wall.

I think of Nan, cold in her forever bed of earth and darkness.

I think of Winnie and Ginger and their endless cycle of death.

I think of Odette, hanging upside down from a bough of Peg Powler.

I promised her.

I would smash it with my wings.

Lyr's body suddenly thrums with energy, and I whisper the words aloud.

"I would smash it with my wings."

I hear Rufus's voice in my head. *There must be another way.*

The wild mettle of the sticklegrass wood calls to me, strange yet familiar. Something stirs inside me—a whisper of the fierce, unrestrained little girl I once was, prowling beneath the leafy embrace of the willow.

Find me, that little girl whispers.

But I don't know how to get back to her. She's been lost to me, along with my magic, ever since Odette and I snuck into Sicklehurst and I made the little twig dolls.

I remember the expression on Nan's face when I came back with Mam.

She knew we'd been to Sicklehurst. She could smell the green magic under my fingernails. I'd wanted to tell Nan what I'd done, about the hole I'd made in her membrane. But Nan had been so angry at Mam. I didn't want her to look at me like that.

"She's a greenwitch," Mam told Nan, her hands shaking and the scent of bitter almond on her breath. "Did you know?"

"Of course I knew," Nan hissed. "Our roses haven't stopped blooming since the day she was born."

"What's a greenwitch?" I asked, but nobody seemed to hear me.

Nan knew what Mam had done. She could see the broken string inside me. Halmoni bundled me off to bed while they argued.

"What's a greenwitch?" I asked again as Halmoni fussed over my blankets.

She hesitated. She knew Nan wouldn't want me to know.

"Someone who can talk to forests, love," she said at last. "Right down in their roots."

I giggled. "Can't everyone do that?"

She shook her head and kissed my forehead. "Time to sleep."

I considered telling Halmoni about the hole in the membrane, but I was so weary, my insides still bruised from where Mam had broken one of my strings. So I let her soothe me the way that only Halmoni can. I let her envelop me with calm—Halmoni's gift is spreading calm. And I fell asleep.

I didn't tell anyone the next day either. Then Mam was gone, taken away by the auditors, and four years later Nan slid the bone-pin brooch onto my shirt.

This will keep you safe.

I glance at the sliver of bone, still pinned there like it always is. Yellowish bone, carved in intricate loops and whorls.

Just like the knife that is buried in Lyr's feathered breast.

Mam tried to destroy the knife, but she could break off only a tiny sliver.

And I've been wearing it this whole time.

The Hollow Knife of Uisnigh. A magical knife that can cut the mettle from a living creature.

Sever the mettle that links all living things.

I let out a little moan of realization, and awkwardly I shift Lyr's bulk to my right arm, so I can reach up to pull the bone-pin from my dress. It slides free, and I hold it against the hilt of the knife. It clicks onto it like a magnet.

Nan tried to contain me. To contain my magic, my wildness. Just as she tried to contain the sticklegrass wood.

"Wild things shouldn't be contained," I tell the knife, and I pull it from Lyr's breast in one smooth movement.

Gripping it in my real hands, I reach out with my witch-hands to grab a loose thread of mettle. It snags in my fingers, and I want to scream in exultation.

My magic.

Not gone at all. Just blocked, by a sliver of the Hollow Knife of Uisnigh.

The call of the ancient sticklegrass wood grows louder. And this time I know I can answer it, the way I did on that strange night with Mam. Because I'm a greenwitch. I can talk to the forest.

So I do.

I let the wild in.

It floods me with power. With *knowing*. My strings thrum, and I turn the knife toward myself, putting the tip against my breastbone and letting it rest there, as my witch-hands, holding the knife, strip the corrupted mettle from my strings as deftly as Halmoni peels an apple. The filaments, silvery bright once more, spark with a kind of electricity that repairs neural pathways and binds tissue back together. My organs reform, pink and new. My blood flows bright once more, pulsing through my veins, filling my nerve endings with sensations I thought I'd never feel again. My skin repairs itself, creeping and thickening over my fingers. My fingernails sprout fresh, brittle and moon-shaped. Hair streams from my head in a muddy tide, whipping up and battering my face in the howling wind. My vision sharpens.

I turn the knife to Lyr and cut the red thread that binds his beak. The crusted blood around his wounds crumbles to dust and is carried away on the wind, leaving only pure white feathers. I feel a stirring in his wings as his bones begin to knit back together.

He *screams,* a wild sound so full of longing and rage and hope that it seems to light something inside my soul. He unfolds his wings, beating them against the air with a heavy booming sound.

He can't carry the weight of us both on his just-mended wings. He flaps in vain, and I know I have to let him go.

So I do.

Feathers float free as he beats his wings—the first creature to fly in the sticklegrass wood for more than fifty years. The feathers surround me as I continue to fall, spiraling and whirling, until all I can see is feathers. One lands on my tongue and melts like a snowflake.

Lyr goes racing off into the sky, and I am alone, still falling.

But I know what to do.

I channel the power of the sticklegrass wood. I whisper to it, tell it what I need, and it whispers back.

My shoulders ache in the place where the swan by the willow

beat me. Then the ache explodes into burning pain. My skin splits open, and I cry out as bone and sinew erupt from my shoulder blades, growing and shifting as they prickle into shafts, and shafts burst into feathers.

I feel the hot stickiness of blood against my skin, soaking into my dress, staining my brand-new wings.

My wings. They are mine, golden and whole. I spread them wide, feeling new tendons pull and stretch. The wind catches me and holds me aloft before I slip between the columns of air and plummet again. I flap, feebly at first, but more confidently as I learn to use muscles I didn't have before, to navigate the air, to feel the push and pull of the wind.

Lyr is high above me now, crying out with wild, unbridled joy at the freedom of flight.

I follow him up, rising with an exhilaration so intense that I can barely breathe.

When I draw next to him, Lyr fixes me with a look that says, *Finally.*

I feel a stab of defensiveness. "You didn't exactly do a good job of explaining it," I yell over the wind.

He lets out a whistling laugh and races away again, wings beating hard. I soar after him, giddy, and we chase each other around the sky, wheeling and circling, rising and then folding our wings and falling, before spreading them wide and rising once more in wide, graceful arcs.

But there is no time for play. I have work to do.

I dive down into the thorny, oily darkness of Sicklehurst, where the roses are battling with sticklegrass. I open my wings at the last possible moment and land gracefully outside the refinery building. The ground beneath me is rumbling.

My wings fold up behind me and I crouch and plunge my arms into the soil, letting my witchsight sink with it as I inhale the rich, thick scent of soil—petrichor, ginger root, monsoon rains, ancient caves, and the snuffling brown odor of burrowing creatures. My attention grows small and close as the soil reveals itself to be an ancient kingdom of its own, built over hundreds of thousands of years, from primeval mountains and long-forgotten seas. It teems with microbes—yeasts and algae and protozoa and nematodes, intricately laced with fungi.

I remember Rufus telling me that there are more microorganisms in one teaspoon of soil than there are humans on our planet, and here I can see that it is true. This world is vast and powerful, and it's been here the whole time.

I enter the rhizosphere. The infinitely branching network of mycorrhizal fungi. The consciousness of the forest. It is foul and oily with corrupted mettle, and I can feel the longing in it. The yearning to be green and good once more.

"Where are they?" I ask the sticklegrass wood.

It leads me along highways built by ants and earthworms. Through the fibrous roots of oak and ash and dandelion. Through sand and clay and silt, and the worn-down bones of long-dead creatures.

Then I surge upward, through layers of rotting leaves and burrowing insects. And I burst free into the air once more. The earth seems so much bigger now. So much more vast and complex than I ever could have understood before.

Odette and Rufus are there, huddled at the foot of the ruined tower. Rufus is unconscious, blood weeping from a cut on his cheek. Odette looks small and scared, her knees drawn to her chest, her cheeks streaked with dirt and tears.

I want to tell them that it will be all right, but I'm not really here, only my consciousness. Instead, I whisper to the forest again, telling it to keep them safe. I watch as a bower grows over them, twisted vines and thick sticklegrass. Odette looks around, panicked, as she and Rufus are encased in green. But she doesn't resist.

"I'll come back for you," I tell them both, even though they can't hear me.

Then I open my eyes, and I'm outside the refinery building, up to my elbows in the kingdom of soil.

I stand up, not bothering to brush the earth from my hands.

I face the door of the refinery and take a deep breath.

We have work to do.

"Let me in," I tell the forest. "Please," I add, because Nan and Halmoni raised me to be polite.

Everything goes very still.

Then with a twisting, leafy noise, sticklegrass rises in twin waves on either side of me before plunging into the earth. I hear cracking and groaning as the ground heaves, and I struggle to keep my footing. The sticklegrass tears the building open and splits the ground, cleaving the concrete and iron, deeper and deeper, until the refinery chamber is revealed below in a cloud of foul, sulfurous steam.

I stand now on the edge of a new cliff. Far below me I can see the pool of roiling corrupted mettle. I step off the edge and glide down to it.

The waves of malice threaten my resolve, and bile rises in my throat.

The sticklegrass will not come here with me.

I am alone.

I grip the knife in my hand.

The forest has told me what it wants. What it needs.

You would need a thousand such forests.

I didn't realize before that forests are connected. Every ancient tree, every blade of grass, joined to one another by billions of glittering silver filaments that cover the globe.

Except this forest.

This forest stands alone.

Nan's spell severed the sticklegrass wood from the network, just as she severed me from my magic.

She meant well.

But it's time to make things right.

I get down on one knee and hold the tip of the knife against the heaving corrupted mettle.

And I cut what remains of Nan's magical membrane away.

The oily mettle pulses violet and acid lime, and I feel its malevolent satisfaction as it begins to spread through the forest, thicker and faster than ever before.

I can't strip it, the way I did the mettle inside me. There's too much, and it's too powerful. I'm just one girl, no matter what trinkets of magic I bear. The forest cannot do it either. It needs a thousand other forests.

I need help.

I don't have thirteen witches to help me. But I don't need witches. I need wings.

I don't have much time.

I beat my wings once more.

"Bring them all back," I tell the forest.

As I rise into the air, birds rise too, resurrected from the soil of Sicklehurst, the three hundred birds that Nan and the other witches buried alive to fuel the triple spell—lapwings and kitti-wakes and fish owls and sicklebills.

"Winnie and Ginger too," I say.

Two birds soar upward from the forest of thorns—a plump partridge and a darting goldfinch. I let out a full-throated cry of pleasure at the sight of them. Lyr comes plummeting from the sky toward me, and we swoop down together to meet Winnie and Ginger. The air rolls under my wings, holding me steady. It's like nothing I've ever felt before.

Ginger's soft partridge wings have to work hard to keep up with us, but she draws even with me, her wingtips brushing mine. I'm so glad she's okay.

The forest gives me the fishy girls too, now with green-gray wings and snapping beaks, their scales sparkling in the sunlight. Glimmer moths explode from the trees like fireworks, and I glance down to see my own body glowing blue in response to them.

The air is alive with the thrumming of wings.

Now that the bone-pin brooch is gone, now that I have my magic back again, I finally know how this story will end. All of the answers were there all along, I just couldn't see them.

I would smash it with my wings.

I wheel in the air and face the birds, aware of my awkward girl-bird shape, but not caring.

"Hear me, birds! Hear me, porphyrio, pelican, spoonbill, redbreast, grouse, peacock, horned owl, teal, bittern, heron, petrel, figpecker!"

The birds start to form a feathered cyclone around me, spinning and whirling. Every beady eye is trained on me.

"For too long you have lain hollow-eyed and still. It is time to rise and take back what is yours! Take back the ancient forest. Take back the deep loam! Take back the topmost air, where you once gathered fresh songs in the clouds!"

Lyr lets out a full-throated cry, and I am filled with a kind of joyful ache at the sight of him.

"It is time for us to tear down the walls of this prison!" I tell the birds. "I am a storyteller, but today I ask you for wings, not for words. Let us get to work with our beaks, our wings, our claws. Forward to the assault! Throw yourselves upon the walls! Tear, pluck, beat, strike, and most of all *smash*. Forward! It is time!"

The air fills with a screaming cacophony of shrieks, twitters, and calls.

Lyr and I lead the way, the feathered army at our backs as we approach the wall.

The wall that my grandmother made—with her blood, with my blood, and with the blood of birds.

Below us, the sticklegrass wood pulses, waiting. The witchmarks are glowing with a power that I couldn't see before.

We surround the wall, each of us taking a post, hovering.

Then I let out a cry, and in that cry is all my frustration, my sorrow, my pain. The grief of losing Mam and Nan. My fury at the world for keeping me penned in. At Nan, for cutting my connection to the forests, to the wildness that runs through my veins.

At Odette, for not loving me the way I loved her. I cry out for every girl who was told to comb her hair and wash the mud from her face. To keep herself contained. To be ashamed of her voice, her hair, her flesh. To be *quiet* and *good* and *nice*. Girls are not *nice*. Girls are wild and fierce and powerful, and I will not let anyone take that away. Not ever again.

The birds around me respond to my call, and as one we drop like stones toward the wall that has held the wildness back for so many years.

And.

We.

Smash.

It.

With.

Our.

Wings.

The red bricks crumble and shatter under the battering of pinions and feathers. The witchmarks explode and shower us with blazing powdered fragments. The mettle embedded in them escapes and flies free into the air, where it infuses our feathers, our hearts, the soil beneath us.

Brick by brick, we smash the wall. I revel in the wild, furious sound—screeches and honks and hoots and shrieks. Shattering brick and thudding mortar.

And then it is done.

The spell is broken, and the sticklegrass is free.

It surges out like a wave, cresting across the onion-weed field. And I know it is traveling even faster underground, the silvery filaments remaking ancient connections. I know it is drawing the corrupted mettle out, spreading it far and wide, until it loses its grim potency and can be absorbed and transformed by the chemical cleverness of plants.

Nan thought she was doing the right thing. Containing me. Containing the refinery, the leaking poison. Did she know she was containing the forest too? Did she know that it had the power to purify the corruption? To carry it to be processed in a thousand other forests, in roots and stems and soil all over Anglyon?

She couldn't have, or else she'd never have made the spell.

We rise once again into the skies, higher and higher, until we are black specks against the sun.

I see the forest, the crumbling remains of the wall and the cooling tower. I see Cygnet Creek and the low spread of Inglenook, fields and hedges, other villages. And, on the horizon, I see the rising dunes of Black Larpent Bay and the glittering sparkle of the ocean. It's the real world. My real world, and it is as wild and beautiful as any fairy tale.

A wingtip touches mine—it's Lyr, his feathers glowing white in the sun. We circle each other, then drop together in a spiraling free fall, breast to breast. The ground comes rushing toward us, and my heart quivers and thrills. At the last minute, we spread our wings and let the air take us, and the feeling as we rise again—held aloft by the wind, wingtip to wingtip—is indescribable. Joy courses through me, and for someone who only a short while ago was very nearly dead, I have never felt so alive.

I swoop and play with Lyr and Ginger and Winnie. But eventually, my arms grow weary and I let the wind carry me back over the rubble of the wall, over fragments of brick and crumbling mortar.

Finally, my feet make gentle contact with the ground, and I'm standing in the ruins of Sicklehurst, in front of the green bower.

I touch my hand to it, and the sticklegrass drops away.

Odette looks at me. Her eyes are wide with fear and awe as she takes in my wings, and the glimmer moths tangled in my hair.

"It's okay," I tell her. "It's over."

I touch the knife to her chest.

"Will it hurt?" she asks.

I smile and shake my head as I strip the oily corruption from her strings. She closes her eyes, and her breathing deepens. Her shoulders slump as she lets go of a tension she's been holding.

She opens her eyes and lets out a shaky laugh.

"You once told me you weren't strong enough to make a set of real wings," she says. "But I knew you could do it."

We stare at each other. There is so much that we haven't said. So many confessions and accusations and apologies.

They will remain unsaid. Odette and I, we're done. There's no animosity left. No resentment. But we know that too much has happened for us to ever be friends again.

Rufus's brow is bloody, and his breath scrapes in his chest. I touch the tip of the knife to his collarbone and cleanse his mettle.

His breath loses its rattle, and the dark hollows under his eyes fade. But he doesn't wake up.

"Is he going to be okay?" Odette asks.

I know how to wake a slumbering prince. Doesn't everyone?

I lean forward and brush my lips against his. The sticklegrass winds around him. A curious tendril slips into his ear and pulses gently.

Rufus opens his eyes. He gazes at me, at my ragged dress, my knotted hair. My spreading golden wings.

And he smiles.

"You did it," he says.

I nod. "You were right," I tell him. "There was another way. Remember you told me about the plants around Glidź and Carrowdown that could purify the corrupted mettle? Turns out my nan's spell was stopping that."

Rufus props himself up on his elbows and looks around at the sticklegrass. "Fascinating," he murmurs, and I hug him impulsively.

Feet land softly on the grass behind us, and I turn to see Ginger and Winnie, back to their true sizes and forms. Their wings fold up and disappear into flesh.

I feel a tightening, shrinking sensation as mine do too.

"Well," says Winnie, rubbing her hands together. "That was fun."

Ginger stares over the rubble, across the meadow of onion weed to the dark greenery of Cygnet Creek. She swallows. "Do you think . . . ?" she says, unable to finish the sentence.

"Only one way to find out," says Winnie, holding out her hand.

Hand in hand, they walk together, barefoot, clambering over the ruins of the wall toward the chain-link fence. When they reach the hole, Ginger looks over her shoulder at me and grins. Then they duck through and stand on the other side, whooping and shouting with joy before splashing through the creek and disappearing into the foliage.

"Now that the sticklegrass is free to roam, the girls are too," I tell Rufus and Odette.

Odette says nothing, but I see a faint pinching in her lips at the idea of her doppelganger wandering around Inglenook.

"Are they human now?" Rufus asks. "Real proper humans?"

I shrug. "I have no idea. I guess we'll find out."

"Magic is weird," Rufus observes.

Odette snorts.

I can still feel it sparking in my fingers, flooding my veins. The threads of mettle are all around me. I brush my fingers against them and thrill to the way they respond.

Rufus turns to me, his eyes serious. "Are you okay?"

"Yeah," I tell him, and for the first time in forever I'm not lying. "I'm good."

Good, but not *nice.*

I hear a whistling cry from overhead. Lyr is wheeling above us as he slowly descends. He is glowing white against the sun, so bright that we shield our eyes from his brilliance.

When he lands on the grass before us, he is human Lyr once more. Achingly handsome, but no longer ghostlike and rimed with frost.

"You did it," he says to me. "I knew you would."

"What do we do about the knife?" Rufus says. "The auditors will come for it."

Lyr inclines his head in a nod. "I will return it to Uisnigh," he says. "The auditors cannot enter there."

I reverse the knife and present it to Lyr, hilt-first. He hesitates before taking it.

"Thank you, daughter of witches," he says formally. "The kingdom of birds is in your debt."

And then in a blur of feathers, he is rising into the sky once more, his wings beating, his elegant neck curving.

"Is that it?" asks Odette. "Is it over?"

It isn't—not really. The auditors will still come for me, and I will need something to tell them, or else I'll end up in a detention camp like Mam. But that's a problem for tomorrow.

"It's over for now," I tell her.

The sticklegrass tugs us gently, leading us away from Sicklehurst, away from the shattered tower and the broken wall, toward the creek and home.

EPILOGUE

HALMONI HOLDS OUT A STEAMING BUNCHEONG stoneware cup, her hand trembling slightly.

It's not the same without Nan. But we're getting by.

I take the tea and put my face over the hot cup, inhaling the fragrant steam.

"How are you feeling?" Halmoni asks, for the fifteenth time this week.

I roll my eyes fondly at her. "I'm good."

I sink onto the couch, and Gwion Bach jumps up with me. He clambers onto my lap and begins vigorously kneading my thighs. Princess Bari eyes me suspiciously from the hearthrug— she doesn't forget so easily.

It's been eleven days since we smashed the wall around Sicklehurst and let the sticklegrass wood free.

Inglenook has been crawling with auditors. Black-armored trucks with men in hazmat suits are poking strange mettle-detecting devices into every puddle and hedge. News reporters are saying that the soil levels of the area are safe, and that there is no leakage from the Sicklehurst site. The walls were brought down by a localized earthquake, according to them.

No official reports have mentioned the sudden wild growth in gardens or the unseasonal fruiting and blooming that has spread through town and all across Anglyon, from Foxford to Scouller.

Most people put it down to the mild, wet winter and early spring—a celadon summer, as it's known as in these parts. But the witches know the truth. Casseroles and fresh loaves and buttery shortbread started arriving at our place only days after it happened. Baskets of strawberries. Homemade preserves and flasks of elderflower cordial. The witches always know.

Nobody is saying anything, though, which I appreciate. And there have been no auditors at our door. Yet.

Odette told them that she had made it all up. She made a deal with her mother—she'd meekly go off to boarding school without complaint if her mother would use her influence to keep the auditors off my back.

They'll come for me eventually, of course. I can't say I'm dreading it entirely. Whether they drag me to a detention camp or a thaumaturgical college, I'm ready to take them on. I have armies at my back, armies of trees and roots and microorganisms. Someone has to challenge the auditors, the big magic corporations, and everyone else who has tried to turn magic into a synthetic commodity, rather than something wild and free.

"Back to school on Monday," Halmoni comments. It isn't a question.

"Yep."

I'm not going to the settlement institute, of course. Dr. Slater was furious when I told him. He said I was letting him, and everyone, down. I held firm. I stayed polite, but I met his eyes without looking away.

"It's just not for me," I told him. I injected a little of Nan's steel into my voice, so he'd know there'd be no arguing.

I can't quite imagine going back to school. Back to everyday life. I can't imagine myself sitting through one of Dr. Slater's interminable lectures about what is *expected* and *appropriate*. I used to love assembly when I was a little girl—not for the lecture but for the uninterrupted dreaming time it provided. I would gaze out the window and imagine myself and Odette tangled up in the most extraordinary adventures—with pirates and battles and fairies and prophecies. I'd work the whole thing out in my head, ready to tell to her on the playground, so we could race to Peg Powler after school and act it all out.

Now that I think about it, the idea of a bit of uninterrupted dreaming time doesn't sound so bad.

Rufus went to school the very next day, of course. He didn't want to miss out on our biology exam, because he is strange. He keeps trying to bring me my homework assignments, but schoolwork can wait a few more days.

Halmoni reaches over to take my left hand, her long fingers wrapping around mine. Her wedding band is dull from years of hot water and witch hazel.

"Your nan would be so proud of you," she says.

I smile.

Would she? I hope so.

We sit there in silence for a while, the absence of Nan an aching hole in our hearts.

"Aren't you supposed to be meeting your friends?" she asks at last.

I nod. "I can cancel," I tell her. "I don't like leaving you alone."

Halmoni snorts. "How can I be alone with a house full of cats, a dog, and the very best memories? Go see your friends. Be young. Enjoy yourself."

I squeeze her hand and stand up.

"Be careful, though," says Halmoni. "No dark paths."

I grin at her. "Definitely not."

"And take a cardigan."

"Okay."

Halmoni smooths my hair and lays a hand on my cheek. "Do you need a lift into town?"

"I'll walk," I tell her. "It's a nice day."

She doesn't pin a rose to my T-shirt, because there is no pin anymore. Halmoni didn't know what Nan did, that she used the sliver of the Hollow Knife to block my magic. She thought the bone pin was just some kind of safety charm.

There are no roses left either. They were just dry crackling twigs when I got home, withered and black. It's probably for the best. I don't like being spied on.

As I step out into the garden, a sparrow hops onto a branch of the cherry tree, fixing me with a beady eye. It feels like a sign of better things to come.

THE EXPLOSION OF PLANT GROWTH throughout Anglyon has brought insects and birds flocking from all over, and the air is full of twittering and buzzing. The hedges are bursting with dog rose and honeysuckle and fat blackberries clustering on brambles. I can feel the deep magic of the forest in everything—even in me. Beneath my feet is the kingdom of the earth—a vast intricate network of consciousness.

Everything smells green and good—spring grasses and fertile soil and rain-soaked moss and nettles.

Dunnocks and yellowhammers swoop and flit among the close-knit branches, and a pair of dormice chase each other through the dappled green. Sticklegrass is winding in the undergrowth among bluebells and stitchwort. I guess it's everywhere now.

If I concentrate, I can *sense* the nearby plants, everything happening in them. I feel the vibrations of a cabbage-moth caterpillar chomping on a mouse-ear cress leaf, and I smell the methyl salicylate that the steeplebush leaves release in order to deter predators and warn neighbors of a potential attack. It's dizzying, the sheer volume of information that is in the air and under my feet.

The farmers market is set up on the football field at the edge of town, and I wander through it, inhaling the scents wafting from the food trucks—grilled corn on the cob, buttery steamed cockles, rich lamb burek, and spiced satay skewers.

I hear a familiar laugh, and I follow it past the cheesemonger's stall, laden with cheerful yellow wheels and crumbling wedges, and a confectioner selling peppermints, licorice bootlaces, and chalky pink hearts stamped with edible-ink love spells.

Someone tries to sell me a psychic energy drink, bright blue and orange, in a glass bottle. I politely decline and keep following the laughter.

Ginger is lingering in front of a stall selling a mouth-watering array of cupcakes, sprinkled with candied violets and a shimmering layer of fairy dust. She's wearing high-waisted floral shorts and a sequined crop top, her hair swept up into a victory roll. She pulls her cat's-eye sunglasses down to look at me as I approach, then crooks a scarlet-nailed finger, summoning me forward. Her posse parts to let me through—in only a few days, she's assembled quite the assortment of suitors and hangers-on. A girl wearing a black-cat glamour narrows her eyes at me, and a tall boy with electric-blue eyeliner sighs longingly.

"How are you?" I ask.

Ginger winks. "Not bad."

"Winnie?"

"Still looking for something new to fight. She taught herself how to ride a bicycle."

The sticklegrass wood sent Ginger and Winnie off with treasure—their pockets weighed down with gemstones. It was enough to set them up in a little apartment together.

"And still no idea about . . ." I wave my hand vaguely at her.

I'm not quite sure what the girls *are* now. Are they human? Will they age? If they die now, will they stay dead? Is the sticklegrass wood still sustaining them, or are they real flesh and blood?

Ginger shrugs. "I can't say it's keeping me up at night."

She says it with a wicked grin that makes it very clear that she has much more enjoyable things keeping her up at night.

I clear my throat. My attraction to Ginger under the scarlet lissom wasn't just enchantment. She's gorgeous, and the sight of her still tugs at something inside me. But we are on different paths now. We'd never work as a couple. She'd get bored, and I'd get jealous and weird.

"I'm going to Osgod Hill," I tell her. "Do you want to come?"

Ginger glances at her posse and shakes her head. "I've got things to do."

She links arms with Black Cat Girl, who purrs with satisfaction. Blue Eyeliner Boy looks crushed but falls in behind them.

"See you around, darling," Ginger says, blowing me a kiss.

I smile. "Sure."

I cross the market and skirt around the edge of town until I reach the looming mass of Osgod Hill, craggy and dark against the afternoon sky. Rufus is waiting for me at the chairlift office. His face splits into a grin when he sees me, and I grin back and give him a hug. He smells like sandalwood and iodine.

The slash across his brow has healed into a puckered pink line. It'll fade with time, but he'll always carry it. We all have scars. Rufus should wear his with pride. If it weren't for him, there's no way I would have made it.

Rufus jerks his head at the hill. "She's already up there," he says.

We buy tickets from the kiosk, board a chairlift, and rise gently up the hill, the gondola creaking and swaying. The squeal of the cable and the knowledge that there's nothing but air beneath us makes my stomach lurch, but not enough to want to walk to the top. I've climbed enough steps to last me a lifetime.

There aren't many people at the top of the hill—a lone man in a stall selling key rings and sticks of starry rock, a few tourists looking through pay-per-view binoculars.

Odette is sitting on the other side of the safety barrier, on a rocky crag that juts out over the edge of the hill, her feet dangling. A faint breeze ruffles her silver-blond hair.

She looks over her shoulder at us as we approach, and I feel a little ache in my heart. Not for her, or for our friendship, but for myself. For the child I once was, unburdened by the world.

Although maybe that child never really existed. Some of my oldest memories are of Mam, black-eyed and stinking of wormwood. Of Nan's disapproving stare. Of the whispers of the forest beneath my feet and the ominous knock of an auditor at the front door.

Perhaps I was always burdened by the world. Perhaps I made up imaginary stories under Peg Powler to escape the harshness of reality, just as Odette did.

I scramble under the barrier to join her. Rufus hesitates before he does too. He doesn't like breaking rules, but I think he's getting used to it.

"All packed?" Rufus asks.

Odette nods. "A car is coming for me first thing in the morning."

"Good riddance," Rufus says cheerfully.

"I won't miss you either."

They continue to bicker as I inhale the violet-drenched scent of damewort, released in the evening to attract nearby hoverflies, and feel the almost imperceptible movements of dandelions as their flowers close up for the night.

Overhead, a murmuration of starlings shifts and moves like one single creature. The two crescent-moon scars on my shoulder blades ache a little at the memory of my wings, heavy and powerful with the promise of freedom. I dream of them every night—of whirling and gliding and thrusting upward toward the sun—but I know I'll never fly again.

I haven't heard anything from Lyr, but I believe that he has returned to Uisnigh, and that the Hollow Knife is safe once more.

From here, we can see the brown glint of Cygnet Creek on the other side of Inglenook, and beyond it, the hazy onion-weed meadow and the rubble of Sicklehurst, already overgrown with thick sticklegrass. It spreads out from the site, a rich green ring, expanding to encircle the village. It travels farther each day, stretching to Foxford and Black Larpent Bay. It seems un-stoppable.

"I heard they've quarantined the whole site," Odette tells us. "With armored guards and everything. Betty Metanee says it isn't the auditors doing it. She says it's the company that owned Sicklehurst."

"Ilium," I murmur. "They also own half the detention camps in Anglyon."

In fairy tales, lost boys get to marry princesses and rule over kingdoms. But lost girls go home and everything returns to how it was. They are grateful to be home and for everything they once took for granted. They swear off adventures for good.

I don't want to be a lost boy or a lost girl. I feel like my story is only just beginning.

I'm happy to be home, happy that Halmoni and Rufus and Odette are all right, as well as Winnie and Ginger. I'm happy to be alive.

But I've glimpsed true magic now. And I want to know more. I understand Nan's fear. I don't want to become like my mother, so obsessed with magic that it tears me away from the people I love. I need to learn to control it. To understand it. I'm a greenwitch, and as far as I know, there aren't any others. But maybe I can find someone who can teach me more.

I want to see the true sticklegrass wood, learn about its past and its power.

And I want to take down Ilium, to make sure that what happened to my mother and father never happens again. I don't believe that Mam did the right thing in stealing the knife, any more than I believe that Nan was right to seal up Sicklehurst. But they were *trying* to do the right thing.

I'm going to try too.

I can see a beetle-small line of black trucks winding their way back to Inglenook from the ruins of Sicklehurst, to whatever motel their drivers are staying at. Their headlights burn against the growing gloom, and I shiver.

As the sky darkens, we see little glints of foxfire and witch-light glowing gold and green in the wilderness. There are already rumors, of course—that following the lights will lead you to your death, that they belong to newly hatched forest spirits, that it's glowing radiation from a radioactive spill. I don't know what they are, but I want to find out.

I turn witch-eyed for a moment, and cast out my mettle, calling for the glimmer moths that never came to my windowsill as a child, when flying creatures wouldn't come near our house because of Nan's spell. The thrill of manipulating mettle is still fresh. It feels like I'm finally myself again, a whole and complete person, instead of just a shadow.

A pinprick of light streaks toward us, and I hold out a finger.

The glimmer moth lands delicately, its violet wings beating softly for a moment as it balances on my fingertip. Its fluffy body glows a gentle cyan, and it waves feathery antennae in the air, tasting the night.

"Pretty," observes Odette.

"See how the hindwing has an elongated tail?" Rufus asks, looking at the glimmer moth with interest.

I nod. It's hard to miss the elegant swoop of iridescent wings.

"I read a paper on it. The theory is it confuses predatory bats, who use echolocation to detect them."

Beautiful and useful, like so much of nature.

A clanging bell sounds from the bottom of Osgod Hill, and the glimmer moth flutters its pearly wings, then launches from my fingertip and disappears into the twilight.

"Last chairlift," says Rufus, and we clamber to our feet.

"I guess this is goodbye," says Odette.

"Finally," says Rufus, but he's smiling.

Odette and I promise to keep in touch, but we know we won't actually do it. We're not characters in each other's stories anymore.

I take one last look over the lights of Inglenook, the dark spread of forest and farmland, and the glowing ring of greenery, twinkling with magic. A breath of wind lifts my hair from my shoulders. It's warm and carries the scent of woodland tobacco and phlox, of crumbling fairy-tale cottages and cold stone dungeons, of brimstone and compost and ancient twisting roots.

"Maude?" Odette is already in the chairlift, but Rufus is waiting for me.

"Coming," I say.

It's time to head home. For now.

ACKNOWLEDGMENTS

A Hunger of Thorns is my eighteenth published book, but in many ways it feels like my first. I've been on an epic quest, writing it, have traveled to many strange imaginary lands and made many friends who have helped to keep me on the right path.

The Call to Adventure came a very long time ago, in a Tokyo art exhibit featuring a Chicago outsider artist named Henry Darger. I became captivated by story ideas about the lost girls of literature (for a long time Alice and Dorothy were characters in the book), inspired by my own childhood, which was rich with imaginary play.

Supernatural aid came in the form of a creative fellowship from State Library Victoria in Melbourne, Australia, which provided me with a little office in one of the most beautiful buildings in the world, where I could escape my toddler and lose myself in enchanted forests. Many thanks to my brilliant roomie, Kelly Gardiner, for her companionship, and to Gail Schmidt for letting me stay long past my welcome. Aid also came as financial support during the pandemic, from the City of Melbourne and the Australia Council for the Arts, and in the form of wise counsel from Cheryl Morgan, who gently steered me away from a story idea that was potentially harmful to some readers.

What is a hero without her squad? Many thanks to the Council (Amie, Eliza, Ellie, Kate, Liz, Nic, Pete, and Skye), who have been my daily companions online through these long, strange years. Your friendship, advice, humor, and empathy are worth all the gold and jewels in a dragon's horde. Many helpers and mentors read various bits, pieces, and versions of this book, and every one of them has made it immeasurably better. Amie Kaufman, PM Freestone, Sarah Dollard, Carole Wilkinson, John Wilkinson, and Kate Armstrong, thank you all for your time, your thoughtfulness, your honesty.

Thanks also to fellow travelers I met along the way who offered wisdom or companionship: CS Pacat, Garth Nix, Susannah Chambers, Paul Gartside, Jay Kristoff, Penni Russon, Kate Whitfield, and Chris Miles. There were many others who shared their own stories, identities, and experiences with me, and I thank them for their honesty and generosity.

A quest is never easy. Trials and tribulations are part and parcel of the whole hero business, and this book walked a long, weary road to publication. I never would have made it without my agent, Katelyn Detweiler. Katelyn, you read more drafts of the book than anyone else did, and you were unwavering in your support. Even when I reached the Innermost Cave and sank into my Dark Night of the Soul, you were there, a candle in the darkness, cheering me on, believing in me and in the book. I couldn't have done it without you. Thanks also to the other people at Jill Grinberg Literary Management who supported me and this project, especially Denise Page, Sam Farkas, and Sophia Seidner.

As we near the climax of our story, the hero (and her book) undergoes transformation. *Thorns* found a home at Delacorte Press, under the noble stewardship of Krista Marino, who got this story in ways that even I didn't. Krista, the editorial support I have received from you, and from Lydia Gregovic, has been incredible. Together the three of us plumbed new depths, uncovered hidden pathways, mixed new metaphors, and emerged from the editorial cocoon transformed and beautiful. I'm so glad we found each other, and I'm already excited about our next adventure together. Thanks also to the rest of the Delacorte team, especially Beverly Horowitz, Barbara Marcus, Colleen Fellingham, Tamar Schwartz, Angela Carlino, and the RHCB Marketing and Publicity teams.

Here in Australia, *Thorns* has a home at Allen & Unwin, under the wise and steady hand of Jodie Webster, who has been my friend and mentor for nearly two decades now. Thank you, Jodie, for your guidance and your unshaking support of me as a writer. I am so grateful to be part of the Allen & Unwin family, and I offer thanks to everyone else there who has supported this book, especially Virginia Grant, Hilary Reynolds, Yvette Gilfillan, Simon Panagaris, Deb Lum, Carolyn Walsh, and the sales team for selling the book across Australia during trying times.

Imogen Oh completed my period of transformation with her gorgeous cover art—you are a wizard, Imogen. I can't even.

A good quest ends with the hero returning to the safety and comfort of home, to nurse their bruises and consider their newfound wisdom. I am so lucky to be able to share that home with my family. Michael, you are the most steadfast and loyal companion a girl could have. You are my Samwise, my Kermit, my

Westley. Thank you for everything, but especially for listening to me blather on about whatever I'm currently writing, for your left-field brainstorming brain, for your thoughtful questions, and for your incredible hugs.

Banjo, you first described the Tatterdemalion to me when you were three years old—"bushes on its back and a mouth full of slugs." Now you are eight. It's been a long road, but I love watching you embark upon your own adventures, and I love it when you come home again for cuddles.

And what is a hero without her animal sidekick? Dame Maggie Galoshes, thank you for being such a faithful hound and comforting muse.

Finally, we made it. It's time to sit by the fire and drink a cup of tea. Maybe read a book. I recommend Merlin Sheldrake's *Entangled Life,* Peter Wohlleben's *The Hidden Life of Trees,* and Nikita Gill's *Wild Embers.* Or perhaps an old favorite? My own childhood was filled with magic written by Diana Wynne Jones, Tamora Pierce, Isobelle Carmody, Garth Nix, Susan Cooper, Lloyd Alexander, and Robert Holdstock, and I thank all of them for making me the writer I am today.

ABOUT THE AUTHOR

Lili Wilkinson is the author of sixteen novels in Australia, including *Pink*, *The Boundless Sublime*, and *After the Lights Go Out*. She established insideadog.com.au and the Inky Awards at the Centre for Youth Literature, State Library of Victoria. Lili has a PhD in Creative Writing from the University of Melbourne and now spends most of her time reading and writing books for teenagers. *A Hunger of Thorns* is her first fantasy novel.

liliwilkinson.com.au